PENGUIN BOOKS

Coming Home to Liverpool

By the same author

Miss Nightingale's Nurses
The Liverpool Nightingales
Daughters of Liverpool

Coming Home to Liverpool

KATE EASTHAM

PENGUIN BOOKS

PENGUIN BOOKS

UK | USA | Canada | Ireland | Australia
India | New Zealand | South Africa

Penguin Books is part of the Penguin Random House group of companies
whose addresses can be found at global.penguinrandomhouse.com.

First published 2020
001

Copyright © Kate Eastham, 2020

The moral right of the author has been asserted

Set in 12.5/15.25 pt Garamond MT Std
Typeset by Jouve (UK), Milton Keynes
Printed and bound in Great Britain by Clays Ltd, Elcograf S.p.A.

A CIP catalogue record for this book is available from the British Library

ISBN: 978–0–241–37126–8

www.greenpenguin.co.uk

Elizabeth Blackwell (1821–1910) was the first woman to obtain a medical degree in America and the first female doctor on the register of the General Medical Council in Britain. In 1857, together with her sister Dr Emily Blackwell (1826–1910) and another physician, Dr Marie Zakrzewska, she founded the New York Infirmary for Women and Children, the very first hospital in America specifically for women.

The pioneering Blackwell sisters were born in England but they emigrated to America with their family in 1832. Determined to be a doctor, Elizabeth withstood many rejections from medical colleges until she finally gained a place, obtaining her qualification in 1849. Sadly, whilst undergoing further training in Europe she contracted an eye disease from one of her patients and lost the sight in one eye. This meant that her dream of becoming a surgeon would never be realized.

Although Elizabeth had warned her younger sister of the grim prospects faced by women doctors, Emily was determined to follow the same path. A brilliant woman, she graduated with the highest honours, and became a surgeon at their New York infirmary. Two years later, Elizabeth returned to Britain to pursue other interests and Emily took over the management of the infirmary, running it successfully for a further forty years.

I

'Not only the life of your patients may depend on your faithfulness to duty, but by it you may also influence for good their virtue and happiness . . .'
Florence Nightingale

Liverpool, 1872

'Nursey, nursey,' called a row of barefoot boys, sitting cheekily on a wall near the Albert Dock, swinging their grubby legs as Eddy walked by. She lunged at them and pretended to tickle their feet, laughing more herself than any of the boys. Then, pulling her nurse's cape back into place, she picked up speed, expertly threading her way through the crowds of people making their way towards the harbour, one or two of them nodding, smiling or murmuring, 'Evening, Sister,' as they went on their way.

She needed to breathe some air, gather herself, as she often did before going back to the hospital for supplies. Her days on the district were demanding; out in people's homes, the nurses were working on their own and dealing with everything. But the work was good and today she was especially pleased, having had a real breakthrough with one of her patients – a young mother of two small children, suffering terribly with consumption. When she'd first visited Sylvia she'd found her very breathless and spitting blood. It was thought by all involved that time would be short. And for the first week, Eddy had cried every single day when she'd closed the door of that house behind her, leaving Sylvia as comfortable as she could be, propped up in bed with little Rosanna nestled under one arm and Archie under the other.

But today, after she'd gently helped her to wash, combed her hair and applied soothing cream to the reddened skin on her elbows and the notches of her spine, Sylvia had smiled and said she wanted to sit out of bed, watch the children play for a bit. Eddy had been delighted to help her and even more pleased to note that her breathing was less laboured: the steam inhaler that she'd advised seemed to be making a difference at last. She knew, of course, that there would inevitably be dark days ahead, but today was the first time that Eddy had seen Sylvia smile, and it meant a lot.

Reaching the waterfront at last, Eddy took a deep breath of salt air and then gazed out across the river, savouring the breeze in her face. Looking out towards the ocean she closed her eyes for a moment, picturing her dear friend Maud as she boarded a steamship in New York, all the way across the Atlantic. She would be back with them in Liverpool in one week. 'Safe voyage, Maudie,' she whispered, blowing a kiss out to sea.

As she walked through the city, Eddy thought back

through the rest of her day and all the other patients that she'd seen, making a mental note of the materials that she'd need to replenish her medical bag: cotton wool, lint, bandages, a new bar of carbolic soap, and another mouthpiece for Sylvia's inhaler. And she'd get a bag of sweets for Rosanna and Archie, and see if she could scrounge a few oranges from a street seller – take one for Sylvia and any of her other patients who needed them.

It wasn't until after she'd collected her materials from the hospital and sat herself down on the steps of the Nurses' Home to wait for her friend coming off duty that Eddy began to feel tired. But just as soon as she saw Alice coming along the path from the Infirmary, she jumped up, waving and shouting enthusiastically. 'Only one week to go till Maud's home!'

'Yes!' called Alice, picking up her uniform skirt and running the rest of the way. 'I can't wait.'

Eddy moved to hug her but then pulled back. 'You smell strange,' she said, wrinkling her nose.

'Oh, sorry, yes, there was a bit of an incident on the ward,' said Alice, indicating the soiled apron that she held rolled up in one hand. 'I should have known better really, but a delirious man on Male Medical hadn't eaten anything for days. I've been trying since this morning to get some bread and milk inside him and I think it must have gone a bit sour. Anyway, just now, I tried again, and he grabbed the bowl and chucked it at me. Then he grabbed me too, and it's a good job the orderlies were at the next bed – I've never seen Michael and

Stephen move so fast – but they had him restrained before he could do me any harm. Most of it went on my apron, but it was all over the floor as well and Sister Cleary nearly slipped in it when she came running over . . . It was quite an episode.'

'And so the life of the hospital goes on,' grinned Eddy, picking out some remnants of sour bread paste that still clung to Alice's hair. 'Best get you tidied up and shipshape before Maud comes back, we both know what a stickler she is . . .'

'Matron Maud Linklater,' laughed Alice, hugging Eddy before they both ran giggling up the stone steps and into the building. They stopped short when the door to the superintendent's room clicked open and Miss Merryweather appeared in her bonnet.

'Well, well,' she said, as they both stood holding their breath, waiting to be told off for making too much noise. 'It looks like you two have some exciting news. Could it be anything to do with our Nurse Linklater's return?'

'Yes,' beamed Eddy. 'We can't wait to see her, and it won't be long now. She's setting sail today from New York on the *Abyssinia* and she'll be back with us in exactly a we—'

'Will there be a position for Maud at the hospital?' interjected Alice, nudging Eddy hard with her elbow to shut her up.

'I do believe there will. Our esteemed assistant superintendent, Miss Houston, has already made a request . . . and we will be very glad to have Nurse Linklater back at the Liverpool Royal, no doubt laden with new knowledge of surgery and theatre gained at the Infirmary for Women in New York.'

'Yes, indeed,' smiled Alice, nodding.

'Imagine that, nurses,' continued Miss Merryweather rather wistfully, as she made her way out through the door, 'a whole hospital run by women, even the doctors and the surgeon, and just for female patients . . .'

'What was that for?' muttered Eddy, still rubbing her arm.

'As you were blabbing on about Maud and exactly when she would be back, all the other nurses were walking past behind us, including Millicent Langtry,' hissed Alice. 'I've tried to keep Maud's return quiet until she's safely back in Liverpool and I've deliberately not mentioned anything at all to Millicent. She was almost certainly the one who somehow found out about Maud's wedding and informed Nancy Sellers, and that's why she turned up in church that day. Thankfully, she left before Maud caught sight of her but we don't want to risk another incident. You know what Nancy's like. Ever since we all started our training together, she's tried to make trouble for Maud, for some unknown reason.'

'Sorry, Alice,' whispered Eddy, 'I forgot about that. Do you think she heard?'

'I don't know, you can never tell with Millicent, and as far as I know she doesn't even see Nancy any more, but we need to keep it quiet.'

'Sorry, Alice. Me and my big mouth.'

'Well, I know what you're like. You get carried away, but you need to be more careful.'

Alice pressed her lips together and tried to stay firm, but in the end she couldn't bear to see Eddy looking sorrowful, so she put an arm around her. 'Look, it's probably just me worrying too much, and besides, what harm can Nancy do? Apart from a few snide comments, what harm can she actually do?'

At that very moment across the city, Nancy Sellers lifted her head as if someone had called her name. She felt a prickling of hairs on the back of her neck but, not detecting any sound other than the spit of the fire, she picked up her china cup and took a delicate sip of tea before replacing it with a chink in the ornately patterned saucer. Removing a lace handkerchief from her sleeve, she used it to pat her face. She was warm by the fire, too warm. She could feel her cheeks starting to flush. Maybe she could make use of that silk fan that her private patient had on her bedside table. That would do very well.

'Nurse Sellers,' called Mrs Davenport from the next room, the weakness of her voice indicating how much more breathless she had become in the last few weeks.

Nancy continued to pat her face with the handkerchief; no need to move just yet, she would wait for the next call.

'Nurse Sellers,' called the weary voice again, and this time Nancy tucked the handkerchief back inside her sleeve and took another sip of tea.

'Nurse,' called the poor woman again, and then there was a crash and the tinkle of broken glass.

Nancy scowled and got up from her chair, taking a moment to stretch her back and then pull the large shawl that she always wore more closely around her shoulders so that it fell and covered the curve of her pregnant belly.

Pasting a smile on her face, she proceeded into her mistress's bedchamber, making soothing noises as she went. 'There, there, Mrs Davenport, don't you worry, we'll soon have you straightened up.'

An elderly lapdog with cloudy eyes lifted his head to yap at her from where he lay curled at the bottom of the bed.

'Be quiet, Henry, you nasty, nippy little pest,' hissed Nancy, as she made her way to the mantle to pull the cord for a maid to come and tidy up the broken glass. As she waited, she took a bottle of laudanum from the bedside table and gave Mrs Davenport a good dose, dropping it into her mouth and making her swallow it down. 'The medicine will help your breathing, you must take the drops,' she murmured, smooth as anything. Then, as she heard the maid's footsteps outside the door, she took her patient's hand, tilted her neat blonde head to one side and stood poised, ready for the door to open.

'Our dear Mrs Davenport has had a little accident with a glass,' cooed Nancy, using her sweetest tone, all the while thinking of how many more days she would need to withstand being here, shut up in this room, waiting for the father of her baby to return.

It thrilled her to think of him going about his daily

business, not having any idea about the baby. She hadn't seen him for all the months of her pregnancy. He was working away, but last week she'd received word that he was coming back to Liverpool. She revelled in the memory of those few nights they'd spent together. The warmth of his body against hers, the smell of him and, when she laid her head on his chest as he slept off the drink, the rhythmic sound of his beating heart. She smiled with pleasure when she thought of his new wife: all prim and proper, she wouldn't stand a chance of keeping him when he found out about the baby. Not a chance.

She'd been angry with him when she'd received the news of his return from one of her sources. He'd promised to write. Clearly, he'd thought he could sneak back into Liverpool without being seen, but he was wrong. She would be ready and waiting for him, and she couldn't wait to see his face when he saw her belly.

Once Mrs Davenport was sleeping and the maid had retreated from the room, Nancy removed the silk fan from the bedside table, ignoring the dog who immediately lifted his head and growled at her. She walked back to her anteroom and settled herself by the fire. She could feel the baby pushing inside her, the movement rippling against the fabric of her dress, she even saw the shawl move when it gave an extra hard kick. Nancy feared what she might have to go through at the birth, but she was weary of all this now. She wanted it over with.

Slipping a piece of paper out from a folded pad, she

took up a quill pen and dipped it into the ink. She'd started to make plans as soon as she'd heard the news of her old lover's return, and she'd been able to secure some lodgings and persuade Mrs Davenport to put her name to a contract securing a tidy sum of severance pay.

'Just seven days to go,' she murmured as the pen scratched on the writing paper, 'seven days and he will be mine.'

2

'. . . a Boston lady, training matron to the
Massachusetts General Hospital, has in a very
spirited manner come to us for training . . .
I think we have as much to learn from her
as she from us.'

Florence Nightingale

New York, 1872

Maud walked behind the boy, not taking her eyes off
him for a moment. The bag she was carrying dragged
on her arms but she was strong enough to manage it
and, thankfully, Alfred had worked out that he could
balance the rest of their luggage, packed in a large cloth
bag, on his head. He was only ten years old, but he'd
walked off in front, calm as anything, whilst she followed along behind, burning with fury.

She was even more furious as they pushed their way
along Broadway amidst crowds of people bumping past
and knocking into them. Not only that, they were up
against a mass of excited immigrants streaming into
the city. On any other day, Maud would have been
heartened to witness this lively procession of people

wearing brightly coloured scarves, heading towards a new life. But thanks to her husband, Harry, their day had started off badly, and this time, there was no excuse. He'd promised to be back at their lodgings in Lower Manhattan in time to escort them safely to the seaport. And they'd waited as long as they possibly could, sitting at the kitchen table, sipping tea, all the while enduring the knowing glances of Mrs Kelly, their Irish landlady, as the clock above the mantle ticked away every second that he didn't come through the door. She knew that when he was out working, he had no sense of time; but surely, just this once, he could have made an extra effort to be back. Not just for her, but for Alfred as well. The boy adored his adopted father.

'For goodness' sake,' she muttered under her breath as Alfred ducked smartly out of the way when a big-boned man carrying a huge trunk almost knocked him off his feet. 'Watch what you're doing!' she shouted after the man, adjusting the weight of her bag as she marched along with two bright red spots of anger burning on her pale cheeks. She was so incensed that she almost walked slap bang into a blue-uniformed policeman as he stood surveying several carriages and an omnibus, noisily jammed side to side across the wide cobbled street.

The closer they got to the port at South Street, the heavier Maud felt. With the effort of struggling through the crowd her anger had started to ebb, only to be replaced by a leaden feeling in the pit of her stomach. And for the first time since she'd made her decision to leave her work at the Women's Infirmary, she started to feel doubt creeping in. When the news had come that her oldest friend was gravely ill, of course she'd wanted to go back to Liverpool to see her. After all, without the support of Miss Fairchild, she would never have been able to leave her position as a housemaid and become a nurse and travel to America in the first place. And even now, as she trudged along behind Alfred, she was sure that it was the right thing to do. But although she'd told herself that she could always come back to New York if she wanted, she had just begun to realize that once she was back at the Liverpool Royal Infirmary, she would find it very difficult to leave. And even though Harry had readily agreed to return to Liverpool, she'd sensed that he'd been thrown by her decision. He had soon been back asking if it was all right if he stayed on for another month, to complete some business deal that he'd been working on.

'Look, Maud! There's the bridge,' shouted Alfred, stopping and turning full circle, with the bag on his head, to give her a beaming smile. That smile gave Maud an instant boost and, as always, seeing the Brooklyn Bridge under construction made her heart beat a little faster.

They didn't need to go much further before the gulls were circling overhead and Alfred was calling out again and pointing to the impressive hull of a ship, carefully attended by cranes hoisting cargo aboard. 'That's ours, Maud! The *Abyssinia*, an iron steamer, just where Harry said she would be.'

And as they moved closer, Maud could hear the

creaking of the ropes, the lap of the water and the urgency of the men shouting to each other as they organized the passengers and loaded the ship.

It took her straight back to the morning when they'd seen New York for the first time. They'd been standing on deck after a week on an Atlantic Ocean where, most days, the sea was so calm that she'd felt like they were drifting in a dream. Excited as she'd been to board one of the small boats waiting to take them on the last leg of their journey, she'd felt a pang of sadness to leave that ship. But as they'd approached the shore and the Emigrant Landing Depot at Castle Garden, she'd sensed the rising excitement of Harry and Alfred, and her own heart had begun to beat faster. Maud and Harry – two newly-weds with their adopted son and the dog – all of them together, standing in line to go through registration, and then waiting on the wooden benches, sharing hot coffee and fresh pastries with families from Germany and Russia and a small boy from Ireland, all alone, with a ticket pinned to his jacket.

'She's a lovely ship, isn't she, Maud?'

'She is indeed,' murmured Maud, thinking of how Alfred and Harry had explored every inch of the vessel on the journey out, learning all the nautical names for things, peering over the side to watch the ship's bow cutting through the water, breathing in the salt air.

'Come on, Maud,' called Alfred, striding towards the ship. 'All aboard!'

Once they'd shown their tickets and were safely on board, she went straight to the side and stood, clutching the rail, scouring the faces of the crowd for any sign of Harry. Despite the fury that had brimmed inside of her all the way to the port, she couldn't help the longing she had for her husband to turn up and wave goodbye. Glancing down to Alfred, she could see the tension in his small body and she knew that he was also willing Harry to appear.

Maud could see the excited faces of those who had gathered to say farewell to their loved ones. It made her feel desolate, knowing that she and Alfred had no one to see them off.

She felt a swell of recognition from the crowd as the crew prepared to pull up the gangplank. Time was short now. Maud knew that it had to be too late for him to come. She let go of the handrail and glanced down at her black woollen coat with its row of neat buttons tightly fastened down the front. She took a deep breath and reached for Alfred's hand, making herself smile at him. She didn't want this sad scene to be his last memory of New York. After all, he had blossomed here. He'd gone to school, he'd made some friends – and Mrs Kelly, she'd absolutely adored him. Thank goodness for that, given that Harry had been so occupied with his business dealings and she'd been at the hospital all hours. Alfred had been required to spend a great deal of time with Mrs Kelly.

She took another breath and gave his hand a squeeze. Then she reached up to check that her felt hat with the bright blue feather was sitting perfectly square on her head. Harry had turned up with it the other day and she'd felt a glow of pleasure, that morning, as she'd swept back her dark hair and pinned it securely in place with the two brand-new hat pins that Mrs Kelly had given her as a leaving present.

The steam whistle sounded and the crew started to pull up the gangplank. Maud could feel her heart hammering in her chest. And in the split second that she gave up hope and reached down to pick up her bag, Alfred pulled at her sleeve. 'He's there, he's there!'

Maud dropped the bag, frantically looking in the direction that Alfred was pointing. Her breath caught when she saw him, with the dog, Rita, bounding at his side.

'I'm sorry,' he mouthed, staring at her in desperation. 'I'm so sorry.'

Maud felt a tightening of her heart before she beamed a smile, waving now and blowing a kiss to her husband, with his mane of dark curly hair and his beautiful face. There was nothing she could do but forgive him.

'We'll see you back in Liverpool,' she and Alfred shouted, their voices lost amidst the clamour on deck.

'One month,' he mouthed in return.

Maud blew him a kiss as the crowd cheered and the ship edged away from the pier. She couldn't take her eyes off him. He stayed there with the dog by his side, watching them leave, until he looked like a small and lonely figure. Only when the *Abyssinia* turned to attain her proper speed, gliding away from the spires of the city, was he gone from view.

'Right, Alfred,' she said, fishing in her pocket for their ticket and the details of the cabin that Harry had managed to arrange for them through a friend of his at the docks, 'let's go and find where we'll be stationed.'

Alfred balanced the bag on his head and hummed a tune as he led the way to the right deck and the right set of cabin numbers.

'It must be just along here, I think,' murmured Maud. 'Yes, this is the one, here.'

She put her bag down and tried the door, but it was stiff, it wouldn't budge. She tried again, but it seemed to be locked, and when she peered in through the small round window, she could see boxes stacked up and bags of what looked like provisions.

'That's strange,' she murmured, checking the number on the door against the ticket that she held in her hand.

'You wait here, Alfred,' she said, 'I'll have to go and find someone, make enquiries.'

She didn't need to go far; there was a steward just along the deck, assisting a woman wearing fox fur who had a great deal of luggage. Maud stood and waited politely until the woman was safely installed in her cabin, thinking to herself that at least she and Alfred would be able to sort themselves out.

'Excuse me,' she said to the red-faced steward, who was pocketing what looked like a large tip. 'I wonder if you could advise me about our cabin?'

The man looked her up and down and then took the ticket that she was holding out to him. He gave a small snort of laughter.

Maud straightened her back and glanced down to

check that the buttons on her coat were still perfectly straight.

'There must have been some mistake, my darlin',' he said with a smirk, 'because this ticket is for a cabin that is not currently used for passengers.'

'Are you sure?' said Maud, setting her mouth in a firm line.

'I'm certain. You might have a ticket but you definitely do not have a cabin.'

'But can you not clear it for us?'

'Not possible,' said the steward, handing back the ticket and starting to move away. 'That particular cabin is always used for stores. Captain's orders. We can offer you a berth in steerage, and that's as far as it goes.'

Maud gasped and scrutinized the piece of paper in her hand one more time before glancing at the retreating steward.

'Well, where is this steerage?' she called, working hard to stem the tears of disappointment that were springing to her eyes.

'Down the ladders,' shouted the steward over his shoulder. And then, turning, he pointed, 'Those ladders, there. Keep going and you'll find it all right.'

Alfred led the way down all the ladders until they found the right place. The further they descended, the warmer it became – and the louder the sound of the ship's engines. On the lowest level they could hear voices and the mournful wail of a man singing. Maud and Alfred exchanged a glance. 'This must be it,' she said, trying to smile. But when they walked through the door into what would be their accommodation for the full week of their voyage, she gave a small gasp. It was packed with bunk beds and full of men.

'That way,' said a man with a fresh red scar down his cheek. 'You women are through there.'

Maud nodded her thanks and turned on her heel, walking through a partition door to be met by an equally crowded area, this time full of women and children and, over to one side, what looked like bales of cotton.

Her stomach tightened and she started to feel light-headed as they stood in the midst of everything. It was hot and stuffy, there was a smell of sweat, and the sound of the engines seemed louder than ever. The passengers were packed into every bunk or sat on the floor, and it seemed that children were shouting and playing everywhere. She couldn't see any free space. It must be first come first served, she thought, and we are the last in. We might have to sleep on the floor at this rate.

Alfred put down his luggage and glanced up at her; even he didn't seem to know what to do.

'Just you and the boy?' called a woman with dark blonde hair, getting up from a bunk with a small child clinging to her.

Maud nodded.

'Right, we can make room for you, my darlin', don't you worry,' said the woman, who was smiling now as she crossed the space between them.

'I'm Tessa Coyle and this is my youngest, Barnaby . . . just one thing to check, though,' she said. 'I don't want to sound rude or anythin' but, given you and the boy are dressed like you are, are you sure you're looking for a bunk in steerage?'

'Yes, there was some mix up with the ticket,' said Maud, trying to smile at the woman, but her face felt tight.

'Right then, we'll make space for you,' she said, reaching out to give Maud and then Alfred a firm handshake.

'I'll have to budge up my girls, so that we're only taking up two beds and not three. They probably would 'ave ended up together anyway, that lot. Would that be all right for you and your boy?'

'Yes, of course,' said Maud, a little breathless. 'It is so kind of you to help us.'

'No problem, we travellers 'ave to stick together – and I think your lad will get on just fine with my lot. Do you 'ave a fella in with the men?'

Maud shook her head. 'He's making his own way back,' she added, feeling the need to offer some kind of explanation.

'Same as me,' said Tessa. 'My Daniel's followin' along in a few weeks' time.'

With her next breath Tessa gave a whistle and all of her girls came running. 'Right, you lot,' she said, 'I want you to clear that bottom bunk for this fine lady and her boy. Go on, look sharp.'

'I'll help,' called Alfred, leaving his bag and running off after the girls.

'I'm sorry we don't have many chairs down 'ere,' said Tessa. 'But maybe you could sit yourself down on that big bag that your boy was carrying while I just get you a nip of brandy.'

'Thank you,' said Maud, lowering herself and perching awkwardly on the cloth bag, with her back straight, her coat still neatly buttoned and her felt hat perfectly square on her head. She tried not to feel sad – she tended towards a mournful expression at the best of times – but she felt like an abandoned child as she sat there amidst the chaos of steerage.

That night, as Maud lay fully clothed in the narrow berth, with her new coat and hat carefully stashed beneath the bunk, she knew that she wouldn't sleep. Every spike of straw from the mattress needled her. The whispering and snoring and giggling of the women and children, and one woman's loud singing, all conspired against her. And the heat and the relentless noise of the engines right next to them were almost unbearable. Her only consolation was the steady sound of Alfred's breathing as he lay beside her on the bunk. There was barely room but he'd gallantly squeezed into the narrow space between her and the partition wall, and he'd fallen straight to sleep.

Maud lay with her dark eyes wide open, staring into the poorly lit hold, hoping that the few candle stubs that she could see would last till morning. She must have fallen asleep eventually, because she woke with a start to the high-pitched wail of a frightened child. It took her a second to realize something was wrong; the bunk was pitching, and she could hear the sliding of what could only be pots and pans across the floor. She heard Tessa soothing her children. 'Hold tight, you lot.'

'Don't worry, Maud,' murmured Alfred from over her shoulder. 'The sea's got a bit rough, that's all.'

Maud lay without sleep for what seemed like for ever. When the light started to flood down from the decks above, some of the passengers moved carefully out of their bunks. Maud knew that she couldn't even try. She was feeling queasy and had started to break out into a cold sweat. 'Alfred?' she ventured. 'I feel very sick.'

Instantly he was slipping out of the bunk and quickly came back with a wooden pail.

'Oh no,' groaned Maud, grabbing the pail and heaving into it.

'Sorry, Maud, it looks like you're in for it, this time,' he said softly, dabbing her forehead.

She tried to reply but her mouth started to water again, her stomach gave another heave, and she grabbed the bucket again.

Maud lay on the bunk for days, taking only small sips of water, drifting off to sleep but then haunted by dreams. She was regularly woken by the heaving of her stomach and the sounds of other women groaning and retching. Each dark night, Alfred lay beside her, his small hand stroking her arm if she became restless and his calm voice murmuring words of comfort as the ship tossed and dipped and scooped through the ocean.

It was three whole days before the sea calmed and Maud could sit upright at the side of the bunk. Alfred brought over a fresh bowl of water and a clean flannel.

He dipped and squeezed the cloth, helping her wipe her face and lips, and then she took it herself and cleaned her hands. Starting to smile, she handed the cloth back to the boy who stood in front of her with his feet planted square and a solemn expression on his face.

'This reminds me of what I did for you when you were in hospital with your broken arm,' she said, reaching out a hand to move a stray lock of blond hair that had fallen over his eyes. 'But you were covered in soot.'

'I will always remember . . .' said Alfred quietly, his pale blue eyes shining. 'You were the one, the special housemaid, who saved me from being sent back up to sweep that chimney, and took me to hospital. At least now I've grown, I'm probably too big to be a climbing boy again.'

Maud gave a small shudder and pulled the boy close. 'You are never going back to that life, Alfred. When we get into Liverpool you're off to complete your studies at the Blue Coat School.'

The boy pulled a tattered exercise book from inside his jacket. 'I've been keeping up with my lessons in mathematics,' he said, opening up a page to show Maud a row of calculations.

'These are wonderful,' she said, taking the book from him and flicking through the rest of the pages. 'And you seem to be able to do this so easily.'

'I *like* doing it,' he said.

Maud's chest tightened with pride. 'You are going to do very well indeed, Alfred,' she said.

Alfred grinned at her before running off in response to a shout from Tessa's eldest, Cathy. She and Alfred seemed to have become firm friends.

Maud lay back down but was soon sitting up again, irritated by the straw prickling through the mattress, needing to stand up, to straighten her hair and eat something. She had to try and keep some food down.

'Good to see you've made it back to the land of the livin',' called Tessa from where she sat, wedged between some sacks of provisions, with Barnaby on her knee.

Maud tried to smile, but her face didn't seem to be working properly. 'Not quite there yet, but I will be soon,' she said, reaching down to straighten her skirt. And then, wondering what might have happened to her belongings, she started rooting around under the bunk.

'Your coat slipped out with all the other luggage, and it was a while before I could find it,' said Alfred, appearing in front of her with the dusty piece of clothing in his grasp. 'But I kept it safe, and Tessa had a go at it with a sponge. It doesn't look too bad.'

Maud took the coat from him. She could see a few stains on the black wool, but all the buttons were still there. Ordinarily, she would have tutted and fussed but, seeing the concern in Alfred's eyes, she merely gave the garment a bit of a brush with her hand and tried to smile.

'We didn't find the hat for a few days,' said Alfred quietly, 'but when we did, well, it hasn't come off too well . . .'

'Not to worry,' murmured Maud, feeling a little sad.

Apart from her wedding ring, it was about the only thing that Harry had ever given her.

Alfred rummaged under the blanket at the bottom of the bed and pulled out a flattened object with a detached brim.

'Ah, I see what you mean,' said Maud, starting to giggle. 'It really is a bit of a mess, isn't it?'

'Tessa saw one of the women wearing it – the one who sings a lot and likes to get drunk. She had to sneak it off her head when she fell asleep.'

'Oh dear. Well, at least the feather's still intact,' said Maud, pulling out the bright blue adornment from the band and running it through her hand. 'I can keep this and use it for another hat, when I get one. Thank you, Alfred, for all your efforts and for looking after me so expertly.'

'I'm just glad you're feeling better,' said the boy. 'And we only have two more days left, and then we'll be home.'

As Maud stood on deck, packed in with all the other passengers waiting to see their first glimpse of Liverpool, she held tight to Alfred's hand. It felt so good to be out in the open air at last; she hadn't realized how cramped she'd felt down in the dark, low-ceilinged hold of the ship.

'There she is! There's Liverpool!' Alfred shouted as the steam whistle sounded and a huge cheer went up from all those on deck. Maud felt her heart soar and then, as a man on the deck struck up a few notes on a fiddle, unexpected tears started to well in her eyes. Fishing for a handkerchief in her pocket, she dabbed at her face. Then she smiled and nodded at Alfred, who had reached to take her hand.

'We're home, Maud, we're home!'

Alfred still held tight to her hand as he balanced the big cloth bag on his head and disembarked – leading the way for Tessa with Barnaby, Cathy carrying Maud's bag, and the other girls running backwards and forwards excitedly up and down the gangplank.

'Come on, you lot! We need to go and find our trunk,' shouted Tessa as they stepped on to dry land.

Maud didn't realize how weakened she was until she took her first steps ashore. 'You all right there, Maudie?' murmured Tessa, appearing at her elbow. 'You're lookin' mighty pale and anxious, now you're out in the light. I didn't realize 'ow much weight you'd lost till I saw you buttoned into that coat of yours.'

'Oh, I'm always pale. I'm going to be fine, don't you worry,' said Maud, trying to smile. 'I can't thank you enough, though, Tessa, for all your kindness to me and Alfred. I don't know what we'd have done without you.'

'Ah, you'd 'ave rattled around in steerage for a bit but you'd 'ave been right enough, especially with a good lad like your Alfred. He's an old 'ead on young shoulders is that one.'

'He is, for sure,' said Maud, glancing proudly at her adopted son who was saying goodbye to Cathy. 'And Tessa, I just want to say, I know you'll be busy with getting the children sorted out and everything, but you know where I'll be in a few days' time, up at the Infirmary, if you need me.'

Tessa nodded and then she grabbed hold of Maud with her free arm, pulling her into a tight embrace. 'I'm so glad that you 'ad the wrong ticket. It's been a pleasure getting to know a bit about you and your boy.'

'Likewise,' said Maud firmly, blinking back tears as Tessa pulled away, wiped her face on her sleeve and called for her gaggle of children to assemble.

Maud heard Eddy shouting before she saw Alice's red-gold head bobbing up and down with excitement. Then Alice was shrieking, 'Maud, Maud,' and jumping with the baby in her arms.

Maud's heart swelled with joy. 'Eddy! Alice!' she cried.

Eddy came running towards her with her nurse's cape flying, grabbed Maud and squeezed her tight, almost lifting her off the ground. 'Jeez, woman, you're as thin as a lath . . .' she stated loudly, before setting her back down.

Maud could feel the new coat bagging around her. 'It was a rough crossing,' she said, starting to laugh. And then she was crying and reaching out to hug Alice and baby Victoria as well.

Eddy grabbed Alfred and gave him a squeeze.

'Is Miss Fairchild all right?' asked Maud, suddenly anxious about her old friend.

'Yes, she's fine, Maud,' gasped Alice, wiping her eyes with the flat of her hand. 'She's back at the big house, with a private nurse, and still trying to rule the roost by all accounts. Driving the new housekeeper crazy.'

'That's good,' said Maud, leaning in to speak softly to the baby and breathe in the scent of her hair. 'Mmmm, you have grown, haven't you, Victoria?' she murmured. 'And your hair is so long . . . and look at that streak of red at the front, it's so bright now, just like your mother's.'

'Right, Maud,' sniffed Alice, 'you're to come with me now and stay at Stella's place tonight, it's all arranged. And then tomorrow, you and Alfred can go up to see Miss Fairchild.'

'And I've managed to finish my rounds early, so I can see you safely along to Stella's,' said Eddy, ruffling Alfred's hair. 'We nurses on the district have to toil almost every hour of every day, not like some with comfortable hospital jobs who get an afternoon off every single week.'

Alice laughed and stuck her tongue out at Eddy, then she put her head close to Maud's as they continued to murmur baby talk with Victoria.

Eddy saw Alfred frown as he looked past her, and when she turned she caught a glimpse of someone stepping out of the shadow of a building. And like a knife, she felt the sharp realization of who it was. 'Nancy Sellers, what the . . . ?' she murmured to herself, knowing she had to act quickly to prevent Maud from seeing the woman. Catching Alfred's eye, she put a finger to her lips and then she stepped directly in front of Maud and Alice, standing with her hands on her hips so that her cape formed some kind of shield. Fortunately, Maud had her back turned to Nancy. When she was certain that neither of her friends had seen the intruder, she glanced over her shoulder, drawing in a sharp breath when she saw the true reality of the situation. Nancy was pregnant – very pregnant – and she was looking past Maud, as if expecting to see someone else coming off the ship. Even though most of the incoming passengers had now dispersed.

As soon as Alice looked in her direction, Eddy opened both eyes wide and pulled an urgent face. Then she stepped aside so that Alice, too, could glimpse Nancy.

Instantly, Alice took Maud's arm. 'Come on, Maud, you look exhausted,' she said, leading her away.

Eddy stood her ground for a few moments and kept an eye on Nancy. She marvelled at the brazenness of the woman, still standing with her head held high, proudly displaying the curve of her belly as she looked towards the ship.

She knew that Nancy had seen her, but there was no flicker of recognition on the woman's face; she merely looked past her. Eddy didn't care. She just wanted to keep an eye on Nancy, to make sure that she didn't make any move towards Maud. If she set one foot in that direction, Eddy would be straight there, blocking her path. No one threatened her friend. No one.

3

'The nurses should be strong, active women . . .
of unblemished character . . .'

Florence Nightingale

'I'll take the bag,' called Eddy, easily catching up with
them. 'Maud, you look fit to drop,' she said in a lively
fashion, trying to hide concern for her friend who'd
returned from New York pale and pinched with black
smudges beneath her eyes, like a ghost of her former self.

'Thanks, Eddy, what would I do without you?' said
Maud, her voice still weak from many hours of seasickness. She was glad of the help; even after a few paces
she was unsteady as she tried to walk in a straight line.

Maud was grateful for Alfred steadfastly walking in
front, still balancing the luggage on his head, and Alice
at the other side, linking her arm, as they progressed
slowly behind Eddy, who was out in front as usual.

Alice leant in towards her. 'Just concentrate on walking, Maud. I've heard that the effects of a lengthy sea
voyage can take some days to recover from, but you will
be fine.'

'I know,' smiled Maud, giving Alice's arm a gentle
squeeze with her own.

'Look at madam, out in front,' giggled Alice. 'Do you remember that first time she led us through the city, when I was pregnant and we were going to seek advice from Stella?'

'Of course,' said Maud. 'We nearly lost her, she was walking so fast. It was a good job she was wearing that big hat of hers with the red silk flowers.'

Alice laughed. 'But she found that place, didn't she? Down the alley, next to Lime Street Station, she led us to the brothel. Three nurse probationers out for the evening. What a sight we must have been, waiting to be shown in for the first time. And who would have thought that I'd still be living there?'

'Not me, that's for sure,' replied Maud. 'I would never have gone through the door if we hadn't been so desperately worried about you and your pregnant belly.'

'Strange, isn't it, Maud? How life unfolds . . . I can't imagine living anywhere else now.'

'I know, look at me back in Liver—' Maud lurched sideways, and Alice had to grab her. And then she started to laugh. Quietly at first, but soon it was taking over her whole body.

'Maud?' said Alice, a crease of worry between her eyes. 'Are you all right?'

'Yes, I'm fine, I'm fine,' gasped Maud, stopping for a moment to force the laughter down. 'It's just that I didn't think it would feel so good to be back home.'

'Well, that's probably because you've been so horrendously seasick . . . wait till—'

'No, it's more than that,' said Maud, softly. 'It's all of

this: being here again with you and Eddy, having my feet on home ground, and smelling the city.'

'Smelling the city?' laughed Alice. 'It pongs!'

Maud laughed again but she knew what she was feeling, and she was surprised at just how good it was to be back in Liverpool. Smiling now, she took a deep breath, savouring the salt and tar of the harbour, the smoke, the horse muck. And as she walked, a man sitting on a step enjoying a smoke tipped his hat and gave her a cheeky wink.

Their progress was slow but Maud didn't worry, it gave her time to take in the red brick and stone of the buildings. And when, at last, she saw the cloud of steam rising above Lime Street Station, her body tingled with expectation and she knew that they didn't have far to go. As they walked through the crowds of people making their way in and out of the station, she smiled to herself as she noted the exact spot where she'd asked Harry to marry her. She could almost see him there, leaning against the brick wall with the dog at his feet and a smoke in his hand. Looking like he didn't have a care in the world.

'Are you all right, Maud?' said Alice gently. 'It's just that you're slowing down. Should I shout for Eddy to come and help?'

'No, no, I can manage,' soothed Maud. 'I was just thinking about times gone by, that's all.'

'I know,' replied Alice, giving her arm a squeeze. 'There's been a lot going on, and it feels like you've been away ages.'

Maud saw Eddy glance back and smile at them. 'Come on, you two,' she called, 'don't let me have to carry you both, one under each arm.'

Alfred started to giggle.

'She *is* strong, she could probably do just that,' grinned Alice. 'But we'd be shaken up and roughed about, that's for sure, knowing what she's like.'

'She's an unstoppable force,' said Maud proudly.

'Come on, you two,' Eddy called again from the step of Stella's place. She'd already removed her hat and hairpins and was running her hands through her thick, curly hair as she waited for them.

'Eddy, you look an absolute fright,' snipped Alice, playfully.

'That's good, then, no change there,' laughed Eddy, opening the door for Maud and Alfred to go in first.

Maud caught her breath as they went in through the blue-painted door, past the reception room with the purple velvet settee and down the passage towards the murmur of voices and the ripple of Stella's laughter.

'Hello,' said Maud quietly as she stood at the threshold of the kitchen, with Alfred beside her.

'Maud! Alfred!' cried Stella and her mother, Marie, turning from their tasks and rushing forward to grab hold of them both.

'Come in, come in! We've got some food ready and the kettle's on,' said Marie, taking the bag off Alfred's head and setting it down on the flagged floor. 'My word, young man, you've done a good job carrying that.' Then she ruffled his hair and gave him a big kiss on the cheek.

'The wanderers return,' smiled Stella, standing for a moment with her hands on her hips, the familiar yellow ribbon pulling back her dark hair. Then, seeing Maud falter, she was straight there by her side, gently helping her out of her coat and leading her to a seat next to the fire.

Maud sat down with a sigh. The furniture in the kitchen looked like it was starting to sway from side to side, and the voices of her friends seemed mixed up. She took a deep breath and forced herself to focus, and then it all seemed to settle. It was so warm, and so nice to be back by the fire at Stella's, with the black cat stretched out at her feet.

'Hello there, Hugo,' she murmured, reaching down to stroke his scraggy fur, full of singe marks. 'It looks like you're still spending too much time in front of the fire.'

Hugo lifted his head and then stretched himself out even further.

'He's still a lazy good-for-nothing,' laughed Marie, placing a steaming cup of tea and a buttered scone next to Maud on the table. 'Last week I had a big fat mouse dancing around the kitchen table and he wouldn't even get up to give chase. I had to run after it myself and shoo it out through the door. I don't know why we keep him!'

'Aw, poor Hugo, you have some purpose, don't you?' crooned Alfred, crouching down beside the cat with his cup of tea.

'We just don't know what it is yet,' laughed Stella.

'Maud, Maud,' shouted Eddy from the far side of the

room, 'when you're feeling up to it, we'll tell you all about Alice and her many romantic entanglements.'

'Stop it, Eddy,' cried Alice, her cheeks flushing pink.

'What's this?' said Maud. 'You wrote to tell me about Jamie coming back from Australia and trying to take Victoria, which must have been terrifying. But what else has been going on?'

'Oooh, just you wait,' teased Eddy. 'There is more.'

Maud laughed but then glanced across to make sure that Alice was all right to be teased. 'You don't have to tell me any of it if you don't want to,' she said quietly.

Alice smiled. 'Oh, I want to tell you, don't you worry.'

'Not only that,' said Eddy, walking across the room, 'she got picked up off the street and taken to the Lock Hospital, nearly ended up being examined inside and out. You remember all that Contagious Diseases Act stuff, forcing women to be examined for syphilis?'

'What! Did you? Is that still going on?'

'It is,' said Alice, 'and the day they grabbed me, Victoria was sick. It was awful. Now I walk to work in a district nurse's cape and hat. And you should do the same when you're ready to go back.'

'Is that really necessary?'

'Believe me, Maud, it is. The plain-clothes police pick up any lone women off the street. You should be safe walking with me but, still, it's best to take precautions.'

Maud glanced down at her thin body. If someone grabbed her off the street right now, she'd probably just crumble.

'Don't you worry,' said Marie, placing a reassuring hand on her shoulder, 'we'll get you built back up in no time, and we'll do our best to make sure you're safe. Now, eat your scone, and drink your tea.'

Maud slept like a baby that night, snuggled in Alice's bed. Alice had insisted that she take the bed so that she'd be properly rested, whilst Alice slept on a mattress on the floor beside Victoria's crib. Alfred had the best spot in the house – a palliasse in front of the fire in the kitchen, with Hugo begrudgingly sharing the space.

Maud woke with a start, her heart pounding. She was expecting to feel the movement of the ship and the noise of the engines. But all was quiet apart from the murmur of voices in the kitchen next door and the sound of someone stoking the fire. She rolled on to her back and stretched, luxuriating in the comfort of a proper bed. She knew that she should be getting up, getting dressed, seeing what needed to be done; but just for once, she lay there, staring at the pattern of tiny cracks on the clean whitewashed ceiling. She pulled the sheet right up to her nose and snuggled down even further, smiling to herself, thinking of nothing except the beauty of lying in bed.

Alice must have gone to work by now, she thought. She hadn't even heard anyone get up. After living amidst so much noise, and feeling so ill for a full week on the ship, it was good not to be woken by snoring or coughing or drunken singing. And not only that, she'd never quite got used to sharing her bed with Harry. She liked to feel the warmth of him next to her, to know he was there, but in truth, she liked her own space.

'You make the most of this,' she whispered secretly to herself, knowing that she wasn't expected by Miss Fairchild until the afternoon. 'Just for one day, you make the most of this,' and then she turned on her side and promptly fell back to sleep.

When she woke again it was to the sound of Marie coming through the door with a tray of tea and toast. Maud shot up in bed. 'I'm so sorry, whatever time is it?'

'Oh, don't you worry, Maud, it's still morning,' smiled Marie. 'Now straighten yourself up so I can put this tray on the bed.'

'But—'

'No buts,' said Marie firmly. 'I know you're not in the habit of breakfast in bed, but just for once . . .'

Maud nodded. Once she was alone, she devoured the toast slathered with butter and drank the strong-brewed tea with relish. Picking two stray crumbs off the front of her nightgown, she then swung her legs over the side of the bed.

The door opened again and Marie was there. 'Let me take your tray. And then I'm going to bring the bath in and fill it for you.'

'No, really, that's . . .' mumbled Maud, preparing to decline. But then she felt the itching of her skin and the faint smell of vomit that seemed to have clung to her hair, and she knew that she had never needed a bath so much.

'Thank you,' she said.

'Now do you want the bath in here or in front of the fire in the kitchen?'

'In here,' said Maud straight away, terrified at the thought of lying naked in the kitchen. What if someone came in?

'Right you are,' said Marie, holding out a hand to assist as Maud made a move to stand up.

'You are to do nothing today except see the old lady, your friend Miss Fairchild. Alice has left strict instructions, and I dare not break them.'

Maud smiled, and opened her mouth to ask after Alfred.

'And the young man is playing draughts with one of our girls, Lizzie, in the front room . . . all decent and proper. We might be running a brothel but we don't have any customers at this time of day.'

As Maud lay in the bath, staring at the bedroom ceiling, she still felt anxious in case someone came in through the door, but the pure pleasure of being able to get properly clean far outweighed it. Marie had frothed up the water with some soap solution, to make some bubbles and preserve Maud's modesty, and she'd told her to soak her hair. She'd be back in ten minutes to help her wash it with soft soap and bring a jug of clear water to rinse it through.

I feel like the Queen, thought Maud, closing her eyes, resting back and gently moving her hand through the warm water. This must be what Queen Victoria feels like every single day.

And when Marie came in to wash her hair, it felt like

heaven. She couldn't remember anyone ever washing her hair, or seeing her naked, apart from Harry. But with Marie, she'd begun to relax and was quite confident to step out of the bath and into the towel that she held.

'Sit on the bed,' Marie said gently, 'and I'll get another towel to dry your hair.'

'Thank you,' breathed Maud, feeling the bubble of some deep sorrow rising unexpectedly up through her chest and escaping out of her mouth as she spoke. It felt like the first time she'd ever been truly pampered like this. She'd been very young when her mother died and although she'd been adequately cared for by her grandmother, she now realized that something had always been missing – something that Harry almost compensated for, but not fully.

'You have beautiful dark hair, Maud, it matches your eyes. I think it will shine with a gloss when it's dry. You'll feel like a new woman,' soothed Marie.

'I hope so,' whispered Maud.

Once she was left alone again, Maud began to smile. She never knew that having a bath could make someone so happy, but she felt warm and relaxed. She ran her fingers through her damp hair and pulled it back from her forehead, feeling the delicate drip of the clean water on her shoulders. Giving her hair another good rub with the towel, she clipped it in a loose knot. Then she removed the towel from her body and lay back on the bed for a few moments, feeling clean and free. It didn't last long; she was instantly worrying about the bed getting damp, so she was quickly up and stepping into her clothes, fastening her buttons, hooks and eyes. But she was still smiling.

Maud was soon sitting by the fire with Victoria on her knee. She unclipped her hair and left it loose so that it would dry, and the baby had both her hands in it, twisting and pulling the locks. 'Ouch,' said Maud, laughing and disentangling the baby's fingers, then reaching for a cloth dog with lopsided button eyes to distract her.

Alfred came through and crouched by Hugo, in front of the fire. He looked up and smiled, the corners of his eyes slightly downturned, giving him a mildly mournful air.

'When will Harry be back, exactly?' he asked, reaching out a hand to stroke the cat.

'Four weeks yesterday,' replied Maud, matter-of-factly. 'And by that time you should be settled back at school and I will be on the wards at the Liverpool Royal, feeling like I've never been away.'

'Are you happy that we've come back, Maud?' he asked, still stroking the cat, who was now twitching his tail, impatient to be left alone.

'Yes,' said Maud, after a short pause. 'If it hadn't been for Miss Fairchild's illness, I think I would have spent longer in New York, got more experience at the hospital, but I would have come back to Liverpool in the end.'

'That's good,' said Alfred, reeling back as the cat hissed and lashed at him with his claws out. 'Although it doesn't feel like Hugo is altogether pleased that we've returned!'

Maud laughed. 'Wait till he's nose to nose with Harry's dog, vying for position in front of the fire.'

'Rita won't win,' laughed Alfred. 'This cat is vicious.'

'Cah,' uttered Victoria.

'Did she just say "cat"?' marvelled Alfred. Then he repeated, 'Cat, cat, say "cat".'

'I do believe she did. What a clever girl!' smiled Maud, giving the baby an extra squeeze.

'Cah,' beamed Victoria, reaching out to be held by Alfred.

'I think you're safer with the baby than the cat,' laughed Maud, handing Victoria over. 'Have you got her? Keep tight hold and make sure she's safe. I'll just fix my hair and then I'll go and find Marie, see if I can do something to earn our keep.'

After Maud had carefully positioned a tortoiseshell comb in exactly the right place to keep her hair neat and tightly drawn back, she straightened her collar, smoothed down her skirt, and knew that she was almost back to her old self. She found Marie in the backyard folding clean sheets that she'd just unpegged from the line. Taking one side without being asked, Maud followed Marie's lead and doubled the sheet, doubled it again and then met hands with her to fold the fresh-smelling sheet into a perfect square. After each one was folded, and Marie had disappeared back to the kitchen, Maud sat for a few moments on the wooden bench against the wall. They would have to be setting off soon to see Miss Fairchild, but Marie had insisted that she take ten minutes.

Maud rested her head against the hard wall, using the time to list in her head what she needed to do before she made her return to work. Almost instantly she heard the click of the back gate and there in front of her, like an apparition, stood a girl with matted pale red hair and a grubby face.

'Where's Alice? Is she in?' asked the girl.

'Sorry, she's at work,' said Maud, noting the instant disappointment in the girl's big green eyes.

'That's all right,' said the girl, lifting her chin in mild defiance. 'It's just . . . I've brought something. Can you give it to her when she comes home?'

'Yes, of course,' said Maud. She was intrigued by the unexpected visitor, who she gauged as being a similar age to Alfred, though she was much thinner.

'Here it is,' said the girl, fishing in her pocket and then holding out a shiny ring on the palm of her hand. 'Tell her it's another special find from Sue Cassidy, just for her.'

'I will,' said Maud, taking the ring. She assumed it was nothing more than solid brass. 'Where did you find it?'

'Oh, it was outside Lewis's, this one. I was sitting there for ages, waiting for my mam to come, and it was on the path, between the flags, right next to me.'

'Well, it's lovely,' said Maud, turning it over and seeing some engraving on the inside.

The girl was leaning in now, her head almost touching Maud's as they scrutinized the ring together. 'It's treasure,' said the girl, 'and I want Alice to have it, because she helped us when Mam was out of work, before she got her job as a flower seller on the market. She gave us money for food.'

'But wait,' said Maud, holding it up to the light and seeing that it was indeed precious, it was almost certainly solid gold. 'It's—'

But with one click of the back gate, the girl was gone.

Maud gave the ring a rub on her skirt. She saw the lustre of it now even more strongly. She was sure of her assessment; she'd seen rings like this on the hands of wealthy visitors to the big house when she'd worked as a housemaid. She knew expensive jewellery when she saw it. Peering closely inside what was almost certainly a wedding band, Maud could see the engraving more clearly – the symbols that showed it was gold were there, and then another simple inscription. 'Love me and leave me not,' she recited quietly. And yet, the ring had been lost like a sixpence or, worse still, wilfully discarded, outside Lewis's Department Store. Maud knew straight away that it would be the right thing to go up there to the shop and ask if it had been reported missing by a customer. She would speak to Alice this evening.

Glancing down to her own thin wedding band, Maud felt a pang when she thought of Harry slipping it on her finger. Obviously, her ring was no match for the one she held in the palm of her hand, but she would never swap it. She knew that she would feel sad when she had to remove it each day before going to work. At the Women's Infirmary in New York, no questions had been asked, but she'd always kept it safe in her pocket before assisting in theatre or performing some of the more unmentionable nursing tasks. No one there really seemed to care if she was married or not, but she knew that that was not the case here, back in Liverpool. It had been decreed by Florence Nightingale herself that there were to be no married nurses in the service.

Maud took a deep breath. She'd never wanted her marriage to feel like a weight around her neck, and she'd never been good at subterfuge. She always told the truth if asked. Alice, Eddy and Miss Houston knew that she was a married woman. But as far as she was aware, no one else did. So now she felt the first inklings of the secret that she would be forced to carry when she was at work. A secret that she hoped would not make her feel too different from the rest of the nurses.

4

'Variety of form and brilliancy of colour in
the objects presented to patients are actual
means of recovery.'

Florence Nightingale

Maud felt Alfred hold more tightly to her hand as they
rounded the corner into the square, the ox-eye daisies
that he held in his other hand bobbing up and down on
their long stems as he walked along. Eddy had run in
with them, just as they were about to leave. 'A gift for
Miss Fairchild,' she'd shouted from the kitchen door,
catching her breath before she dived back out on her
way to the next case. Maud had managed to rescue
most of the flowers but some were too battered to make
up a posy. It had made her smile most of the way, thinking about how kind Eddy was.

As they neared the big house, however, she began to
feel a little apprehensive. And seeing the white stuc-
coed buildings, so clean and new, reminded her of the
day that she'd first seen Alfred walking this same route,
following along behind the chimney sweep, Mr Greer.
As senior housemaid she'd been waiting for them to
arrive, watching out of the dining-room window. She'd

seen Alfred desperately trying to keep up with his master and getting a clip around the ear when he failed to do so. Then she'd been horrified to witness the mindless cruelty that had taken place after Alfred had become wedged in the chimney and Greer had wrenched him down, breaking his arm. If she hadn't intervened and prevented the sweep from sending him back up the chimney, she dreaded to think what would have happened to her precious boy. Just thinking about it made her shudder.

As soon as they drew closer to the house, Alfred glanced up and gave her a cheeky smile. 'Go on, then,' she said, laughing to herself as she watched him run full pelt down the alley at the side of the house, the one that led to the tradesmen's entrance. When she caught up with him, he was still knocking on the door. 'Alfred!' shouted the kitchen maid, taking his arm and dragging him in off the step.

'And Maud!' called the cook, Mrs Watson, from the other side of the kitchen where she stood, red-faced and resolute, in front of the range full of copper pans bubbling away.

After the greetings and the fuss were done, Mrs Watson took Maud's hand and leant in to speak quietly. 'Before you go in to see Miss Fairchild, I want you to be prepared. You will find her somewhat changed – the weight's dropped off her, she's very out of breath and very melancholy at times . . .'

Maud could see that the cook was almost in tears, and she took her hand. 'I'm sorry about all of this, Mrs

Watson, she seemed to be in such good health when I went away last year.'

'Yes, she did to me as well, but you know what she's like. She'd been having the vapours at times and not telling anybody. All of it leading up to that day when she collapsed, here in the kitchen, right in front of me. I knew it was her heart right away. So I called for the footmen and they carried her to hospital in a cane chair. I didn't even think we had time to prepare the horse and carriage.'

Mrs Watson took a hankie out of her pocket and gave her eyes a wipe. 'Thank goodness for your friend, Alice. She was on duty that day and she did a fine job of looking after her. But would Miss Fairchild write and let you know what had happened to her? Would she hell as like! Sorry, Maud, 'scuse the language. And she sorely tried my patience with her stubbornness. Well, I knew I had to do it in the end without telling her – and I didn't feel good about writing that letter behind her back – but it was for the best, you and Alfred had to know . . .'

'You did absolutely the right thing, Mrs Watson,' soothed Maud. 'And thank you for all that you've been doing here. I know that you'll have been trying to feed her up, and you're probably helping out with the nursing as well.'

'Hmph,' grumbled the cook. 'Well, I had to with that first private nurse the mistress brought in. She was useless, couldn't have nursed a small child with a runny nose, never mind a fine lady like Constance . . . erm,

Miss Fairchild. But the new one, Nurse Ashworth, she's a bit straight-laced but she does seem to be doing a reasonable job. Anyway, you go through to Miss Fairchild, see what you think. She still has the two rooms adjoining, where she always was. But we had to move her desk out and give it to the new housekeeper.'

As they walked the familiar route to Miss Fairchild's room Maud's chest started to feel tight with the expectation of how she might find her old friend. To steady herself she glanced down at Alfred as he trotted by her side, the heads of the daisies still bobbing up and down. Knocking gently on the door, they both stood and listened. Not able to hear any response, Maud knocked again, more firmly.

'Come in,' called a muffled voice.

Maud felt a lump in her throat as she opened the door. It was a good job that Mrs Watson had warned her. It was a real shock to see her old friend sitting straight-backed in the chair with her starched cap perched on top of her grey hair but looking so thin and much altered. And for a moment Maud didn't think that her old friend had even registered who they were. Then her face broke into a watery smile, and she was reaching her arms out for Alfred.

Maud followed along behind as Alfred ran to Miss Fairchild with his posy of ox-eye daisies. 'Give the flowers to me,' she said quietly, so that Miss Fairchild could hug him and kiss him and cry happy tears at the sight of him. As Maud stood by the chair she noted her friend's bluish lips and fingertips, the laboured rise and fall of her breathing and the sallowness of her skin, stretched like parchment across her clearly defined cheekbones. And most of all her eyes, which had once been so full of life; her eyes were dulled and now seemed full of pain.

'Take your time,' soothed Maud, as Miss Fairchild broke away from Alfred, leaning back in the chair with her hand pressed over her heart. 'Just breathe,' said Maud, her voice perfectly calm although her own heart was beating like a drum in her chest. When Miss Fairchild was sufficiently recovered, Maud took her hand and leant in to give her a kiss on the cheek, the familiar smell of her lavender water scent somehow affirming the housekeeper's continuing hold on life.

'I've missed you, Maud,' she said, her eyes shining with tears. 'I've missed you but I never wanted you to drop everything and come back to Liverpool . . .'

'I know that,' said Maud. 'But we wanted to come back, once we heard the news, we wanted to come and see you.'

'But what about your work at the Women's Infirmary, all the exciting new ideas, the stuff you put in your letters?'

'I've brought them all back with me, up here,' said Maud, tapping her forehead.

'And what about Harry? Where is he?'

'Well, he had to stay a little longer. He was in the middle of some business deals that he needed to see through, but he'll be back next month.'

Miss Fairchild still didn't look convinced that their

premature return was a satisfactory arrangement but she held on to Maud's hand and then put an arm around Alfred. 'Now, young man,' she said quietly, 'I was wondering if you would be able to read to me for a little while. I keep nodding off every time I open a book, and I'm so missing my favourite novel. Look over there, on the side, you'll see a Jane Austen. Yes, that's the one. Now come and sit beside me here, on the footstool.'

'Read on,' ordered Miss Fairchild, once she could see that the boy was settled with the book on his knee.

'Chapter one. Emma Woodhouse, handsome, clever, and rich, with a comfortable home and happy dis-po—'

'Disposition,' smiled Miss Fairchild.

'Disposition,' repeated Alfred and then, continuing without further hesitation, 'seemed to unite some of the best blessings of existence . . .'

Maud quietly excused herself from the room, making her way to the kitchen to find a vase for the flowers. And as she walked along the familiar corridor, she began to feel sad. Even though, in her work as a nurse, she'd got used to seeing people altered by disease, it only went part way towards preparing her for witnessing an old friend struggling so much. She felt shocked by the change in Miss Fairchild, more so because with her nursing experience she could predict the sad, inevitable course that her condition would take.

'Sit down,' said Mrs Watson, 'I'll get you a glass of port wine.'

For once, Maud didn't object.

In the warmth of the kitchen, with Mrs Watson

fussing over her, Maud felt once more like that thirteen-year-old girl who'd been sent to train as a maid all those years ago. Fresh from losing her grandmother, she'd sat here at the kitchen table for the first time, an orphan. And like the orphan that she'd been back then, she now started to cry.

'There, there,' soothed Mrs Watson, 'that's it, just let it out . . . now let me find you a piece of cake.'

'No cake, thank you,' sniffed Maud, taking a lace handkerchief from her sleeve and wiping her eyes. Then, straightening her back, she made a physical effort to blink back the tears and cleared her throat. 'Please can you find me a vase for the flowers, Mrs Watson . . . and is there anything else that you think I can do to make Miss Fairchild more comfortable?'

'Well, that's easy,' smiled the cook, placing a large hand on Maud's shoulder, 'now that you and Alfred are home, all you need to do is come here and see her occasionally. It will make a world of difference to her. She's done nothing but talk about you two since the day you left for New York . . . and she's been sending out orders left, right and centre for new clothes and books and pens for Alfred to take up to the Blue Coat School. She probably hasn't shown you yet, but she's got a whole trunk of stuff ready and waiting.'

Maud started to well up again, and then she patted Mrs Watson's hand where it still rested on her shoulder. 'I'm so glad that we came back from New York. It was absolutely the right thing to do.'

She was even more sure of that when she ventured

back to the housekeeper's room. As she opened the door Miss Fairchild lifted her head, her eyes shining with pleasure. In that moment Maud glimpsed all the grace and dignity of the woman she had known, someone with a bit of fight left in her. Alfred was still reading and Maud moved as quietly as she could.

'Where do you want the vase?' she whispered, not wanting to interrupt the reading.

'You might as well put it over there, on the sewing machine,' said Miss Fairchild, pointing to the corner of the room and then taking Alfred's hand so that he paused at the end of the next sentence.

'Is this new?' asked Maud, running a hand over the shiny wood of the sewing machine and admiring the ornate pattern on the drawers before placing the vase of flowers on a cork mat.

'Yes, it's a brand-new Singer,' confirmed Miss Fairchild. 'I still have a tidy sum of money saved up – it will all go to you and Alfred – no, don't wave your hand like that Maud, who else am I going to leave it to? So I thought I might as well spend a bit of it and I ordered the machine when I got back from hospital, thinking I could help out in the house by doing some mending, or sewing tea cloths or something. But I'm completely out of breath just working the treadle.'

'Oh, I'm sorry,' soothed Maud, walking back towards her friend, 'that's such a shame. Maybe I could help you have another try?'

'No,' replied Miss Fairchild forlornly. 'No more tries.' And then she looked up with a gleam in her eye.

'I want you to have it now, Maud. I will ship it to your address when you get your accommodation settled.'

'No, I couldn't possibly . . .'

'You could and you will,' smiled Miss Fairchild, lifting her chin in a determined way, and reaching out to take Maud's hand. 'A beautiful modern machine like the Singer needs to be used, Maud. It needs to be working. Have you ever used a treadle?'

'Well, my landlady in New York had a new machine, almost identical, and she let me use it a couple of times. I didn't even know you could buy these yet in England.'

'You can now – these are some of the first – and I know you will get good use out of it, Maud. I remember how adept you were with your fingers, and how quick you were to learn. You were the best housemaid this place had ever seen.'

'Well, thank you, Miss Fairchild,' said Maud, blushing.

'Right, well, at least we've got that settled. Now pull up a chair and let's both listen to the rest of this chapter. You are going to be a fine scholar, Alfred,' said Miss Fairchild, quietly. 'Your reading is beautiful. And you'll be very pleased to know that I've got lots of new pens and books for you to take with you to school—'

There was a firm knock on the door and a woman wearing a nurse's starched cap walked in carrying a medicine glass on a porcelain plate. 'Time for your medicine, Miss Fairchild,' she said, matter-of-factly. Then, seeing the visitors, she gave a hint of a smile, revealing two very prominent front teeth.

'Here is Nurse Ashworth with my medicine,' grumbled Miss Fairchild, 'and this is the stuff that tastes bad.'

'I've mixed some honey in it for you, this time,' lisped Nurse Ashworth, holding out the plate unflinchingly.

Miss Fairchild muttered another grumble before taking the medicine glass and knocking the mixture back. She pulled a face as she swallowed and gestured for a glass of sherry that she kept at the side. Once she'd had a sip, all seemed to be well.

'What medicines is Miss Fairchild taking?' enquired Maud.

The nurse pursed her lips for a moment, considering her response. Then, as if a light had dawned behind her eyes, she spoke. 'Ah, you must be Maud, the nurse.'

'Yes,' replied Maud, taking the hand that was proffered. 'I am Maud Linklater.'

'I've heard all about you, and I've already met your friend Alice, when she was here visiting. I trained at the Liverpool Royal Infirmary too – a good few years before your time, though.'

'Really?' said Maud. 'You must have been in one of the very first sets of probationers.'

'I was. We bore the brunt of it from Miss Merryweather and some of those sisters on the wards. Miss Fairchild has been telling me all about Sister Fox. She doesn't seem to have changed at all. But I found real solace when I was there with one of the assistant superintendents, Miss Merryweather's sister, Elizabeth. She is so quiet and kind, and very well spoken. Did you have any dealings with her?'

'Not really. I did meet her a couple of times, though, and she did seem a very pleasant person,' said Maud. Then, changing the subject in case Nurse Ashworth started making enquiries about her personal situation, she asked again, 'What are the medicines that Miss Fairchild is taking?'

'Oh, I'm afraid that I can't disclose that information. Miss Fairchild's private physician likes to keep these things confidential.'

Maud caught an amused glance from Miss Fairchild and decided not to pursue the issue any further.

Nurse Ashworth started to turn away, but then she looked back at Maud and smiled again, more broadly this time. 'I forgot to ask your friend, Nurse Sampson, when she visited, but I have an acquaintance that probably trained at the Liverpool Royal around the same time as you two. Did you know a Nurse Sellers, Nancy?'

Maud felt the hairs at the back of her neck prickle. She hadn't seen or heard of Nancy since the day they received their certificates in the boardroom of the hospital. She took a deep breath. 'Nurse Sellers was in my set.'

'Was she?' grinned Nurse Ashworth.

'Yes. But how do you know her?'

'Oh, I handed over one of my patients to her. I'd been nursing a lady called Mrs Davenport in her own home for a number of years, a chronic case. I would still have been there now but, unfortunately, I was called home to a family illness. So Nurse Sellers took over the care of my patient and, as far as I'm aware, she's still there. She seemed such a lovely person, such a sweet smile and so gentle with Mrs Davenport. I only had a half day with her, to hand over, but she made a real impression on me.'

'Did she?' offered Maud, not knowing what else to say.

'Well, I must get on, I need to go and prepare a coddled egg and some aspic jelly for your tea, Miss Fairchild.'

'I can't wait,' muttered Miss Fairchild, turning to Alfred and pulling a face.

Well, well, thought Maud, feeling a tightness in her chest, I didn't expect to have to listen to an account of our Nurse Sellers again so soon. Then she straightened her back as she sat in the chair and tried to force any thoughts of Nancy right out of her head.

'Do you know what your medicines are?' she asked, turning to Miss Fairchild.

'Yes, of course,' she said with a conspiratorial gleam. 'I'm having a digitalis infusion each morning and some kind of tonic, afternoon and evening. And I can have laudanum drops for my aches and pains if I need them. No big mystery.'

'That sounds about right,' murmured Maud. 'They might be able to increase the digitalis a little, perhaps, if you need it.'

'Well, I'm on quite a big dose already,' said Miss Fairchild quietly. 'And I suppose you might say I'm as good as I can be. I've got enough breath for sitting here and talking to you and Alfred. But once I start to move . . .'

'I know,' said Maud, taking her friend's hand, 'and I wish there was something else to offer. But apart from an injection of morphia, if the breathlessness gets very severe . . . However,' she mused, looking around the room and seeing the window tightly sealed, 'you might find some relief from opening the window, letting a bit of air in. And you could try facing that way, so that you can see out to the street. In her *Notes on Nursing* Miss Nightingale strongly advises that we not only nurse the patient but also the room, paying particular attention to ventilation, light and air.'

'That sounds like a very good idea,' said Miss Fairchild. 'I'll speak to Nurse Ashworth.'

'Well, I can open the window for you now,' said Maud, getting straight up and opening the curtains to their fullest extent before pulling up the sash. 'Let's get more light in here, and some air,' she murmured. 'Not too much so there's a cold draught, but just enough to circulate.' Satisfied with her efforts, she then gestured for Alfred to help her swivel the chair with Miss Fairchild sat in it.

'Right, we'll turn you around so you can see what's going on out there. Is that all right?'

Miss Fairchild nodded, and then Maud and Alfred together heaved the chair and managed to turn it just enough.

'Oh, what a difference,' sighed Miss Fairchild, 'just being able to look out of the window. I can see the people passing by. Oh, look at that little boy, pulling a naughty face. And I can see the horses . . . I've always loved horses. And now with the window open, I feel like I can breathe just a little easier. And I've got Alfred's lovely flowers on the side table. Thank you, Maud. Thank you so much.'

Maud didn't know what Nurse Ashworth would make of the changes in her patient's environment but she felt very satisfied with her efforts as she made her way back to Stella's. As they walked she held tight to Alfred's hand. Miss Fairchild had already organized the sending of his trunk to the Blue Coat, and arrangements had been made for him to start school tomorrow morning.

That evening, as Maud sat on the wooden bench in the backyard listening to Alfred's reading practice, she could hear the murmur of voices from the kitchen. A shriek of laughter made Alfred glance up from his book. 'Just Alice back in from work,' said Maud, indicating for him to continue. She smiled to herself at how much life Alice had now. Last year when she'd been a probationer, hiding her pregnancy, she'd been a shadow of the person that Maud had found on her return to Liverpool.

Maud knew that Alice would be out to see them just as soon as she'd checked on Victoria. Sure enough, within moments, she was peering through the back door. 'There you two are,' she said.

Maud beckoned for her to come and sit next to them until Alfred had finished his passage. 'Right, that's enough for tonight,' she said gently, placing a hand on his cheek. 'Do you want to go and pack your things ready for tomorrow?'

Alfred nodded and got up from the bench.

'You're such a good lad,' said Alice, ruffling his bright blond hair as he walked past her.

'He's excited about going back to the school,' said Maud, watching him disappear through the door.

'Really?' said Alice, her eyes wide. 'He's one on his own, isn't he? But, then again, if I'd had to grow up in the workhouse, maybe I'd have a different way of looking at things.'

'True,' said Maud, standing up from the bench to straighten her skirt before sitting back down again with her hands neatly folded in her lap. 'What?' she asked, bewildered by the amused expression on Alice's face.

'Oh, nothing,' laughed Alice. 'It's just that I'm used to sitting here with Eddy spread-eagled all over the place.'

'Ha,' laughed Maud, 'I sometimes wish I could be so carefree. Harry has really tried to "loosen me up", as he calls it, but it just doesn't work. I need to have order and tidiness, and there really doesn't seem to be any way round it.'

'Well,' smiled Alice, sitting down beside her, 'we love you just the way you are, Maud. And what's more, you've been the talk of the whole hospital today – in a good way. Sister Law and Sister Pritchard were especially excited about your return. But I suppose that makes sense, given that they're in charge of the surgical wards and you are the queen of theatre.'

'I wouldn't exactly say that,' said Maud steadily. 'I still have a lot to learn.'

'You sound just like Sister Law,' laughed Alice.

Maud puffed out her chest and pretended to tie the strings of a sister's cap very tightly beneath her chin. 'We'll have no skulking in the sluice, Nurse Sampson,' she said, trying to keep a straight face.

'Sorry, Sister,' sniggered Alice, 'but I was just polishing the sink and emptying the sputum pots and washing the urinals in between making the beds and applying leeches and poultices to every single patient.'

Maud laughed out loud. 'Have you been on Male Surgical today?'

'No, I had to help out on Female Medical.'

Maud pulled her mouth down in mock horror.

'I know, Sister Fox. She is truly evil, you know. She's so evil that I've almost come to admire the perfection of her evilness. But thank goodness I'll be back on Female Surgical with our lovely Sister Pritchard tomorrow. Anyway, that's not what I came out here to tell you. I wanted to tell you that I've spoken to Miss Merryweather and Miss Houston and they can't wait to get you back on the wards. So much so that they not only gave me a district nurse's cape and hat for you to wear so that you can safely pass through the city, but they also gave me express instructions to make sure that you report to the Nurses' Home and Training School in the morning and start work as soon as possible.'

'Really?' said Maud, her eyes wide. 'They don't even want to interview me first?'

'No, of course not. They know you and they know your work. They want you back as soon as possible.'

Maud smiled. 'Well, I need to take Alfred up to the Blue Coat first thing, then I'll go straight to the hospital. Will that be all right?'

'Yes, of course,' said Alice. 'They wouldn't give anything away as to where you'll be placed, but it would be such a shame if they don't let you work in theatre.'

'Oh, I'll fit in wherever they need me. Although it might be a bit strange working on the male wards again, after nursing just women for so long. But I'll manage.'

'That's the spirit,' said Alice, resting her head back against the brick wall. 'And how did you find Miss Fairchild today?'

'I'll tell you in a minute but first, before I forget, you had a visitor this afternoon – Sue Cassidy, she brought this,' said Maud, rooting in her pocket for the gold ring. 'She said it was a special find, just for you, and I thought at first it was brass. But I think it's the real thing, I think it's pure gold.'

'Really?' said Alice, taking it from Maud. 'Difficult to see in this light, and I have no real idea what gold looks or feels like.'

'She said she found it outside Lewis's, between the cracks in the pavement. If it is gold, maybe we should go back, see if anybody's reported it missing.'

'Yes, of course we should,' said Alice, slipping it into her pocket. 'How did Sue look, was she all right?'

'She was unkempt. I felt like I wanted to give her a good wash and hold her head over a dolly tub to clean that lovely red hair. With those big green eyes, she's a real beauty under all that muck, isn't she? But she didn't stay long, she was gone before I could offer her any food or drink.'

'She's been coming to see me, on and off, all the time you've been away. The first time I met her she tried to steal a pillowcase off the washing line so she could sell it for a few pennies to buy food. She was starving hungry that day. There's something really special about Sue. She helped me when I was going through things whilst you were away. It felt like she was some kind of guardian angel, turning up just at the right time.'

'Maybe she is an angel,' smiled Maud, 'someone who's been sent to both of us.'

'You're very fanciful this evening, Maud. Maybe you have come back from New York with a whole new side to your personality.'

'Mmm, I don't know about that,' said Maud, leaning back and resting her head against the wall.

'Well, how did you find Miss Fairchild?' murmured Alice, turning to face Maud. 'And did you meet that nurse of hers?' she asked, tapping her two front teeth with the tip of her index finger.

'Stop it,' laughed Maud. 'Don't be mean. And yes, I did meet Nurse Ashworth.'

'Did she tell you that all details of her patient's case are confidential, like she did with me?' laughed Alice. 'Even though I was the one to provide Miss Fairchild's case history when she was discharged from Female Medical.'

'She did tell me that, yes,' replied Maud.

'And I thought all of us nurses were supposed to be working together – hospital, district, private – all trained together under the same system,' continued Alice, her cheeks flushing pink with indignation as she spoke.

'We are supposed to be. But maybe having sole charge of just one patient, it makes things seem different sometimes.'

'Might make you go a bit crazy, you mean! Some of the patients I've nursed, if I had them all day and all night . . . just imagine.'

'Imagine what?' called Eddy, pulling off her district nurse's hat and unpinning her hair before throwing herself down on the bench at the other side of Maud.

'Having the same patient, day and night, like a private nurse.'

'Oh, I don't know, that might not be so bad . . . not after the day I've had,' breathed Eddy. 'I not only had all of my usual cases, but the daughter of a patient – who was only visiting, mind, not resident in the house of my patient – she only started to give birth, right there and then. So I had to roll up my sleeves and deliver a baby. It was chaos. My patient lives in one room with two cats, so I had to shoo all that lot out first. And move him to a chair, so we could use his bed. And then, despite my best efforts with the rubber sheet that I always carry, the bed had to be changed. But it was an easy delivery, thank goodness, and what a beautiful baby boy, with a full head of blond hair. Oh, and you should have seen the face of my patient – the baby's grandfather – such a poorly man, but he was laughing and crying and singing songs in his native tongue.'

'Where is he from?' asked Alice, her eyes wide.

'He's a sailor from Riga, used to work the Baltic timber ships but hasn't been able to go home due to a back injury. So one of his daughters came here to look after him and she fell for a local man. And now Mr Indars Berzins has a grandson called Eddy!'

'Ha, ha, well done,' laughed Alice. 'They'll be wetting the baby's head in the Baltic Fleet pub tonight.'

'What a lovely thing, though, for a man who might never see his homeland again,' said Maud quietly. 'To witness the birth of his own grandchild.'

'Yes,' smiled Eddy, 'and he didn't bat an eyelid. I don't know why men scurry off as soon as women go into labour. I think we should encourage them to stay and bear witness to it. After all, seeing a baby come into this world is an absolute wonder. However, it might have been better from my point of view to have assisted with the absolute wonder at the end of the day, rather than in the middle, and then I wouldn't have been put so far behind. But at least I can sleep well tonight thinking of little Eddy Berzins.'

'I'll get you a sip of brandy to celebrate,' offered Alice, jumping up from the bench.

'I just don't know how you do it, Eddy,' marvelled Maud, 'out there on your own, with all sorts coming your way. You must have to think on your feet.'

'Yes,' said Eddy, running her hands through her hair. 'It can be exhausting, but it's such good work.'

'I brought a sip of brandy for us all,' said Alice, re-appearing with three glasses.

Maud was about to say her usual, 'Not for me, thank you,' but then she thought better of it. 'Cheers,' she said as they all chinked glasses. 'Here's to us, back together at last.' She coughed a bit with the first sip, and Eddy slapped her on the back, but she managed to get the rest of the brandy down and it gave her a lovely warm glow. 'Oh, I know what I was going to tell you both,' she said, putting an arm around Alice on one side and Eddy on the other.

'That nurse of Miss Fairchild's, she knows Nancy Sellers.'

Maud felt as if she'd dropped a stone down a silent well. She sensed both of her friends freeze, then Eddy stammered out something about Nancy, here, there and everywhere, and who'd have thought it, not seen her for ages.

Maud narrowed her eyes and looked from Eddy to Alice. She knew there was something that she wasn't being told.

'What's going on?' she said, meeting Alice's bright blue gaze.

Alice gave a tight smile, her face flushed bright pink. 'Oh, nothing more than usual. It's just that . . . I saw her a few times when I went back to the wards and was finishing my training. She was still trying to cause trouble . . . you know what she's like.'

'What kind of trouble?'

'Well,' said Alice, 'you know those romantic entangle-ments that Eddy was hinting at.'

'I was . . . I was hinting at them, wasn't I?' gabbled Eddy.

'Well, apart from Jamie, there was another man I was involved with. I fell for him very badly indeed, but he didn't tell me he was married. Nancy found out and she took a great deal of pleasure in letting me know.'

'Oh, I see,' said Maud, wanting to believe that this was all there was to it. And as Alice continued to tell of her various romantic entanglements, Maud could have been fully convinced. But as she sat between her two dearest friends on that bench in the backyard, with the light beginning to fade, just as surely as the moths came to tap at the lamplight in the small window beside the back door, so her nagging, nudging thoughts would not let her settle on one story. She knew there was more to it, and she knew that her friends were hiding something from her.

5

'The good nurse can often only answer, if examined how she nurses, "With brains and heart, sir, and with training and practice." '

Florence Nightingale

Maud wore her district nurse's cape and hat with pride as she walked towards the Blue Coat School early the next morning. She was surprised to see passers-by doffing their caps or calling out a cheery, 'Morning, Sister.' It was disconcerting, even though Alice had told her it might happen. And she wasn't sure whether she liked it or not. But she could see Alfred grinning beside her as he carried his bag of books.

To distract herself she thought of Harry and wondered what he might be doing. It seemed odd, thinking of her husband going about his usual business all the way across the Atlantic Ocean. She had an image of him in his dark green jacket, walking down Broadway with a bit of a swagger, the dog trotting by his side. And as he got closer to the port, he'd be exchanging banter with some of the men and buying merchandise to sell on to the shops in the city. She'd asked him many times about the detail of his work but never really got a full answer. He always managed to slide instantly into some other conversation and then tell her one of his stories and make her laugh. She never really knew what he was up to and wished now that she hadn't agreed so readily to him staying behind in New York. It would have meant a great deal to her and to Alfred for Harry to be with them now as they walked towards his first day as a boarder at the Blue Coat School.

Glancing at Alfred, steadfast by her side in his blue uniform jacket, she felt a stab of grief. She would miss being able to see him every day and she had to force herself to smile when he grinned up at her.

Their goodbye in the impressive courtyard at the front of the school was brief; a uniformed man was standing at the door and as soon as he saw them he came down the steps to escort Alfred inside. Maud was ill prepared for the pain that tightened her chest and made her breath rasp as she gave Alfred one final hug. She found tears stinging her eyes as she tried to say some hurried words, promising that she'd be up to see him as soon as she had an afternoon off – and she would, of course, make arrangements for him to come with her to meet Harry on the day of his return – all the while speaking firmly to hide the waver in her voice.

'That's all right, Maud, I won't be worrying,' he smiled. 'I've lived here at the school before, I will be just fine.'

'Of course you will, I know you will,' she said, blinking back tears.

And then he was gone, walking away with just a

single glance over his shoulder before disappearing inside the building.

As Maud stood alone at the bottom of the steps in the now empty courtyard, she felt bereft. Gazing up to the impressive walls of the historic brick building, she saw the stone-cast cherubs above the windows and felt their ornamental faces seeming to look down at her, passing judgement. She slipped her handkerchief out of her sleeve and wiped her eyes. Then she lifted her chin and looked back up at them. They were just ornaments, and she couldn't work out if their stony expressions were happy or sad, but at least they marked the use of the building as a place specifically for children. That must count for something, she thought. She always worried that Alfred might come to harm at the hands of some person in authority. She'd never been able to shake it off – not since she'd heard the stories that Alfred had told, very stoically, about his early life in the workhouse and then as an apprentice to the chimney sweep who had later tried to sell him on, just to make some money. Maud had had lengthy discussions with Harry about Alfred's safety if they returned to Liverpool. In the end, they'd agreed that it was very unlikely that the sweep would threaten the boy again. But feeling the separation from him now, Maud had to fight off the uncomfortable feeling that prickled at the back of her neck that something was lying in wait for him or for her, or maybe for both of them.

She took a deep breath to calm herself and then she looked across to the ancient parish church that sat opposite the school. With its octagonal tower and soot-blackened walls, St Peter's was a landmark in Liverpool. She remembered her grandmother telling her that she'd attended services there as a child, and Maud seemed to remember that the church had been built in the early seventeen hundreds when Liverpool was no more than a small town, set amongst green fields. It was hard to imagine that her crowded, smoky, ever-expanding city, full of grand buildings, had once been a quiet, rural place.

Strange, thought Maud, as she walked across School Lane and in through the church gate, my grandmother used to watch the children from the Blue Coat walking in line across to St Peter's and filing into their special pews up in the gallery.

Maud glanced up to the church clock and her pulse began to quicken. 'I need to get going,' she murmured to herself, 'I don't want to be too late for my first morning at work.' She could imagine Miss Merryweather already tapping her fingers impatiently on the polished wood of her desk. And that sense of the hospital waiting sent a ripple through her body as she walked towards her work – she could almost smell the disinfectant of the wards.

As she made her way up Brownlow Hill towards the Infirmary, the street was busy. One carriage came so close to the footpath that Maud felt the swish of the wheel as it brushed by her. And there were street sellers with their stalls at the side of the road, and women and children milling around. It was a good job that she could step lithely around her fellow pedestrians or she would have been delayed.

Just as she was approaching the final stretch, Maud noted a child with tousled red hair up ahead and took a second to recall where she remembered her from. It was her visitor to the backyard – Sue Cassidy. She called out to the girl but her voice was lost in the hubbub of the crowd. She picked up her pace so that she could reach out to her, say hello. She could see the girl's head still bobbing along in front. She was moving fast, dodging her way through the busy street. Then Sue stopped dead in her tracks and Maud began to gain ground, keeping her eye on that head of tangled red hair. She was almost there, half a dozen strides away, when Maud saw the girl clutch her head with both hands and shout something inaudible amidst the rumble of carriage wheels and the sound of horses' hooves. Then, to Maud's absolute horror, the girl darted into the road, right in front of a horse and carriage.

'Sue!' Maud screamed, her voice instantly drowned out.

What came next was the terrified shriek of a rearing horse, followed by screaming and shouting. Maud's heart contracted for a split second, then she lifted her skirt and ran, pushing her way through the people on the pavement. The whole street had come to a standstill. Maud looked past a woman who stood frozen at the side of the road, her hand over her mouth. Maud gasped when she saw Sue lying, bloodied, on the ground. And there, next to her, was a small boy with bare feet who lay clutching a dusty loaf of bread. Both casualties were unconscious.

A coachman in full grey livery had got down into the road, along with the driver of the carriage.

'Let me through,' shouted Maud, her heart thudding in her chest. 'I'm a nurse.'

Maud's instincts led her first to Sue, who had a pool of blood now forming around her head. Glancing across to the boy, even as she assessed the girl, she saw the driver kneel down by the side of him.

'Is he breathing?' she shouted.

The man nodded.

'Stay with him,' instructed Maud, shutting out the sound of a woman who had started to weep and the frenzied snorting and stamping of the horses around her. As she inspected the extent of Sue's injuries, somewhere in the distance she heard the sound of a policeman blowing his whistle and shouting, 'Stand back, everyone!'

It was easy to see the source of the bleeding. Sue had a gash on the left side of her face, stretching from her forehead, skimming past her eye and down her cheek. Maud could see the white glint of bone. It was deep.

She pulled out her clean handkerchief and pressed it to the wound, her hands instantly covered with blood.

'I need more clean cloths,' she shouted. 'Anything. But it has to be clean.'

The passers-by that surrounded her looked at each other frantically, appearing helpless. Then the coachman in grey livery handed her a linen handkerchief.

Maud took it without a word and pressed it to the

wound on Sue's face. It was soon soaked through with blood, but now other people were catching on, too. They began passing their handkerchiefs and then a tea cloth from the bread stall at the side of the road. Maud soon had a compress on the wound and the bleeding under control. Sue was still unconscious so Maud checked her limbs carefully with her free hand. She couldn't detect anything that felt obviously broken.

The coachman crouched down in the dust of the road. 'I can put pressure on there for you,' he said, 'if you want to go and check the boy.'

Maud went straight over to the boy, who lay covered in dust, as if asleep, the loaf of bread still tucked under his arm. She knelt down beside him, her eyes scanning his body. He was breathing but his skin was white. Maud gasped when she saw the mark of the carriage wheel right across his body. She felt a stab of pain as she realized that there would be too much damage inside his small body to repair. There was no hope for the tiny child. When she saw the frozen expression on the driver's weather-beaten face, she knew that he too understood the consequences of the boy's accident.

'He ran right out in front of me,' said the driver, holding back a sob. 'Right in front of me. He must have grabbed the bread off that stall. And then the girl came straight after him, she tried to pull him back. There was nothing I could do.'

Maud put a hand on his arm. 'Just stay with him,' she said.

The coachman was doing a good job applying

pressure to Sue's wound. He seemed unfazed by the amount of blood that covered his hands. 'We need to get moving right now, up to the Infirmary,' Maud said firmly.

'I'll take over from here, Sister,' said a policeman with a red face, pushing his way through. 'I'll organize transport for these two up to the workhouse infirmary.'

'No,' said Maud firmly. 'No. They are going to the Royal Infirmary.'

'They're just waifs and strays, Sister, no need to concern yourself,' replied the constable.

Maud stepped in front of him with her teeth gritted and her right hand balled into a fist at her side.

'As you well know, Sister,' said the policeman, frowning, 'they don't accept riff-raff from the streets at the Infirmary. The only place they can go is the workhouse.'

'I work at the Royal Infirmary,' she said, feeling the quickening of her pulse as she tried to control her anger, 'and that is where I am taking these children.' Then, turning her back on the policeman, she leant down to speak to her helper. 'It isn't far. Can you manage the girl, if I carry the boy?'

'Of course,' said the coachman, instantly slipping his arms beneath Sue and lifting her up from where she lay in the street.

'Right,' nodded Maud. 'We need to get moving.'

'Now, Sister—' tried the policeman once more.

'I need to move these casualties to the hospital,' she called over her shoulder as she stooped down towards the boy. 'I happen to know the girl's name. She is Sue

Cassidy, and her mother works as a flower seller on the market. I want you to get word to her and send her up to the Infirmary. And you need to try to find out who this boy is, and if he has any family.'

Not waiting for any further discussion, Maud murmured to the driver, 'I'll take him now,' and she slipped her arms carefully beneath the boy and lifted him up from the ground. Her heart almost broke when she felt the slightness of his starved frame and saw his small face, white beneath the muck, with a bubble of bright red blood forming at the corner of his mouth. She could feel him still breathing but his body felt broken in her arms.

Maud almost ran to keep up with the coachman as he strode ahead at some pace, easily carrying Sue, without any regard for the blood that was undoubtedly soaking into his grey livery.

As soon as they reached the door of the Infirmary, he stopped and waited for Maud to catch up. 'Follow me,' she said breathlessly, knowing exactly where she was going – straight to Alice and Sister Pritchard on Female Surgical.

As they ran down the corridor, Maud could feel her heart pounding in time with the sound of their echoing feet. She caught the familiar carbolic tang of the hospital and it somehow reassured her. As soon as they were in through the door of the ward, she saw the tall figure of Sister Pritchard further up the ward. 'We need some help,' she cried, and Sister came running.

'Maud?' she said, as soon as she recognized her, but there was no time to ask any more questions.

'These two ran out in front of a carriage at the top of Brownlow Hill. I know this girl, her name is Sue Cassidy. She has a nasty facial injury and she's been unconscious since the accident. This boy is breathing but he has the mark of a carriage wheel across his body.'

Sister Pritchard glanced at the boy in Maud's arms. The fleeting look of sorrow was unmistakable in her eyes but she was already giving instructions. 'Well, we are a female ward but small boys are also welcome. See those two beds there, next to each other,' she said firmly, turning to point towards the bottom of the ward. 'Put the boy in the corner bed, it will be quieter, and the girl next to him.'

As Maud walked with her helper, carrying the children in their arms, she saw the line of female patients in beds down each side of the ward look in their direction. One or two crossed themselves.

'Nurse Sampson!' called Sister, and Maud saw the shock on her friend's face when she popped her head out from behind a set of wooden screens midway up the ward. 'I need you to finish up there with Mrs Jenkins and come here directly, we have two new admissions. Find one of the probationers, Nurse Latimer, and ask her to go and locate Mr Jones and inform him that he's needed in theatre on Female Surgical as soon as he's finished up what he's doing. And send the other probationer, Nurse Devlin, down here to me.'

'Yes, Sister,' called Alice.

Maud settled her boy carefully in the bed, the dirt

75

from the street instantly smearing the spotless white bedding as she slipped him between the sheets. There was more bright red blood now at the corner of his mouth, and she wiped it away with the flat of her hand. Then she pulled up the top sheet to cover his body and gently tucked it beneath his arms. With his grubby face belying the deathly whiteness of his skin, the boy looked as though he was peacefully sleeping. Maud noted that his breathing was very shallow. And when she picked up his wrist to check his pulse, it was barely palpable.

She heard Sister Pritchard directing the probationer, Nurse Devlin, to stay with the boy, quietly telling her that there was nothing else that could be done for him. As the young nurse, a slender girl with wide grey eyes, slipped by her, Maud gave her a grateful smile for what she was about to do. When she turned back to Sue's bed, she could see the tension in Sister Pritchard's thin body as she leant over to check her patient's breathing and pulse and then, as Maud had done earlier, feeling up and down her arms and legs for any sign of a fracture.

Straightening up, Sister looked across at Maud. 'You've done well. We'll leave your makeshift dressing in place for now, it's doing a good job of staunching the bleeding. I'll just add some clean lint on top and a bandage to keep it in place.' And then, with a wry smile, she added, 'I knew you were coming back to join us, Nurse Linklater, but I didn't expect you to be rescuing injured children from the streets of Liverpool just yet.'

Maud just nodded. 'Mercifully, from what I can see,

the eye seems to be undamaged. The facial wound is deep, it will need to be seen by a surgeon as soon as possible, but at least we've managed to slow down the blood loss,' she said. 'Thanks to this coachman here, who has provided excellent assistance . . .'

The man stood as if in a dream, still gazing down at Sue as she lay unconscious on the bed. His hands were covered in blood and Maud could see the bright red stain of it on the sleeve of his grey jacket.

Maud saw Alice coming down the ward. She walked quickly towards her friend and took her hand. 'One of the new admissions is Sue Cassidy, Alice. I saw the whole thing. She was hit by a horse and carriage on Brownlow Hill. She's breathing, she doesn't seem to have any broken bones or internal damage, but she does have a deep wound all the way down the side of her face.'

Maud saw Alice frown as she tried to take in all the information, and then her eyes widened. She bowed her head for a second, but when she looked at Maud her mouth was set in a firm line. 'Thanks for forewarning me,' she said. By the time she reached Sue's bed, her voice was steady. 'I know this girl,' she said.

Maud turned to speak to the coachman, who still stood at the bottom of the bed in his ruined jacket. 'I cannot thank you enough for helping me. I would never have got her up here to the hospital if it hadn't been for you. And I don't even know your name . . .'

'I'm Thomas Wright,' he said, reaching out to shake her hand but then realizing that his was full of blood.

He gave a wry smile. 'Well, that's what you get for helping out at the scene of an accident, I suppose.'

'You did a good job,' said Maud.

'I witnessed the Charge of the Light Brigade during the war,' he said. 'We had to deal with all kinds of injuries.'

'Oh, I see,' breathed Maud, reaching out to place a hand on his bloodstained sleeve. 'Thank you for stepping up again today.'

He was nodding, lost in his own thoughts for a moment, and then he looked up with the semblance of a smile.

'Now, I'll ask one of the nurses to get you a bowl of water and you can wash your hands and try to sponge those marks off your jacket. It is rather a mess, I'm afraid.'

'It's of no importance,' he said, glancing once more towards Sue and then across to the boy. 'These children are all that matter.'

Maud was quickly back at the bedside.

'Right, nurses,' said Sister quietly. 'Sadly, I've had a good look at the boy and I think that time is very short. I'm assuming that he was alone, no family with him?'

Maud nodded. 'There was a policeman in attendance, and I asked him to try and find out who the boy was. But you know how many stray children there are on the streets . . .'

Sister nodded, her face sombre. 'And the girl?'

'Her mother is a flower seller on the market,' Alice said quietly.

'And I asked the policeman to find her,' added Maud. 'So, hopefully, we might see her here in due course.'

'Good, well, there's no more that can be done for the moment. Now, given that the bleeding from the girl's wound has been contained, we can afford to wait for our surgeon to attend. I'd like to get her treated within the next couple of hours, but we do have time. She is deeply unconscious, so we need to keep a careful eye on her. If you could do that, Nurse Sampson. We need to wash her and change her out of that filthy dress and into a clean nightgown. But I don't want to move her just yet and risk disturbing the wound – so if you two could do that when we've got her into theatre.'

'Yes, Sister,' said Maud.

Then Sister turned to gaze at the small figure lying so very still in the next bed. 'But the boy . . .' she said wistfully. 'There is nothing more we can do, I'm afraid, except keep him comfortable. Nurse Linklater, perhaps you could help Nurse Devlin to give his face and hands a wash. Again, I don't want to disturb him too much, so don't change him out of his clothes . . . just be gentle with him.'

'Of course,' said Maud.

'Oh, and Nurse Sampson, bring the wooden screens down here, will you? Let's create a quiet space for the boy in the corner of our ward . . . and when Nurse Latimer returns I will tell her to go and fetch the chaplain to say a few prayers. The Reverend Seed needs to know about both of these admissions.'

As Maud walked up the ward to collect a bowl of

water from the sluice, she slipped the dusty nurse's cape from her shoulders and folded it into a square. Seeing one woman silently crying, Maud took a moment to go to the side of her bed. 'We'll do all that we can for the boy, to keep him comfortable,' she said gently.

'I know,' murmured the woman, taking a handkerchief from the sleeve of her nightdress and wiping her eyes. 'It's just that he looks about the same age as my William was when he died. He was killed in the street, crushed by a cart when he was out playing. I should never have let him out of my sight that day . . .'

'I'm so sorry,' soothed Maud, feeling her chest tighten with sympathy for the woman. After what she'd just witnessed out on Brownlow Hill, she could have knelt down by the side of the woman's bed and cried alongside her, there and then. But there was so much that still needed to be done. And, of course, she could never do that – a nurse had always to be strong for her patients.

'I'll come back and see you later,' Maud said quietly, and the woman nodded.

Once she was safely inside the sluice, Maud leant back against the closed door for a few moments and took some deep breaths. Everything had happened so fast, it was hard to believe that she was instantly back to work on the wards. But here she was, and she needed to keep moving. Still clutching the soiled cape in her hands, she found a place to leave it, then gave her hands a good scrub with carbolic soap, seeing the red blood dissolving quickly into the water. But even with a brush she was not quite able to get it all out from under her nails.

With no time to waste, Maud reached for a nurse's apron from a neat pile of spares at the side. She shook it open and tied it tightly around her thin waist, smoothing down the white starched material before collecting her bowl of water. A steaming kettle stood by the side, ready to use, so she poured just enough into the cold water to make it a comfortable temperature. Then she quickly took a soft flannel and a clean towel from the shelf, placing them neatly over her arm so that once she was out through the door she could carry the bowl with both hands as she walked down the ward.

When Maud slipped behind the wooden screens, she found Nurse Devlin crouched by the boy's bed. The probationer hurriedly stood up and tried to compose herself but Maud could see that she had tears in her eyes.

'It's all right,' said Maud quietly, placing her bowl of water on a small side table. 'You can be upset. But we just need to be aware that sometimes patients can still hear us, even though they seem to be out cold. So let's talk to him and reassure him.'

Nurse Devlin nodded. 'Yes, I can do that,' she said, her lilting voice gentle and distinctly Irish.

As they worked together, Maud used the soft cloth to wash the boy's face and hands whilst her assistant gently dried them with the towel. She was glad of Nurse Devlin's big grey eyes, glancing to her for reassurance or for instruction. It helped her to keep exact focus on the crucial work that they were doing for their small patient.

'Now, young man,' said Maud softly, 'we're going to lift your legs and bend your knees so we can soak your feet in a nice bowl of warm water to give them a gentle wash.'

Covering the boy's upper body with a warmed blanket that Sister had provided, Maud indicated for Nurse Devlin to spread a towel over the bottom sheet. Then, placing the bowl on top of the towel, she took each small leg in turn and placed both feet in the bowl, gently washing and cleaning the dust of the streets from the boy's poor ragged feet.

'He must have always been without shoes,' murmured Nurse Devlin, as the cuts and calluses became visible.

Maud could see her blinking back tears again. 'Yes, like so many others,' she said. 'But we're washing your feet now, aren't we, young man? And I'm going to find some soothing cream in a minute to make them shine.' Maud made herself smile, even though all she wanted to do was kneel down by the bed and weep.

When she came back with the cream, Maud found Nurse Devlin quietly humming a gentle tune. 'An Irish song me mother taught me,' she said, looking up with a tentative smile.

Maud nodded her approval. 'Right, young man,' she said, 'we'll just dry your feet and apply the cream, and then we'll get you comfortable.'

As soon as they had him settled beneath the small

blanket and covered with a clean sheet, Maud asked Nurse Devlin to go and find a stool so she could sit with the boy. When she was gone and Maud was alone, she took the boy's hand, instantly noticing how cold it was, and when she checked for a radial pulse, there was nothing. He was still breathing, but only just, and Maud knew that he was very close to death.

Kneeling by the bed, she took his tiny hand in her own again and whispered, 'My lovely boy. I'm so sorry that this world hasn't treated you any better than this . . . I hope you can find some peace now.'

Maud saw Nurse Devlin's face change as soon as she came back behind the screen. Her eyes filled with tears again and she wiped them away with the flat of her hand before placing her stool beside the boy and gently taking his other hand. She looked up at Maud and nodded, indicating that she was all right, she wanted to do this.

Maud stood up and gave her a small smile. Even if this was the girl's first ward, Maud knew that she would have already seen death by now. But seeing a child so young, that was different. It seemed, however, that despite the girl's youth and her wide grey eyes, she was a person with some resilience.

'You will make a good nurse,' Maud told her, quietly, before turning from the bed, feeling confident to leave Nurse Devlin behind the screen alone, whilst she went back to check on Sue Cassidy.

Five minutes later, the Reverend Seed was there, just in time to say prayers. After he had spoken briefly to Alice, Maud saw him slip behind the wooden screen and then the whole ward full of women were listening to the words of his prayers as the boy took his final breaths.

When the chaplain's voice fell silent, Maud heard small gasps and some gentle sobs from those patients awake or alert enough to know what was going on. The collective grief was palpable in the air as the chaplain emerged from behind the screen and stood looking down the ward towards all of the women.

As if from nowhere, a patient started to sing. Quiet, almost inaudible at first, and then her voice swelled within the silence of the ward. The words were Welsh. Maud knew the song right away, she'd heard it many times in Liverpool. It was 'Suo Gân', a lullaby. And as another woman's voice joined the singing, the two voices seemed to soar up to the high ceiling of the ward. Maud's arms prickled with goose bumps as she stood by Sue's bed, reciting in her head her understanding of the song's translation. 'Nothing shall disturb your slumber . . . Nobody will do you harm. Sleep in peace, dear child. Sleep quietly on your mother's breast.'

Maud blinked back tears as she stood by Sue's bed. When she looked up the ward, she could see Alice crouched by the bed of a woman who was weeping and Sister Pritchard speaking to another patient. The Reverend Seed was now carefully making his way from one patient to another. But the other probationer, Nurse Latimer, stood impassive at the top of the ward. Maud made a mental note to check on the girl later, make sure that she was all right.

Maud's head began to swim a little and she took hold of Sue's hand to steady herself. But when she looked back down at the girl, lying on the bed with the blood-soaked dressing on her face, Maud felt her heart thud as if she were feeling the shock of the accident all over again. For a split second she heard the terrified scream again and she almost felt the moment of impact. It made her gasp. And then her head was crowded with thoughts. If only I'd managed to get to Sue a few seconds sooner. If only I'd walked faster, or set off with Alfred a few minutes earlier, I might have managed to get to her in time. I might even have seen the boy about to run and been able to grab him. *If only* . . .

6

'. . . our great English hospitals are places
in which more is done for the relief and cure
of human misery . . . than in any other
places in the world.'

Florence Nightingale

'You're still wearing your district nurse's hat, Nurse Linklater,' said Miss Merryweather as she joined Maud at the bottom of Sue Cassidy's bed.

Maud reached up her hand and gestured towards removing it.

'No, leave it,' smiled the superintendent. 'I hear you've been far too busy to think about nurses' caps. And you've certainly made your mark back here already. Sister Pritchard has given me all of the details. This is a very sad business, isn't it? And on your first day, as well.'

Maud nodded. There didn't seem to be any words.

'I'll just go in and see the boy,' said Miss Merryweather.

'Yes,' said Maud, glad of a few moments to compose herself.

When Miss Merryweather emerged from behind the wooden screens she was dabbing at her eyes with a lace handkerchief. 'Such a poor, tiny boy,' she murmured. 'And as far as we're aware no family have been located?'

'Not as yet. But if the police do manage to locate someone, I'm sure they'll send them here.'

'Well, we are his family now, if no one turns up, and we'll make sure that he is dealt with in the proper manner. My sister, Miss Elizabeth, has some money set aside for such eventualities . . .' Then, clearing her throat, 'I was going to allocate you to Female Medical, Nurse Linklater – we have long-standing staffing issues on that particular ward – but given the start you've made here, I think there is no choice but to offer you a position with Sister Pritchard. Subject to, of course, any requests for additional help on other wards. Is that satisfactory?'

'Yes, very much so,' replied Maud.

'Now, I won't delay you any further, Nurse Linklater, except to say, well done. And do call by when you get the chance to fill me in on your exploits in New York.'

And with that the superintendent turned on her heel and was gone.

'I can stay on and help in theatre,' offered Maud as soon as Sister Pritchard came back to Sue's bed.

'Really? Are you sure? That would be an enormous help. I've already lent a nurse to Sister Law on Male Surgical because they've had a big case in theatre this morning.'

'I'm sure,' Maud said as Sister Pritchard slipped behind the screen to assist Nurse Devlin. 'But before I do anything else,' she murmured to herself, glancing up the ward to the other probationer, 'I just want to go and have a word with Nurse Latimer, make sure that she's all right.'

She spoke to her colleague gently, taking a step back when the sharp-faced probationer turned on her with an empty stare.

'I just wanted to make sure that you were all right, with what happened to the little boy?'

'I lost a brother and a sister before I was ten years old. I am fine,' replied the probationer.

'I see,' said Maud, knowing that the girl's response was decidedly askew. But from the glassy stare that was levelled at her, she also knew that there was no way she could pursue the issue any further.

'Well, just let me know if you need help with anything,' Maud said, offering a small smile.

The girl nodded and started to turn away but then she switched back. 'And you are?'

'I'm Nurse Linklater, a trained nurse. I'll be starting, officially, tomorrow. I'll be helping Sister Pritchard with the supervision of the ward,' Maud said. 'You can speak to me at any time.'

Nurse Latimer didn't reply but continued to gaze at Maud with her too bright eyes. The probationer made Maud feel out of kilter, unsettled. In a way that she hadn't experienced since she'd worked with Nancy Sellers.

Maud started to feel more uncomfortable, as if she needed to apologize for something that she knew she hadn't done.

She started to speak again, but Nurse Latimer had already turned away and was walking towards the sluice. Maud frowned, trying to make sense of what had just happened, but she had more pressing concerns so she put it out of her mind as she walked back to Sue Cassidy's bed.

As soon as she reached her patient she saw the tall, slightly dishevelled figure of the senior surgeon, Mr Jones, coming through the ward door. Maud gave an involuntary sigh of relief; she had worked with him many times in theatre, and he was always a very reassuring presence. He seemed thinner than she remembered him, though, and more distracted.

'Ah, Nurse Linklater,' he smiled. 'So pleased to see you back, we are desperate for a true theatre nurse. Now, I believe you have a patient for me already . . .'

'Yes,' replied Maud, giving the surgeon all the details of the case.

'Well,' he said, checking Sue's level of responsiveness, 'I can see she is knocked insensible and, given that our man with the chloroform, Dr McKendrick, has been called away to a difficult case, I think that we should get her straight into theatre, before she wakes up.'

'Righto,' said Maud, 'I'll call for the orderlies to come with their stretcher.'

'They too are busy with Dr McKendrick,' said Mr Jones. 'But given that she's only a slip of a lass, I think I can manage her,' he said, pulling back the sheet and carefully sliding both his arms beneath the girl.

'Come on, dear girl,' he said gently as he straightened

up from the bed and turned to carry her up the ward as if she were the most precious thing in the world.

Maud gestured for Alice to follow. Once they were in through the door of theatre, they stood one at each side of the high wooden table as Mr Jones positioned his patient.

When they heard the dull clunk of something on the solid wood of the theatre table, as Mr Jones shifted Sue's position, Maud exchanged a glance with Alice. They both knew what it would be: some special 'find' in the girl's pocket. Alice slipped her hand in and pulled out a red painted earring, a wooden dice and an empty glass bottle with an etched pattern.

Maud could see tears springing to her friend's eyes. 'You keep them safe, for good luck,' she soothed. 'Put them in your pocket for now.'

Alice nodded mutely and carefully took the items.

'Now, Alice,' said Maud, as Mr Jones headed quietly to the sink to scrub his hands. 'Whilst I start to wash the worst of the muck from her face and hands, I want you to go and get a clean nightdress and the big scissors – this dress is filthy and too far gone to go to the laundry, we'll have to cut it off her.'

When Alice returned they soon had the ragged dress removed, but they left the grey vest and underclothes in place – even with Maud's concerns for cleanliness they didn't have the heart to strip the poor girl of all her worldly goods. Once the clean nightdress was in place, Alice seemed desperate to try and wash the worst of the dirt from the girl's matted hair but, for now, the best that she could do was go over it with a dampened cloth.

'We'll make sure we wash it properly when she's recovering,' murmured Maud, turning to give a nod to Mr Jones, who'd gone from scrubbing his hands to having his ritual smoke in the corner of the theatre.

'Just stay with her, Alice, a second, will you? Whilst I wash my hands.'

As soon as Maud was back at the table, Alice stooped to collect Sue's dress from the floor. 'I'll be at the top of the ward if you need anything,' she said, glancing at Sue for one last time. 'Just shout.'

As Mr Jones was finishing his smoke Maud removed the bandage and the lint and then peeled the layers of blood-soaked handkerchiefs from Sue's face. She was careful with the final one, not wanting to set off any further bleeding just yet. Mr Jones walked around to the other side of the theatre table and leant over to peer at the wound.

'Now, what do we have here? Mmmm, it only just missed the eye, didn't it? A nasty, vicious wound. What is the definition of a wound, Nurse Linklater?'

Before she could open her mouth to reply, he continued, 'Wounds are the divisions of soft parts produced by external direct mechanical force. Classified according to their direction, depth, locality or their mode of infliction. Here we have an open, contused wound caused by a sharp object, and given that the girl was found in the road following a collision with a carriage, there is little doubt the object was a horseshoe. Fortunately, the wound seems clean – thanks to whoever applied that dressing at the scene – and, as you can see, even though the edges of the wound are swollen, they can be brought together quite easily. The eye is very bruised, but seems intact, and all of that should settle with time.'

'Will you be using a fine silk thread to reduce scarring?' asked Maud.

'I will indeed, Nurse Linklater,' he replied, his eyes shining with interest. And then he pursed his lips. 'But I'm afraid there are no sutures in the world that will leave this girl without a substantial disfigurement.'

Maud nodded. Sadly, she too was aware of that reality. She'd witnessed a number of women at the Infirmary in New York, victims of knife wounds – slashed across the face by vengeful husbands or deranged men.

'But we will do our best for her,' said Mr Jones. 'I'll take my time with the sutures, keep them small.'

Maud nodded as she checked that all the instruments were to hand, and then she took up the bottle of carbolic acid and sprayed it over the wound.

'Good practice, Nurse Linklater, good practice. I too am a devotee of Mr Joseph Lister, and we need to do all that we can to try and prevent deep suppuration.'

As Mr Jones explored the wound before commencing his suturing, the unmistakable white glint of a cheekbone made Maud's stomach tighten. But once he had the first suture in and fresh blood was welling up, she was straight there with clean swabs, taking each one from the pile at her elbow and discarding the blood-soaked ones into a bowl on the floor.

He was painstaking with the sutures, taking his time with each and every one as his deft fingers continued their work down the long wound on Sue's cheek, fashioning a scar that would dictate what she saw in the mirror for the rest of her life. Maud could see the sheer concentration on his face. Even when his forehead began to glisten with sweat, he continued to work, only pausing for a few moments when Sue gave a low groan and looked like she might be going to wake up. Thankfully, she settled back into her unconscious state and they were able to finish without calling for Dr McKendrick and his chloroform.

When the final suture went in and Maud stood back to check the wound, she could see the true extent of it. She almost wept. The scar was disfiguring; she had known women with similar wounds choose to wear a veil rather than expose themselves to the world.

Maud took a deep breath and swallowed hard to quell the lump in her throat. She could see the side of Sue's face swelling angrily against the insult of the sutures and she knew she needed to get on and make sure that the area was as clean as possible and apply a good dressing. Giving the wound a final wipe with a clean swab, she gave another spray of carbolic acid. Then, placing one neat square of white lint over Sue's closed eye and another oblong piece over the long wound, Maud selected a two-inch-wide muslin bandage. She knew that it would be a tricky manoeuvre to secure the dressing and so she asked Mr Jones to hold Sue's head in position whilst she made two turns of the bandage around her head, crossing the fore-head and then down to the nape of the neck, before passing beneath the ear and then obliquely across the affected eye.

'That might just do it,' she murmured as Mr Jones carefully lowered Sue's head back down to the table. 'We'll need to check that it remains secure, and it might be a good idea to unwrap the whole thing tomorrow just to check on the swelling. Leaving the lint dressing over the wound, of course, if it's clean and dry . . .'

'That sounds like a first-rate plan, Nurse Linklater,' called Mr Jones over his shoulder as he stood washing his hands at the sink.

Maud could see the slump of his shoulders. He'd done the best job he could with his sutures but she knew that he was probably experiencing the same feeling that burned inside of her – the desire for better methods so that they could fix wounds more cleanly, do less damage. Maud hoped that in her lifetime they would see more improvements in the art of surgery.

'I have something for you, Nurse Linklater,' said Mr Jones, turning from the sink as he dried his hands. Then, reaching up to a high shelf, he pulled down a book. 'I want you to have this. It's a new edition of Timothy Holmes's *A System of Surgery*. Read it through, you might find some useful detail. I'm giving a copy to each of my medical students.'

'Thank you,' said Maud, quickly wiping her hands on a clean swab before eagerly accepting the volume. Once she had it in her grasp, she ran a hand over the cover and then looked up and smiled at the surgeon. 'I will treasure it,' she said.

As Mr Jones opened the door to leave theatre she heard him call to the orderlies to come through and move Sue back on to the ward. Michael Delaney came in first, red-faced and shaking his head when he saw the girl with her bandage. 'Such a bonny young lass,' he muttered. 'Such a shame.' And Stephen Walker followed with his long, mournful face.

Maud couldn't stand it. 'Come on, you two,' she said firmly, 'let's get the girl comfortable in bed.'

Once she was left alone to clean the theatre, she scrubbed and scoured and sprayed with all her might, venting all of the pent-up fury that she'd kept back from the events of the day. Over and over in her head she could still see Sue bobbing along in front of her, tantalizingly close. If only she'd managed to get to her in time, stop her from running out. If only she'd been able to grab the boy as he shot away from the bread stall.

She nearly took the polish off the theatre table, she was scrubbing so hard. 'And what about poor Alice?' she murmured out loud. 'She is clearly fond of Sue Cassidy. What a mess,' thought Maud, as she took a scouring pad to the tin bowls, shining them up till you could almost see your face in them.

By the time she'd finished, she was out of breath and the theatre was spotless.

As Maud walked out, back on to the ward, she saw Alice look up and point to the far end. A careworn woman, with greying hair curled in a loose knot, stood twisting a handkerchief in both hands as she waited by Sue's bed. It was undoubtedly her mam, and Maud felt for her as she dipped her head to kiss her daughter.

When she reached the bed, Maud could see that Mrs Cassidy had brought a pink rose for Sue. It lay on the pillow next to her mass of red hair.

'Are you the nurse that found her?' she asked, and when Maud nodded, tears started to well in the woman's eyes.

'The flower is lovely,' murmured Maud. 'Did you bring it from your stall?'

'I did,' nodded the woman, wiping her eyes with the flat of her hand before picking the bloom up between her finger and thumb and breathing in the scent. 'I brought the last of the roses for her, the ragged ones that nobody wants to buy. These are her favourites,' she said, laying it back down on the pillow.

'I brought two,' she continued, her voice beginning to steady, 'but when I heard about the little boy, I gave one to him as well. Poor little mite.'

Maud glanced to the next bed where the boy had lain. The bedding was still crumpled from the shape of him. On the pillow lay a single pink rose. She felt a stab of sorrow and if she hadn't been holding fast, for the sake of Sue's mam, she would have cried. Instead, she took the woman's hand. 'What a lovely gesture,' she said.

'The other nurse,' the woman said, glancing towards Alice, 'has told me about the injury, the extent of it . . . and I know Sue could have been killed outright. But what will it be like for a girl living with that, people staring at her, for the rest of her life . . . ?'

'It will be hard,' said Maud, 'I'm sure it will. But it will be up to Sue, in the end, to find the best way she can of managing it.'

Mrs Cassidy was nodding, and then she started to cry again. 'Can you take the bandage off, while she's still out of it? Then I can see it for myself.'

'I can't, I'm afraid,' Maud said gently. 'It's very important that we keep it sealed with the dressing for at least four days to prevent suppuration.'

'I understand,' said the woman wearily, and then she gave a huge sigh. 'I want more than anything to stay here with her until she comes round but I need to get back to the stall. My neighbour on the market, she's looking after it for me, but she'll be struggling to run two. And I can't afford to lose my job, especially now . . . not with her like this.'

'I understand,' said Maud kindly. 'But your daughter will be in good hands, Mrs Cassidy, I promise we'll take very good care of her – don't you worry.'

'Oh, I know that for sure,' she said, glancing up the ward to Alice and then grasping Maud's hand very tightly. 'Thank you. And I'll get in to see her as often as I can, but it might not be every day. If you need me, come to the market. I'm the third stall on the right as you come down the street.'

Then the woman kissed her fingers and laid them lightly on the bandage that covered half of her daughter's head and she was gone.

Maud took a deep breath and straightened her apron, and then she was scanning the bandage for any sign of blood seepage through the dressing. She took Sue's wrist – her pulse was strong and steady. No cause for concern, as yet, but they'd have to be on guard for signs of any fever. Alice had told her that each of the wards now had a medical thermometer, and she was glad of that. It was reassuring to have an exact measurement of a patient's temperature and be able to chart it – morning and night.

As she held Sue's wrist she felt a movement. The girl was showing some resistance, she was waking up. She was moving her head gently from side to side, emitting a low moan. Maud knew that it was a good sign, the girl couldn't stay unconscious for ever. But with her awakening would come the awful realization of what had happened to her and the boy. And she would have to be told exactly what she would see on her face – a disfigurement she would bear for the rest of her life.

Alice appeared beside Maud as Sue moved her head again. Alice looked at Maud, her eyes wide, and then they both turned their attention to their patient, who now seemed to be settling back into her unnatural slumber.

'It's best for her to get more rest,' Maud said gently. 'It will be soon enough for us to start telling her what she needs to know tomorrow.'

Seeing Nurse Devlin walking down the ward with clean bedding for the boy's bed, Maud went straight over to help her make it up. The pink rose still lay on his pillow and they both stood looking at it for a moment. Then Maud picked it up gently, between her finger and thumb. 'We'll find some water for this,' she murmured, but even as she spoke, the petals began to fall back on to the bed.

'Ah well, maybe that's more appropriate, after all,' she said, looking over to meet Nurse Devlin's wide grey eyes.

They both took a breath, and then Nurse Devlin started to collect up the petals and put them in her pocket. 'I'll press them,' she said. 'Keep them in memory of him.'

'That's a nice idea,' said Maud quietly, starting to remove the pillowcase as Nurse Devlin loosened the sheets.

'And roses are special to me, too,' said Nurse Devlin, pulling off the bottom sheet with one clean movement. 'After I was born, or so the story goes, Grandma Devlin went out to her cottage garden and brought in an armful of roses. Me mother used to say the smell of them in the room was divine. Well, after that, I had to be called Rose, didn't I? And every year until she died Grandma Devlin brought me roses on my birthday.'

'That's a lovely story,' said Maud with a smile. 'And did your mother continue the tradition?'

'She did, but then she died herself, just four years later . . . so.'

'Oh, I'm sorry,' said Maud, reaching out a hand as she stood with the linen bundled in her arms.

'That's how it goes for many people, isn't it?' said Rose Devlin, pressing her lips into a firm line.

'Yes,' Maud replied, quietly. 'Yes, it is.'

As Maud walked back that evening through the city, with her arm linked firmly through Alice's, she held on tight to her friend. They'd thought that Eddy might be waiting for them, but there was no sign of her.

'No doubt she'll be running late with a case, but she'll be along to Stella's later on and we'll be able to tell her what happened today,' murmured Alice.

'What a day, hey?' replied Maud.

Alice tried to say something else but her voice caught on a sob.

'Oh, Alice, I'm so sorry about Sue, I know how special she is to you . . .'

Alice sobbed once more, clinging to Maud. 'She's such a beautiful girl and I know she could have been killed out there on the street . . . but her face will be such a mess . . .'

'It's such a shame,' said Maud, and then she glanced towards the road and stopped in her tracks, with the hairs on the back of her neck prickling. 'This is where it happened, about here.'

They both stared forlornly into the road. It was almost deserted now, just one or two carriages passing by at a leisurely pace. There was no sign of anything any more. The dust had already settled and resettled many times. It was as if nothing had happened.

'Come on,' Maud said gently, 'let's get going.'

Alice nodded and Maud led her away as she continued to talk. 'And the boy couldn't have been more than five years old, and he was out on the street. So many children with no homes to go to. When the orderlies came to take him to the mortuary, Michael carried him out from behind the screens wrapped in a blanket with his little feet peeping out. The boy looked just like he was sleeping. And Michael was crying and Stephen was just standing there with his head bowed. It was so sad.'

Maud gave Alice's arm a squeeze with her own as they continued to walk. There were no words of comfort to offer, she just needed to let her talk. When at last she fell silent, Maud said gently, 'But providing Sue comes round properly from her head injury, she is going to survive this. We'll make sure that she makes the best recovery, we'll make her strong again.'

Alice nodded.

Maud glanced down at her stained cape. She'd tried to sponge it with water from the sluice but it was still a miserable reminder of what had happened that day. She would clean it again when she got back to Stella's.

'Talk to me, Alice, talk to me about something else, will you? Tell me more about the married man you fell for.'

'Mmmm,' said Alice slowly, 'I don't really know what to say, except the last time we spoke I told him that I never wanted to see him again.'

'Did you mean it?'

'I did then. Funny you should ask, just a few weeks ago I saw him ahead of me, on the street. He didn't turn around, he didn't see me. But I was holding my breath, willing him to glance over his shoulder . . . and just seeing the back of him, it gave me the shivers. So, there you go . . . I suppose that means I'm definitely not over him.'

'Oh, Alice,' murmured Maud, 'I'm so sorry that he's married.'

'Don't be sorry, it's just one of those things, isn't it? At first I kept saying to myself, well, if I'd known he was married, I'd never have gone near. But I was probably lying to myself. There was something there, so strong. You know what I mean, Maud, you have that with Harry, don't you?'

'I do. But I took a while to trust him. I could see straight away, that second time he was admitted to the ward, you remember, after he'd been knocked out again in one of those bare-knuckle fights. I knew then he was a flatterer, popular with the women . . . you know the sort.'

'I do,' smiled Alice. 'But Harry adores you, Maud. Anyone can see that.'

'I suppose he does,' smiled Maud, knowing, in that moment, just how much she missed him.

As Maud and Alice walked on, they passed an alley lined with buildings offering rented accommodation to those with means enough to afford a comfortable room. If they'd turned their heads and looked more closely, they might have seen the outline of a woman at the end of the alley, a private midwife, waiting to be admitted to one of those rooms. She'd been newly appointed by her patient, a Nancy Sellers, and judging by the wailing that was rising to a crescendo as the midwife stood in the street, the labour was progressing very well indeed.

'Get it out of me,' growled Nancy, as soon as the midwife stepped in through the door. 'Get it out of me now . . . aaargh,' she screamed, gnashing her teeth and flailing around in the bed.

'Let's have a look at you,' soothed the midwife, used to angry responses from her patients but never having seen a woman with quite such a look of fury in her eyes.

'Just lie back for me on the bed, that's it. How often are the pains coming?'

'How should I know!' screamed Nancy. 'Just give me some chloroform, will you?'

'I don't have any. You can only get it at the hospital.'

Nancy emitted a low growl.

As the midwife stood with her hand over the swollen belly of her patient, she knew that she was in for a very long night indeed. The uterus beneath her hand was showing no sign of another contraction, indicating that the labour was mid-stage, if that.

'Oh dear,' she sighed quietly to herself.

Through the watches of the night Nancy thrashed and screamed and moaned her way through one contraction after another. She got up and walked about, leant against the wall, sat down, rocked backwards and forwards, but nothing eased the pain that ground away deep inside her body.

The midwife mopped her brow, rubbed her back and sometimes tried to hold her hand. But, after being pushed away and shouted at and nipped very hard on the arm, she took to a chair in the corner of the room and pulled out her knitting, leaving her patient to snarl and growl at her from a safe distance.

Just as the first light began to peek through the window of the rented room, the midwife heard a change in Nancy's breathing and she knew, at last, they were getting close to deliverance. She walked cautiously towards the bed where her patient lay sweating profusely, strands of blonde hair plastered to her face and the remnants of red paint from her lips now smeared around her mouth.

With the next pain Nancy emitted a guttural sound, and then she was pushing.

The midwife was all prepared. She couldn't wait to get this one delivered.

'Push,' she urged her patient, 'push as hard as you can. Let's get this baby out!'

Nancy was good at the pushing. Enough rage still burned inside her to really engage with this stage of labour.

'Good, keep going, keep going,' the midwife encouraged, until at last she could see the dark shape of a baby's head.

'God love ye,' she murmured to the baby, and then she saw the tiny eyes and nose emerge and, as always, her breath caught in her throat, just for a second, at the sheer wonder of that moment.

With a few more pushes the baby was out on the bed.

'It's a girl!' cried the midwife.

'Ugh,' said the mother, 'are you sure?'

'Yes, I'm sure,' laughed the midwife, as she expertly tied off the cord and divided it with a knife. 'And she has a full head of black hair. What a beauty!'

Swaddling the baby – the bonniest that she'd seen all year, without a doubt – the midwife took her up to the head of the bed for the mother to hold.

Nancy just stared at the child and had to be urged to take her. The midwife had seen the reaction before, in women exhausted by labour. But even when the after-birth was safely delivered and her patient was cleaned up and padded, she could still see that the mother wasn't interested in her baby.

It'll just take her some time to come to terms, thought the midwife. After all, there doesn't seem to be a father of the baby on the scene. But she feared in her heart that this bonny little girl, who hadn't asked to be brought into this cruel world, would risk being sold for adoption or, God forbid, being left on the steps of the workhouse.

'Do you have a name for the baby girl?' asked the midwife.

Nancy roused herself, gesturing for the midwife to take the baby and put her in the crib that lay ready next to the bed.

'Flora,' she said, almost as if it were an afterthought. 'She's called Flora.'

7

Maud was awake early the next morning. She tiptoed
quietly out of the room, collecting her bag as she
went. Still in her nightgown, she shivered a little as
she lit the oil lamp before slipping into a chair at the
kitchen table and then removing from her bag a writing pad and an ink pen. She'd been meaning to write
to Harry ever since she'd got back and the days were
going by. She needed to get the letter sent; it would
take at least a week on the ship to get to New York
and then another week for a reply to come. Not that
she was expecting him to reply. He'd never written
anything – apart from a brief note to tell her what
time he'd be back, or a betting slip. Anyway, that
didn't matter, she needed to write to him, so she
flipped open the lid of her ink pot and dipped in the pen.
The new nib scratched softly on the paper as she sat

at the table, her nightgown glowing brilliant white in the lamplight.

Dearest Harry,

I wanted to let you know that we are arrived safely and our dear Alfred is already settled at school. We had a rough crossing and Alfred was fine but I did have some seasickness. I am now, of course, fully recovered and yesterday started my work at the hospital. I witnessed a terrible accident on . . .

No, thought Maud, scrunching up the piece of paper, I can't tell him that. Beneath all his bluster he can be sensitive, and he loves children. I can't tell him about the accident in a letter, I'll wait till I see him.

Dearest Harry,

I wanted to tell you that we arrived safely and Alfred is settled at the Blue Coat. We had a rough crossing and I was seasick but all fine now. I started back at the hospital yesterday and I was fortunate to be placed back on my favourite ward — Female Surgical. No questions have been asked, as yet, about my status but I have, of course, taken the precaution of removing my wedding band — I keep it safe, in my pocket, and will get a chain for it so that I can keep it close to my heart.

I didn't realize until I returned to Liverpool just how much I'd missed the hospital and the city — I hope that you will feel the same when you arrive and won't miss New York too much. I'm lodging at Stella's place with Alice and Victoria, they have made me very welcome, and I am content to stay here until you arrive and we can look for a place of our own — only just over three weeks and we will be reunited. I do miss you, Harry, and can't wait to see you coming off the boat.

Ever yours . . .

As she signed her name – carefully, as always – Maud heard the door creak open, and someone gasped. Her hand slipped and the final letter of her name gained an uncharacteristic flourish.

'Oh, Maud, it's you, thank goodness,' breathed Marie, coming through the door and grabbing the back of a kitchen chair to support herself.

'Sorry, Marie, are you all right?' said Maud, readying herself to stand up from her chair.

'Oh, no, I'm fine, it's just that . . .' And then she started to laugh, trying to keep quiet at the same time, which made her laugh even more. 'I thought you were the ghost of my great-aunt Jemima.'

'Who was she?' asked Maud, starting to giggle. 'She must have been a fearsome woman.'

'Oh, you don't want to know about her,' gasped Marie, pressing a hand to her heart. 'That bloody woman has been trying to haunt me ever since the day she died, over thirty years ago. I've always known she'd be "turning in her grave" with the line of work I ended up going into. And one that turns in her grave . . . well . . . if there are such things as ghosts, they'll be up there with the worst of 'em.'

'Sorry to give you a shock,' laughed Maud, 'but at least I'm not Aunt Jemima.'

'Ha,' laughed Marie, shaking her head and making a move. 'I'll get on and light the fire,' she said. 'That'll keep her at bay. It's a bit cold in here, isn't it? Oh, you're writing a letter, are you?'

'Yes,' smiled Maud, sitting back in her chair. She checked that the ink was completely dry before she slipped it into the envelope. 'It's for Harry.'

'That scoundrel,' laughed Marie, turning up the oil lamp and slipping a woollen shawl around Maud's shoulders. 'Now give it to me. I need to send some letters of my own, so I'll make sure it's posted today. We need to do all that we can to feed the fires of young love,' she said, taking up the poker and vigorously breaking up the cold cinders that lay in the bottom of the grate.

Once the fire was lit, Hugo sidled in and stretched himself out in front of the stove. Seeing the cat there made Maud think about Alfred and how he loved to crouch by the fire next to Hugo. She felt a little sad as she thought about him getting up from his bed amongst a row of other beds occupied by Blue Coat boys. She knew in her heart that he would be fine, but as soon as she had a half day she would go up there to see him, just to make sure.

Later, Maud reached down to stroke Hugo as she sat eating her toast at the table, with Alice making sure that Victoria had her breakfast. It made Maud smile to see the little girl clutching a finger of toast, squashing it in her hand with such a look of glee on her face.

'You're supposed to be eating that, madam,' tutted Alice, offering her a drink of milk from a spouted cup.

Maud started to giggle as Victoria turned her face away.

'Stop it, you two,' said Alice, glancing from Maud to Victoria.

'Oh, don't you worry, Alice,' said Marie. 'Give her to me, I'll make sure she has her breakfast. And there's not much point getting you dressed until we've done that, is there, madam?' Victoria was screeching with laughter now as Marie pulled her off Alice's knee and blew a raspberry against her cheek.

Maud was ready to go. She'd made sure to have all that she needed organized and laid out the night before. As Alice got dressed she cleared the breakfast table and washed up the pots. And as soon as her friend was all set, they both kissed Victoria and waved goodbye, and then they were stepping out through the door into the alley with the cat trotting behind them.

'Oh, he often does that,' said Alice, seeing Maud's puzzled face. 'Shoo, shoo, you lazy good-for-nothing,' she said, waving a hand in his direction.

And to Maud's surprise, the cat turned tail and made his way back towards the house.

'He doesn't usually do as he's told,' said Alice as they marched along, side by side, in their nurses' capes and hats. 'After all, he's male. He's a law unto himself.'

'Hmph,' replied Maud.

As she walked, Maud glanced down at her cape. She'd sponged it and re-sponged it last night, trying to remove every scrap of dust from the street. She'd stayed up beyond the time she liked to be safely settled in bed, but it had been worth it, and she was proud of her efforts. There were no visible traces of the events of yesterday. What she felt inside, however, was a different matter; she'd dreamt about the accident and she'd woken thinking about Sue Cassidy. And now she was anxious to find out whether the dressing had stayed in place overnight and if it had been comfortable for the girl.

As Alice walked quietly beside her, Maud could sense that she too was thinking about Sue. When they arrived outside the Nurses' Home, however, Maud couldn't help but feel a tingle of excitement. She halted with Alice at the bottom of the stone steps, looking up to the beautiful brick building with its ornate iron balustrade leading to the heavy wooden door. Maud couldn't help but think about her first day as a probationer when she'd stood in the exact same spot, all alone with her small bag of belongings and her copy of *Notes on Nursing*.

Alice looked at her and then took her hand. 'Welcome back, Nurse Linklater,' she smiled.

As they both ascended the steps together and Maud pushed open the door, she had the sensation of going backwards in time. It was immediately wonderful to be in the entrance of the building, walking across the coloured floor tiles, breathing in the smell of the varnish. Maud felt truly at home.

'Just one moment,' she said as Alice turned to the pegs where they would leave their capes and hats. 'I just need to do something.'

Walking through to the open space, Maud looked

up to the glass skylight that covered the heart of the building. She took a deep breath. In her moments of anxiety when she was new to the work at the Women's Infirmary in New York she'd had to imagine this space. But now she was back, and as she glanced to the stone stairs and the two galleried landings that rose above, she felt the strength and the beauty of the building greet her like an old friend.

'You've really missed this place, haven't you, Maud?' Alice called from the entrance.

'I have,' she said, walking back across the patterned floor tiles. 'Much more than I thought I would. Now is this cap for me?'

'Yes. I hope it's got enough starch for your liking?' laughed Alice.

'It'll do,' replied Maud, placing it exactly square on her head and pinning it expertly into place, then taking a moment to straighten Alice's cap.

'I know, it's limp,' she laughed. 'It's a good job I'm not heading to Male Surgical with Sister Law. She'd definitely have a go at me.'

Maud laughed.

'It's not funny, Maud. Even though I'm now a trained nurse, she still treats me just the same, hounding me about my cap and telling me I'm a daydreamer.'

'Well . . .' said Maud, tipping her head to one side.

'You're just as bad as her, Maud. One day you'll be a horrible old harridan, just like Sister Law . . . and I'll be a kind and very beautiful senior nurse, like Miss Ada Houston.'

'Are you taking my name in vain?' said a voice from behind.

Alice clapped a hand over her mouth and flushed pink to the roots of her hair.

Maud turned to face Miss Houston, her dark curly hair pinned neatly in place and her bright eyes shining with amusement. 'Miss Houston, so lovely to see you,' said Maud, reaching out a hand.

'Good to see you back, Nurse Linklater . . . my protégée,' she said, leaning in to give Maud a kiss on the cheek. 'And you too, of course, Nurse Sampson. I know all about what happened yesterday and I can only say that I'm very proud of you both. As for the girl, Sue Cassidy, I've been on the ward this morning and she's starting to come round. Sister Tweedy, on nights, said that she's been asking for a drink and muttering a few words. She seems to have understood that she's in hospital. But no more, as yet. She became distressed with pain, so Sister gave her a tiny dose of laudanum around six a.m. and she's been sleeping ever since. I think when she starts to rouse, she will be asking questions. She might never remember the full details of the accident, but we will, of course, provide her with any appropriate information. Given that you were at the scene of the accident, Nurse Linklater, and you assisted Mr Jones in theatre, you'd be best placed to answer any questions that she might have.'

'Yes, I'll speak to her as soon as she's ready,' said Maud, tying her apron extra tight as she felt her stomach clench with the sadness of the situation.

'I am, of course, desperate to hear all about your adventures in New York. You must come to my room at the earliest opportunity and give me all the details. The experience that you've had over there, especially with regard to surgical nursing, is unique. My friend John Lampeter, the doctor who gave us your contact for the Infirmary in New York, he learnt so much from his time in America. Now I need to get going, I'll try and catch up with you both on the ward,' called Miss Houston, as she headed towards the door.

'That Dr Lampeter,' whispered Alice as soon as the door was firmly closed behind the assistant superintendent, 'I have reason to believe that he might be more than just Miss Houston's friend.'

'Oh, Alice, you know what this place is like for rumours. There are probably all sorts of stories going round.'

'No, I think there might be proof – well, not so much that. It's just that when you were away, Miss Houston confided something in me that I think is significant. She made me swear to keep it secret.'

'Well, you must keep it secret then,' said Maud, straight out. 'Don't think you can go telling me or anyone else.'

'I know, but isn't it hard to keep a real secret? I just want to be able to tell one other person . . . and I can't tell Eddy, you know how she is for opening her mouth when she shouldn't.'

'Don't even think about it, Alice. You promised Miss Houston. You can't tell anyone, and that's that.'

'But if I tell you, I know that you won't tell anyone else.'

'That might be the case,' said Maud. 'But, Alice, you promised Miss Houston to keep her secret. You have a responsibility.'

'I suppose,' sighed Alice. 'And there's something else as well. You know Dr McKendrick – the doctor with the chloroform?'

'Yes, of course I do,' smiled Maud. 'I haven't been away for all that long.'

'Well, he definitely really likes Miss Houston. I've seen the way he looks at her—'

'Alice, for goodness' sake. Just stop it, will you? Haven't you got enough of your own intrigues to be worrying over? And now we really do need to get going,' she said, pulling her friend out through the heavy wooden door. 'Come on. The ward awaits.'

'You sound just like Miss Merryweather,' Alice groaned. And then she sighed. 'No, you're a cross between Miss Merryweather, Sister Law and Sister Fox.'

'Oh no, I'm far worse than that,' growled Maud as she stepped smartly down the stone steps. 'Now, come on, will you? Speed up! We don't want to be late. This reminds me of the times I had to wait for Eddy – always running late, always rushing, with her hair a mess and her cap all over the place.'

'She's still the same, just the same,' laughed Alice.

'Morning, Nurse Linklater, Nurse Sampson,' called Nurse Devlin as she skipped past them on the steps. 'I'll see you on the ward. I just need to go to the laundry – I dropped my cap in the washbowl this morning.'

'She's a lovely girl, isn't she?' smiled Maud.

'She is indeed. But I'm not sure of the other one, Nurse Latimer,' murmured Alice.

Seeing Nurse Latimer up ahead, making her solitary way to the hospital, Maud and Alice exchanged a glance.

Alice frowned and muttered, 'She reminds me of Nancy.'

'Well, I must say I'm inclined to agree . . . but we still need to give her a chance. After all, it's up to us senior staff to guide and nurture the probationers.'

Alice stifled a laugh. 'I agree, but with some of them . . .'

'Let's give her a chance,' said Maud firmly. 'We have to be fair, otherwise we'll all end up like Nancy.'

'True,' murmured Alice. 'You're such a good person, Maud, but you know that I'm right, don't you?'

'Well, let's see, shall we? And, as for me, I'm not always a good person. You should have seen me that day I confronted Nancy in the sluice, I nearly throttled her . . .'

'Maud!' laughed Alice, taking her friend's arm. 'You never fail to amaze me – all quiet and ladylike, but underneath that neat starch and tidy appearance . . . you might just be a dangerous woman!'

'Grrrr,' replied Maud, making Alice giggle.

As they were approaching the door of the hospital, Maud heard a shout from behind and two men ran past with a patient on a window shutter. He was lying very still and his face was bright red, with the skin peeling away.

'He's badly burnt, isn't he?' she murmured to Alice as they both instantly picked up their pace.

As soon as they were in through the ward door, they could see that Sister Pritchard was harassed. 'I'm having to send both the probationers to Male Surgical,' she said. 'There's been a boiler explosion at a factory. They've admitted two men with severe scalds and there might be more on the way. They might need you over there to help in theatre as well, Nurse Linklater. It all depends. Sadly, those with extensive scalds, they seem all right on arrival, but they can sometimes die within hours.'

Sister was glancing up and down the ward, and then she turned to Maud.

'So, Nurse Linklater,' she said with a frown, 'if you are required to go, then we'll need at least one of our probationers back. And Miss Houston said that she can come and lend a hand, if need be. But Sister Law's more likely to need her as well.'

'Where do you want us now?' offered Maud.

'Well . . .' replied Sister, glancing up and down the ward, making a rapid assessment. 'You two go down that end,' she said. 'And then you can speak to Sue Cassidy when you get the chance. And I'll be up this end with the nurse assistants. If we get any admissions, though, we are definitely going to be overstretched . . .'

Maud and Alice worked together, as if the time that

Maud had spent in New York had never existed – helping those who needed a wash, re-dressing wounds, applying poultices, getting patients out of bed, straightening sheets, making beds, taking and recording temperatures with the ward thermometer, checking pulses. They both kept a careful eye on Sue as she slept propped up in bed, leaving her till last, till the other duties were done, so that they could spend more time with her.

At last, they were able to attend her, one at each side of the bed, and Maud saw Alice glance nervously across. She knew that she would have to take the lead.

'Sue,' she murmured gently, 'Sue.'

But there was no response from the girl.

'We can't leave her in one position and risk a bed sore,' said Maud, matter-of-factly. 'So I suggest we give her a gentle wash, hands and face, and then we move her position and change her sheets, if need be. Then I'll remove the bandage, check her eye, and the dressing.'

'Good plan,' said Alice. 'I'll go and get a bowl of water.'

As they worked together, talking to Sue and explaining everything that they were doing as if she were wide awake, the girl never flinched. It was satisfying to remove even more grime from her hands. Maud could see that Alice was still itching to wash the girl's hair but that would have to wait until the wound was healed properly. Before they moved her on to her side to change the sheet, Maud unravelled the bandage that she'd applied yesterday in theatre. She held her breath, hoping that all was well with the dressing. And it looked to be. There was still a good deal of swelling, especially around the eye, and the purple bloom of a bruise all down the side of her face, but no exudate on the dressing. Maud removed the pad that she had placed over Sue's eye. It was closed shut with the swelling but appeared clean.

'Please could you get me the carbolic spray from theatre and a fresh bandage?' she murmured to Alice.

As soon as Alice was gone from the bed, Sue began to stir herself, opening her good eye, creasing her brow, and licking her dry lips.

'Hello,' said Maud.

The girl moved her head and emitted a groan. And then she tried to speak. Maud offered her some water from the spouted cup that sat at the side of the bed. She took it readily and then wanted more.

'What is this place?' croaked the girl at last, her voice tiny against the background noise of the ward.

'You are in hospital.'

The girl tried to move her head again, and she put a hand up to her face.

'I can't see, I can't see,' she said, starting to move her head from side to side.

'Sue,' said Maud calmly, 'you have been in an accident. You have one eye that is very swollen so it won't open at the moment. If you open your right eye properly, then you will be able to see.'

Maud breathed a sigh of relief when the girl opened her eye. But then the poor child started to cry and tried to move herself in the bed, struggling to get out.

'You must lie still, Sue,' said Maud calmly, holding her firmly. 'Look at me, look. Do you remember me?

I'm Alice's friend, you saw me in the backyard, at the house, the other day.'

Still Sue tried to struggle against her.

'Sue,' said Alice gently, appearing at the side of the bed.

'Alice?' said the girl, starting to cry again. 'Alice!'

The girl clung to Alice as if she were the only person in the world. Alice held on to her with both arms, gently rocking her from side to side, murmuring words of comfort.

'Now, Sue,' said Alice gently, 'my friend, Nurse Linklater, needs to put another bandage around your head, so you need to keep still. Is that all right?'

Sue nodded, and then she gasped. 'Why, what is it for? What have I done?'

'You ran out into the road yesterday and you were hit by a horse and carriage. You have a long cut down the side of your face,' Maud said gently.

Sue reached up a hand and felt the dressing.

'The dressing needs to stay in place, Sue. It's important for healing.'

The girl nodded. 'Will it get better?'

'Yes, the doctor has put stitches in and the wound will heal.'

Sue nodded, seeming satisfied with that. 'But what about Mam, does she know?'

'Yes, she came to see you yesterday, after the accident.'

'That's good, then, as long as she's all right. And she needs to keep her job on the market, so she won't be able to keep coming in.'

Then Sue sat forward in the bed and put a hand to

her head, murmuring something, shaking her head. And then she drew in a sharp breath. Maud glanced at Alice.

'I remember now, I saw a little boy without shoes grab a loaf of bread from the stall at the side of the road,' she said quietly. 'I saw him start to run and I shouted to him to stop, but he couldn't hear me. I ran after him . . .' more agitated now, 'I tried to pull him back. I felt my hand brush his back but then a horse reared up over me and there was screaming . . . and I fell?'

'That's exactly what happened,' murmured Maud.

'Where is the boy? I want to see him. Is he injured?'

Alice opened her mouth to speak but no words would come.

'I'm sorry to have to tell you this, Sue,' said Maud, standing resolute by the bed. 'But the boy also fell in the road and he was very badly injured. We brought him here, to the hospital, but his injuries were so severe that he died very peacefully shortly after he was admitted.'

Sue's chin wobbled and then she started to cry, silent tears from her good eye flowing steadily down one cheek.

'He was only a tiny boy,' she sobbed. 'He was just hungry.'

'I know. I'm so sorry,' said Alice, putting her arms around Sue and holding her tight.

As soon as Alice started to release her hold, Maud said quietly, 'What you did for that little boy was very brave. You risked your own life to save him. You couldn't have done any more.'

'But what if I'd run faster, got to him before he ran into the road?'

'It just wasn't meant to be,' soothed Maud. 'You couldn't have done any more.'

Sue was still crying, but she took the handkerchief that Maud proffered and wiped her one good eye.

'You can ask as many questions as you like about the accident. We will always answer what we can,' continued Maud, 'but right now I need to put some special spray over this dressing on your face and secure it with a fresh bandage.'

Sue nodded.

As Alice supported Sue, Maud applied the bandage. Then, after the pair had helped her stand out at the side of the bed for a few minutes so that they could change the bottom sheet, they got her settled back against the pillows.

'We'll come back and see you soon,' murmured Alice as they moved to their next duty.

'That was so hard,' said Maud once they were out of earshot. 'And as we know, this is only the beginning for her. In another three or four days' time we'll be removing the dressing and then, when she's ready, she'll have to see the face that she'll have for the rest of her life.'

Alice nodded grimly but there was no time for further discussion as Michael and Stephen came running through the door with a new admission.

'This is Dolores Williams,' called Michael as Maud directed him to the empty bed next to Sue Cassidy. 'Her husband brought 'er in, she's been doubled over with pain in 'er belly since the middle of the night.'

Maud could see the terror on the young woman's

face as she lay curled up on the stretcher, her hair plastered to her head with sweat. 'Let's get you into bed,' she said firmly, 'and then we can see what we can do to help.'

The woman started to cry.

'It's all right, Mrs Williams,' she soothed, 'please try not to distress yourself.'

But the woman was wailing now. 'Don't cut me open, I don't want to die.'

'Shhh, shhh,' soothed Maud, but still the woman wailed, and when Maud glanced up the ward she could see a murmuring of concern from the other patients.

'That's enough, now, Mrs Williams,' said Alice, appearing at Maud's elbow. 'We don't even know what's wrong with you yet. Getting worked up will only make the pain worse, so please try to calm yourself.'

Something about the exact tone of Alice's voice seemed to soothe the woman and, almost instantly, she quietened.

'There, there,' said Alice, 'nobody's going to do anything without your consent. All we want to do is have a look and try to work out what's going on.'

Maud gave her friend an appreciative glance. 'I'll go and get the wooden screens,' she said, 'and find Sister Pritchard.'

When Maud returned, with Sister in tow, she found Mrs Williams gently sobbing in the bed but much more settled as she clung to Alice's hand. Maud erected the wooden screens as Sister Pritchard moved straight in to examine the patient.

First she laid a hand on the woman's forehead. 'You feel hot, Mrs Williams, I think you might have a fever.'

'I'll check with the thermometer afterwards,' offered Maud.

'Now, let's have a feel of your belly,' Sister said, gesturing for the woman to lie flat on her back.

Maud scrutinized the expert way that she moved her hand over the woman's abdomen, concentrating on the pelvic area just above the symphysis pubis.

'So, Dolores,' she said, 'when did you get married?'

The woman looked puzzled but answered the question. 'About four months ago.'

'And have you had any monthly bleeding since you got married?'

'No, I don't think so,' said Dolores.

Sister placed a hand on the woman's lower abdomen again, pressing gently just in a particular spot. 'Well, I can't be exactly sure,' she said, 'but what I'm feeling here feels very much like an enlarged womb.'

'Oh no, what's that?' cried Dolores.

'Stay calm, Mrs Williams,' said Sister firmly. 'What it means is that you are very likely to be pregnant. Of course, there is no real way of knowing for sure until you start to feel quickening, but it shouldn't be long before you feel that as well.'

'What is quickening?'

'It's the first movements of a baby. I've heard it described as the fluttering of a butterfly's wings.'

Dolores was almost in tears now, and then she was

drawing her knees up in discomfort. 'But what about this bad pain?'

'Well, yes, you are right, the pregnancy wouldn't cause the pain, but it might make you much more prone to inflammation of the bladder. Have you had any discomfort whilst passing water?'

'Yes, I have,' said the woman, almost gleeful now. 'It's been like passing pins and needles.'

'Well, there you are then. I think what you have is no more than severe cystitis. We'll need to get you to drink plenty of barley water to try and flush it out. And if your symptoms don't settle, we might try dry cupping or some leeches over the area to help relieve internal congestion . . . but I'll ask our surgeon to check you over, just in case—'

'No, no, he'll want to cut me open.'

'He won't want to do any such thing,' said Sister firmly, 'he's far too busy. Nurse Linklater, Nurse Sampson, do you want to feel an early pregnancy?'

Alice, still holding Dolores's hand, responded automatically, 'Oh, that's all right, when I was—'

'Yes,' said Maud, covering the revelation that Alice was about to make, 'yes, we would.'

They soon had Dolores settled, with a full jug of barley water by her bed and the beginnings of a smile on her face. Maud went to find the husband. Michael had left him waiting in the corridor near the hospital entrance. Sister Pritchard had advised that they tell him, for now, that all was well with his wife, she was in no danger, and he needed to come back at visiting time.

She thought it best that his wife tell him that she might be pregnant.

Maud found Mr Williams pacing up and down the corridor, his pale hair almost standing on end where he'd run his hands through it and his face flushed pink with anxiety.

'Mr Williams?'

'Yes,' he said, walking towards her, his face blanching with anxiety.

'No need to worry. Your wife doesn't need any surgery, she has some inflammation of the bladder. But Sister is happy with her condition and advises you to come back at visiting time.'

The man couldn't speak. His whole body slumped with relief, and he needed to reach out and rest a hand on Maud's shoulder to support himself. And then he looked up and smiled, flashing a mouthful of discoloured teeth.

'Thank you, Nurse,' he said. 'Thank you very much.'

'Oh, and bring her some flowers,' called Maud as he turned to flee the hospital as quickly as he could.

Later, Maud saw Mr Williams file in with the rest, at visiting, clutching a ragged bunch of pink carnations. 'Mmmm,' commented Alice as she walked by, 'looks like it might be a baby girl they're expecting.'

Within moments of his arrival he was shouting the news to the whole ward. 'A baby, it's a baby, she's going to have a baby!'

As Maud and Alice walked towards the Nurses' Home at the end of their shift, they found Eddy perched on the step, waiting for them. She ran and hugged them both at the same time and then, as they all walked together through the city in their nurses' capes and hats, she told them more news of Indars Berzins. 'What an improvement in him since his grandson was born. He's moving in and out of bed much more easily, he doesn't have as much pain. He'll sit for hours with the baby, rocking him to sleep. And the ulcers that he had on his legs, I've been treating them for months, no change. But now, they're actually starting to heal. It's like a miracle . . .'

'The miracle of Eddy,' said Maud, linking her arm and pulling her close.

'No more so than the work that you two do,' grinned Eddy. 'And you, Maud, with what you did yesterday at the scene of an accident.'

'And can I just say, here and now? And I know I've said it before,' smiled Maud, 'I love working on Female Surgical with Sister Pritchard – and with you, of course, Alice.'

'Ha,' laughed Eddy, 'you and Female Surgical. You do know you'll end up going back to Sister Law and the male patients at some stage?'

'Oh, yes. I know it won't last for ever, and I also know I'll have to go where I'm put. But for now, I'll just enjoy it. I've never felt as comfortable nursing men. I don't really know why but, well, they're so male, aren't they? With all that hair on their bodies . . .'

Alice and Eddy both cracked up laughing.

'Maud, you're so prim. But you're right. Yes, the men on Male Surgical are male,' snorted Eddy.

'Uh oh,' said Alice, stopping dead in her tracks and turning towards them, her eyes wide. 'That's Miss Fairchild's private nurse, Nurse Ashworth, across the road. Is she looking this way?'

'What? Who?' called Eddy.

'Shush, Eddy. Stop gawping,' hissed Alice, grabbing her arm and trying to lead her on. 'We don't want her prying, asking questions about me and Maud and our living arrangements.'

'Too late,' said Maud, quietly. 'She's coming over.'

'Yoo hoo,' called Nurse Ashworth as she trotted across the road. 'Good evening, Nurse Linklater, Nurse Sampson. How lovely to see you both again. Oh,' she said, narrowing her eyes as she glanced from one to the other, 'I didn't know you were working on the district. I thought you both worked at the hospital.'

'We do . . .'

'We don't . . .' said Maud and Alice at the same time.

'We do,' said Maud firmly, proffering a polite smile. 'We've just been . . . helping out for one day, that's all. And this is our friend, Nurse Pacey.'

'And have you been helping out for one day, also?' asked Nurse Ashworth.

'Oh . . . er . . . no. I work full-time on the district. I had a rush of new cases, some crew off a ship, all at once. So I needed help.'

'I see,' smiled Nurse Ashworth, swallowing the story but clearly not altogether convinced. 'Well, I've just been to see my ex-private patient. The lady I told you about, Maud. Mrs Davenport, poor lamb. Her condition certainly doesn't get any better. I was hoping to catch up with our mutual friend, Nancy. But sadly, the housekeeper told me that she has very recently left her position. Have any of you seen her?'

'Oh no,' blustered Alice.

'Definitely not. No, not for ages,' said Eddy.

Maud knew straight away that they were lying. And as they all stood together in an awkward group, she couldn't help but feel like her two friends had taken a step away from her and left her in the cold. She had to believe that they had her best interests at heart, but in that moment of isolation she felt sad and alone. She knew that they were probably covering something up to protect her. But she also knew for sure, as Nurse Ashworth bade them goodbye and crossed back over the street, that whatever it was would probably not stay hidden for ever. The truth had a way of coming out, eventually.

8

'Hospitals are not tea-gardens . . . Great quiet
and some severity of discipline are necessary,
and ought to be exacted.'

Florence Nightingale

The next day, Female Surgical looked busy as soon as
Maud and Alice walked through the door. All the beds
were occupied, and Maud could hear a number of women
groaning in pain and one calling for a nurse. Thankfully, they had a nurse assistant on hand to see to the
immediate needs of the patients whilst the trained staff
and probationers gathered at the top of the ward to
receive their orders.

As Sister Pritchard gave her report on the patients
and assigned duties, Maud couldn't help but notice, yet
again, the difference in the two probationers. Nurse
Devlin, with her eyes wide, listening intently; whereas
Nurse Latimer seemed indifferent, her dark eyes shining, but not with interest, with something else that
Maud could almost sense lurking beneath her outward
appearance.

'Nurse Devlin, you work at the top of the ward with
Nurse Sampson, will you? And Nurse Latimer the

other end, please, with Nurse Linklater. Now, let's get moving, Nurses. We're busy, busy.'

'Nurse Latimer,' called Maud, seeing her moving off down the ward, 'just a moment. Let's make our plan of work.'

Maud watched as Nurse Latimer walked back in her direction – not too slow, to evince comment, but just slow enough to cause irritation. Mmmm, thought Maud, we'll see about this. I'll get you moving.

'We'll work together to get the more poorly patients sorted first, and then we'll split up to do our separate duties.'

Nurse Latimer stared at her, offering no sign that she'd even heard what was being said.

'Nurse Latimer?' Maud said, raising her voice a notch. 'Do you understand?'

She nodded.

'I want you to say "Yes, Nurse Linklater",' said Maud, never before having felt it necessary to speak to a more junior member of staff in such a fashion.

'Yes, Nurse Linklater,' the probationer replied, her voice flat.

Maud knew that the worst thing she could do, at this stage, was show irritation, so she smiled at the probationer. But when she spoke again she made it absolutely clear what her expectations were for the course of their work that morning.

'So, we'll start with Mrs Rattigan in bed six – she will need a blanket bath and a change of position, and then we'll need to re-dress her wound and check her temperature. I want you to go now to collect what we need whilst I check on Miss Cassidy and Mrs Williams.'

As Maud watched Nurse Latimer walk up the ward, she felt like running along behind her with a stick. The girl was infuriating.

Thankfully, Sue was sleeping peacefully, propped up in bed, and Sister Pritchard had reported that the night staff were pleased with her progress. All set for taking down the dressing in a few days' time, thought Maud, feeling a prickle of anxiety as she pictured what lay beneath the innocent white bandage.

Maud glanced to the next bed, to see Dolores Williams lying flat on her back with her eyes wide open. Something about the way she was staring at the ceiling made Maud approach her.

'Are you all right, Mrs Williams?'

'Not really,' Dolores replied, big tears starting to leak from her eyes and run down both sides of her face.

'Have you got more pain?'

Dolores moved her head from side to side.

'Are you worrying?'

Dolores nodded, pressing her mouth into a firm line and taking a deep breath through her nose. And then she started to cry even more.

Maud crouched down by the side of the bed. 'Whatever is the matter, Mrs Williams?'

'It's just that, well, I know Jim is very excited about the baby and everything. But honestly, Nurse,' she said, turning her face in Maud's direction, 'the thought of a baby, growing inside and coming out . . . through there,' she said, nodding in the direction of her abdomen, 'it terrifies the living daylights out of me.'

'Oh, Mrs Williams,' said Maud, taking her hand.

'Well, for a start,' sniffed Dolores, 'I've never had anybody to ask about these things. Me mother died when I was a baby, and I grew up with two brothers, so there's things I should know . . . but I haven't a clue.'

'What kind of things, Dolores? You can ask me anything.'

'Well, I don't even know properly what happens when, you know, when it starts to come.'

'You mean when the baby starts to be born?'

Dolores nodded, and then she whispered, 'I don't even know properly where the baby comes out of. Will it come out of my belly button?'

'No, it will not,' said Maud quietly. She saw the look of relief on her patient's face. 'Babies come out through the same part of your anatomy where they're made,' smiled Maud. 'Through a passage called the vagina.'

'That's a fancy word, va— What?'

'Vagina,' repeated Maud.

'Right,' said Dolores, reaching down to feel her belly through the sheet. 'And I know Sister could feel something – that's why she thinks I'm pregnant – but when will I be able to see it properly, like a bump.'

'You can only just about feel the top of your womb at your stage of pregnancy, but as the baby grows it will move further and further up until it's right up under your ribs. And that's when you'll be able to feel the shape of it in your belly and feel it properly kicking you.'

'Oh, Nurse, you know so much . . .'

'Not really, just the basics of midwifery,' said Maud. 'But I'll come back later, and you can ask me as many questions as you want,' she said, glancing up to see Nurse Latimer waiting by Mrs Rattigan's bed.

'Thank you, Nurse,' said Dolores. 'Wait till I tell my Jim about this vagina thing!'

Maud directed Nurse Latimer as patiently as she could during the blanket bath, and then she talked her through the dressing and, finally, she demonstrated how to take their patient's temperature with the mercury thermometer. Throughout it all, Nurse Latimer barely spoke. It frustrated Maud; she didn't want a chatterbox of a probationer but, by the end of a morning cajoling and directing an almost silent Nurse Latimer, she wasn't so sure.

'What do you make of our Nurse Latimer?' murmured Sister Pritchard, appearing by Maud's side as the probationer removed the mercury thermometer from the wooden box at the bedside of their final case and slipped it under the patient's arm, without a word.

'I'm not sure,' frowned Maud. 'I think we need to give her more time, certainly. But we need to keep a careful eye on her.'

'I agree entirely,' nodded Sister Pritchard. 'Now, I just need to nip up to see Miss Houston in her office for ten minutes. Can I leave the ward in your capable hands?'

'Yes, of course, Sister,' said Maud, feeling a small glow of pleasure. And as she looked around the ward she realized, despite the morning she'd had with Nurse Latimer, why she loved the work on this particular ward so much. Some of the women were chatting from one bed to another, Nurse Devlin was helping a patient out of bed at the top of the ward, and a cheery assistant nurse was singing a song to an elderly patient who was cackling with laughter. Just in that moment, as she glanced back to Nurse Latimer, she even saw her say a few words to the patient. Maud was pleased; it seemed that they had done a good job caring for their patients, and the ward was happy.

She was still smiling to herself when she saw a familiar figure, with a lace cap tied tightly beneath her ample chin, stalking down the ward towards her, glancing from side to side with her eyes narrowed as she went.

'Uh oh, Sister Law,' murmured Maud, bracing herself as she saw the woman scowl in her direction. She felt like a target as Sister homed in towards her, planting her feet squarely and puffing out her chest.

'Nurse Linklater,' she said, 'good to see you back in the fold. I was just wondering if you have any idea where Sister Pritchard might be?'

'Ah, she's gone up to see Miss Houston, I'm afraid. She said that she'll only be ten minutes.'

Sister Law pulled her shoulders up to her ears and puffed out her chest even further. 'Ten minutes is far too long,' she said. 'Tell her to come and find me on Male Surgical when she returns. In the meantime, Nurse Linklater,' she said, casting her eyes up and down the ward, 'I'm assuming that you have been left in charge of this . . .' She didn't seem able to find the right word but gestured with her hand to the whole of the ward, including the array of flowers in vases crowded on to a long table.

'Yes, Sister,' said Maud, steeling herself.

'Well, Nurse Linklater, I realize that you are fresh off the boat from New York, and over there they will have different methods . . . but can I just remind you that a ward should not be run like some tea-garden. Nurses singing, patients chatting, it's chaos.'

As if on cue, the elderly patient singing with the nurse cackled very loudly once again.

'You need to do something about this, right away, Nurse Linklater, right away. Remember what Miss Nightingale has said about quiet and order and discipline.'

'Yes, Sister,' replied Maud, straightening her back and almost standing to attention in an effort to impress Sister Law sufficiently for her to leave the ward.

'I'll expect to have you back in theatre on Male Surgical very soon, Nurse Linklater. Then you can leave this . . . tea-garden . . . behind.'

'Yes, Sister,' said Maud, relieved to see Sister Law turning on her heel at last and marching back down the ward.

Maud held her breath until she could see that Sister was safely out through the ward door.

'Alice, where have *you* been?' gasped Maud, as her friend appeared at her elbow.

'Hiding in the sluice, of course,' she replied. 'I opened the door to come out, saw her and went straight back inside to do a bit of tidying and cleaning until the coast was clear. What did she want?'

'Well, she was looking for Sister Pritchard, but she took the opportunity to remind me that a ward should not be run like a tea-garden!'

'Ha,' laughed Alice. And then Maud started giggling, holding on to Alice's arm until they could both get a hold of themselves.

Maud and Alice were still laughing about tea-gardens late into the afternoon when, unexpectedly, they were summoned up the ward by Sister Pritchard.

'Thank you so much for all of your good work this morning, Nurses. Given that we seem to be fairly straight, I wonder if one of you would like to take your afternoon off today? It's just that tomorrow the probationers will be attending one of their lectures, and who knows what we might have through the doors! What do you think?'

'I've only just got back,' said Maud straight away. 'You take some time off, Alice.'

Alice was already shaking her head.

'Look, Maud, even before your official first day you were dealing with casualties in the street, and you've barely had time to breathe since you got back. You can go and see Alfred or Miss Fairchild.'

'Yes, I suppose . . . but what if you get busy again this afternoon and—'

'No ands or ifs or buts, Nurse Linklater, take the half day. You won't be getting any more time off this week, so make the most of it,' ordered Sister Pritchard.

Alice was nodding.

'Well, if you're sure.'

'We're sure,' said Sister.

'Go on, off you go,' urged Alice.

Maud knew she'd have just enough time to nip over to the Blue Coat School and catch Alfred towards the end of afternoon visiting hours, and then she could make her way to see Miss Fairchild. It would be a rush to do both. But who knew when her next half day off would be? She changed quickly into her cape and hat, running down the steps of the Nurses' Home and then out towards Brownlow Hill. As always, when she passed the stretch of road where Sue's accident had occurred, she felt her stomach tighten and she said a silent prayer for the little boy. Then she was running, dodging around pedestrians, almost colliding with a street seller who waved an apple in her direction.

Out of breath, she saw the octagonal tower of the parish church and knew she was almost there and, thankfully, as she approached she could hear children's voices and the murmur of conversation in the walled courtyard where visiting took place. She saw him straight away, sat on a bench with the other boys who had no visitors. He was reading a book and the sheer concentration on his face almost brought tears to her eyes, she was so proud of him. She approached him quietly, smiling to herself, hoping that he would lift his head so that she could see the spark in his bright eyes when he saw her there unexpectedly. But he was too absorbed in the book, even though she stood there for a few moments.

'Alfred,' she said gently, at last.

'Maud,' he cried, grinning from ear to ear and jumping up from his seat to give her a hug, still with the book in his hand.

'Oh, Alfred,' she murmured, holding him close and breathing in the scent of him. 'I'm sorry I've not been able to come sooner, but this is the first half day I've had off.'

'That's all right, Maud. I told you it is.' His voice was muffled against her as she continued to hold on to him.

At last she was able to release him. She reached out a gentle hand to straighten his hair, before taking his hand and leading him to the bench. 'What are you reading? Is it a Jane Austen?' she said, still smiling, and needing to put an arm around him and pull him close to her side.

'No Jane Austens here, I'm afraid. It's a book of mathematics.'

'Oh,' said Maud, 'is it a set text, one you have to read?'

'Oh no, I asked the master for it. I've gone through all the others we have in class. He gave me this one from his own collection.'

'Really?' smiled Maud. 'Are you enjoying it?'

'Yes,' giggled Alfred. 'I know it sounds strange, because most of the other pupils hate the maths lessons, and the master is very severe. Some of the boys spend most of the lesson standing in the corner of the classroom. And I never say anything to the rest, but I find it easy and I always want to learn more and more.'

'Oh, Alfred,' sighed Maud, savouring the last few moments with him as she saw the man in uniform walk towards the bell that signalled the end of visiting. 'You are so clever, but that's not . . .'

And as the bell clanged loudly, Maud told him that she loved him for being who he was – kind and true and the best adopted son that anyone could ever have.

Leaving the Blue Coat School with a smile, Maud made her way in a more leisurely fashion towards the big house and Miss Fairchild, taking time to stop by the street seller's fruit stall to buy two oranges. Something fresh, something colourful, she thought to herself, as she walked the familiar route.

Cook reported, as soon as Maud was through the back door, that she was still very worried about Miss Fairchild. 'Since that day you and Alfred came, I've not really seen her smile much. I go in there as often as I can, but she always seems to be irritated with me somehow. Then again, she's always been irritated with me . . . See what you make of her but I'm sorry to say, Maud, I think she might be starting to go downhill.'

Maud stood waiting after she'd tapped on Miss Fairchild's door, but there was no reply. She could hear muffled voices from the direction of the stairs that led up to the rooms used by members of the family. It sounded like some housemaid chattering with one of the footmen. She needs to be getting on with her work, thought Maud, as she knocked again, more firmly this time. Still no reply. So she went straight in.

Seeing her friend slumped in her chair, with the

room growing darker around her, Maud was instantly concerned.

'Miss Fairchild,' she said gently, approaching the chair. And then, not getting any response, she spoke again, more firmly. 'Miss Fairchild.'

'What . . . what? No, thank you, I don't want any . . .' Then, opening her eyes, Miss Fairchild squinted for a moment and tried to smile.

'How are you?' Maud asked softly, crouching down beside the chair and taking her friend's hand. 'Take your time. That's it . . . let your breathing settle.'

'Oh, I'm all right,' murmured Miss Fairchild. 'Better now, seeing your lovely face. But as we know, I'm not going to get any better, am I?'

Maud gave her hand a squeeze. 'That might be the case, but there still might be things we can do to help you at least feel a bit better.'

Miss Fairchild sighed and then tried to say something else about not being sure if it was worth it – mumbled words that Maud couldn't quite catch.

'Well, let's see, shall we?' said Maud, glancing around the room. 'Right, for a start, are you happy for me to light the lamp? I know it's not completely dark outside, but it does feel a bit gloomy in here.'

'Mmm,' murmured Miss Fairchild, turning her mouth down. Then, with a dismissive gesture of her hand, 'Do what you want, Maud, I don't really care.' And then she closed her eyes.

Once the lamp was lit, there was an instant warm glow in the room. Then Maud went straight to the window and pulled up the sash, just a little, to let some air in. Turning her attention to the open fire that had died down almost to ash, she took some kindling from the side and used the bellows to give it some draught. Just the crackle of the wood as it caught and bloomed into flame made a difference and then, when it was well alight, Maud took the fire tongs and placed some choice pieces of shiny black coal carefully on top of the wood.

When she glanced back to Miss Fairchild, she could see that her eyes were open and she was starting to smile.

'You are just as skilful as you ever were, Maud. None of the housemaids, either before or since, have been able to manage a fire as well as you. They either neglect it, and let it go out, or they throw on too much coal and leave a smoking, smouldering mess.'

'Well, I learnt from the best,' said Maud, straightening up from the fire and surveying the room again.

'Move my chair a little, will you, Maud, if you can? So I can see out of the window.'

Maud managed to twist the chair just enough to afford her friend a view.

As she did, Miss Fairchild gave a wheezy sigh. 'I'm so useless,' she said. 'Even if I stand up for a few moments, I'm completely out of breath. Nurse Ashworth has to get two of the footmen to carry me to bed now. Just imagine . . . I'm such a useless lump.'

'Nonsense,' said Maud.

'Bless you, Maud, but you know that's not true. I'm not even half the woman I was. Remember how I used to stride through this house with the keys at my belt? Making sure all was in order, and the staff were doing as they were told.'

'I do,' smiled Maud. 'And I'm sorry that you are having to bear all of this now, it just doesn't seem fair. I wish I could do more . . .'

'Oh no, don't you worry yourself, Maud. This is the reality of my condition, I just have to withstand it. You know that, don't you, being a nurse? But even when you were a young girl, coming here straight from your grandmother's funeral, you knew how life could be. I could see it in your face, that first day. Sat at the kitchen table, no more than a child, with your white face and your big dark eyes. You never spoke one word, but I could see that depth of understanding in you.'

'I remember that day,' smiled Maud. 'I'd never sipped tea out of a china cup before. I thought that it must be the Queen's crockery. I was terrified that I'd drop the cup and break it.'

'Oh, Maud, we've both come a long way since that day, haven't we? And do you know what? Just talking to you about the old days, it seems to work better than any amount of tonic that Nurse Ashworth can administer.'

'Poor Nurse Ashworth,' murmured Maud. 'She does seem to do her very best for you, though.'

'She does her best by forcing medicines down my throat,' chuckled Miss Fairchild.

Resting back in her chair, she looked at Maud with some of the old life in her eyes. 'Is there enough light for you to read to me? Our Nurse Ashworth has been proceeding with the book, but she has such a dull reading voice, I always end up falling asleep.'

'Well, I'll try, but I can't promise to add any more colour than Nurse Ashworth,' said Maud, taking the Jane Austen off the side and pulling over the footstool so that she could sit close to the lamp. She sat upright and held the book square, with both hands, and then cleared her throat. 'Chapter nine. Mr Knightley might quarrel with her, but Emma could not quarrel with herself . . .'

'Ha,' laughed Miss Fairchild, 'I love the way Emma is so self-satisfied. So sure of herself . . . such a madam. Read on, Maud, read on.'

Maud was surprised at how much she enjoyed the reading – the act of focusing on the words, feeling the rhythm of them, and being transported back in time to a world that existed well over sixty years ago. She found it very diverting. And as she sat there by the fire, on her footstool, with the scent of Miss Fairchild's lavender water in the air around her, Maud felt content. She read until she could read no more, and then she remembered the oranges in her bag and pulled one out.

'Ooh, an orange. I haven't had an orange for years,' said Miss Fairchild, taking it from Maud's hand and pressing it to her nose, breathing in the scent of it. 'There's a small knife over there on the side . . . that's it, yes. It might help you get the peel off.'

Maud spread her clean handkerchief on her knee as she used the knife to peel and segment the orange. She didn't like the mess of the juice on her hands, but it was worth it to smell the freshness and see her friend taste the first piece. By the third piece Miss Fairchild had juice running down her chin.

There was a firm knock at the door and Nurse Ashworth came in, carrying her porcelain plate with the glass medicine pot.

'Miss Fairchild!' she gasped, glaring at her patient, who was sucking the last of the juice from a segment of orange and holding her hand out for more.

'My dear Miss Fairchild,' she said, with authority, 'you must not eat any more. Orange is far too acidic for an invalid. I have prepared some ground rice pudding for your tea.'

'Piffle,' said Miss Fairchild, with more juice running down her chin. 'Absolute piffle. Of course I can have an orange.'

'Miss Fairchild, Maud!' insisted Nurse Ashworth, almost stamping her foot.

'I am eating the rest of this orange, Nurse Ashworth, whether you like it or not,' insisted Miss Fairchild, lifting her head and tilting her chin at a certain angle.

Maud saw a glimpse of the housekeeper that she had once known, in that one simple movement. And the glint in her eye was unmistakable.

'Well, don't blame me if your constitution is upset,' snipped Nurse Ashworth, leaving the porcelain plate on the side table with a decided clatter.

'I won't,' smiled Miss Fairchild.

'And Nurse Linklater,' she said, 'I trust that I can

leave you to ensure that my patient receives her tonic, as prescribed.'

'Yes, of course,' smiled Maud, feeling a little sorry for the nurse. She was, after all, only trying to do her duty.

'Thank you,' huffed Nurse Ashworth as she left the room.

Miss Fairchild started to chuckle as soon as the nurse had clicked the door shut. 'I enjoyed that, Maud,' she said, rooting up her sleeve for a handkerchief and wiping the juice from her chin. 'And don't worry, I'll soothe her ruffled feathers later. And I'll take her nasty-tasting tonic. She's not a bad sort, really, just very rigid with her ideas ... How are you getting on at the hospital?'

'Very well, I think,' said Maud with a smile. 'Even after only three days it feels like I'm completely at home again. And I love the work on Female Surgical.'

'That's good, Maud. Thank goodness,' breathed Miss Fairchild. 'Oh, and I forgot to say, I've had a letter from Alfred, already. He says that he's doing well and the lessons are excellent.'

'Yes, I've just come from the Blue Coat. He seemed very well indeed, and he was doing extra maths. He's so good, isn't he?' laughed Maud.

'Yes, he is. We did a good job there, didn't we, Maud, rescuing him that day? I know I keep saying this, but you and he are like family to me now, and when something happens to me – and we both know it will – I've left everything to you.'

'Oh, Miss Fairchild, don't be talking like that, honestly—'

Miss Fairchild held up a hand. 'No, Maud, I need to know that arrangements are in place.'

'Are you sure?'

'I'm sure. I have no family. You are very special to me, Maud. And all that you've achieved with your nursing. I'm so proud of you.'

'Just take a moment,' soothed Maud, 'and get your breath back.'

'No, I need to tell you . . . I have a tidy sum put by, savings from all the years I've worked as a housekeeper . . . Oh, and don't forget, I want you to have the sewing machine as well,' she said, pointing to the Singer sitting idly in the corner of the room. 'As soon as you have an address . . . I'll send it for you.'

'Yes, of course, that's fine,' said Maud. 'Now just catch your breath . . . that's it. You have helped me so much already. You have been a friend and a mentor, there is no need to give me any inheritance.'

'But I want you to have it, Maud. It will make me very satisfied indeed to know that I am leaving behind the means for you to continue to flourish in your work, to set up a home with that new husband of yours. And, of course, there will be money for Alfred's education . . .'

'I understand,' said Maud, more moved than she could express adequately. 'I suppose all I can say, then, is thank you.'

Miss Fairchild nodded. 'Is that a deal, then?'

'It's a deal,' smiled Maud. 'I don't know what—'

Miss Fairchild held up her hand again. 'No need to say any more, Maud. Now, tell me, when will Harry be back?'

'In about three weeks' time. And I just can't wait to see him! I never thought I'd miss him as much as this. I hardly ever saw him when we were in New York together.'

'Ah, but you knew that he was there and he was coming home to you. That's all that matters,' said Miss Fairchild, wistfully. 'You are drawn together, you and Harry, that's the important thing, and no amount of distance can change that . . .'

Miss Fairchild slipped a lace handkerchief from her sleeve and dabbed at her eyes before rousing herself. 'Now, make sure you send him to see me as soon as possible. I want to have a word with him about the inheritance and his responsibilities . . . And when you two get settled into a comfortable place of your own, then and only then, will I be ready to depart this world.'

As Maud walked back through the city, she had no idea how to be or what to feel. The sorrow that she felt for Miss Fairchild's condition weighed her down. But the prospect of an inheritance was something that, as an orphaned child, she would never have dreamed possible. Even though Miss Fairchild had mentioned it before, Maud had never presumed . . . but now, after today, she understood that it was important for her friend to know that she could pass something on. That her 'tidy sum' could do some good in the world. It was unbelievable, and Maud would have been lying to herself if she tried to deny the excitement of it.

Just wait till Harry finds out, she thought, as her feet measured the ground beneath her. What a homecoming he will have.

9

'. . . no living thing can less lend itself to a
"formula" than nursing. Nursing has to nurse
living bodies and spirits. It cannot be
formulated like engineering.'
Florence Nightingale

As they were approaching the door to Female Surgical
on their way to work the next morning, Maud and Alice
met Miss Merryweather head on.

'Nurse Linklater,' she called, 'I need you to go
straight to Male Surgical. They have an urgent admission for theatre, and Mr Jones has asked specifically for
you.'

'See you later,' grinned Alice, giving Maud a pat on
the arm.

'There's been a bad accident at the Tate sugar refinery
on Love Lane. Some incident involving an out-of-
control hoist – two men crushed to death against an
iron girder, and another badly injured after jumping
down. Sister will give you all the details. Ah, Mr Delaney,' said Miss Merryweather, catching sight of the
orderly tiptoeing by, 'we need you on Male Surgical in
fifteen minutes. Don't be late.'

Maud heard his deadpan, 'Certainly, Miss Merry-weather,' as she turned to walk briskly towards Male Surgical.

Sister Law was waiting just through the door. 'Your theatre awaits, Nurse Linklater. But first, let me give you a brief outline of our patient. He is Wilhelm Langer, forty years old, a sugar boiler by trade, originally from Hamburg but moved to Liverpool ten years ago to work at the refinery. Whilst trying to save two men from a hoist ascending at speed, he fell from a height, sustaining a compound fracture of the tibia. They brought him in lying on a window shutter, and the men carrying him came at quite a pace so he was fairly shaken up when he arrived. But we've managed to settle him and put a temporary dressing over the wound.

'Mr Jones is keen to reduce the fracture, get the leg straightened and immobilized as soon as possible. So time is of the essence. I've already prepared a bowl of egg white, camphorate of alcohol and subacetate of lead, to use for setting the limb. Don't forget to leave a decent aperture over the open wound when you bandage. And anything else, just ask. Are you clear?'

'Yes, Sister,' said Maud, keen to get into theatre.

'Mr Delaney has brought us a fracture box from the store room and left it propped against the wall in the-atre,' Sister called over her shoulder as she marched up the ward, with Maud following. 'It's best to give extra support for the leg in the box, as well as using the egg white bandage. Are you familiar with its use?'

'I am, Sister,' called Maud.

'The rest you should be able to work out for yourself, Nurse Linklater,' she said, stopping abruptly and turning towards Maud, with narrowed eyes. 'As you know, I keep the theatre room in very workable order.'

Maud was nodding, and then Sister gestured to the patient lying in his bed. 'It will be a long job,' she murmured. 'The ones who survive a compound fracture, and the inevitable manifestations of a suppurating wound, always are . . . But this man is the main bread winner for his wife, Clara, and their three children, so we have to make him well. His wife will get some temporary support from Tate's, though. They do tend to look after the families of their valued workers, at least for a period of time . . .'

'Mr Langer,' Sister called gently, as she approached the bed. 'Mr Langer, this is the nurse I told you about, the one who will be assisting Mr Jones in theatre today.'

Maud saw the man open his eyes and look in her direction, and then he was scrunching his face up in pain.

'I'll get you some more laudanum drops immediately,' said Sister, walking away towards the medicine cabinet.

Maud crouched down beside Mr Langer's bed and took his hand. She could see the beads of sweat standing out on his pale forehead, and he was almost in tears with the pain. 'Sister won't be long,' she murmured, 'and when we get you into theatre, they'll give you some chloroform. So even if the drops don't work, you will be out of your pain, at least for a while.'

'*Danke*,' murmured the man.

152

As Maud waited quietly with Mr Langer, she noted that he was so broad-shouldered that he filled the width of the bed. And his work clothes were encrusted with so much sugar that he actually smelt sweet. His pale brown hair was neatly parted, his chin showing just one day's growth of stubble, and there were gentle laughter lines around his eyes.

As soon as Sister returned with the laudanum, Maud went straight into theatre. Seeing the high wooden table in the middle of the room made her pulse quicken, and she was instantly checking the preparations that had already been made. She noted the bowl of egg white solution and the wooden fracture box, with its hinged sides and footplate. Then she rolled up her sleeves and went to the sink to scrub her hands with carbolic soap, before gathering together some compresses, made from folds of linen, and two muslin bandages and submerging them in the bowl of egg white solution. After rinsing her hands, she gave the table a wipe down and then she prepared the bowls and instruments, laying out a surgical knife with a wooden handle, long-handled dressing forceps, straight forceps, curved forceps, a silver probe and a pair of sharp, pointed scissors. She took a large enamel bowl and positioned it carefully on the floor for the used swabs. Finally, she took the bottle of carbolic acid and sprayed a liberal amount over everything.

Peeping out through the door into the ward, Maud could see the orderlies with their stretcher waiting by Mr Langer's bed. Michael stood red-faced, with a fixed smile on his face, as Sister wagged her finger at him. Stephen stood quietly, as always, with his jacket hanging loose around his thin frame. She saw Michael roll his eyes as Sister Law marched away, and then the orderlies made a move to place the stretcher beneath the patient and carefully slide him into position.

'We have no surgeon, or chloroform, yet,' murmured Maud, glancing behind to ensure that her own preparations were still faultless. When she looked back to the ward, she could see the tall, shambling figure of Mr Jones striding through the door with a smoke in his hand and slim, dark-haired Dr McKendrick keeping pace at his side, carrying a wooden box.

That's more like it, thought Maud, taking a moment to untie her apron and refasten it tightly around her thin waist.

'Nurse Linklater,' cried Dr McKendrick, his dark eyes sparkling with life. 'Welcome back. We have missed you,' he said, laying the wooden box down with a firm clunk on a small table. 'Although your friend Nurse Sampson was able to do some of the work, it wasn't quite her speciality.'

'Ah, yes, she wrote to me and told me that she'd fainted,' smiled Maud, as she adjusted the position of the small table where McKendrick had placed his wooden box.

Mr Jones gave a grunt of recognition as he stood in the corner of the theatre, finishing his smoke.

'And Miss Houston has been telling me all about your adventures in New York,' continued Dr McKendrick, as he unpacked a bottle of chloroform, some squares of lint and a glass dropper.

Then the door swung open and Michael and Stephen were there, both red-faced, as they heaved either end of the stretcher that was barely wide enough to carry the man's large frame.

Mr Langer looked groggy from the laudanum but as they slid the stretcher from under him he shouted out in pain.

Michael winced visibly and grabbed the man's hand. He didn't leave him until Dr McKendrick was speaking quietly to him as he prepared to administer the chloroform. Maud saw him use the dropper and carefully count the drops as he delivered them on to the lint. Seeing him work, the sureness of his movements and the way he observed his patient took Maud back to the very first time she'd been in this theatre room and witnessed her first operation. The magic of chloroform never failed to impress her, no matter how many times she saw it used. And the smell of it, that heady aroma, made her feel that she was definitely back where she belonged.

'Have you seen those new chloroform masks that some have started to use?' she asked, once their patient was anaesthetized and she was busy loosening the temporary dressing that covered the wound on Mr Langer's shin.

'Yes,' said Dr McKendrick, scrunching his brow with interest. 'In fact, I have a friend coming to see me soon who has been using one. I'm certainly going to look into it. Did they have them in New York?'

'Yes, the surgeon who I worked with, Dr Emily Blackwell, she found that the right mask can deliver chloroform much more evenly. She very much approved of their use.'

Maud saw him raise his eyebrows at the mention of Dr Blackwell's name.

'Oh,' he said, 'a woman surgeon. There is great progress going on in the world, Nurse Linklater. Great progress. I don't know how long it will be in Britain, or in my country of birth, India, before they are admitting female doctors. But we can only hope.'

'What's that?' frowned Mr Jones. 'Women surgeons?'

'Yes, indeed, Mr Jones.'

'Hmph,' he said, mumbling something else that Maud couldn't quite catch.

As Mr Jones was washing his hands, Maud used the dressing forceps to remove the lint from the wound. She had to take a deep breath when she saw the broken end of white bone protruding from a bloodied mess on the man's shin.

'Good work, everything laid out in a logical order,' smiled Mr Jones, glancing at the instruments as he walked towards the table drying his hands. 'There's a good strong tibia,' he said, peering closely at the wound. 'Just a shame that it's now on the outside of the man's body. At least, though, it looks like our Mr Langer has a decent circulation to his foot, so we've got time to make a good job of this. First things first, we need to tie off all the bleeding vessels with ligatures . . .' Just as Mr Jones took up his forceps, the door swung open and a young man with thin hair and small, deep-set eyes entered.

'Ah, Mr Stafford,' said Mr Jones, with an edge to his voice. 'So glad that you could escape the clutches of your fellow medical students and find time to join us.'

The young man didn't offer any apology but, instead, pursed his lips and went straight to the table, making a move towards the pile of clean swabs.

'Please stop right there, Mr Stafford,' said Maud.

She had never seen anyone look properly down their nose, but that's exactly what the young man did.

'I need you to go first, please, and scrub your hands with carbolic soap. Before you even think of assisting,' she said, with cut-glass precision.

'And who are you?' blustered Mr Stafford.

'I am Nurse Linklater,' Maud said steadily, tilting her chin towards him. She heard Mr Jones almost snort, to stifle a laugh, as the medical student huffed and puffed and flushed bright red.

'Mr Stafford,' insisted Mr Jones, as he stood with his instrument poised above the patient's leg, 'Nurse Linklater is a senior theatre nurse. She knows what she's about. And not only that, she is following the direct guidance of Dr Joseph Lister of Glasgow, the master of germ theory. Do as she says, otherwise I will most certainly have you removed from this theatre.'

Maud saw the young man glare at her with something approaching hatred, but she met his gaze with equal fire. She didn't care what some medical student thought, all that mattered was the welfare of her patient.

And if he overstepped the mark again, she would boot him out of theatre herself.

As Mr Jones started to swab with one hand, searching for bleeding points, Maud stood ready to collect the swabs. There were some small pieces of dead tissue and slivers of bone that he also pulled out, and Maud collected each one reverently on a piece of lint. She avoided looking at Mr Stafford. It was enough to feel him there, still glowering as he stood ready with a clean swab in his newly washed hand. In due course, there was a great deal of bleeding, and so he was kept very busy mopping up the blood and throwing each saturated swab, with a satisfied grunt, into the enamel bowl on the floor.

'Now, Mr Stafford,' murmured Mr Jones, as he scrutinized the mess of bone and muscle exposed before him, 'there isn't any way that I can suture this wound. The whole thing will have to heal by granulation, from the bottom up. But let's see if we can get this broken bone back into some kind of line. And maybe I could use some adhesive lead tape to stretch across and try to bring the edges of the wound at least partly together – we do, of course, need to leave space for the pus to escape when suppuration commences. Are you ready with the compresses and the muslin bandage, Nurse Linklater?'

'I am,' stated Maud, glancing down to check that she also had a dry roller of bandage to hand. 'We're all ready.'

'We need a pillow as well to support the leg in the fracture box.'

'There's one there, on the shelf,' said Maud, grateful to Sister Law and her exquisite organization.

'Right, Mr Stafford, I need you to put some traction on this leg by grasping the patient's ankle and giving it a good, strong pull.'

The medical student nodded and took up his position at the end of the table.

'Nurse Linklater and Dr McKendrick, you'll both need to hold on to our man at the top end. Are we all ready? When I say pull . . . you pull, Mr Stafford, and I'll push the tibia back into alignment. Are you ready? Go!'

Maud and Dr McKendrick looped their arms under the patient's arms and clung on for dear life as Mr Stafford's face turned bright red with the effort and Mr Jones did his work within the wound. She heard the grating of bone on bone as something went back into place. It made her feel a bit light-headed, but she held on to Mr Langer with all her might.

'That seems to be a reasonable position,' murmured Mr Jones. 'Hold fast where you are, Mr Stafford,' he said, holding on to the leg to maintain position. 'Now, Nurse Linklater, if you could apply the compresses to the sides of the leg and bandage them in place. And then, finally, we'll get the leg positioned in the fracture box.'

'Righto,' said Maud.

'We might need your assistance as well, McKendrick,' said Mr Jones. 'If we, all three, lift the leg together then we might be able to avoid disrupting the position of the bones. Nurse Linklater can then bandage around us – leaving the wound at the front of the leg exposed, of course. We'll dress that separately.'

Maud worked like fury, her hands covered in the slimy egg white solution.

'Good work, Nurse Linklater. Now, in with the pillow,' directed Mr Jones, as he and Mr Stafford lifted the leg once more.

Maud turned and grabbed the pillow, and then slid it smoothly beneath the leg.

'Finally, we all need to lift the leg again, whilst Nurse Linklater slides the fracture box into position.'

Maud went to the wall and picked up the wooden structure. She opened up the hinged sides, laying it flat, and as they lifted the leg, still on the pillow, she slid it beneath.

'Good show,' breathed Mr Jones.

Maud already had a dry bandage to secure the patient's foot to the wooden base of the box, and then they were ready to fold up the sides.

'Right,' said Maud, checking the position of the leg in the box, 'I just need to apply a dry dressing to the open wound and give one final spray of carbolic acid. But we will, of course, have to continue to be scrupulous with wound care and handwashing,' she said, glancing directly at Mr Stafford. 'And make an accurate recording of temperature, three times daily.'

Mr Jones stood nodding. 'I think, given your plan, Nurse Linklater, Mr Langer's leg will have no choice but to heal.'

'Isn't it all a little over the top, all this handwashing and spraying with carbolic acid?' added Mr Stafford, looking down his nose again.

Mr Jones sighed. 'You need to keep up with the times, Mr Stafford. Lister's ideas on germ theory are making a huge difference in hospitals throughout the country. Mortality rates have fallen from something like forty to as low as four per cent in some cases. Not even the most hidebound old surgeon, mired in tradition, could ignore results like that. Surely?'

Mr Stafford cleared his throat and looked a little downcast. Maud almost felt sorry for him.

'I'll ask the orderlies to come in and move our patient back to his bed,' called Mr Jones as he moved towards the sink, with Mr Stafford in tow. 'Let's get our hands scrubbed, and go and see how things are fixed on the Female ward.'

After they were gone, Dr McKendrick gave Maud a sympathetic glance. 'I think our current medical student still has a great deal to learn.'

'Yes, I think so too,' breathed Maud. 'But it's more a frame of mind than anything else, isn't it? And I'm not sure that any amount of learning can change that. Now, how is our Mr Langer? Is he showing any sign of waking up?'

After the orderlies had been in to move the patient, and Maud had almost finished the scrubbing and cleaning in theatre, Sister Law came through the door. 'My word, Nurse Linklater, you're doing a thorough job in here,' she said, coming to a halt at the opposite side of the theatre table. 'And Mr Jones has been singing your praises, loud and clear, out on the ward. Well done.'

Maud halted in her final polishing of the surgical instruments. It was unprecedented for Sister to say such a thing.

'Thank you,' she stammered, 'but I do still have a great deal to learn.'

'Of course, don't we all?' smiled Sister, her eyes gleaming. And then she actually grinned.

Maud nearly fainted on the spot. She never thought that she'd ever be faced with the sight of Sister Law grinning from ear to ear.

'You have done very well, Nurse Linklater,' repeated Sister. Then, clearing her throat, she regained her composure. 'Now, I need to tell you about another new admission – a fifty-three-year-old man with abdominal pain, suspected inflammation of the appendix. You know the drill. Dr Jones is just completing his examination of the patient, and he'll be back in theatre directly. I've sent for Dr McKendrick, and the patient should be with you in about ten minutes. Will you be ready?'

'I will,' said Maud, starting to arrange the instruments the minute Sister Law turned and made her way to the door. Then she removed her soiled apron and reached for a fresh one from the pile that was ready and waiting.

In fact, they had yet another case after that, and her work in theatre kept her busy for the rest of the day. She'd hoped to have some time to nip over to Female

Surgical and check on Sue and Dolores, but there was no chance. Her work was all-consuming.

Maud emerged, at last, through the door of the theatre room, just as the night staff were coming on duty.

'Good evening,' she murmured to Sister Tweedy, as she made her way up the ward with her assistant nurse. Then she went straight to Mr Langer's bed and was pleased to find that he was resting peacefully, flat on his back, with what even looked like a satisfied smile on his face. You get some rest, thought Maud, you've got a long road ahead of you. Then, lifting the sheet to expose his injured leg, she made one final check of her dressing.

'You get off now, Nurse Linklater,' called Sister Law, sternly.

It's a good job I know her better now, thought Maud, smiling to herself as she walked off the ward. Otherwise I'd be spending all night wondering what the heck I'd done wrong.

As Maud walked back with Alice, through the city, Alice recounted all the details of her day on Female Surgical. Maud was heartened to hear that Sue was stronger and she'd been up out of bed for a short walk. 'Oh, but that medical student, Mr Stafford, it's a good job I caught him. He was going to take down her dressing! It's perfectly fine – clean and dry, not a sign of any exudate. And the earliest we can remove it is tomorrow, all the nurses on the ward know that. So I stopped him. And he wasn't too pleased.'

'Thank goodness you saw him,' said Maud, proceeding to tell her all about the incident that she'd had with him in theatre.

'Well,' said Alice, 'this'll amuse you. You know you explained to Dolores Williams all about how babies are born? Well, she only went and told the Reverend Seed about it – and how you'd told her the proper name was "vagina".'

'Oh no,' said Maud, mildly horrified.

'Nurse Devlin heard the whole thing. She said he went bright red, even his ears. But he continued to stand by Dolores's bed and listen to everything that she had to say. And you know what she's like, she talked on and on.'

Maud giggled. 'Well, at least she's remembered all the information I gave her. But what about the poor chaplain?'

'Oh, he'll be all right,' said Alice, confidently. 'Lawrence is very shy, but he's a good sort, and much more worldly wise than you'd think.'

'Ooh,' giggled Maud, 'Lawrence. You and he are on first name terms, then?'

'Yes,' said Alice, flushing pink. 'But that doesn't mean anything. I'm on first name terms with you . . .'

'But, Alice, I'm not a man,' smiled Maud, linking her friend's arm and pulling her close. 'A man who, by all accounts, has been following you around like a puppy ever since you went back to work at the Infirmary.'

'Well, yes, but it's complicated. I thought, at first, he was just being friendly and welcoming me back to finish my training. But then, well, he made it clear what his intentions were, and he was very kind to me when all that stuff was going on with Jamie. We've been going out for afternoon tea, and he is very sweet. But the problem is, I still can't think of him as anything more than a nice friend.'

'Even so, Alice. Clearly, he really likes you. And even from the little that I know about him, he seems to be such a lovely man.'

'Yes, he is,' said Alice, 'and I do like him. But I'm not sure if that's enough. I mean, look at you and Harry – that was always clear from the start. I saw your face after he was admitted to the ward that day, all beaten up. You took one look at him and you fell for him, there and then. Even though he had a busted, broken nose. And, as it turned out, in due course, he felt the same about you. Isn't that how it's supposed to be?'

Maud sighed. 'Don't ask me. I've no experience of men, apart from Harry. That was how it was for me and him, but it makes more sense to think that it's all probably a bit random. There shouldn't be any right way or wrong way for it to start, and there certainly needs to be a lot of work invested in keeping any kind of union between two people going. So, I've really no idea how it all works. I thought that I would be the last person in the world to even consider getting married, especially after I started nursing. But now look at me, waiting excitedly for my husband to return home.'

'Mmmm, life does have a habit of playing mysterious tricks at times, doesn't it?' mused Alice as they walked along. 'Ooh, the other thing I wanted to tell you. We need to get Sue some new clothes. Her mam came at visiting time and I asked her if she could bring something in. That old dress she was wearing – the one we cut off – had to go to the incinerator. We did manage to find a whole set of hospital nightgowns, but even the smallest are swamping her. She needs something her own size. And I think, in a few days, when she's feeling stronger, it would be good to have her up and dressed in proper clothes. But her mam said that the one dress was all Sue had. So I was thinking, you know that gold ring that she found, the one she gave to me? I thought that maybe we could take it to the pawn shop and get some money for it, use it to buy her some clothes.'

'We can't do that,' said Maud, outright. 'We said that we'd take the ring back to Lewis's, ask if any of their customers had lost it.'

'Yes, but Maud, that was before Sue had her accident. Surely things have changed now?'

'Not really, it's still the right thing to do. Think about it, Alice. What if you'd lost something really precious, something of sentimental value? Wouldn't you want the chance of getting it back?'

'Yes,' sighed Alice, 'I suppose you're right. But what if someone does claim it? What can we do about Sue? I mean, I could find some extra money, out of my savings, that might work . . .'

'No, Alice, you need that money for Victoria. But I might have some to spare, and I could ask Miss Fairchild if she would help. After all, look what she's done for Alfred. But first, we'll take the ring to the shop and see if we can find the rightful owner.'

'All right, Maud,' said Alice, pulling her closer. 'You have a way of always making me do the right thing. I think you must hypnotize me, or something . . . So, are you back with us on Female Surgical tomorrow, or has Sister Law found a way of hypnotizing you so you never leave her ward?'

'Oh, I'll be back tomorrow.'

'That's goo—'

'Aargh!' screamed Maud and Alice together, as a black shape wearing some kind of cloak lunged at them from the shadows.

'Rarrrr!' roared their assailant.

Maud immediately stepped in front of Alice, with her right hand balled into a fist. Until, that is, she heard their assailant stifling a laugh. And as she stepped closer, in the evening light, she could see it was Eddy, laughing her head off.

They both pounced on her, pretending to rough her up as she doubled over with laughter.

'I saw you both coming,' she gasped at last. 'Tripping along and chit-chatting as you went, I couldn't resist it. I had to leap out. Oh, that was so good!'

'Well, what if I'd really walloped you?' said Maud, balling her fist again.

'And me,' said Alice, pretending to throttle her.

Eddy was still laughing. 'I thought I could safely take my chances,' she said at last, holding her ribs. 'After all, I had the advantage of surprise . . . oh, that was so good. Anyway, you two,' she said, straightening up and removing the hat that was hanging off her head. 'What were you talking about?'

They were almost back at Stella's before they were finished telling Eddy all of their news. She listened carefully, glancing from one to the other, as they linked arms on either side of her.

'What about you, Eddy?' asked Maud, as they headed through a cloud of steam outside Lime Street Station. 'What have you been up to?'

'Busy day, as usual. Mr Berzins is still doing well. But I've got another consumptive case, a young one. And you remember me telling you about Sylvia, the one with the two young children – Rosanna and Archie? She's deteriorating again, I think. It's so sad, seeing them rally, these cases. And then, inevitably, they start spitting blood again and, bit by bit, they fade a little further. Until they're so weak they've no resistance. Tuberculosis is such a cruel disease.'

Maud gave Eddy's arm a squeeze with her own.

'At least they've got you and all the other district nurses to look after them,' she said.

'Mmmm,' replied Eddy, 'but I just wish we could do more. If there was only some effective treatment, or some vaccination, like the smallpox one. I know it doesn't work every time, but at least it's something that can stop it dead in its tracks.'

'All we can do is hope,' said Maud, 'and there are scientific discoveries being made all the time. Let's hope it's not too long before they find a vaccination for tuberculosis as well. It's strange, though, isn't it, how you district nurses don't often catch it yourselves? I've heard of many nurses catching typhus fever, some cholera, pneumonia, even diphtheria . . .'

'Jeez, Maud,' laughed Eddy, 'you need to stop going through the list. I'll be too scared to go out there again at this rate. It's bad enough dealing with the dogs and the sticky-fingered children!'

'Sorry,' said Maud, 'I do have a tendency to get a bit grim sometimes.'

'You do,' said Eddy. 'Thank goodness Harry will be back soon. There's a man who knows how to lighten the mood.'

As soon as they reached the blue door, Maud stood back whilst Alice went through. She was followed by Eddy, already fluffing out her hair.

'Come on, let's all get a cup of tea,' called Alice, leading the way down the corridor and into the kitchen.

The nights were cooling now. Maud could feel the difference even in the short time that she'd been back in the city. It wouldn't be long before the biting cold started to seep in from the Mersey. It was still just warm enough for them all to sit out in the backyard, though, snuggled up in their capes. These times that they could spend together, like they used to when they were all living in the Nurses' Home, were special to Maud. She knew that it was only a short while before she would be moving out to be with Harry. It made her feel a little sad as she sat there, seeing the steam rise from her hot cup of tea, listening to the murmur of voices and the insistent tap, tap of the moths against the window as they were drawn inexorably to the glow of lamplight from within the house.

10

'A nurse should be . . . cheerful, hopeful, not
allowing herself or her patient to become
discouraged . . .'

Florence Nightingale

'In case I forget, will you remind me to ask Sister Pritchard about booking my half day off for when Harry comes back?' said Maud as she stood tying Alice's apron for her, three days later.

'Yes,' grimaced Alice. 'That's a bit tight, Maud. Just slacken it off a bit, will you?'

Maud untied the firm bow and retied it with less force.

'I know it's a couple of weeks off yet, but I want to get it booked. And given that I seem to be working between the two surgical wards, I might have to ask Sister Law as well,' she continued, as they made their way out through the door and ran down the stone stairs.

'I would, just to make sure,' said Alice. 'You know what Sister Law's like, unless you make it clear. In fact, give it to her in writing so there's no mistake. Though, of course, you can't tell her what you need it for. As far as she's concerned, you're a single woman.'

'That's true,' said Maud, 'I'll need to get my story straight.'

'Think of something good. You have to make sure she agrees,' insisted Alice. 'You have to be there to greet your husband, for goodness' sake.'

As they walked up the ward, Alice called by Sue's bed to give her the customary morning greeting. When Maud saw Sue sitting there, all smiles, her chest began to feel tight – today was the day that the dressing would be removed. Maud felt confident enough of her dressing, and the rigorous checks she'd made post-operatively, to be hopeful that all would be well beneath that pad of innocent white lint. But the thought of seeing Sue's beautiful face, and having the extent of that cruel wound exposed for all to see . . . it filled her with dread.

When Mr Jones's ward round approached Sue's bed, Sister Pritchard gestured for Maud to attend.

'Now, my dear,' murmured Mr Jones, perching himself at the edge of Sue's bed. 'We are very pleased with your progress. You are doing well,' he smiled.

Maud felt proud of Sue as she sat up in bed in her clean white nightie, beaming.

'I can't watch,' murmured Alice in Maud's ear as she passed by, on her way to Mrs Jenkins at the top of the ward.

Maud felt her stomach tighten as she stood waiting.

'The time has come for us to remove the dressing,' continued Mr Jones.

Maud wasn't sure but she thought even his voice

sounded a little nervous. It felt like the whole ward was watching.

Mr Stafford tried to step forward, but as Mr Jones got up from the bed, he beckoned for Maud to approach.

Here goes, she said to herself, pasting a confident look on her face and mustering a smile for Sue.

'Now, Sue,' said Maud, 'you don't need to do anything. I'll just unwind the bandage, and then I'll tell you when I'm going to remove the dressing pad – it might catch a bit and pull on the stitches underneath.'

'That's all right, Maud,' said Sue, taking her hand just for a moment. 'I'm ready.'

Maud nodded and went straight to the unravelling. It looked good so far; there was no sign of any suppuration, and the swelling around Sue's eye had gone down very nicely.

'I'm just going to remove the pad over your eye now . . .'

Sue blinked a few times and then opened the injured eye.

'Can you see?'

'Yes!' smiled Sue. 'I can see with both eyes now.'

'Right, so here goes with the dressing pad. I'll be as gentle as I can.'

Sue nodded.

Maud grasped the top corner of the dressing and carefully peeled it away. She saw the first black silk suture and the top end of the wound. It looked good – clean and dry and well knitted together. The lint snagged on the next couple of stitches but Maud found only a little resistance as the pad came away. As she continued to gently peel the dressing, the whole row of black stitches was revealed, bit by bit. Maud didn't look at the full extent, not yet. She concentrated on removing each section, one at a time. Finally, after some gentle persuasion, the dressing came away from the girl's face and the wound stood bare.

There was a moment of complete quiet around the bed as Sue sat there smiling.

'Well done,' Maud murmured, 'you've been so brave.'

Mr Jones cleared his throat and approached, scrutinizing the suture line. 'This is healing very well indeed,' he said, frowning. 'I think we can leave the wound exposed now and remove the stitches in a few days' time, once they've loosened a little.'

'Does that meet with your approval, Nurse Linklater, Sister Pritchard?'

'Yes, of course,' smiled Sister Pritchard.

Maud nodded warmly. And before she knew it, the ward round moved to the next bed and she was left with her patient.

'It feels so much better now that the bandage is off,' said Sue, reaching a hand up towards her face.

'Try not to touch the stitches, Sue,' Maud offered gently. 'It's good for them to have the air, but we need to keep them as clean as possible.'

'All right,' said Sue, swinging her legs over the side of the bed. She'd got used to wandering up and down the ward in her nightie, chatting to the other patients.

'Just stay at the side of your bed until Mr Jones has finished the round,' said Maud. 'Then you can go for a walk.'

Sue nodded and rooted out the small drawstring bag that she kept under her pillow. Alice had brought it in for her to store her small treasures in. She'd already added to her trove: a pebble that she'd found on the hearth of the ward fire and a shiny penny that one of the patients had given her. And now she brought them all out together, arranging them into different patterns on the bed.

Glancing back as she walked up the ward, Maud swallowed hard to get rid of the lump in her throat as she saw Sue still happily swinging her legs at the side of the bed. The girl was smiling to herself, completely unaware of the scarlet line of the wound, punctuated by harsh black sutures, puckering one side of her face.

Alice passed her on her way down the ward and they exchanged a glance. Maud could see the sadness in her friend's eyes but she knew that Alice would muster a bright smile and speak confidently to Sue. They'd already talked about what they would do and agreed that they would wait for her to ask to see the wound. That's when they would show her.

Later on, Maud found Dolores Williams very excited. She'd just been given the all clear to go home.

'My Jim's coming at visiting, and he can take me home. I mean, I never thought that I'd enjoy coming into hospital – and I'm not saying I've exactly done that – but when I came in, Nurse Linklater, I don't know if you could tell, or not. But I was scared stiff.'

'Yes, you did look worried,' smiled Maud, remembering how terrified Dolores had been.

'And I want to say thank you, to you in particular, Nurse Linklater, for telling me about all the things related to the baby. And I've been meaning to ask you something else . . . well, do you think you would be able to come and deliver it for me?'

'Oh,' said Maud, taken aback for a moment, 'well, that's very nice of you to ask, but I've only ever delivered one baby. I don't have any real experience, I'm afraid. You'll need to find yourself a local midwife – ask the women on the street where you live, they'll know who to use – or you could come in here, to the hospital, on to the lying-in ward.'

'Oooh,' said Dolores, 'I might like to come back to hospital. What do you think?'

'Well, to be honest, if everything is straightforward and you have a good local woman who knows her stuff, then you're probably best staying at home. They have doctors on the lying-in ward, but that doesn't mean to say that the service the women get is any better.'

'Mmm, I see what you mean. I'll have to think about it. I've got a good few months to go, anyway. But thanks, Nurse Linklater . . . for everything.'

'You are very welcome, Mrs Williams. And don't forget to keep drinking the barley water once you get home. You know how to brew it up, don't you?'

'Oh, me mother used to brew it all the time. I was born and raised on that stuff,' she laughed.

Maud nodded to Jim Williams as he came through

the door at visiting, with his eager face and measured stride. He'll be pleased when he finds out he can take his new wife home, she thought to herself, silently wishing the newly married couple well as she walked along the corridor towards Male Surgical to see Sister Law about her afternoon off.

As she walked up the ward she raised a hand to Mr Langer. She'd been into Male Surgical every single day to monitor the wound on his shin. He'd been fevered and mildly delirious for two days, but this morning, as the natural suppuration of the wound had begun and there was a promising flow of light yellow pus, he was much more settled. It was good to see him sitting up in bed with his visitors around him. The small woman with dark hair must be his wife, Clara, and she could see the three children. The eldest one was tall for his eight years of age, and he had pale brown hair, like his father. And the two little girls, with blonde hair and ribbons, she knew were only five and three. He'd told her just this morning that they were called Frieda and Martha, and they were the light of his life.

Maud would keep an eagle eye on Mr Langer's wound. She knew that they were at an early stage, as yet. A wound like that had to heal from the bottom up: a very lengthy and laborious process with, all the while, the ever present threat of deep suppuration or gangrene setting in. She prayed that Mr Langer would stay the course.

Sister Law was standing to attention at the top of the

ward, surveying her patients and the visitors who were emerging tentatively through the ward door. When she saw Maud, she seemed to almost smile, but then thought better of it. Maud took a deep breath and ploughed ahead.

'If possible, Sister, I need to book a half day off in advance,' she gabbled. 'I know that I'm based on Female Surgical and I've asked Sister Pritchard and she has approved. But given that I work in theatre on Male Surgical as well, I thought it best to book the date with you also.'

Sister Law pursed her lips. 'Mmmm,' she said, narrowing her eyes, 'a half day, is it?'

'Yes, please,' said Maud, her heart racing.

'And when is it?'

'In two weeks. It's a Thursday.'

Sister puffed out her chest. 'And what is so special that you need to book your half day off so far in advance?'

Maud was stumped for a moment. She'd been so busy on the ward, she'd forgotten to practise a reason. And she couldn't very well tell Sister Law that she was meeting her husband off the ship from New York.

'Well, I have a . . . I have a dear friend, a very respectable lady, who is ill, and I've promised to spend the afternoon with her.'

Sister Law frowned.

'It's her birthday,' blurted Maud. 'It's her birthday. That's . . . why I need that particular day.'

Sister Law narrowed her eyes again. 'And so, Nurse

Linklater, you've promised this time, this Thursday afternoon, to your friend, without consulting me first?'

'Yes, sorry,' said Maud, starting to feel desperate.

'Well, Nurse Linklater . . .' said Sister, moving her face closer so that she could scrutinize Maud's expression.

For a moment there was complete silence. Maud held her breath.

'. . . you have worked extremely hard since your return from America. And I am impressed with the time you have spent ensuring that our Mr Langer's wound is satisfactory. Therefore, just this once . . . I will grant your request.'

Maud breathed again. 'Thank you, Sister. I've written the details here, in a letter,' she said, passing her the envelope, before turning on her heel and retreating down the ward as quickly as she could.

The interaction had temporarily made Maud feel that two weeks hence was a distant place, set far in the future. But in fact, she was so busy with her work that the time was flying by. She hadn't even been able to get up to the Blue Coat again to see Alfred. And given the way that things were going, she knew that she would have to reconcile herself to the fact that she wouldn't see him until the day of Harry's arrival. She'd written to him and they'd already arranged that she would collect him at two fifteen on the day. The ship was due in about three. But depending on tides and the sheer number of other vessels vying for position on the river, Maud knew that it could vary. But now that she had confirmation of her half day off, she was on countdown, and she would be there, waiting with Alfred, no matter what.

As Maud walked back towards Female Surgical, she was startled by a piercing cry that came from the ward. Her heart thudded and she instantly picked up her pace. Coming through the door, she could see the anguished face of Sue's mam as she held on to her daughter, and now she was sobbing uncontrollably. Alice was coming down the ward very fast, and Maud headed straight to the scene, too.

'Mrs Cassidy,' she soothed, trying to put her arm around the woman's shoulder.

'My poor baby, my little girl,' wailed Mrs Cassidy, 'what an awful thing to happen to you.'

The girl sat rigid in the bed, her eyes wide and her face terrified.

Alice was there with her now at the other side of the bed.

'Mrs Cassidy, please try to calm down,' Maud tried to coax. Clearly, the woman was in shock, but Maud could see how frightened Sue looked.

'Look at her,' wailed Sue's mam. 'How will she get a husband now?'

Something clicked inside Maud's head then, and she took a firmer grip of Mrs Cassidy. 'You need to stand back for a moment,' she said calmly. 'Let your daughter have some space.'

But Mrs Cassidy clung to her child more tightly.

Sue was crying now, big tears rolling down her face, trickling through the black sutures.

Maud and Alice exchanged a glance.

'The wound has healed very well,' said Maud steadily. 'Sue could have been killed that day. You could have lost her completely, but you will have a healthy daughter to leave the hospital.'

'What use will that be?' spat her mam. 'When she's ruined for life!'

Maud was shocked. 'Now just one minute,' she retaliated, 'a woman doesn't have to be beautiful to marry. And she doesn't even need to be married, or have a man, to be something in this world.'

'Doesn't she?' screamed Mrs Cassidy. Then, as if she'd shocked herself, her voice was quieter when she spoke again. 'Look at me, Nurse, just look at me. Working for next to nothing on that flower stall. And if I lose that job, then I'll be back to nothing and Sue will be out on the street begging for food again. When I had a husband at home, he was bringing in a wage as well. We didn't have much, but we had enough for food on the table and a bit of life.'

Maud did understand what she was saying, of course she did, but a bright girl like Sue . . . Maud could have put the case for her finding work in nursing. But she knew that there was no point, not yet. Mrs Cassidy was heartbroken, devastated. There was nothing that anyone could have said, right then, that would have made a jot of difference.

'I can't stand 'ere and look at her like that,' said the woman, wiping her face on her sleeve. 'I'll be seeing you, Sue,' she called as she walked away.

'I didn't know it was so bad,' sobbed Sue. 'I must look like a monster.'

'No,' soothed Alice, 'you are a beautiful girl with an unusual mark on the side of your face that will start to look much better when the stitches are out. And when you're ready, we'll get the mirror and we'll let you see for yourself.'

Sue nodded.

'You just let us know, Sue,' said Maud, 'as soon as you're ready.'

'I'll wait till you're taking out the stitches,' said Sue, lifting her chin in a mildly defiant gesture.

By the time the day for removal of the stitches came, it felt like Maud and Alice were more nervous than Sue. Her mam hadn't returned to the ward, as yet, and beyond monitoring the wound for suppuration and checking her temperature twice daily, they'd been working closely with the girl, trying to build up a bit of confidence. They'd encouraged her to show her face, not even think of hiding away, so she'd been up and down the ward as usual, chatting to the other patients. And after the scene with her mam, many of the women on the ward were giving Sue pennies or finding her an old brooch or an embroidered handkerchief. Her draw-string bag was now bulging with treasure and no longer able to slip under her pillow.

Maud had devised a plan. She'd bought a brand-new tortoiseshell mirror and matching hairbrush, and she'd suggested that they take Sue up to theatre where they could have some privacy to remove the sutures. Mr Stafford had tried to insist that a medical man was required for the procedure, but Mr Jones had put him straight. Maud smiled every time she remembered his words, and she'd repeated them to Alice on request more than once. 'My dear Mr Stafford, our surgical nurses are more than competent to snip one side of a stitch and pull it through the skin. The advances we are currently making in theatre rely upon their skill. Where would we be without their assistance in theatre and the crucial post-surgical nursing that they perform? They are with the patients twenty-four hours a day; we come and go on the wards. If I was a patient, I'd much prefer a nurse to attend me, not some bumbling medical student!'

Maud carried a stool as she walked up to theatre, with Sue and Alice following behind. Many of the other patients were calling out to them, wishing Sue luck or blowing a kiss. The strength of feeling on the ward for their youngest patient was almost overwhelming. As Maud turned to open the theatre door with her hip, she saw Alice desperately trying to blink back tears.

'Right, Sue, you come and sit yourself down here,' called Maud, indicating the stool, which she had placed right by the open window where the best light could be found. 'Now, Nurse Sampson . . .'

Sue giggled and whispered, 'You can call her Alice in here, Maud. Sister Pritchard can't hear us.'

'Now, Alice,' smiled Maud, pulling a length of bright green ribbon from her pocket, 'if you could tie Sue's hair back with this whilst I scrub my hands.'

'It matches your eyes, Sue,' said Alice, making a show of pulling back her tousled red hair and tying the ribbon with a luxurious bow.

After Maud was satisfied with the cleanliness of her bright red scrubbed hands, she removed a pair of small pointed scissors and some forceps from a bowl of carbolic acid, placing them on one lint swab and drying them with another.

'Now, Sue, if you could twist round a little, so I've got the best light. Good girl, that's it.' Maud surveyed the line of sutures set close together.

Mr Jones had really sweated over them, and the mastery of his skill showed. The scarlet line of the wound was healing well, with only one small area that appeared raised due to an ever so slight misalignment of the edges of the wound.

'These look very good indeed,' Maud said. 'Now, I'm going to start at the top and work down. You will feel them tugging a little as they come out, and one or two might sting, but there shouldn't be any really bad pain. Are you ready?'

Sue nodded and then took Alice's hand.

Maud worked her way meticulously down the line of sutures, ensuring that each stitch was drawn cleanly through the wound, then placing it in a small white enamel bowl positioned carefully at the side.

As each one came out of the skin, it left a red dot either side of the scar – a pattern that stretched from Sue's eye, over her fine cheekbone and then curled in to skim by the corner of her mouth. The more stitches that were removed, the more Maud could see the consistency of the lasting damage to Sue's face, and her stomach began to tighten. They all remained silent as the process continued. All anyone could hear was the steady rhythm of Maud's breathing as she concentrated on the job in hand.

At last, the final stitch was pulled through. Maud placed it in the enamel bowl with the rest.

'All done,' she murmured, straightening up, then taking a step back. 'It has healed very well,' she said. 'Do you want to see?'

Sue nodded, her lips pressed into a firm line.

As Maud brought the hand mirror, Alice held tight to Sue's hand.

'Are you ready?' asked Maud, holding the mirror in front of Sue's face but with the tortoiseshell back towards her.

'Yes,' said the girl, with her chin tilted and her big green eyes wide.

Maud turned the mirror.

Sue just stared at her reflection for what seemed like an age. And then her chin began to tremble and a single tear started to roll down her face. She couldn't speak.

'Do you want me to take the mirror away?' asked Maud, her throat tight.

'No,' gasped Sue. 'No.'

Maud held on to the mirror and Alice held on to Sue's hand for as long as it took.

Eventually, Sue reached up a hand to her cheek, to touch the scar. She prodded it with a finger, frowning.

Then she moved her hand over the whole of it, wiping it over and over, as if trying to scrub it away. Tears were now streaming down her face.

She turned her face to the side, glancing at her good side and then at the side with the scar. Then she did it again and again, sighing at last and motioning for Maud to lower the mirror. With her shoulders slumped and her head bowed, she muttered, 'I hate it. It's so ugly.'

And then she got up from the stool, pulled the green silk ribbon out of her hair, threw it to the floor and walked silently out through the door.

Alice made a move towards the door but then stopped, realizing Sister Pritchard had seen Sue, and would look after her.

Maud sighed. 'That's one of the most difficult things I've ever had to do,' she said. 'Maybe there would have been a better way?'

'I don't think so, Maud. We waited until she was ready to see the scar, we did our best to prepare and support her . . .'

'But now all we can do is wait and see what she makes of it,' added Maud, moving to the bin with the enamel bowl to empty out the discarded black sutures. Then she took the instruments to the sink and scoured them vigorously.

'When she's ready, Alice,' she said, as she scrubbed, 'we'll see if she'll let us wash her hair. Fluff it out a bit, arrange it around her face. I'm not much good with hair but I'm sure we can do something. Oh, and I brought that gold ring. Like we said, I'm going to call by Lewis's this afternoon to see if anyone has reported it lost. If not, then I'll take it up to the pawn shop. Are we still agreed?'

'Yes,' said Alice, dabbing at her eyes, 'good thinking. Let's get her some money for a whole new set of clothes. Stella and Marie have already been knitting – they've got a hat, a scarf and a shawl made from knitted squares of bright wool.'

'She'll like that,' said Maud, putting her arm around Alice's shoulders. 'She's going to come through this, Alice, and be even stronger. Just you wait and see.'

Despite her encouraging words for Alice, Maud's heart felt like a heavy weight in her chest as she made her way to Lewis's that afternoon in the pouring rain. She'd taken a sturdy umbrella from the stand just inside the door of the Nurses' Home and it did keep the worst of the downpour off her. However, the footpath was crammed with other people and similar umbrellas, so as she walked she had to keep holding it up above her head or squeezing it sideways just so she could get through.

Nevertheless, she walked on. Even though the water was soaking up from the hem of her dress, she walked on through the rain.

Arriving, dripping wet, at the glass-fronted shop on Ranelagh Street, she stood for a moment looking up at the grand sign that read Lewis's & Co Clothiers & Bootmakers. She'd regularly passed the shop and admired the window displays but never once been in through the door. And she had no idea why she was hesitating in the street, with the rain drumming on her umbrella. Come on, Maud, she said to herself, taking a deep breath and pushing through the door. She heard the tinkle of a bell as she emerged in the shop and folded her umbrella.

'Please, miss,' tutted a sharp voice behind her, 'don't stand there dripping on the tiles, put your umbrella in the stand at once.'

Maud turned to find a tall woman with scraped-back hair and pince-nez glasses on a fine chain pinching the bridge of her long nose.

'Apologies,' said Maud, immediately walking in the direction of the umbrella stand that the woman was indicating with a very straight and pointy finger.

'You're not a regular customer,' continued the woman, as Maud turned back to find her almost blocking her way.

'No, I'm not,' bristled Maud. She'd had too busy and distressing a day to trifle with the petty details of a shop assistant's world. 'I just need to see your manager about something and then I'll be on my way.'

'I'm Miss Madden, I am the manageress,' snapped the woman, glaring down her long nose.

'I see,' said Maud. 'Well, perhaps you will be able to help me.'

Maud fished in her pocket and produced the ring that Sue had given her in the backyard. It glinted deep gold, even in the dim light of the shop.

'We are not a pawn shop,' said Miss Madden immediately, pulling her mouth down in disapproval.

Maud held the woman's sharp gaze; she was not in the mood for snobbishness. 'I realize that, Miss Madden. I just need to ask if any of your customers has reported the loss of this gold ring. It was found on the pavement immediately outside the shop.'

Miss Madden held out her hand to receive the ring. And then she removed her pince-nez and used them like a magnifying glass to inspect the item.

'No, I've not heard of any losses being reported,' she said, as she continued to scrutinize the ring. And then she looked at Maud with narrowed eyes. 'Who found it? It looks like an expensive ring.'

'I found it,' said Maud, knowing that if there was any hint of it having been retrieved by a girl from the street then the police might be called.

'I see,' said the woman, replacing her pince-nez and handing the ring back to Maud. 'Well, I'm sorry, but we at Lewis's cannot help you today, madam. Now, good day.'

'Thank you,' said Maud politely, slipping the ring back inside her pocket.

The woman still stood there, right in front of Maud, scowling and waiting for her to leave.

Maud neatly sidestepped her, moving further into the shop, surveying the range of women's clothing. She didn't need anything but there was plenty of time before the pawn shop closed, and the devil in her wanted to prolong Miss Madden's agony for as long as she possibly could.

After she'd browsed the women's clothing, she moved to a selection of the men's. Hearing Miss Madden tut as she stood behind her made her all the more determined to view the full range. Then she saw a display of shiny silver pocket watches, and she was genuinely interested. They were of a simple design, functional more than anything, and she was immediately drawn to them. She'd been trying to think of a suitable homecoming gift for Harry and had brought some money that she'd saved from her wages, thinking that she might find something at the pawn shop. But seeing these brand-new watches, at a surprisingly affordable price, she couldn't resist. After all, a watch was a personal item and he could make it his own. And given that he never could turn up on time for anything, it would be ideal.

After paying Miss Madden, who seemed to almost begrudgingly agree to the sale, she watched her painstakingly wrap the watch in a tight layer of tissue paper before slipping it into a small brown paper bag. Maud waited patiently as Miss Madden secured the bag with a length of string. Eager now to leave the shop, she walked straight to the stand to pick out her folded umbrella and then heaved a sigh of relief as she heard the shop bell tinkle behind her.

The rain had stopped completely, and when she glanced up to the sky there was even a patch of blue. She took a deep breath and started to smile as she turned over the package in her hand before slipping it into her pocket. Not long to go now, my love, she murmured, counting off the days in her head as she started to walk away from the shop, with the weight of the gift for Harry tapping satisfyingly against her thigh.

11

'Moral activity? There is scarcely such a thing possible! Everything is sketchy. The world does nothing but sketch.'

Florence Nightingale

Sue Cassidy hadn't let them near her all the next day. She would only communicate with Sister Pritchard or Nurse Devlin, and she averted her eyes whenever Maud or Alice walked by. Maud had tried to approach her a number of times but she'd sat with her head down and stubbornly refused to speak. Maud could sense how sorrowful Alice was beginning to feel about the situation, but there seemed to be little that she could do to help.

'She'll come round,' soothed Maud. 'Just give her time. She's firing all of her rage in our direction because we're closest to her. What else can she do? Her mother hasn't been back to visit since she walked out that day. Her anger has to go somewhere, and we are the ones who are best placed to deal with it. You know we are.'

Alice was nodding. 'I know you're right,' she murmured, glancing once more in the direction of Sue's bed. 'I just hope it doesn't take much longer, that's all.'

Maud was all set to make another approach to Sue again later that day but, in the end, there was no need. She'd seen her sneaking a glance towards Alice as she walked down the ward and then, later on, she heard her call out as they were passing by.

Maud continued on her way up to the sluice, with the bowl that she was carrying. 'Sue wants me to wash her hair,' Alice called excitedly as she came in through the door after her.

'Phew!' said Maud, turning with a smile. 'At last! Well, why don't you bring her in here? We can get her head over the sink, and I'll go and get another kettle full of hot water so that we can have as much warm water as we need. There's soft soap on the shelf up there, Alice.'

When Sue came quietly into the sluice with Alice, she looked a bit sheepish. But as soon as she glanced to Maud and started to mouth sorry, Maud was straight there, reaching out to her. 'There's no need to apologize. You needed to do what you had to do, that's all there is to it. Now come on, let's have a look at this mane of hair. Yes, it certainly does need some attention, doesn't it?'

Sue leant over the sink, with a towel pressed over her eyes, and Alice poured the first lot of warm water over her matted hair. By the time Maud returned with the extra hot water, Sue's head was a mass of bubbles. 'I think I might have overdone the soft soap,' laughed Alice, 'but we're giving it a good do, aren't we?' she said, getting her hands right in and massaging down to Sue's scalp.

'Are you all right in there?' Maud whispered in Sue's ear.

'Yes, just about,' was the muffled response.

Maud mixed the hot into the cold and they poured jug after jug of water over the girl's head. When at last there were no suds left, Sue stood up, flushed in the face and slightly out of breath. Alice was already giving her hair a good towelling and Sue started to laugh as her head was jolted from side to side.

'This really is squeaky clean,' beamed Alice, clearly delighted. And it was very satisfying indeed to see the true colour and the first shine of Sue's glorious locks.

Maud led the girl back through, to sit by the fire on one of the benches at the end of the ward. Another patient shoved up to make room for her. 'Come on, lass,' she said, 'you'll be catching pneumonia if you don't get that lot dry soon.'

And as Sue basked in the warmth of the fire, her hair dried and rose into a glorious crown of red curls.

'My word,' said Maud, as she came to help Alice finish the untangling and the cutting out of the more obstinate knots, 'your hair really is very beautiful.'

'Mam says it's my crowning glory,' grinned Sue.

Alice fluffed it up one more time, bringing the curls down over both sides of Sue's face. It didn't cover the scar completely but it definitely softened the appearance of it. When Maud brought the tortoiseshell mirror again, she could feel a flutter of anxiety in her chest. And she held her breath when she glimpsed the girl's bright eyes and deep frown as she looked into the glass, meeting head on the angry red line that dominated her reflection. Then she saw her reach up a hand to feel down the full length of the scar.

'Always remember, Sue,' said Maud quietly, crouching down by the side of her, 'your scar tells a story of how you tried to save a boy's life. You should be proud of it and not hide it away.'

Maud saw Sue's chin tremble ever so slightly as she blinked back tears. Then she was moving her head from side to side, adjusting her hair.

'My hair looks nice,' she said.

'Yes, it does,' smiled Maud. And when Sue tried to give her the mirror, 'No, you keep it,' she said. 'We bought it for you. And the brush as well.'

'Thank you,' said Sue, starting to smile as she ran her hand over the smooth tortoiseshell pattern on the back of the mirror.

From that day, there was no question that Sue was anything but ready for discharge. Word was sent to her mam and arrangements were made for her to be collected at visiting. Maud had given the pawn shop money to Alice, and she'd been out to buy two new dresses – one light brown and one blue – in a soft woollen fabric, new underclothes, two nightdresses, three pairs of fine wool stockings, and some brand-new boots that fitted properly. Along with the knitted items that Marie and Stella had sent, Sue had a fine new wardrobe.

'Good work,' smiled Sister Pritchard, seeing Sue all packed up and ready to go in her new light brown dress, with the green silk ribbon in her hair and the brightly coloured chequered shawl neatly folded and waiting on the bed.

'I hope her mam approves,' whispered Alice, as they waited at the top of the ward for the visitors to come in. 'What if she starts yelling again?'

'She won't,' said Maud, sounding confident. But inside she was nervous as well.

Alice grasped Maud's hand when they saw Sue's mam come through the door carrying a scuffed leather bag. Old beyond her years, with thin hair and a weary resigned expression, she looked like someone who had given up. They saw her stop in her tracks when she saw Sue sitting at the side of the bed with her head down, playing with her treasures from the drawstring bag.

Alice drew in a sharp breath and Maud gave her hand a squeeze.

They saw Sue's mam start to move and then stop, stock still, at the bottom of the bed, still watching her daughter. She put the leather bag down on the floor.

When Sue looked up, she instantly put a hand to her cheek to try and cover the scar. Her mam didn't make a move, she stood with her back stiff, still gazing at her daughter. Sue slipped off the bed and stood in front of her mam, looking up to her, her eyes wide and beseeching. Still her mam stood with her shoulders held square.

'Go on, go on, just give her a hug,' murmured Alice.

And in that moment, as if she'd heard and taken note of the encouragement, Mrs Cassidy seemed to fold in on herself, and then she reached out and drew Sue to her in a tight embrace. Her shoulders were shaking, she was crying, but she was holding on to her daughter with all her might.

'Thank goodness,' breathed Maud, as Alice exhaled loudly and pressed a hand to her heart.

'Oh no,' gasped Maud, a moment later when she saw Sue's mam reach into the leather bag and pull out a large black hat. 'She's only brought her a hat with a heavy veil.'

There was nothing that either Maud or Alice could do to dissuade Sue's mam from insisting that her daughter wear the hat. And as Sue left the ward that day, it was so sad to see her walking with her head down as if the weight of the black hat and dark veil were dragging her down. There wasn't anything at all that they could do, except make Sue promise that she'd still come to visit them at the house – and if they weren't there, to ask for Marie or Stella.

'I'll try,' said Sue, quietly, from behind her veil.

As Maud walked back through the city that evening, with her arm linked through Alice's, they talked through Sue's situation again. At least they had an address; they could go and visit her if she didn't turn up like she always used to in the backyard.

'I think she'll come,' soothed Maud, sensing Alice's anguish. 'After all, she's determined enough, we know she is, and her mam will have to go straight back to work on the market. She'll be back, like our little guardian angel, just you wait and see.'

'Yes, you're probably right, Maud, I know you are. But until she had that accident, I didn't realize just how fond I've become of her. I was so terrified that we might lose her, and now I'm worrying how she'll manage at home and back out in the city.'

'I know,' soothed Maud. 'She is a very special person – and it's always the way, isn't it? We never know what we've got till there's a risk that it might be gone. I suppose, in a way, Alice, we're privileged, doing the work that we do. We learn just how precious life is from our first days on the wards. It makes you realize what's important in life, doesn't it? We are witness to immense suffering and incredible joy – often all in the same day.'

'You're right there,' agreed Alice, with a wry smile, 'and Maud, you always have a wonderful way of seeing into things and putting it into words.'

'Mmm, I don't know about that. Eddy would probably say that I'm a bit too gloom and doom.'

'Ha! Yes, she would,' laughed Alice, straightening up and giving Maud's arm a squeeze. 'But I'm the one who's being all gloom and doom this evening, Maud. And I'm so sorry, I know how excited you must be about Harry coming home tomorrow.'

'Well, it has been on my mind a little, yes,' smiled Maud. 'I just can't wait to see him.'

It was four o'clock in the morning on the day that Harry was coming home. Maud was wide awake, and she knew there was no chance she'd be able to go back to sleep. From where she lay on her mattress on the floor, she could hear the sound of Alice's steady breathing from the bed above, and Victoria snuffling in her sleep. And she could feel the creeping cold that seemed to seep upwards from the stone-flagged floor. She half wished now that she'd accepted Alice's offer of staying in the bed. But she'd refused point blank – she was a guest, after all, and it was the right thing to do. And what's more, it would only be a matter of days now before she was moving out to be with Harry. She'd saved up enough money for them to find somewhere decent, and he'd promised to put some aside, too. She couldn't wait to sleep in a proper bed again and feel the warmth of his body next to hers. Hearing the rustle of a mouse behind the skirting board, Maud felt a tiny shudder go through her body, and she pulled the blanket more tightly around her.

She did in fact manage to doze off again, eventually. But Alice and Victoria were still sleeping soundly when she woke again. This time, she was very cold. She lit the candle at the side of her bed so that she could find her clothes. She shivered as she got herself dressed, all fingers and thumbs with her buttons and hooks, due to the cold and the sheer thrill of getting ready to see Harry.

Maud walked to work so fast that Alice had to almost run to keep up.

'Slow down, Maud,' she called. 'I know you're excited and everything, but I'm going to be worn out even before we get to work.'

Maud turned and laughed. 'Come on,' she said, 'the

sooner I get there, the sooner I can get through the work. And I'm just praying that there won't be any urgent theatre cases.'

'Well, remember what Miss Houston said,' puffed Alice, out of breath and still trying to catch up. 'She said not to worry, that she'd make sure to pick up any work that might keep you back.'

'Yes, she did,' called Maud over her shoulder. 'Thank goodness our assistant superintendent is also an excellent theatre nurse. But what if she gets busy with another case? What then?'

'It will be fine, Maud. You could go on and on with "what if" this, that or the other. There are enough people to cover for you. I promise we can make this work.'

Maud pressed on, still anxious but very excited.

The morning did go to plan for Maud. And even though there was an urgent theatre case, she still managed to visit Male Surgical and supervise the dressing of Mr Langer's wound. He seemed to be getting stronger every single day, and there were healthy signs that the process of granulation might be starting. The dry dressings were barely able to cope with the exudate from the wound, though, and so they'd started filling the fracture box with bran to absorb it – a bit of a messy business when they emptied it the next day, but at least it kept the smell down.

Miss Houston appeared at the other side of the bed, just as Maud was throwing a clean sheet over the hooped bamboo frame that kept the bedding off Mr Langer's leg.

'Good morning, Mr Langer,' she smiled, before beckoning to Maud that she wanted a quick word.

'I hope it all goes well today,' she whispered. 'You must be so excited.'

'I am,' grinned Maud, glancing to the door. 'But I'm just worried that there'll be another urgent theatre case.'

'Don't worry,' urged Miss Houston, 'I've told Sister Law that I'll cover anything else that comes in. So you can be sure to get off on time. After all, it's not like you're asking for special consideration every single week.'

'Thank you so much,' beamed Maud. 'Oh, and just so you know, I've told Sister Law that I'm visiting a dear friend to celebrate her birthday. Just in case she tries to check up on me.'

'Ha,' said Miss Houston, 'she may well do that. Anyway, you have a wonderful time, Maud. You've worked extremely hard since you got back from New York, and even Sister Law has been gushing about your prowess in theatre.'

Maud felt her cheeks flush a little.

'So, your half day is more than well deserved. And I'll be coming on to Female Surgical just to make extra sure that you can get off on time.'

Miss Houston was true to her word and, for the first time ever, Maud was able to leave the ward exactly on time. She almost ran to the Nurses' Home to get changed, desperate to remove her starched cap and put on the black wool coat that she'd bought especially. She'd taken extra time with her hair that morning, and all she needed to do was tidy up a couple of strands. Once that was done, she took a deep breath, thrust her hand into her pocket to make sure that the watch she'd bought for Harry was safely stashed, and then she was grinning to herself and opening the door. Still grinning, and with butterflies in her stomach, she walked down the stone steps. I'm going to see Harry, I'm going to see Harry, she thought, as she sped away from the hospital. She felt as giddy and excited as she'd been before they were married, when she knew that he'd be waiting for her to come off duty, right there, on the street outside the Nurses' Home.

She walked fast to the Blue Coat School to collect Alfred. As she approached the door, she glanced up at the stone cherubs on the wall; they seemed to be smiling down at her today. Even before she reached the bottom of the steps, she saw the heavy wooden door swing open and Alfred appeared, stopping for a moment to grin at her, before running down the steps and throwing himself at her.

Maud was crying with joy already, even before she'd got to the harbour. She grabbed him and pulled him close. 'Alfred,' she said, her voice breaking.

And then they were both laughing together as the excitement of Harry's return ricocheted between them.

'Come on, let's get going,' she urged, feeling the delight of holding his small hand in her own. Glancing down at him as they sprang along together, she felt proud, as always, to see him in his smart uniform, and when he glanced at her with his pale blue eyes her heart melted.

'I've brought this to give Harry,' he said, pulling a piece of folded paper from inside his jacket and passing it to her as they walked along.

Maud paused momentarily and took the paper from his hand. She unfolded it. It was a line drawing of a sailing ship, detailed and expertly done. 'Is this all your own work?' she gasped.

'Yes,' he smiled.

'You have a very good eye, Alfred.'

'I copied it from a book that we have in class,' he said.

'Harry will like it. He'll like it very much indeed.'

'And I brought this for the dog,' smiled Alfred, pulling a piece of ham wrapped in a handkerchief out of his pocket as they continued to walk. 'We had it for supper last night, so I saved a bit for Rita.'

'Ha,' laughed Maud, 'she'll be your best friend for ever. She'll love you even more than she does already.'

Maud could barely stand still as they waited at the pier head for the first sign of Harry's ship, the next transatlantic crossing due to arrive. Alfred smiled at her as he leant against the barrier, watching the ships out in the estuary. 'It's too early to even think about it yet, Maud,' he called, but she paced back and forth amidst the group of people that were steadily gathering to greet the passengers. She kept scanning all of the ships. None of them were heading in their direction.

'Just you and the boy, my darlin'?' called a woman's voice from behind.

Maud turned instantly. 'Tessa!' she cried, as her friend from on board the *Abyssinia* stood laughing, with little Barnaby clinging to her.

'I'm waiting for my Daniel. Don't tell me you're waiting for your fella as well, on this next ship?' beamed Tessa, grabbing hold of Maud with her free arm and pulling her into a tight embrace.

'Yes,' gasped Maud, 'I'm waiting for Harry.'

'How wonderful,' cried Tessa, releasing Maud at last. 'And you've got your Alfred over there as well.'

Alfred waved cheerily in their direction.

'And where are your girls today, then?' enquired Maud, grateful to have lively company to take her mind off the waiting.

'They're with me mother-in-law, she'll be tearin' her 'air out when I get back. And this one here, he kept me up all last night. I think it's the excitement, he's always the same when his father's comin' home . . .'

As Tessa continued to chatter, Maud kept glancing out to the estuary, and she kept an eye too on Alfred who was still leaning on the barrier, never taking his eyes away from the landing stage. As she listened and nodded, and sometimes contributed a snippet of information, she became aware that the group of people to the side and behind them was gradually increasing in number. All eyes were turned out to sea, all expectantly awaiting the arrival of their loved ones.

'Here she comes!' Alfred shouted, turning to grin at Maud the moment he saw the ship approaching.

The ship's whistle sounded, and a ripple of excitement went through the crowd.

'Come on,' said Maud, laughing, taking Tessa's hand and pulling her across to stand with Alfred. Right at the front.

'Your daddy's comin' home,' cooed Tessa, and Barnaby chuckled with glee.

Maud could see the delight in Alfred as he bounced on the balls of his feet, clutching the barrier with both hands, whilst her own excitement slow-burned in the pit of her stomach. That was until she saw them readying the gangplank, and then she felt a ripple of expectation go right through her body.

She could see all of the passengers crammed on the deck as she clung to Alfred on one side and Tessa on the other. The ship was getting closer now. Soon, very soon, the passengers would be disembarking. She strained her eyes for a glimpse of a dark green jacket, but it was impossible to see.

As a steady flow of passengers disembarked, Maud's heart leapt and fell. She was frantic. There were so many people streaming on to dry land, and so many excited reunions going on around her, she was almost disorientated. Alfred had moved to stand even closer to her now and she could see that he held the folded piece of paper in his hand.

'Where is he? Where is he?' she murmured, as the

number of passengers coming off the ship seemed to be dwindling.

'Daniel!' shouted Tessa, flinging herself forward as a tall red-headed man with broad shoulders loomed into view.

Maud was touched beyond words, seeing the look on his face when he saw his wife. He ran towards her, throwing his heavy bag to the ground with a thud, so that he could reach both arms around her and the baby and lift them both off their feet.

Still Maud scanned the passengers. Still there was no sign of Harry.

'There he is!' screamed Alfred, jumping up and down and then running full pelt, zigzagging through the crowd.

Maud's heart was pounding against her ribs as soon as she caught sight of his familiar dark green jacket. She wanted in her heart to follow Alfred, to run at full pelt, but she was rooted to the spot. She could see his mop of black curly hair, the glint of amusement on his face. She saw him throw his head back and laugh as the dog bounded, clumsy and comical on her long legs, towards Alfred, her thin brown body alive with excitement. Then she was wagging her tail as Alfred reached up to give his drawing to Harry. Still Maud couldn't move. But Harry was looking in her direction now and he gave her a smile that made her heart jump. Then he glanced away, scanning the crowd for a few seconds. And now he was walking towards her, saying her name, and he was pulling her into his arms. She had forgotten how green his eyes were and how his slightly crooked nose made his face even more beautiful. She breathed in the musky smell of him as he held her fast. She never wanted to let him go.

'Maud,' he murmured against her ear, 'my Maud.'

When at last he loosened his grip, Maud could see that he was close to tears. She reached a hand up to his face, gently stroking his bristled cheek, feeling the dampness of his tears. Then she stepped back a little, remembering the watch in her pocket. She'd unwrapped it so that it would fit snugly in the palm of her hand and she could surprise him with it.

When she looked back at Harry, she opened her mouth to speak but in that moment she saw his expression change as he looked past her and then his whole body stiffened. He took a few paces away from her.

'What is it?' she gasped, turning around to look in the direction he was gazing.

'Nothing, nothing,' he muttered, pulling her back to face him, and then he held both her arms firmly.

'What?' she asked, seeing the colour draining from his face.

'Come on, we need to get going,' he urged, glancing over his shoulder as he put an arm around her and took Alfred's hand and started to walk purposefully away.

Maud glanced at his profile and saw the determined set of his stubbled chin. She couldn't work out why he was moving them away so fast, she didn't even know where they were going.

He glanced over his shoulder again, and she felt the heaving of his chest as he sighed heavily. He stopped dead in his tracks.

'Stay there!' he called, stepping around her.

Maud reached for Alfred and held tight to him. The watch was still ticking in her hand as they both turned to see Harry striding away, with the dog trotting obediently at his side.

A woman with blonde hair was standing directly in Harry's path. She was holding a baby in her arms. Maud knew who the woman was immediately and the realization sent a sliver of pain through her heart. She watched as Harry stopped in front of her. She could see the square set of his shoulders, and it looked as though he was shouting at her. And then he turned to walk back towards them but the woman stepped around him, thrusting the baby at him. He pushed past and started walking back to her and Alfred. She could see the anguish on his face, and she watched as the woman followed him, grabbing hold of his arm, trying to hold on, remonstrating with him. Harry was shaking his head, trying to pull himself free, and then he looked back at Maud. She could see the frozen horror on his face and she felt it go right through her body. She stared at him, not wanting to accept what was going on between him and the woman.

Nancy Sellers.

Time froze as Maud stood perfectly still.

She heard Tessa's voice behind her. 'What in God's name is Maud's husband doing there, with that woman?'

And then Daniel murmured, 'Jeez,' and whistled softly through his teeth.

Something clicked inside Maud then. She had no choice but to accept what was being played out between Harry and Nancy. And in that split second of realization the watch fell from her hand, shattering to pieces as it hit the ground. Alfred was down on his knees immediately, collecting up the broken glass. He'll cut his hands, she thought, somewhere at the back of her mind, but she didn't seem able to do anything to stop him. And when she spoke, she could hardly hear the sound of her own voice. 'Stay here, Alfred. Stay with Tessa.'

As she walked, Maud kept her eyes on Harry, stock still, with his head bowed now, as Nancy ran her hand up and down his arm. Her eyes were able to pick out tiny details of the scene – the delicate stitching of the baby's white shawl, the shiny patent leather of Nancy's shoe peeping out from beneath her gown, the glint of the gold-loop earring that Harry always wore. Then the forlorn cry of a gull as it circled overhead pierced the frozen silence and made the baby stir in Nancy's arms. Maud felt the reality of her situation register, with a sense of dull inevitability.

She didn't even glance at Harry, she went straight to Nancy.

Face to face.

'What are you doing with my husband?' she asked, surprised by the strength and the clarity of her own voice. And when there was no reply, 'I said, *what* are you doing with my husband?'

Nancy had a strange smile on her face now, and her blue eyes were bright, too bright. Maud leant in; she could hear the rasp of her breathing and the small snuffles of the baby. She breathed in Nancy's lily of the valley scent, and when she moved her lips to speak Maud noted the fine cracks in the paint on her lips.

'Well, Maud, this is quite a homecoming, isn't it?' Nancy sneered. And then, nodding towards the tiny baby in her arms, she said, almost casually, 'This is your husband's daughter.'

'How can you be so sure of that?' gasped Maud, her breath coming in quick bursts. But when she glanced down to the baby girl in Nancy's arms, she saw the full head of dark hair and the perfect rosebud mouth. And she knew, in that instant, she knew that there was no question about it. The beautiful child that lay innocently in Nancy's arms was indeed Harry's.

She felt something tilt and slip sideways. And when she looked up, she could see the triumph in Nancy's eyes and the curve of her mouth. She knew that she would never forget the expression on her face in that moment. And now it was too late, there was nothing more that she could say.

As she turned to walk away, she saw Harry's silhouette out of the corner of her eye. He was trying to follow and speak to her, but her head felt muffled. All she could hear was the dog, whining miserably, and it made her feel agitated. Harry tried to grab her arm but she wrenched free. All she wanted was to get away from him, from them, and go back to Alfred.

Then Harry was standing in front of her, his face pleading, his voice breaking. He was sobbing.

She pushed him away. 'Go to her, Harry. Go to the mother of your child.' And she turned her back on him then, not in fury, not yet, but with immense sadness. Sadness that, if she let it, would drag her to her knees, there and then. And then she saw Alfred, standing dejected, with the broken pieces of the watch in his hand, and she knew that she had to try and take charge of the situation. She took deep breaths, forced her chin up and made herself walk steadily towards him.

'Put the pieces of the watch in here, Alfred,' she said, shakily, rooting in her pocket for a handkerchief and then turning around with Alfred so they were both facing away from the grim spectacle.

She could see Tessa and Daniel waiting, and she forced herself to walk towards them, drawing Alfred along with her. Then she glanced behind, to check that they weren't being followed by Harry or Nancy.

'Do you need anything, Maud?' murmured Tessa, putting a hand on her arm. 'It's easy to see what's been going on there, so you don't need to tell us anything. We understand, and if there's anything that we can do . . .'

Maud felt her breath catch. If Alfred hadn't been there, she would have sunk on to Tessa's shoulder and wept. But instead she straightened up and set her mouth in a firm line and said, 'No, that's all right, thank you, Tessa.'

'Well, my darlin', I'm so sorry that you've had such

a day. Men can be such pigs, and it can take a long time before you find one that you can trust. You come and find me if you want to talk,' she said, slipping a piece of paper into Maud's hand. 'This is where we're living now.'

'Thank you,' said Maud, trying to smile, but her face didn't seem to work properly.

As Maud watched Tessa walk away with Daniel and Barnaby, she felt the first stirrings of anger. Seeing them, arm in arm, heading home with their child, it brought into focus exactly what had just happened. She felt her heart pick up its rhythm as the anger started to build within her. She took a deep breath to try and control it, but when she saw Alfred, still standing dejected, with big tears rolling down his face, that's when she felt the full force of it. Pure, clean anger. She could have stood there and howled with the intensity of it, but instead she took a deep breath and swallowed it all down, deep inside. With her shaking hand she took the handkerchief containing the shattered watch carefully from Alfred and pushed it into her pocket. Then she crouched down and put her arms around him, pulling him close, murmuring that she was sorry for what had happened.

'I didn't even get time to speak to him properly or stroke Rita. And I forgot to give her the piece of ham.'

'I'm so sorry,' repeated Maud, kissing his head, wiping his tears with her hand. 'I'm so sorry.'

'When will we see him again? Will he come back?' Alfred hiccupped.

'I don't know,' said Maud, 'I really don't know. We'll just have to wait and see, I suppose.'

Alfred nodded his head. 'At least I got to give him my drawing. And he said that he liked it.'

'Oh well, that's good, then,' murmured Maud, squeezing his hand so that she wouldn't cry. 'What do you want to do now, Alfred? Where do you want to go?'

'Back to school,' he said. 'I just want to go to my lessons.'

'Are you sure?'

'Yes,' he said, trying to smile as he looked up at her with tears still in his eyes.

'All right, then.'

They walked in silence for a while as Maud still held tight to his hand. She could sense how weighed down he was with everything but still he tried to hold up his head, occasionally glancing up at her with a small smile. He is such a special boy, thought Maud, gaining strength from his stoical approach.

As they neared the school, Maud sensed Alfred slowing his pace. She wondered if he'd changed his mind, after all, about going back to his lessons. But then he looked up at her and spoke quietly. 'That woman with the baby, she worked on the ward with you when I was in hospital, didn't she?'

'Yes, that's right,' replied Maud, squeezing his hand again.

'And she was at the harbour that day we came back from America. And I could see then that she was going to have a baby.'

'What?'

'She was at the harbour when we came back,' he continued innocently. 'Eddy and Alice saw her, too.'

Maud almost gasped. So that was it, that was the thing they'd been hiding from her.

She cleared her throat. 'Well, Alfred, I don't want you worrying about this thing with Harry. He'll be back to see you soon, I'm sure he will. He's just got some other business to attend to at the moment. You know what he's like.'

'Maud,' said Alfred, stopping in his tracks and holding her gaze with his clear blue eyes, 'I know that what has happened between Harry and that woman with the baby isn't about his business. And I'm thinking that it might not be easy for us to see Harry again.'

Maud felt tears stinging her eyes.

'But I will make sure that I try to stay happy, for your sake, and for the sake of my lessons. I don't want to fall behind with my work.'

Maud swallowed hard and held back a sob. 'I am very proud of you, Alfred. I promise that I'll do all that I can to find out exactly what's going on with Harry, and I will tell you properly about everything in future.'

As they entered the courtyard of the Blue Coat, Maud pulled Alfred into a tight embrace, whispering words of comfort and promising that she would come and see him just as soon as she had another half day off. He was nodding as he drew away from her and Maud reached out a hand to straighten his hair, placing one final kiss on his smooth cheek before letting him go.

'I'll see you as soon as I can and I'll write to you,' she called as he ascended the steps.

He turned with a nod and closed the door, with a heavy click, behind him.

The moment he was gone from view, Maud felt her legs weaken. She took a deep breath, she knew that she would have to find somewhere to recover before she could make it back to Stella's place.

She looked over to the solid structure of St Peter's Church and knew that was where she needed to be. The blackened stone and bulky octagonal tower had substance, and she was drawn to the building and the green grass that surrounded it. She walked through the wrought-iron gate straight up to the walls of the church. The patchy blackness of the stone showed layer after layer of accretion – soot and dust – the ongoing life of an industrious city. She placed the palms of both hands against the stone and rested there for a few moments. She'd hoped, somehow, that the building would give her some comfort, but the blackened walls had nothing to offer. She stepped back and scanned the tall arched windows but their leaded glass was dark and empty. Maud made her way around the church, past the ancient graves, still looking for something. She needed to sit down, rest somewhere. She saw a low wall that edged the path leading through the gate out on to Church Street. She slumped down on it, hardly able to take in the murmurings of life from the street. As she sat, she plucked at the weeds growing out of the wall. A gust of wind, coming as if from nowhere, caught up some dried leaves from the path. And then the wind swirled again and some leaves and dust blew over her. She brushed at her coat and picked them out of her hair. It seemed that in one day the whole city had turned against her. She felt alone and betrayed. Like the child that she'd been in the weeks after her mother died, when her grandmother had turned on her angrily one day, slapping her hard across the face. She'd never spoken out of turn again after that.

Maud's chest felt so tight she could hardly breathe. She saw a small boy with a grubby face and bare feet walk by, his shoulders slumped. His head had been shaved but he looked about the same age as the boy that she'd carried to the hospital. She wanted to reach out to him, try and help him, but she was barely able to breathe and she knew that her legs wouldn't hold her. The boy gave her a wide-eyed glance over his shoulder before he slipped out through the church gate and went on his way, soon lost from sight amidst the busy street. She felt shame. Shame that she was letting what had happened overwhelm her. Shame that she couldn't chase after that poor boy, who was starving hungry, and press some coins into his hand. Maybe the few coins would save his life. But he was gone now, wandering through the city all alone, and the opportunity had been missed.

'Come on, Maud,' she murmured to herself, feeling the cold dampness of the wall seeping into her bones. 'Get yourself moving.' She could have cried, but instead she made herself get up.

She bit it all down, just like she'd always done, making herself stand tall, pulling her skirt straight. And as she walked away from the ancient soot-blackened church of St Peter's, she felt something that had rested inside of her from when she was a child – a toughness that she'd always needed – starting to harden.

12

'Women dream till they have no longer the
strength to dream . . .'

Florence Nightingale

As Maud walked out on to Church Street she glanced
down to check that her black wool coat was perfectly
straight. She felt a strong urge to walk in the direction
of the hospital, there and then, and get straight back to
work. She'd been left high and dry. If it hadn't been for
the knowledge that she'd have to explain herself over
and over to all the people that she'd told, so excitedly,
that she was going to spend an afternoon with her dear
friend to celebrate her birthday, she would have definitely gone back to the ward and put herself straight back
to work.

And there was another thing, of course. There was
Alice. She couldn't confront her on the ward about
Nancy; that wouldn't be fair to the patients. She would
need to deal with Alice – and, of course, Eddy – this
evening. Why, oh why, had they thought that the best
option was to keep quiet about Nancy and the pregnancy and all that indicated. Why?

So her only option was to head back towards Lime

Street and Stella's place. Maybe she could help Marie with some of the chores, start to think about what her next move might be. She tried to make some kind of plan as she walked, but her head felt heavy on her shoulders and it took all of her concentration to weave her way through the people on the street and cross the road between vehicles. Even when a carriage wheel whisked by her, very close, and she was inches away from injury, Maud felt nothing. She was numb. When she reached Lime Street Station, the sound of a steam whistle shocked her and then, as a cloud of steam emerged, she felt lost within it. She was bumping into people, blindly stumbling along.

'Watch where you're going,' hissed a woman's voice.

Maud felt tears stinging her eyes. She felt as if she might never find her way. But then a kindly gentleman with silver hair took her by the elbow, leading her along like some maiden aunt. 'There you go, my dear,' he said, tipping his hat as he left her, clear of the steam and only a very short distance from home.

The quiet of the house met Maud as she walked through the door. She could feel the emptiness of the place, and then she remembered that Stella was out on some business and Marie had said she would be taking Victoria to see friends and they were going to visit the new Sefton Park. They'd told her this morning, when she was full of excitement at the prospect of seeing Harry. Now the emptiness of the house, and the cold dregs of tea in the cups on the table, made her feel even sadder.

Hugo lifted his head to look at her, as if asking a question, as he lay stretched out in front of the fire.

'No, it didn't go well,' she murmured.

He gazed at her for a second, blinked, and then put his head back down.

Hmph, that's about right, Hugo, thought Maud, trying to unbutton her coat. But she was all fingers and thumbs, feeling like she just wanted to rip it wide open and send the buttons flying across the kitchen. But she made herself take her time, one by one, and soon she had the coat off and hung up in a neat row with the others behind the door.

She made herself a slice of bread and butter to try and fill the empty feeling inside her. But the plate sat on the kitchen table, untouched. She couldn't manage one crumb. She brewed herself some tea with two big spoons of sugar, good for shock. But she put it down and forgot to drink it. All she seemed able to do was sit in the chair and stare at the fire, or pace the room. She needed to make a plan but all she could see in her head were flashes of Harry's dazed face, the triumphant look in Nancy's eyes, and the sweet face of the baby, Harry's baby. A child that should have been hers.

Maud swallowed hard against the lump in her throat. Tears were welling up and she couldn't stop them this time – the thought of the baby, sleeping like a tiny angel in Nancy's arms. Maud sobbed, her throat so tight now that she could hardly breathe, and then she cried and cried. She rooted in her pocket for her handkerchief but only found the broken watch—

'Aaargh!' she screamed, flinging the whole thing on to the back of the fire.

Hugo shot up and fled the kitchen.

Maud grabbed a clean tea towel and buried her face in it. She pressed the rough fabric to her eyes, making the tears stop, drying her face, over and over, with the towel.

'Maud?' said a voice. It was Stella.

There was no way that Maud could hide her despair. She gave her face one more wipe and then pulled the tea towel away.

'Oh, Maud,' whispered Stella, looking close to tears herself as she covered the ground between them. 'Whatever has happened?'

Maud took in a deep, shuddering breath and then the whole story poured out of her.

'Oh, Maud, I'm so sorry,' said Stella, shocked. 'Wait till I get my hands on him. I'd never have thought he'd pull a stunt like this. I've known Harry for years – he's been a regular in that pub where I play the piano. He's always drunk too much, and then he was involved with the bare-knuckle fighting. He's always been a rogue. But then when you came along, I could see that he was different – changed, even. But this, well, this is terrible and so, so awful for you and Alfred.'

'It is,' croaked Maud, not knowing what else she could possibly add. The facts were plain, and that was that.

'What are you going to do?'

'I'm just going to carry on with my work,' hiccupped

Maud. 'At least I've got that. They can't take my nursing away from me. And I've got Alfred to think about as well. I'll just keep going.'

Stella was nodding as she tried to take Maud in her arms, but Maud felt her body stiffen and drew back. She didn't want too much sympathy, she didn't want to soften, and she heard herself saying matter-of-factly, 'I'll just clear these pots from the table.'

'There's no need to do that,' soothed Stella, trying to take her hand.

But Maud was already collecting the cups. 'I'm always best when I keep busy,' said Maud, forcing herself to smile and show Stella that she was fine.

'Well, all right, then,' said Stella, dubiously. 'But don't overdo it, you need to save your energy for getting very angry with that man. Stupid good-for-nothing idiot.'

After the washing up, Maud wiped the sink, mopped the floor, took a scrubbing brush to the kitchen table and then swept the hearth. Damp with sweat, she did – at least for a while – feel calmer with the activity. But still her head was full of all that had happened.

Later, as she sat in the backyard, she began to feel restless again, so she took up a broom and started to sweep up some dead leaves that lay scattered and untidy. She'd got them all into a nice pile and was just about to find a shovel when the gate clicked open and brushed through them, sending the leaves flying again.

Maud tutted as she readied herself to sweep them up again. But then she noticed a solemn figure, wearing a multi-coloured shawl and a large black hat with a veil, coming slowly through the gate.

'Hello, Sue,' said Maud, with as much energy and warmth as she could muster.

'Hello, Maud,' replied a tiny voice from behind the veil.

'Come and sit down,' said Maud, finally finding the strength to pull herself together for the girl she'd become so fond of, and indicating the bench. 'Can I get you a drink or a piece of cake?'

Sue shook her head, a clumsy gesture in the large hat. 'I've come to ask you something,' she said, starting to swing her legs as she sat beside Maud on the bench.

'All right,' said Maud. 'What is it?'

'Well, I know that Mam wants me to wear this hat because she thinks my ruined face will shock people and she doesn't want them staring at me. But I've been thinking about what you said to me on the ward, about not hiding away, and being proud of the scar because it tells the story of how I tried to save a boy's life . . . well, that isn't as easy as it sounds, for a start.'

'Of course not, it can't be,' soothed Maud.

'But I've been thinking about all the work that you and Alice and the other nurses do at the hospital. And one day, when I'm old enough, I'd like to do that kind of work as well. And if I did, I'd have to wear a uniform and a starched cap. I wouldn't be able to wear this big hat, covering my face, would I? So, even though Mam wants me to wear the hat, I think that I should try to persuade her to let me leave it off. What do you think?'

'Well, you need to talk to your mam, as you say. But I think you're absolutely right to be thinking of the future. After all, if you were to become a nurse you would be able to earn a good wage, and you could support your mam. And I think you'd make an excellent nurse, Sue. Especially with all you've been through yourself. And yes, you're right, you wouldn't be able to wear a hat with a veil, if you were working on the wards.'

'I thought so,' said Sue, removing the hat with a flourish and turning to face Maud with a slow smile.

All Maud could see and think of in that moment was the smile and the twinkle of mischief in this lovely girl's green eyes.

'It's so nice to see you,' said Maud, meaning it heartily and blinking back tears as she reached out a hand to brush a few stray locks of hair away from Sue's face. And then she ran her fingers along the scarlet line of the wound. 'This is healing very nicely,' she said, reassuringly, before kissing the girl gently on her scarred cheek.

Sue raised her own hand to the spot where Maud had kissed her. And then she smiled again, put her hand into the pocket of her dress and pulled out an orange silk flower. A little crushed, a little dusty, but bright and cheerful all the same.

'This is for you,' Sue said, jumping up from the bench and holding out the silk flower.

'Thank you very, very much,' murmured Maud, more touched than she could express by the girl's gesture.

'I found it on the steps of St George's Hall,' she said. 'It was blowing in the wind, I had to chase after it, and with the veil on I couldn't quite see what colour it was. But when I had it in my hand, I was able to see how lovely it was.'

'Thank you,' murmured Maud, reaching up to stroke the girl's cheek. 'I will treasure it.'

'I need to go now. Mam's expecting me at the flower stall. I'll tell her what you said about me being a nurse,' called Sue, as she skipped across the backyard, pulling her hat on as she went.

'Goodbye, Sue,' called Maud as the gate clicked to. She looked at the orange flower and turned it over in her hand. 'It's beautiful,' she murmured. 'Unexpectedly beautiful.' And then she smiled, the warmth of it momentarily pushing back her emptiness. Sue Cassidy must actually be a guardian angel, thought Maud, remembering what Alice had said about the girl.

Later that afternoon, after Marie had returned with Victoria and Maud had helped make a meal for all the women of the house before their evening of work began, she made herself a cup of tea and went to sit out in the backyard. She knew that Alice and Eddy would be returning to the house soon.

When she heard them both come laughing into the kitchen, she listened carefully and then she heard them fall silent. Stella had agreed to tell Alice and Eddy the whole sorry story, so that Maud didn't have to keep retelling it. She'd kept back the information that Alfred had let slip about Nancy being at the docks the day of their return to Liverpool, and her dear friends being aware of that. That was something she would broach with them herself. Everything needed to be out in the open now.

Within minutes, they were both coming out of the back door and into the yard.

'Maud, we're so sorry. Stella's just told us the terrible news. Are you all right?'

They both stood in front of her, and Maud could see that Alice was in tears.

'I think I might be in shock,' Maud said quietly. 'I'm very hurt. But most of all right now, I'm concerned for Alfred. His whole world has been turned upside down, he adores Harry . . .'

'Oh, Maud,' murmured Eddy, reaching out to hug her.

Maud held up a hand, and Eddy stopped dead in her tracks. 'There is one more thing, however,' she said, as Eddy stood over her, with her eyes wide. 'And I think you both know what it is.'

Neither of them spoke.

'Alfred told me, in all innocence, that he'd seen Nancy at the docks the day we came back from America.'

Eddy took a deep breath, and Alice was crying properly now.

'He also told me that both of you saw Nancy that day, too.'

They stood in front of her like naughty children with their heads bowed. Maud could see Eddy's tousled locks sticking out all over the place, and Alice put a hand up to wipe her eyes.

'I asked you about Nancy a number of times. You didn't even tell me that you'd seen her, never mind that she was pregnant.'

'It was my fault,' stated Eddy, holding up her hand. 'I was the one who saw her first, and shushed Alfred and then Alice.'

'But I would have done the same,' said Alice, immediately. 'It wouldn't have made any difference, it could have been either of us.'

'But why?' cried Maud, her voice breaking.

'You were so thin and ill-looking when you got off that ship,' said Eddy. 'I was just worried about giving you a shock, that's all.'

'But I was soon recovered from seasickness. You could have told me later — you could have told me at any time.'

'I suppose so,' offered Alice. 'But I think we both hoped that there'd been some mix-up, that we'd been mistaken. Yes, Nancy was pregnant, but that didn't necessarily mean that Harry was the father.'

Eddy cleared her throat. 'When I saw her waiting at the docks, first of all I thought, uh oh, Millicent Langtry must have overheard me telling Miss Merryweather about Maud coming home, and here's Nancy wanting to stir up trouble as soon as she's back. But then, she stared right through me and she didn't make any move in your direction. It was like she was looking beyond us, waiting for someone else to come off the ship. So it all seemed strange, and I couldn't help but put two and two together. After all, before Harry was courting you I'd seen him out and about with Nancy. So, here she was . . . pregnant. But then I reckoned up the amount of time you'd been away, and the months that Harry had courted you before you married, and it didn't tally. He couldn't be the father of her baby, not unless he'd . . . well, he'd been seeing her in between times . . . and we still don't know if that is the case, do we?'

'Except that the baby has his black hair and his features,' said Maud, flatly.

'Are you sure?'

Maud pressed her lips together firmly and then she lifted her head. 'Yes, I'm as sure as anyone can be that the baby is Harry's.'

'So that means that Harry must have—'

'Shush, Eddy,' called Alice, nudging her friend with her elbow.

'Yes,' said Maud, firmly, 'it means that Harry must have slept with Nancy during the time that we were courting. When I was all excited about the wedding and going to America and being a proper family with him and Alfred.'

'Oh, Maud,' sobbed Alice, 'this is so awful. And we are so sorry that we didn't tell you everything before now.'

Eddy was nodding violently. 'There is no real excuse, but once you were recovered you were so happy and excited and waiting for him to come home – in the end, too much time had gone by, and we couldn't say anything.'

Maud sighed heavily and slumped on the bench for a few moments. Then she lifted her head. 'Well, I knew you two were keeping something from me. Neither of you are very good liars.'

Alice and Eddy exchanged a glance.

'Oh, just come and sit down, will you?' she said at last, patting the bench on either side of her. 'I've had a terrible day, and I need you both. I can't stand this. You're not the ones who've caused the trouble, you just tried to protect me from it. Of course I can forgive you.'

Alice started to cry even more and Eddy threw herself down on the bench, grabbing Maud and pulling her close.

'Come on, Alice, come and sit down,' urged Maud, 'before she smothers me or something.'

Alice sniffed loudly and wiped her eyes, and then she was next to Maud on the bench.

Even though she was drained of everything, Maud felt such ease from having both her friends close by. And as she sat there, feeling the warmth of Eddy and Alice, one on each side, there was no need for words. Even Eddy was quiet as they listened to the murmur of voices inside the house and the sounds of the city beyond the back gate. Maud began, at last, to feel some easing of the pressure that she'd held tight inside her. She felt that she could breathe more easily and allow her body to relax a little. That's when a thought came to her, fully formed, and she knew exactly what she needed to do next.

'I'm going to ask Miss Merryweather if I can move back into the Nurses' Home,' she quietly announced.

'Ooh,' said Eddy, turning to her with both eyebrows raised. 'That sounds like a good idea. In fact, I've been thinking of moving back in myself. That rented room I've got isn't quite far enough away from some of my patients. One fella keeps coming and shouting up to me in the early hours of the morning – Nurse Pacey, Nurse Pacey. I mean, of course I want to do my best for them, but I do need to get some sleep.'

'Oh, Eddy,' laughed Alice, 'of course you need to get some sleep. Is that the same man who followed you down the street, pretending to have a bad leg?'

'The very same . . . now he thinks he's got consumption, but his chest's as clear as a bell. And his breathing can't be that bad if he can shout up to my bedroom window in the middle of the night.'

Alice guffawed with laughter.

'It would be nice if you came too, Eddy,' said Maud quietly. 'But do you think there'll be any spare rooms in the Nurses' Home?'

'There are some at present,' said Alice. 'Sister Fox and Sister Law have been weeding out the new recruits.'

'It would be just like old times,' mused Eddy.

'But that means I'll be here on my own,' murmured Alice, sounding a little forlorn.

Maud took her hand. 'It would be the best thing in the world if you could move back in as well, Alice. But you couldn't bring Victoria with you, could you?'

'No, of course not. I was just having a pang for the old days, that's all.'

'But we can still meet up with you after work. And we can visit you here as well, Alice,' offered Eddy.

'Yes, of course,' said Alice. 'Don't pay any attention to me. Times have moved on for all of us since we were probationers.'

Maud nodded, lost in her thoughts again. Yesterday she was so sure of the direction her life was taking, but now it all felt like one big tangled mess. Except, of course, for her work – she was still sure of that.

'Oh, Alice,' she said, pulling out the silk flower from her pocket, 'look at this. I had a visit from Sue this afternoon . . .'

After Maud had told the story, and Eddy had stretched and told them it was time to make tracks, Alice heard the whimpering cry of Victoria and went straight in to check on her. Maud, left in the backyard alone, knew that it was time to go inside, but she didn't want to leave just yet, dreading the thought of going to bed. She could already feel her thoughts creeping back to the events of the day, so she made every effort to go over the details of her current surgical cases, and then she put her hand in her pocket and felt the silk flower and thought about the smile that Sue Cassidy had given her. But her mind and body were exhausted and, inevitably, even though the nights were too cold now for the moths to be out, it was as if she could still hear their tap, tap against the glass whilst her thoughts returned, over and over, to the moment she saw Harry's face when he caught sight of Nancy with the baby in her arms.

13

'What is it to feel a *calling* for anything? Is it not
to do your work in it to satisfy your own high
idea of what is the *right*, the *best*, and not because
you will be "found out" if you don't do it?'

Florence Nightingale

Maud woke at four again the next morning. She sat up
in bed, with her heart pounding and tears stinging her
eyes, and for a split second all she knew was that she
had been hurt, badly hurt. And then the reality of what
had happened swept over her and she felt a cold shiver
go through her body. She knew that there was no
chance she would go back to sleep. It was even colder
now in Alice's room, and she could hear rain on the
window. And even though she could hear the steady
rhythm of Alice's breathing, and she knew that she
could easily slip into bed beside her, still she felt like
she was all alone in the world.

She reached for the stub of her candle, made herself move, get up. There was nothing else that she
could do to try and stop the thoughts that were running through her mind. As soon as she was dressed,
she went through to the kitchen and lit the oil lamp.

She would rake out the ashes of the fire and get it going. Try to make some warmth.

As Maud riddled the cold embers in the grate, she saw the blackened metal remains of the pocket watch. She was surprised at how little she felt as she shovelled it up with the rest of the grey ash and disposed of it. She sighed. The sorrow was still there, like a hard lump in her chest, but she seemed to have completely used up the means to express it. Marie had left some newspaper and kindling next to the stove, as always, so she made use of it and soon had some flickering light from the flames that made shadows on the walls. She raised her palms in front of the fire, trying to draw in the first meagre glimmers of warmth.

Finding her pad and pen, Maud pulled out a chair at the kitchen table and set to work on a written plan – listing what she needed to do, the items that she would take, and who she would need to see – to move back into the Nurses' Home. She'd already settled the money owed for board and lodgings with Marie, but she would need to plan carefully to be able to cover the expense of the move and make sure that Alfred had all that he needed, too. As she wrote with her new pen, Maud glimpsed the thin wedding band on her finger. She felt nothing more than a dull ache in the pit of her stomach as she slipped it off, without ceremony, and made to throw it to the back of the fire. But something stopped her. She didn't even know what it was – maybe the whisper of some misplaced sentimentality – but whatever it was made her push the ring into the case where she kept her pen and snap it shut.

Maud walked to work with Alice, as usual. The rain had stopped but the streets were cold and wet. She pulled her cape around her more closely as she walked silently next to Alice, her head heavy on her shoulders.

'Are you sure you're all right to go in?' Alice had asked earlier.

'Yes, of course,' she'd replied immediately.

What else could she have done? The wards needed nurses, and she needed to speak to Miss Merryweather, because making arrangements for moving back into the Nurses' Home was at the top of the list that she'd made that morning.

But as she walked, she became aware of just how different today was to how she'd imagined it would be. This should have been the first exciting day after Harry had arrived; the beginning of the next phase of their lives together. Instead, she was trudging along with a dull ache behind her eyes after her whole life had been turned upside down.

She gave an involuntary sigh and hoped that she would, eventually, stop thinking about how things should have been. There was no mistaking the events of yesterday – and no changing them, either. All she could do was keep going, carry on with her work. And in time, that would lead her to something else.

Maud lifted her head and linked Alice's arm, pulling her close.

'Oh, Maud,' said Alice, softly.

'I'll be all right, don't you worry,' she said quietly, taking a deep breath and starting to pick up her stride as they reached the bottom of Brownlow Hill.

As soon as they were in through the front door of the Nurses' Home, Miss Merryweather's door clicked open and she appeared, in her bonnet, closely followed by her sister, Miss Elizabeth Merryweather, in her leather gloves.

'Nurse Linklater,' said the superintendent, before Maud could open her mouth to ask about her move back to the Nurses' Home. 'We need you to go straight to Male Surgical. I'm afraid Mr Langer's condition has deteriorated overnight. He's spiked a fever and become delirious. The night staff have been sponging him down with cool water, but there is very little change. They need a capable nurse with surgical experience.'

Maud looked at her blankly for a moment, her heart skipping a beat with concern for her patient.

'They need you, Nurse Linklater, they need you.'

'Yes, Miss Merryweather,' she said, automatically.

Sister Law was beside Mr Langer's bed when Maud arrived promptly on the ward. She glanced up with a frown. 'He's in a bad way, Nurse Linklater. I'm afraid that we might well be heading towards poisoning of the blood, if we can't turn this situation around.'

'How is the wound? Have you been able to examine it?' asked Maud, already laying a hand on Mr Langer's forehead.

He opened his eyes and muttered something in

German, moving his head from side to side. His skin was hot and dry.

'Not as yet. You know how dark the wards are at night, and Sister Tweedy didn't feel that they would gain anything by emptying the fracture box and examining his leg by candlelight. So, Nurse Linklater, the task is yours.'

'Yes, Sister,' she said, already moving away from the bed to scrub her hands and collect her materials.

As soon as she uncovered the fracture box, Maud could detect a change in the wound. The bran was soaked through with exudate, and it stank. After emptying it all out, thankful that she'd taken the precaution of separating the loose material from her patient's leg with a piece of cotton cloth, Maud noted dark green pus striking through the dressing. She knew straight away that this was deep suppuration. A very dangerous and life-threatening complication.

Mr Langer called out again and started to writhe in his bed.

Maud was already making her plan. First, he would need a dose of laudanum, not enough to knock him flat – his body would need to battle hard – but enough to settle him. Then, in terms of localized treatment of the inflamed leg, there was really only one option, something that she had read up on in Holmes's *A System of Surgery*. They would have to douse the wound with dilute carbolic acid and then pack it twice a day with soaks of the same antiseptic solution. If the poisoning was in the early stages, they had a chance of saving the leg and the man's life. But if it had gone too far . . . No, Maud couldn't think like that, not yet. They had a fight on their hands.

'We need to clear all of the contaminated materials from Mr Langer's bed,' said Maud to the nurse who had appeared at the other side of the bed. Not until the woman spoke did she realize that it was Nurse Devlin, and then she remembered that the probationer had told her a couple of days ago that they were about to change wards and she would be going to Male Surgical.

Maud flashed a grim smile at the probationer. 'I'm glad it's you, Nurse Devlin. Now, whilst I go and update Sister Law and collect my materials, I want you to remove all of these soiled dressings and create a clean area for the treatment of this patient's wound. He is Wilhelm Langer, forty years old, and he sustained a compound fracture of the tibia about three weeks ago. The wound has been suppurating cleanly and showing signs of healing and has been very satisfactory, until today. How we treat this now is of the utmost importance for this man and his family. Do you understand?'

'Yes, Nurse Linklater,' said Nurse Devlin firmly, already starting to gather the soiled dressings with her bare hands.

Maud mixed a whole bucket full of carbolic acid solution with extreme care. She wanted it to be strong enough to have an antiseptic effect but not so strong as to cause damage to the wound and the surrounding skin. She placed a white porcelain jug in the bucket and then gathered an India rubber sheet and a stack of towels to protect the bed. This was going to be a messy business.

Sister Law had already administered the laudanum drops, and she nodded to Maud as she withdrew from the bed. 'I've sent word to Mr Jones and he'll be here as soon as he can,' she said.

'Thank you,' said Maud, turning away to take a deep breath as she was hit afresh by the stench of the wound. Then she gestured for Nurse Devlin to help her open the hinged sides of the fracture box and slip the rubber sheet between Mr Langer's bandaged leg and the pillow. She was tempted to remove the box completely but didn't want to risk any disruption to the bone that would only be half healed, at best.

Before she started to irrigate the wound, Maud instructed Nurse Devlin to pack towels down each side of the leg, to absorb the solution as it spilled out of the wound. And then she went to the head of the bed. Mr Langer had gone quiet, not really a good sign, as the laudanum hadn't had a chance to start working yet. She explained to him in simple terms what they were about to do to his leg and why they needed to clean the wound. He opened his eyes briefly but showed no other sign of understanding anything that she had said.

'Right, Nurse Devlin,' said Maud steadily, 'I'm going to pour the carbolic acid solution from this jug on to the wound. The towels will catch some but it will spill out on to the bed, so your job is to mop it up as best you can. It won't be a pleasant job; the idea is to flush out all of the bad pus and decaying tissue.'

Nurse Devlin nodded, her grey eyes wide with expectation.

'Here we go,' murmured Maud, starting to dispense the cleansing solution. As she poured she made sure to cover every inch of the wound and wash away all sign of suppuration. In due course, she saw the white glint of bone appear but still she continued with the process. Nurse Devlin valiantly mopped up as much of the solution as she could, the sleeves of her uniform and her apron becoming saturated with the stuff.

After the last half jug was poured, Maud straightened up and surveyed her work.

'Thank you, Nurse Devlin. That looks much cleaner,' she said, 'and I think the smell has improved also. Now we need to make the best job that we can of drying this fracture bandage and then, if you could clear away the saturated towels and the worst of the debris, I'll go and mix some more carbolic acid solution and collect some material for packing the wound. And if you could bring some clean linen back with you, we'll change the bed first and then we have a clean area for re-dressing the wound.'

'Yes, Sis— I mean, Nurse Linklater,' said Nurse Devlin.

Mr Langer was barely responsive as they changed his sheets, ably assisted by Sister Law who'd rolled her sleeves up for the procedure. As Maud pulled the final creases out from beneath him and smoothed the bed linen with her hand, she thanked Sister Law and then explained to Nurse Devlin about the dressing they were going to use.

'This is called "charpie",' she said, indicating a mound of soft fluffy material. 'It's linen that's been unravelled, thread by thread, and it's ideal for packing wounds. It will absorb the carbolic acid and bring as much of the solution as possible in contact with the suppurating surface.'

Maud submerged a couple of handfuls of the material in the large bowl of antiseptic. She squeezed it out a little and then packed it expertly inside the cavity of the wound. 'We'll cover it with a piece of lint for now,' she said. 'We'll change the dressing later today, and then twice per day, until we can see the healing process resume.'

Nurse Devlin nodded and then glanced to the head of the bed. 'I hope this works for you, Mr Langer,' she murmured.

Once the process was complete and Maud was satisfied with the secureness of the dressing, the neatness of the bed sheets and the positioning of their patient's pillow, she asked Nurse Devlin to check Mr Langer's temperature and then to try him with regular sips of water from a spouted cup.

'Get yourself a stool and sit by him,' she said quietly. 'And you must come and find me if there is any change at all in his breathing, pulse or his colour, or if he starts to shiver.'

'Yes, Nurse Linklater.'

As soon as Mr Jones appeared on the ward, Sister Law summoned Maud to give a full account of Mr Langer's treatment.

'My dear Nurse Linklater,' he smiled, 'the Surgeon General himself could not have devised a better plan. All I would suggest is that you try some kind of stimulant to rouse him – a teaspoon of brandy every two hours should do the trick. And the toes of his foot on his affected leg do look rather congested. Maybe you could cut away some of the bandage, and apply a poultice to encourage circulation – camphor or horseradish, or both. Yes, use the camphor and grate some horseradish on there as well. We need to do all that we can.'

Maud nodded and made a mental note to start the brandy straight away and show Nurse Devlin how to make the poultice. She didn't want any chance of it being applied too hot and causing a burn.

'Now all we can do is hope and pray that our measures are enough to save the fine fellow,' continued Mr Jones. 'There is nothing more we can do for now. We are, as Miss Nightingale would undoubtedly remind us, at the mercy of the healing powers of nature.'

There was little change throughout the day in Mr Langer's condition. Maud and Nurse Devlin checked on him regularly and made sure to give him small sips of water. The teaspoons of brandy made him cough, so most of it came back up, but they persevered. When his wife and children visited, they did what they could to comfort them as they wept miserably by his bed. Maud had to blink back her own tears when she saw the older daughter, Frieda, her voice husky from crying, hugging her younger sister, Martha. Mrs Langer stood by the bed with her arm around her son, staring at her husband's face, stroking his cheek. It was a desperately sad scene.

All Maud could do was explain to the family exactly what she had done and what they might expect, but she could see that they were struggling to take it all in. Only yesterday they'd visited and Wilhelm had been sitting up in bed, smiling and joking, with Frieda on one side and little Martha on the other.

Later on, Maud hovered hopefully by the bed as she supervised the final reading of temperature.

'Still one hundred and five degrees Fahrenheit,' reported Nurse Devlin, her eyes downcast, 'and Mr Langer has only taken sips of water all day.'

Maud's heart was heavy but she showed no sign of it to her probationer. 'It's too soon to see any real change yet. All we can do is stick, without fail, to our treatment plan. Now, come on, let's get on and renew the carbolic acid soaks in the wound. You can do it, this time.'

As Maud watched and directed Nurse Devlin, she said another silent prayer for Mr Langer. What she had told Nurse Devlin was correct. It was too soon to see any improvement, she knew that in her head, but her heart yearned to see him open his eyes, smile at them, ask them what had been going on.

Maud was last off the ward, apart from Sister Law who was giving the report to the night staff. As she walked down the corridor, she felt strangely light-headed, as if she wasn't quite in charge of her own body. But at least she'd been so involved with her work that she'd had no time to think about Harry or Nancy or any of that.

Out through the door of the hospital, she kept up her pace as she walked along the path to the Nurses' Home. I must speak to Miss M first thing in the morning, she thought, and enquire about a room. And I'll write to Miss Fairchild, tell her what's happened with Harry, not the full details, not with how frail she is, but enough for her to know that there has been a clear change in our arrangements and Harry won't be coming to see her. And fingers crossed, I'll be asking if she can send the sewing machine to the Nurses' Home. Maud sighed, she'd have much preferred to have gone up there to see her friend, but she knew that she simply wasn't going to have time, not for a while at least.

'Maud,' said a voice behind her.

The voice made her breath catch in her chest. She was tempted to run and keep running. But instead, she stopped in her tracks and turned around. It was Harry, with Rita by his side, the dog's ears laid back flat against her head. Maud must have walked straight by him, so immersed in her own thoughts that she hadn't even noticed him waiting in the place he always used to.

She noted the black smudges beneath his eyes, and his slumped shoulders. He looked like he'd aged at least ten years overnight.

'I need you to listen to me, Maud,' he said, his voice husky.

'No,' she said, shaking her head.

'Please, Maud, just listen to me for a minute, please.'

'No,' she repeated, more firmly, holding up her hand. She could hear the dog whining miserably. Poor Rita, she thought, desperately wanting to reach out a hand to comfort her.

'But Maud, I was drunk, I had no idea what I was doing, I couldn't even remember being with her. I—'

'No,' shouted Maud, 'don't say anything else. Whether you were drunk or sober, it's clear that you were with her whilst we were courting. You must have been!'

He was shaking his head, trying to speak.

'No, I don't want to listen to you. I don't even want to see you. No!'

'Maud,' he sobbed, desperate now, his voice ragged.

Maud felt her heart pounding against her ribs. She couldn't stand it, she couldn't bear to see the wretched figure that was, or used to be, her husband.

She turned on her heel and started to run. She had to get away.

'Maud, please,' he called once more, his voice weak, trailing off.

And just the tone of his voice made her sob, and then she was crying as she ran.

If it hadn't been for Alice stepping out through the door and grabbing hold of her, shouting to Harry, telling him to stay away, and then pulling her inside, Maud knew that she might have collapsed in a heap on the ground.

'Men!' spat Alice. 'Bloody men!'

Maud could hear the dog still whining out on the street. It made her feel desolate.

She held on to Alice until she could stand upright. Then, without saying a word, she walked through to the space inside the building. It was dark outside now and the sky was overcast, so she couldn't see even one star. But still she gazed up to the skylight.

'Maud?' said Alice, quietly, beside her.

'I will be all right,' she murmured. 'I have to be all right.' And then she reached out to take Alice's hand.

'Nurse Linklater,' called Miss Merryweather, softly, 'Nurse Sampson has been telling me that you would like to move back into the Nurses' Home. Is that correct?'

'Yes,' said Maud, fishing in her pocket for a handkerchief to wipe her eyes. 'Yes, I would like that very much.'

'Well, we have a room up on the top floor. It's a little more commodious than the single dormitory you will remember from your probationer days. I think it will suit you very well, and you can bring a few sticks of your own furniture, if you wish, something to make it your own.'

'Thank you,' croaked Maud. Then, clearing her throat, 'How soon can I move in?'

'The sooner the better,' sniffed Miss Merryweather. 'I think it would be of great benefit for you to have the seclusion of our four walls as soon as possible, don't you?'

'Yes, I think it would,' said Maud, wiping her eyes. 'I will come tomorrow.'

Miss Merryweather nodded and then strode back to her room, leaving Maud and Alice to walk back over the coloured floor tiles towards the entrance and make ready to don their capes and hats.

'I never thought he'd dare to show his face,' murmured Alice, 'and if he did, I thought he'd come to Stella's. After all, he used to be a regular visitor there at one time. But coming here, well, it's not acceptable.'

Maud tried to form a response but no words would come.

'Now, I'll check that the coast is clear and he's not hanging around outside,' offered Alice, slipping out of the door for a few moments.

Maud walked down the steps of the Nurses' Home like a machine. It was cold and starting to mizzle with rain as they made their way back through the city. She held on tight to Alice, glad to have her friend by her side. Whatever would we women do without each other, she thought to herself, as she felt the warmth of Alice's hand in her own.

14

'A careful nurse will keep a constant watch over
her sick, especially weak, protracted and
collapsed cases . . .'
Florence Nightingale

Maud carried one bag and Alice managed the other as
they wove their way quietly through the city on their
way to work the next day. As Maud walked she tried to
raise a smile for Alice, as she chatted of this and that.
She felt relieved somehow to be moving back to the
Nurses' Home. It felt like she was reclaiming something that she'd mistakenly given up. Even the thought
of living there, on site, right next to the hospital, and
having the heavy wooden door of the Nurses' Home
that was routinely locked by ten p.m., gave her a feeling
of satisfaction and safety. She wanted to retreat from
everything else and feel even closer to the work that
she intended to live and breathe from now on.

Maybe, once she was back in her own room, with her
copy of *Notes on Nursing* resting on the bedside table, and
her uniform hanging neatly in the closet, she would be
able to get some proper sleep at last. She'd lain awake for
a good part of the night again, with fragments of recent

and long-gone conversations and flashes of Harry and Nancy, all jostling for attention in her head. And even though they'd started lighting the fire in Alice's bedroom, the dank cold still continued to seep up from the flags. She'd got up from her makeshift bed in a state of despair, in the end, and decided to keep her mind busy by sitting at the kitchen table to write her note to Miss Fairchild, telling her not to worry, that all was well, that she'd be moving back into the Nurses' Home for the time being. She told her that she would be up to the house to see her as soon as possible but, in the meantime, please could she send the sewing machine to the Nurses' Home on Dover Street? When Miss Merryweather had mentioned bringing her own sticks of furniture, Maud had thought instantly of the Singer – she knew that she could put it to very good use, making up bandages and compresses and hemming cotton squares for theatre.

Miss Merryweather's door clicked open as soon as they were in through the door of the Nurses' Home.

'Put the bags in here for now, girls,' she said firmly, holding the door of her office open. 'I'll show you up to the room this evening, when you've got time to unpack. Just knock on my door when you come off duty. It's good to have you back, Nurse Linklater,' she called over her shoulder as she marched towards the nurses' dining room.

'Are you really all right, Maud?' asked Alice. 'I hope you're going to manage on your own. I was hoping to keep you with me at Stella's for longer, so that I could make sure that you were back on form.'

'Oh, don't worry, I'm fine,' said Maud distractedly, as she fumbled with the fastening of her apron.

'You keep saying that, Maud. But how can you be fine?' Alice stepped around to fasten Maud's apron. 'It wouldn't be natural for you to be fine,' she continued, blinking back her own tears as she turned to face Maud and took hold of both her hands.

Maud sighed heavily and then looked Alice straight in the eye. 'You're right,' she said, quietly. 'I'm not fine . . . but once I get on the ward, I know that I will be able to lose myself in the work, and I'm hoping that the rest of me will catch up in due course.'

'That's a better response,' murmured Alice, giving Maud's hands a squeeze. 'And are you sure about moving back in? I was feeling a bit jealous of you. But seeing Miss Merryweather stepping out of her door, with her face all stern – and knowing, for sure, that the woman can almost detect the sound of a pin dropping in the wrong place – I'm thinking it might be much better, after all, to be out through that door every evening.'

Maud gave a wan smile. 'Well, we'll see, I suppose,' she said, reaching up to the shelf for her starched cap. 'She's always been a good sort, though, really, Miss Merryweather, underneath it all.'

'Maud, she is terrifying,' laughed Alice, 'but not as terrifying as Sister Law. So we'd best get a move on, or she'll be on your back. You're on her ward again today, aren't you?'

'Yes,' said Maud, 'we have a very poorly patient, Mr Langer, a collapsed case. If he's made it through the night, I'm hoping that he'll be showing some signs of recovery.'

'Well, Sister Tweedy on Male Surgical nights is excellent. But you know what it's like around three or four a.m., that's when the patients are at their weakest. I'm sure there are more deaths around that time of day than any other. So if he's made it through the night then that has to be a good sign.'

Maud went straight to Mr Langer's bed, relieved to find him alive and breathing, but she could see immediately that there was no sign of recovery for him. She picked up his wrist to check the radial pulse. It was rapid, but at least she could see from the chart by his bed that his temperature, although still worryingly elevated, had come down a notch.

'Just keep going, Mr Langer,' she murmured, as she moved away from the bed and made her way to the group of nurses assembled at the top of the ward. She saw Sister Law's steely glare soften a little when she met her own.

But then Sister was glancing around the group, narrowing her eyes, and Nurse Devlin nearly jumped out her skin when she pointed a finger at her and shouted, 'You!'

'Yes,' said Nurse Devlin, her voice sounding small against the background noise of the ward.

'Where is your apron?'

Nurse Devlin glanced down and looked up, wide-eyed. 'Bejasus, I forgot.'

'Forgot!' cried Sister Law. 'Would you forget your

head, if it were loose? It's a very good job that you worked so well with Nurse Linklater yesterday, otherwise there would be no excuse for this. Now go to the sluice, you will find a pile of clean aprons there.'

As soon as Nurse Devlin had left the group, Sister glanced at Maud and gave her a small conspiratorial smile.

Maud nodded. She knew what Sister Law was like and, after all, she had a reputation to uphold. But Maud knew already that if she ever did become a ward sister, she would have a very different approach, something much more akin to Sister Pritchard's – a real stickler but also fair and kind.

When Nurse Devlin returned, she was in full uniform and they were ready to receive Sister's report.

'That's better,' proclaimed Sister Law, lifting her chin and puffing out her chest. 'Now we can begin. And Nurse Devlin . . . I want you to work with Nurse Linklater again this morning.'

Maud was pleased to be given the job of supervising the probationer. 'We'll start with a blanket bath for Mr Langer,' she said, checking first the dressing and then the condition of his foot. It still appeared congested, but no more so than yesterday, and there was no darkening of colour.

'You wash and I'll dry, Nurse Devlin. You know the drill: start with his face, then his hands and arms, and then the torso, legs and private parts. Then we change the water and get a nurse assistant to help us roll him on to his side, and we'll wash his back – even though he is in a comatose state, he will feel the benefit. And we can make sure that he has clean sheets underneath him with no creases, Nurse Devlin, no creases!' Maud kept a watchful eye on the probationer. 'That's right, yes, use a little bit of soap on the flannel. And don't forget to rinse the cloth in the bowl of cool water and then sponge him down again.'

Maud liked the way that Nurse Devlin applied just the right amount of pressure as she used the flannel. She noted how she took care with the angles of Mr Langer's face, and when she washed his hands she cleaned between the fingers and gave a soothing wipe to the palm of his hand.

Maud had chosen the softest towel that she could find to dry him, and when she wiped his chest she could feel the muscle tone. He was a very strong man and she knew, having nursed other men who worked at the sugar refinery, that the work there was heavy. The men had to be tough to manage the heavy lifting, and they worked in extremes of heat. The sugar boilers, like Mr Langer, were skilled workers, and no doubt he would have served a long apprenticeship in Hamburg or Hanover before he came to Liverpool. She'd heard stories that the men worked almost naked and drank gallons of beer each day just to survive.

After the blanket bath was complete, and Maud had rubbed some liniment on to the reddened areas of skin on Mr Langer's shoulders, sacrum and right heel, she made sure she was satisfied with the smoothness of the sheets, his change of position and the placing of the pillow, complete with fresh pillowcase, before she checked his mouth. His tongue was dry and furred, and his lips were dry.

'This is a very important job in the nursing of any patient, but especially a fever patient, Nurse Devlin. I want you to go and find the small sponges that we use for mouth care and give his mouth and lips a good clean with water. Let him suck the sponge if he shows the inclination – the more fluid he has the better. And when you're finished, apply some salve to his lips.'

After Nurse Devlin had performed the mouth care to Maud's satisfaction, it was time to re-dress the wound. Maud breathed with relief when she saw that it was still clean after the carbolic acid irrigation. They repacked it with saturated charpie and covered it with a dry dressing. Thankfully, the stiffened bandage that supported the fracture seemed to have dried out and it was still doing the job of immobilizing the leg.

'All seems well with the wound, at least. But we still need to come back every two hours, on the dot, to move his position. We need to keep an eye on those reddened areas of skin and prevent a bedsore,' said Maud, firmly. 'It is the fault of the nursing if a patient develops a sore whilst in hospital, Nurse Devlin. And in a debilitated patient a bedsore can prove fatal.'

Nurse Devlin nodded, soaking up all the information.

'Now, Nurse Devlin, I'm going to move along to our next patient. Can I leave you to take Mr Langer's temperature? Oh, and we need to apply another poultice to his foot, exactly the same as yesterday. And don't make it too hot, bring it to me for checking before you apply it.'

'Yes, Sis— I mean, Nurse Linklater.'

There was no stopping Maud that morning, her whole being was attuned to the needs of her patients. Every tiny detail was accounted for and dealt with promptly. If she'd stopped for a moment, she would have been exhausted. But she didn't stop, she couldn't stop, because if she did, thoughts of Harry and the baby would sneak in and then build and build. No, she wanted to work, she needed to work. And that was that.

Every two hours, Maud and Nurse Devlin checked Mr Langer, changed his position, administered his teaspoon of brandy and offered him a sip of water. He was still swallowing, at least there was that, and maybe he was taking a little more fluid than yesterday. And when Nurse Devlin removed the six-inch-long mercury thermometer from his armpit for the second reading of the day, it was still down a notch from the previous day.

'Any change, Nurse Linklater?' queried Mr Jones. He'd already seen Mr Langer on the ward round but he'd returned for another look.

'Not so far. But thankfully, there doesn't seem to be any further deterioration.'

'Mmm,' sighed Mr Jones, 'let's give it a bit longer. But if there's no improvement by the end of the day, we'll have to start treatment with mercury drops.'

Maud nodded, praying that Mr Langer rallied. In other cases where she'd seen mercury drops used to treat inflammation and prevent poisoning of the blood, they'd made a terrible mess of the patient's mouth, causing sores and bleeding gums. And invariably the patient had died anyway.

'There is nothing more we can do, other than keep up with the routine of care and maintain a constant watch,' offered Maud when Nurse Devlin gave a sigh, after they'd moved Mr Langer's position for the fourth time that day.

'But only the other day he was laughing and joking,' murmured Nurse Devlin.

'I know,' breathed Maud. 'But we can't lose hope. If we do, then what about his family? They'll be visiting soon. We need to keep fostering hope for the patient and for the family.'

'Yes, of course,' murmured Nurse Devlin, with the glint of realization in her eyes. If she stayed the course as a probationer, Maud had no doubt whatsoever that she would become an exemplary trained nurse. She'd learnt in the first year of her training that the trick was to feel for your patients but learn to manage it, so that you could stay strong, still do the work and, most of all, help those in your care. A nurse wracked with sorrow would struggle to provide effective support for her patients or their families. It wasn't easy, she knew that, but if Nurse Devlin could learn to manage it, there was a lifetime of rewarding work that lay ahead of her.

'Are we all set for visiting?' called Sister Law, down the ward, glaring at Nurse Devlin and then smiling at Maud.

'Yes, Sister,' shouted Maud, casting her eyes up and down each side of the ward, just to make sure.

Maud saw Mrs Langer and the children come slowly into the ward, the two eldest glancing sorrowfully at their mother when they could see that their father was still lying flat in the bed. Maud smiled as she saw three-year-old Martha break away from them and run up the ward, her blonde curls bouncing as she made her way to the bed. She might look like a little angel but the girl was full of mischief.

'Daddy, Daddy,' she called, reaching up to pat his hand. 'Daddy!' she shouted, frowning now and pulling at his hand.

Maud was instantly there and about to gently restrain the girl when she heard Mr Langer groan and, to her astonishment and great relief, he half opened his eyes.

'Daddy!' the little girl squealed with delight.

'Hello there,' said Maud, catching her breath and laughing now as her patient rubbed a hand weakly over his face and then looked down at his daughter.

'Martha,' he whispered, his voice husky. 'Martha.'

Mrs Langer was crying and the other two children were jumping up and down with excitement, and all the while Maud was doing her best to try and explain to Mr Langer exactly what had been happening over the last few days. Nurse Devlin came out of the sluice. She ran over to the bed and was hugging the children. Sister Law appeared at the bottom of the bed – her face impassive, as she took in the whole scene – and then even she beamed a smile at Mr Langer and his family.

Maud was still smiling as she walked down the ward. Then she heard someone calling, 'Psst, psst,' from just outside the door. She went straight there, realizing, just too late to withdraw, that it was Harry. She stepped through the door to confront him as he stood swaying, with the dog at his side, his face flushed from drink.

'I need to ask you to leave. And do not try to see me again,' she said firmly, her steady voice belying the tightness in her chest and the pounding of her heart. She couldn't look him in the eye but she was sorely tempted to reach down and stroke Rita, who was wagging her tail furiously.

'Hear me out,' he pleaded. 'Please, Maud.'

She put her head back in through the door and glanced up the ward. She could see Sister Law and Nurse Devlin, busy with a patient; she didn't want to risk him following her in through the door, if she turned and left him standing there.

'Just one minute, that's all. And you're not supposed to bring dogs in here, you know that.'

'All I want to say is, I don't even remember what happened with her . . . I was drunk, I'm ashamed to say. When you walked away from me at the docks that day, I didn't want to go to her place, I told her I was going to stay with a mate of mine. But she was stamping mad, she tried to push me, and the baby slipped from her grasp – the poor little mite would have fallen to the ground if I hadn't grabbed hold of her. So I had to go home with her then. I didn't trust her to look after the baby. And now, she's threatening me with all kinds of things. She's not in her right mind, Maud. I don't know what to do about her, and I fear for the baby. Little Flora, she never asked for any of this, but it's like Nancy doesn't want to look after her properly. I've been up all night with her, and she's feeding from a bottle. But she's only tiny. I'm worried that she might get sick.'

Maud was shaking her head now. Just hearing the baby girl's name made her want to cry. 'I don't know what you expect from me, Harry,' she gasped, and then her voice was wavering. 'There isn't anything I can do. This is your situation with her . . .' She couldn't even say her name. 'You need to deal with it, and I think it's only fair that you leave me alone from now on.'

'Oh, Maud,' he croaked, starting to cry, and then the dog was whining as well.

'I'm sorry, Harry. I need to go back to the ward. Sorry,' she said, leaving him there, knowing that he was watching her as she walked away.

'Are you all right?' said Nurse Devlin, a frown creasing her smooth brow.

'Yes, I'm fine,' said Maud, gritting her teeth and heading for the sluice. She closed the door behind her and leant back against it. Hard, bitter tears erupted from her as she stood, all alone. Swallowing the pain, feeling her chest sore and aching with it, she grabbed a clean towel off the shelf and wiped it round her face. Then she got a flannel and dipped it in cold water, ruthlessly wringing it out over the sink and then pressing it to her eyes. 'I will be all right,' she murmured, wiping her face again, straightening her back, then making sure that her apron and her cap were perfectly positioned before she took a deep breath and went back out on to the ward to finish her shift.

Maud was wary as she left the hospital. She peeped out from the main door, making sure that Harry wasn't waiting, before walking quickly along the footpath to the Nurses' Home and running up the steps, grateful of the heavy sound of the door as it closed behind her.

Alice came in right behind her, and Maud filled her friend in. 'Harry came to the ward today,' she said.

'What! He needs to leave you alone,' cried Alice. 'I'll find out where he's living, if you want. I'll go along there and see him.'

'No, it's all right, Alice,' sighed Maud. 'I've already told him. He was a bit drunk, but I think he understood what I was saying. And at least now I'm back here, in the Nurses' Home, I'm less likely to bump into him or have him harassing me.'

'Mmm,' said Alice, narrowing her eyes, 'we'll see. But me and Eddy can sort him out for you, if you want.'

'I know,' said Maud, 'but . . .' And then she was stuck for words, her mind tripping up on what she wanted to say.

'Right, come on,' said Alice, taking charge. 'Let's get your bags from Miss Merryweather, and then we can get you moved in.'

Maud and Alice definitely felt like probationers again as they knocked on Miss Merryweather's door and stood waiting to be admitted. When she called for them to come in, they stepped through the door to find her at her desk, wearing her bonnet and scribbling frantically in some kind of ledger.

'The monthly reports for our current probationers,' she muttered, without glancing up, still busy with her ink pen. 'We have one or two rising stars but already two dismissed for drunkenness, another for lateness, and one that I am watching very closely indeed.'

Maud and Alice exchanged a glance.

'I'm not sure if our Nurse Latimer has the correct moral fibre or demeanour for our line of work,' she announced, reaching for the blotter and then sniffing, as if disgusted, before closing the book with a snap and, at last, looking up from her work. 'Now, Nurse Linklater, I'll show you to your room,' she said, pushing back her chair. 'You'll be on the second floor, as befits your status as a trained nurse. You have risen above the mishmash of probationers now. And I want you to keep your ears and eyes open,' she said, leaning across the desk. 'We need to weed out those who are not going to provide our patients with the best possible care.'

Maud swallowed hard before replying, 'Yes, of course, Miss Merryweather.'

Within moments, they were hastily picking up the bags and following Miss Merryweather out through the door. Moving swiftly as they tried to keep up with the superintendent, they marched up the stone stairs to the first floor. Maud glanced towards her old room, the first in line to the left, and felt an unexpected wave of nostalgia for her time as a probationer. But they were already moving on, up to the second floor where, even though she'd previously lived in the Nurses' Home for over a year, she had never dared to venture.

As they walked along the galleried landing, the layout was familiar, with rooms on either side. Some were single dormitories, as on the probationers' floor, but there was a slightly different arrangement of rooms at the far end. Maud glanced over the balustrade to the floors below. It really did feel like you could see everything from up here.

'There you go, Nurse Linklater,' said Miss Merryweather, turning ceremoniously to indicate the door of a room. 'These rooms are for trained nurses, district nurses and valued servants. And at the far end we have two rooms that serve as the nurses' sick bay. Fortunately, we have no occupants at present. Now, I'll leave you two girls to get unpacked and organized. Oh, and a piece of furniture arrived this afternoon, Nurse Linklater. I supervised its installation in the corner of your room.'

'Thank you,' said Maud, as Miss Merryweather strode away.

Alice was stifling a nervous giggle as Maud pushed the door open. They both stood for a moment on the threshold.

'Oh, it is much bigger than our single dormitories,' cooed Alice. 'I didn't even know what these rooms were like up here. Wait till Eddy sees it.'

Maud walked through the door with her bag of

belongings and stood in the middle of the room. Instantly, she felt soothed by the clean smell and the simple lines of the furniture. This will suit me very well, she thought, eyeing the narrow bed – neatly made up with clean bedding – a chest of drawers, a clothes closet, and the brand-new sewing machine waiting in the corner of the room. Miss Merryweather had even found a small spindle-backed chair and placed it in front of the Singer, and she'd made sure that Maud had paper and kindling sticks and a shovel of coal to light a fire in the small cast-iron grate.

'I'll go down and wait for Eddy,' said Alice, placing Maud's other bag on the bed. 'This is perfect for you, Maud, perfect,' she said, with a smile.

Maud began to unpack, easily finding drawers for her clothes and hanging the two gowns that weren't uniforms in her closet. As she removed the light grey one that she'd worn for her wedding, she felt a lump in her throat. She swallowed hard to keep it down as she hung up the gown and closed the door on it. And then, wiping invisible tears from her eyes, she took her two books from the bottom of one of the bags and placed them square on the chest of drawers – Holmes's *A System of Surgery* at the bottom and her now dog-eared copy of Florence Nightingale's *Notes on Nursing* on top.

In less than ten minutes she was unpacked and already removing the shiny wooden dome that covered the sewing machine. She placed it carefully on the floor and then sat down on the chair. Slipping both feet on the iron treadle, she used her right hand to gently move the small wheel on the body of the machine. Immediately, she had a satisfying rhythm with her feet and she could see the needle bobbing up and down. She ran her hand over the black painted cast-iron metal of the machine, noting the simple decorative design and the gold Singer lettering.

Finally, opening up the ornate carved wooden drawers, one on each side of the machine, she found bobbins of white, black and coloured thread, buttons, hooks and eyes, a packet of new sewing machine needles and a box of pins. She had all that she needed to sew bandages and cloths for the ward and, if she got some lengths of material, she could even make nightdresses or a new gown.

'Thank you, Miss Fairchild,' she murmured, pleased that her friend had responded instantly to her request. 'Thank you very much indeed.'

The door burst open and Maud shot up from her seat.

'Maud,' shouted Eddy, launching herself across the room and giving her friend a hug that almost took her breath away. 'Look at the size of this room,' she cried, plonking herself down on the bed and starting to bounce up and down. 'And these mattresses are much better than the horsehair we got as probationers. I'm definitely going to ask if I can move back in, too.'

'Well, you'll have to keep the noise down,' tutted Alice, closing the door behind her and then sitting next to Eddy on the bed. 'But somehow I don't think that's possible, do you? I'll have to gag her,' she said, grabbing a pillow and pushing it against Eddy's face, knocking her hat off and pushing her back on the bed.

'That's a clean pillow. Stop it,' ordered Maud.

'Oooh, I think Matron wants us to leave,' laughed Eddy.

'No, of course not. I just want you to show a little decorum, that's all,' she said, struggling to keep a straight face as they sat like two naughty children, side by side on the bed.

'Well, we do have some things to discuss,' said Alice, putting an arm around Eddy. 'Maud told me that Harry turned up again. He came to the ward at visiting.'

'What?' frowned Eddy. 'I wouldn't have thought he'd keep showing his face. What can he possibly hope to achieve?'

'I don't know,' sighed Maud. 'But this time, it made me feel very sad. And even maybe a little bit sorry for him.'

'Don't,' said Alice, fiercely. 'Do not feel sorry for that man. All of this, everything that's happened, is his doing.'

'She's right,' said Eddy.

'Well, when he talked about the baby, I just wanted to cry. She's called Flora.'

'Let's not get all sentimental about the baby,' said Alice. 'She's Nancy's daughter, remember.'

'I know,' said Maud, 'but she's also Harry's. And from what I saw of her, she is very like her father. It's as if Nancy had no part in it whatsoever.'

'But it's just not fair of him to keep turning up like

this. It's not fair on you,' muttered Alice. 'And if I see him hanging around the hospital, I'll tell him so myself.'

'I've told him to stay away. And do you know? I have a feeling that, this time, he might just do that. He was a bit drunk but he seemed to have a resigned look about him. I wouldn't be surprised if I never saw him again,' said Maud, her voice breaking.

'Oh, Maud,' they both cried, jumping up from the bed and hugging her. 'This is such a mess.'

Maud took a deep breath and instantly dried her tears. 'There's no use sitting around and crying all the time, though, is there? What good will that do? Now, let's see if I can get this fire lit. And maybe I can get a little kettle and some cups and saucers, and next time you come I can make some tea.'

As Maud turned to the fire grate, Alice and Eddy exchanged a worried glance.

'Let's help you with that, Maud,' said Alice.

'And do you know what?' said Eddy. 'I'll ask Miss Merryweather if there's room for me to move in up here as well, as soon as I can.'

Alice was nodding vigorously. 'Good idea. I'm often running a bit late in the morning, but I can catch up with you on the ward – and call by in the evening, before I go home.'

Maud lay in bed that night with the flickering light from the dying fire playing on the whitewashed ceiling and a murmur of voices from the room next door. She felt content, in a way, and was starting to feel sleepy. But just when her body tried to slip into a deep sleep, she gasped and shot bolt upright in bed. She was sure that she'd heard the piercing cry of a baby. In her head it had been clear and unmistakable. She was so convinced that she got up from her bed and opened the door to her room, putting her head out, listening intently. But all she could hear was the murmur of voices from the next room and the gentle snoring of another resident on the opposite gallery. She looked hard in both directions but the darkness of the landing gave nothing away, apart from the tiny escape of candlelight from beneath the doors of those who were still awake.

15

'Honour lies in loving perfection, consistency,
and in working hard for it . . .'

Florence Nightingale

Maud was up very early and getting ready for work before the other occupants of the second floor were even starting to rise. Effortlessly, she seemed to have slipped back into a routine that she'd held dear whilst living as a single woman in the Nurses' Home. By the time she was ready, fully dressed in her uniform and with almost an hour to wait for the opening of the dining room for breakfast, she started to hear sounds from other rooms along the corridor and she knew that she could safely use her sewing machine without causing any untoward disturbance.

She removed the wooden dome and ran a hand over the cast-iron body of the Singer. She'd already seen a full shuttle of white cotton in the drawer, with very little of it used, and she slotted it into the compartment lying just beneath the needle. Although she'd only used their landlady's Singer a couple of times in New York, Maud could remember all the details of how to thread the machine. She soon had a matching white bobbin in place on top, and then she was deftly pulling the cotton through the various hoops and holes before licking the end and passing it through the needle in one expert move. Then she held it between her finger and thumb whilst she turned the top wheel of the machine so that she could pick up the shuttle thread.

She looked around for something to sew as a test piece. She would make sure to obtain a supply of white cotton, muslin and flannel as soon as possible for the bandages and compresses that she intended to make, but right now she needed something else. There was a handkerchief with an unravelled seam at the bottom of a neat pile in her top drawer, she would use that.

As Maud positioned the handkerchief and heard the clunk of the sewing foot when she lowered it into place, she felt real satisfaction. She could see the line that she needed to take, no need for pins or tacking. So she held the handkerchief in position with her left hand and used her right to turn the small top wheel that connected with the treadle. In one easy movement she had the steady rhythm of both feet on the treadle and she could use two hands to guide the piece of cloth. It was one short seam, so it took only a few seconds, but she felt a surge of jubilation as the machine delivered perfect, even stitches, completing the task in a mere fraction of the time that it would have taken to use a needle and thread. All of the years in which Maud had hand-sewn repairs, or made clothes, towels, pillowcases, faded now as she sat back, admiring the new machine. She repositioned the handkerchief, running over each seam in turn. It was effortless, and the sound of the treadle and the rhythmic hum of the machine only added to her pleasure. In the drawer she'd found a pair of ornate-handled sewing scissors, and she used them now to snip the two threads neatly to the required length so that she could use a sewing needle to turn them in and secure the finished work.

She tried out the machine until she could hear doors closing along the landing and she knew that it was time to go down for breakfast.

'Good morning,' Maud said politely to her next-door neighbour, and then again to the wiry nurse with a severe parting in her dark hair who was emerging from a room on the opposite gallery. She recognized her immediately. It was Millicent Langtry, a probationer from their set – someone who she remembered, to her dismay, had been a close friend of Nancy's. She saw Millicent give her a curious glance, but Maud was determined not to falter. For all she knew, Nurse Langtry didn't even see Nancy any more. But if she did . . . then she would know all about the baby and about Harry.

Maud shot along the balcony, desperately trying to make sure that she didn't collide with Millicent at the top of the stairs. In the end, there was no danger of that; she'd forgotten just how slowly her colleague moved. Maud was already safely seated in the dining room before she even emerged through the door.

But on the way out, Millicent was lying in wait for her, ready to accompany her to the hospital. Maud looked around, desperately trying to find Alice, but there was no sign of her. She knew that she had no other choice than to speak to Nurse Langtry, so she offered, 'How are you, Millicent?' with a polite smile.

'Oh, I'm fine. I'd heard that you were back from New York but I've only just returned from a stint at the convalescent hospital in Southport myself, so that's why we haven't had the opportunity to catch up before now. I must say, I'm a little surprised to see you back here at the Nurses' Home. I thought that you—'

'Oh, I thought it would be good to live in again. Now that I've fully re-engaged with the work on the surgical wards,' said Maud, talking quickly, desperately trying to move the conversation along and prevent Millicent from asking any further questions. 'How did you find your time in Southport?'

'Well, the wards are much slower and quieter, but the nursing is very much the same, and the sea air was a real tonic . . .' As Millicent droned on about tea rooms and donkeys on the beach, Maud lined up another topic of conversation. Fortunately, Millicent talked so slowly that it wasn't even required.

'Well, Millicent, I'm on Female Surgical, so I'll see you—'

'Oh, I'm on . . .'

Maud held her breath as Millicent worked through her thoughts.

'. . . Male Medical.'

'Phew,' said Maud, without thinking. 'I mean, good, that's good, Millicent,' she added, already walking briskly in the opposite direction.

Just before she reached the ward, Alice caught up with her. 'Hello, Maud,' she said, breathlessly. 'Sorry, I was hoping to be there on time to wait for you coming out of the dining room, but Victoria was fully out of sorts this morning. And then I couldn't find my nurse's hat, so I ended up being late.'

'It's good to see you,' breathed Maud, taking her hand as they went in through the ward door. 'I ended up having to walk in with Millicent Langtry, and she's living opposite me.'

'Oh no,' said Alice, wide-eyed.

'Do you think she's still in touch with Nancy?'

'I've no idea,' said Alice, 'but, as you know, Eddy and I think that she must have been the one to overhear a conversation and let Nancy know when you were coming back. And do you remember what I told you about Nancy turning up at your wedding? She must have been the reason for that as well.'

Maud gaped at Alice. She had been told no such thing. 'You didn't tell me that she turned up there as well!'

Alice slapped a hand over her mouth. 'Sorry, Maud,' she murmured, not able to say any more as they made their way up the ward to join the group of nurses, ready and waiting to be given their instructions by Sister Pritchard.

Maud could feel Alice glancing at her all the way through report. Even though she'd thought that nothing more could shock her after what had happened on the day of Harry's return, she felt rocked by Alice's unwitting revelation.

'I'm sorry, I'll speak to you later,' mouthed Alice, before she moved off to her designated tasks.

Maud took a deep breath and made herself snap out of the irritation that niggled her. She'd have to leave the issue for now – there was work to be done. And what's more, she'd been assigned to the supervision of Nurse Latimer, who hadn't been moved, as was usual, to her second ward. Maud assumed that was because Sister Pritchard had requested to keep her – still evidently trying to make something of her – knowing that the cause would be completely lost if she was moved to the charge of Sister Law or Sister Fox.

'Let's make a start, Nurse Latimer,' called Maud from up the ward, seeing her probationer lagging behind already.

Although Maud made herself be extra patient with Nurse Latimer, there was little change. If anything, there were even fewer signs of her being able to engage properly with the patients. The only thing that she seemed to be competent with was the use of the thermometer. That gave her no trouble at all, and she was very accurate with her recordings. But there was much more to nursing than the mastery of some new technique so, despite Sister Pritchard's supposed hopes for the probationer, it didn't seem likely that there was any real chance of her surviving the year of training.

Maud did her absolute best to both supervise and encourage Nurse Latimer. But when an admission came through the door later that morning, she was straight there with Sister Pritchard. And she couldn't help but feel relieved when she realized that she might be able to escape into theatre.

'This is Mrs Freda Martin, fifty years old, reporting nausea and sudden pain in the lower abdomen. She doesn't have any family but her neighbour, a Mrs McCluskey, was very concerned about her and will be along at visiting,' called Michael Delaney, leading the way on to the ward at the head of the stretcher, with Stephen Walker almost running at the rear.

Maud smiled to herself. It seemed that the orderlies were now gaining so much knowledge and experience that they might well be ready to help out in theatre themselves soon.

'Bed six, please, Michael,' ordered Sister Pritchard, as Maud took the patient's hand.

'You're safe now, Mrs Martin,' she soothed, noting her patient's pallid face and grey hair, plastered down with sweat. 'We're just going to get you into bed so that we can have a proper look at you.'

Mrs Martin tried to speak but then she scrunched up her face and groaned in pain.

'Let's try to make you more comfortable,' urged Maud, suspecting that this was indeed a genuine surgical case – possible appendix, or maybe a ruptured ovarian cyst.

'Bring the screens, please, Nurse Latimer, and then could you get the ward thermometer and make a recording of her temperature,' she called, as she assisted Sister Pritchard with settling their patient in bed. The poor woman was still scrunching her face up, and gripping Maud's hand so tight it hurt.

'I'll just get you something for the pain,' Sister said, turning to speak quietly to Maud. 'I don't want to mask her symptoms before Mr Jones is able to examine her, but let's try some laudanum to take the edge off.'

Maud nodded, speaking softly to the patient, telling her what they were going to do.

Whilst Sister was away, she checked the radial pulse – it was rapid – and then she assisted Nurse Latimer with the use of the thermometer, making sure their patient remained still for the required time. She left Nurse Latimer sitting with the patient whilst she attended to other duties. But as soon as Mr Jones was ready to examine, Maud was there by the bed.

'If you could move over on to your back, please, Mrs Martin,' she said gently. 'That's it, now if I could just slip up your nightdress.'

Mrs Martin groaned sleepily and nodded.

Even before the nightdress was lifted, Maud could see that the woman's abdomen was very distended, almost like a pregnancy. She suspected that her potential diagnosis of a ruptured ovarian cyst might well be correct.

'Ah,' said Mr Jones, glancing across to Maud, as he pressed Mrs Martin's abdomen, 'you seem to have quite a collection of fluid in your belly.'

'What?' groaned Mrs Martin. 'That can't be good, can it?'

'You're right, my dear,' confirmed Mr Jones, 'but it might not necessarily be very bad. We will, however, have to take you into theatre and make an incision in your abdomen to find out exactly what the problem is.'

The woman started to cry.

'Try not to upset yourself,' murmured Mr Jones, pulling down the nightdress to cover the bump of her belly. 'Surgery such as this is starting to become almost routine, these days.'

The woman was still crying, and Maud took her hand.

'Will you stay with me, Nurse?' she pleaded. 'I want you to stay with me.'

'Yes,' Maud reassured her. 'But they will give you some chloroform to put you to sleep before the operation, so you won't know anything about it.'

'Will they?' said the woman, her eyes wide. 'Are you sure?'

'Yes, I'm sure,' smiled Maud, patting her hand.

'Thank the Lord for that,' murmured the woman. 'I lost me mother and me father on the operating table. They died screaming.'

'Well, we don't have anything like that, these days,' soothed Maud. 'We have very modern techniques now.'

'You're an angel,' smiled Mrs Martin, and then her face convulsed as the pain struck her once more.

'I'm going to leave you now with Nurse Latimer whilst I go and get things ready for the operation, but I'll see you in theatre. I promise.'

The woman was writhing on the bed now. Maud gestured for Nurse Latimer to take her hand and was relieved to see the probationer do so with a flash of genuine concern for her patient. Maud walked briskly up the ward, speaking first to Sister Pritchard about the suspected diagnosis and then confirming that she could take charge of theatre.

Maud took a deep breath as she entered the hallowed space. In less than ten minutes, she had her hands scrubbed and the shiny instruments, enamel bowls and the wooden theatre table ready and waiting and sprayed with carbolic acid. As soon as Michael Delaney appeared through the door, leading the way with the stretcher, Maud was there by her patient's side, giving reassurance.

Mrs Martin was starting to groan again with pain as Mr Jones came through the door. He nodded to Maud and went straight to the sink to scrub his hands. Maud could feel her patient clinging tightly to her hand now. She spoke soothingly, telling her to take some deep breaths, in and out, telling her that the doctor with the chloroform would be there soon.

Mr Jones was finishing his customary smoke in the corner of the room before Dr McKendrick slipped in through the door. Maud smiled with relief.

'So sorry,' he murmured, 'I was called to Male Medical to give a morphia injection to a heart failure patient. It took him a while to settle.'

Mrs Martin was starting to draw up her knees and cry out with pain now.

'One more minute,' soothed Maud. 'Now let's put this piece of lint over your nose and mouth. No need to worry. Now we're just going to put the drops on to the lint, and I want you to take some deep breaths. It will smell strong, but don't worry, it will put you to sleep. And when you wake up, the operation will be over.'

Maud could see the terrified look in the woman's eyes above the mask formed by the lint. 'It's all right, Mrs Martin,' she soothed, 'I'm going to stay with you, and I'll be here when you wake up. Now, the drops are going on, breathe deeply. Just breathe.'

Mrs Martin hung for a moment in a place of pain, her eyes wide.

'Try to let go,' Maud murmured, breathing with her. 'That's it,' she said as, finally, the woman closed her eyes.

'You nearly put me to sleep there as well, Nurse Linklater,' smiled Dr McKendrick. 'You have a very soothing voice.'

Maud pursed her lips. Harry had always liked her voice . . . 'Right, Mr Jones,' she said, energetically, 'do you have all the instruments that you need?'

'Yes,' said the surgeon, casting a careful eye over the side table. 'And do we have a bucket and plenty of towels? If this is an ovarian cyst, given the size of her abdomen, I think there will be a great deal of fluid in there.'

Maud indicated the bucket placed ready on the floor and the towels waiting on the shelf. And then she pulled up the patient's nightdress to reveal the distended abdomen. Once she'd sprayed the skin with carbolic acid, she indicated that they were ready.

'Let us begin,' said Mr Jones, brandishing his surgical knife.

He made an expert incision, about seven inches long, from the patient's umbilicus to the top of the symphysis pubis. Maud saw the first dots of red springing from the cut and readily applied lint swabs.

'Now, Nurse Linklater, I'll cut down through the muscle to the peritoneum. What is the peritoneum?'

'The membrane that lines the abdominal cavity and covers the internal organs,' replied Maud.

'It is indeed,' murmured Mr Jones, applying the knife carefully to complete the next stage of the incision. 'And there it is.'

Maud peered into the wound, nodded her head and then started dabbing with swabs again.

'Now, I'm going to puncture the peritoneum,' he said, picking up another knife. 'Do we have the bucket ready to collect the fluid? I think it will burst out very quickly once it's released.'

'Ready,' said Maud, reaching down to pull up the bucket. 'Could you take some towels as well to the other side?' she asked Dr McKendrick.

With one stroke Mr Jones punctured the peritoneum, and a spurt of pale yellow fluid gushed from the abdomen. Maud was able to catch some in her bucket but most of it needed to be hastily mopped up with towels. The fluid flowed and flowed as Mr Jones pressed on the woman's abdomen.

'There must be pints of serum there,' he murmured, still watching as more and more poured out. 'That was a hell of a cyst.'

Unable to capture a clearly defined leakage of fluid

now, Maud had abandoned her bucket and was using towels to mop up alongside Dr McKendrick. She could see that his neatly rolled shirt sleeves were already saturated, as were the sleeves of her uniform and her apron.

When at last the flow of fluid subsided, Mr Jones pulled apart the wound with his hands and peered inside. 'There's our cyst,' he remarked, triumphantly.

'How is she doing, McKendrick? Sometimes a sudden release of pressure like that can significantly weaken the patient.'

Dr McKendrick was already checking Mrs Martin's pulse and observing the rise and fall of her chest wall. 'Her pulse is still rapid and a little weaker but her breathing is strong. We're not going to lose her just yet, but we do need to proceed quickly, if at all possible, so that I don't need to administer any more chloroform. I don't want to suppress her vital functions any more than necessary.'

'Righto,' said Mr Jones. 'Stand ready, Nurse Linklater, I'm just going to puncture the cyst and release the remains of the fluid.'

Maud had a towel there at the ready as more fluid gushed from the wound.

'Now, let's cut the blighter out, and the ovary as well,' said Mr Jones, both hands now deep inside the patient's abdomen.

Maud passed a knife and, minutes later, Mr Jones pulled out the mass of the cyst. The way he delivered it through the longitudinal incision in the woman's abdomen reminded Maud of a Caesarean section that she'd seen at the Women's Infirmary in New York. It made her feel sad and even more determined not to lose this patient, remembering that both the mother and the baby had died that day.

Maud had a bowl waiting – she was surprised by the weight of the cyst. No wonder the woman had been in so much discomfort.

'Clamp,' wheezed Mr Jones. 'I need to secure the pedicle and apply ligatures.'

Finally, Maud passed swab after swab so that Mr Jones could mop up the residual fluid in the abdominal cavity. Deftly taking the used swabs with one hand and giving him clean ones with the other, she soon had a mound of sodden swabs in the bowl on the floor.

'Righto,' he said, straightening up. 'We can close now.'

Maud passed needle, forceps and suture thread as Mr Jones prepared to secure the peritoneum, muscle and then the skin. By the time he had tied off the final suture, Maud could see beads of sweat standing out on his forehead. She used a lint swab to mop his brow.

'Thank you, Nurse Linklater. These are always a messy business,' he murmured, looking down to his stained trousers and the sleeves of his shirt, saturated to the elbow. 'I'll scrub my hands and then go to my rooms for a complete change of clothing. Will you two be able to manage the rest?'

'Yes,' replied Maud and Dr McKendrick, together.

Maud wiped the whole area surrounding the wound with swabs soaked in carbolic acid, before applying a square of lint. Then Dr McKendrick helped her roll the patient so that she could apply a flannel bandage around the woman's torso to secure the dressing.

'What do you think, Nurse Linklater?' he mused. 'Will she be at least a stone lighter without that huge cyst in her belly?'

'Probably, yes,' agreed Maud, just as Mrs Martin let out a groan.

'Sounds like she's waking up,' said Dr McKendrick. 'And with all that she's been through, she'll have a great deal of pain, so I've already prepared a fifth of a grain of morphia that I'll administer as a subcutaneous injection.'

'Yes, good idea,' said Maud, taking hold of Mrs Martin's hand.

'Hello. You've done very well,' she said gently, as the woman blinked open her eyes. 'We've removed a very big cyst from your belly and all of the fluid has gone.'

Mrs Martin managed a weak smile. 'Bless you, Nurse,' she said, squeezing Maud's hand.

'Now we're just going to give you an injection. You'll feel it sting, but that's to help with the pain that always comes after an operation.'

'That's fine . . .' murmured Mrs Martin, still smiling.

Once her patient had been removed from theatre, Maud surveyed the scene – bowls of sodden swabs, a bucket full of serous fluid, a mound of wet towels. The floor and the table were awash with fluid and blood and a pile of used instruments. She looked at her hands, stained with blood, and then at her sodden apron.

'Phew,' she breathed, wondering for a moment where to make a start with the cleaning up.

The door opened and Alice came through. 'I've come to help you clean up,' she said, starting to roll up her sleeves.

Maud bowed her head. She felt too exhausted to still feel irritated at not being told about Nancy turning up at her wedding. And yet, she couldn't help but feel let down, once again, by Alice and Eddy.

'I'm sorry, Maud,' said Alice, quietly, from the other side of the theatre table. 'It's just that we would have had to tell you at your wedding, and it didn't feel right to do that. And for all we knew, you were going away to America for a very long time and you'd be well out of the way of Nancy. We had no idea that she might be—'

'It's all right,' said Maud, lifting her head, 'I understand. And I probably would have done the same. You weren't to know . . . about the baby.'

Just in that moment, standing amidst the mess and disorder of the used theatre, Maud could have wept. She took a deep breath and looked Alice in the eye. 'None of this is your fault, Alice,' she said. 'It's Harry and Nancy's doing. But please tell me now if there are any more secrets that you've been keeping.'

'That's it, I reckon,' murmured Alice. 'I'm sorry, Maud.'

'Oh no, please don't worry, Alice,' soothed Maud, making a move to hug her.

But her friend drew back. 'Ugh, you're all full of stuff.'

'I am, aren't I?' said Maud, looking down at her apron and starting to giggle, and then she was laughing out loud and not wanting to put her soiled hand over her own mouth.

Alice placed her own clean hand over Maud's mouth as she stood there, desperately trying to hold back her laughter, and then she led her to the sink so that she could start to wash her hands.

'I love you, Maud, and Eddy does, too. You know that, don't you?' said Alice, her voice husky with emotion.

'Yes,' said Maud, 'of course I do.'

16

'Remember, every nurse should be one who
is to be depended upon . . . she must be no
gossip, no vain talker . . . she must be strictly
sober and honest.'

Florence Nightingale

Maud and Alice scrubbed and cleaned the theatre until it was shiny and new and not a single instrument was out of place. When they finally emerged back on to the ward, Sister Pritchard took one look at their bedraggled state and sent them straight to the laundry for clean uniforms.

'Have you met the new laundress?' said Alice as they walked along the corridor and then out through a side door.

'No, I haven't,' replied Maud, looking down at her ruined uniform. 'But now that I see all this in broad daylight, I know that I'm desperately in need of her services.'

'Me, too,' laughed Alice, linking Maud's arm. 'And I only helped with the cleaning. Well, the laundress is called Dolly, and she was with Miss Houston, Ada, out in the Crimea.'

'Really?' said Maud. She was intrigued, as always, by any mention of the Crimean War or her personal hero-ine, Florence Nightingale.

'Was Dolly a nurse?'

'No, she was a laundress out there, too. I think, before that, she'd been an army wife who'd disguised herself as a rank-and-file soldier so that she could go to war with her husband. Or so the story goes.'

'No, that can't be true, surely?'

Alice was nodding. 'That's what Ada told me. And apparently, there were other women who did that as well. One of them even gave birth when she was serv-ing alongside her husband.'

'Really?'

'Yes, really.'

'Well, it must be true if Miss Houston told you. She would know.'

'She told me other things about her time in the Crimea as well, about that doctor she worked with out there. And I know you said that I wasn't to tell you—'

'No, Alice. You must not tell me. That's one secret you have to keep. You promised Miss Houston.'

Alice sighed with exasperation. 'Well, I'm not really sure about part of it, but there is one thing that is obvious . . . and I can only hope that Miss Houston tells you about it herself, one day. Because it's burning a hole in me, having to keep it all to myself.'

'Oh, Alice, you are so dramatic sometimes,' smiled Maud, pulling her close. 'Come on, let's get our clean uniforms and get back to the ward.'

As soon as Maud returned to the ward, she went straight to Mrs Martin and was relieved to find her still sleeping peacefully from the injection of morphia. Discreetly lifting the corner of the bed sheet, she checked the dressing for any seepage of blood and was pleased to find it clean and dry. Then she placed two fingers on her patient's wrist to check the radial pulse and glanced at the temperature chart. She could tell by the careful hand that the most recent reading had been made by Nurse Latimer and was pleased to find that there was only a slight elevation of degrees Fahrenheit.

Catching up with Nurse Latimer at the top of the ward, Maud tried to thank her for the work that she'd done and mentioned the careful recording on Mrs Martin's chart. The probationer barely smiled and, as ever, offered nothing back. It really was very infuriating.

'Could you please make sure to offer her regular sips of water from a spouted cup when she starts to come round? And then once she's more awake, maybe a teaspoon of brandy or some wine might help her to recover.'

Nurse Latimer nodded and set off down the ward.

At visiting, a small woman with a quick, anxious manner bustled over to Mrs Martin's bed. Maud spotted her straight away and knew that it must be the neighbour, Mrs McCluskey.

'Oh, Nurse, however is she?' frowned the woman. 'I thought she was going to die there, in her bed, at home. I truly did.'

'Well, she needed to have surgery and we removed a large cyst from her abdomen.'

Mrs McCluskey gasped and took hold of her friend's hand. 'Oh, Freda, what have they done to you,' she wailed.

'If we hadn't done the surgery, she would not have survived.'

'Oh my goodness. Is she going to be all right?' clucked Mrs McCluskey.

'So far so good,' smiled Maud. 'It's early days yet, and she's still sleeping off the chloroform, but by tomorrow she should be sitting up in bed and feeling much better.'

Mrs McCluskey pressed a hand to her heart. 'Oh, God love her, she's not had an easy life. What with her husband dying, years ago, and then losing all those babies.'

Maud gave her a questioning look.

'She always wanted children did Freda. As soon as she moved in as a young wife, she always wanted them. And we both got caught about the same time, but when we were about four months, she came to me and said that she'd miscarried the child. I'll never forget how she cried that day, and I tried to comfort her, but she was beside herself. So I said, "Never you mind, Freda, this one wasn't meant to be, but there'll be others, you're a healthy young woman, there'll be others." And come the next year, she was with child again, but then she miscarried. And, do you know, every year until her husband died, it was the same story. Ten babies she lost in all. Ten. And I don't know how she did it but she mourned each and every one of them, and then she got on and kept herself busy by helping out with other people's children. She used to say to me, "Let me look after yours," if I was struggling, or she'd take a sick child from a mother who was needing to go out to work or help the poor waifs and strays off the street. She even started helping out the local midwife, and then she was able to deliver babies herself. But, poor Freda, she never did have any of her own.'

Maud had to blink hard to stop tears welling up.

'Well, at least she's got a good neighbour like you,' she said, mustering a smile. 'And don't you worry, we'll look after her here on the ward.'

'You have to, Nurse,' smiled Mrs McCluskey. 'She's a woman who does good works.'

Maud asked permission to go along to Male Surgical at visiting to check on Mr Langer and was pleased to find him sitting up in bed, with his wife and children around him. Little Martha had snuggled herself up on to his bed and he was even managing to sing a song to her. She waved to the family as she walked by and then went to find Nurse Devlin.

'I did Mr Langer's dressing today, all by myself.' Nurse Devlin beamed, the smile reaching her wide grey eyes.

'Well done,' said Maud. 'Did you notice any signs of granulation?'

'Well, Sister Law scared the living daylights out of me by coming up behind and asking the very same question. And I didn't know what she was talking about, but she explained and then she pointed out the small red lumps of first healing. So, yes, there are signs of granu—'

'Granulation,' repeated Maud.

'That's the one, and it shows the wound is healing,' smiled Nurse Devlin. 'I was wondering, Nurse Linklater – and I need to ask Sister first – but if I get any time, please could I come along to Female Surgical and ask you some questions about surgical nursing?'

'Yes, of course,' said Maud, warmly. 'And if you don't get time, I can meet up with you in the Nurses' Home, if you like.'

'Oh, that would be just grand,' beamed Nurse Devlin.

As Maud left the hospital that evening, despite the jangled start that she'd had to the day, she felt a real sense of satisfaction. She was even looking forward to having her evening meal with the other nurses in the dining room. And then she would have time to use her sewing machine. She'd spoken to Dolly, the laundress, about the bandages, when she'd gone in for her new uniform. Dolly had promised to leave a supply of muslin and cotton outside her room so that, tonight, she could make a proper start on the sewing.

She didn't really care any more that Millicent Langtry had the room just across from her on the opposite gallery – or whether she knew, or didn't know, about Nancy and the baby and Harry. If she already knew then there wasn't any way of untelling her and, instinctively, she knew that Miss Houston – and probably the Misses Merryweather – would support her. So there was little that she could do, except manage the consequences, if any information leaked to the wrong person. Having said that, she was now separated from her husband. She was, in fact, a single woman, once again. So what would it matter anyway?

Her thoughts were interrupted by raised voices further along the path and Maud saw Nurse Devlin in tears, with someone who looked like Nurse Latimer beside her. Maud was straight there between them and, turning to Nurse Latimer, asked icily, 'What is the meaning of this?'

Nurse Devlin started to cry even more. Alice had arrived by now and was there, with her arm around her, trying to comfort the probationer.

'Nurse Latimer, I need to know the meaning of this right now, or I will have no choice but to go straight to Miss Merryweather,' threatened Maud.

Nurse Latimer stood sullen and silent, with her head bowed.

'No,' sobbed Nurse Devlin. 'No. It's not her, she hasn't done anything. I'm crying because she said she's going to leave the hospital and I don't want her to.'

'What?' frowned Maud, switching her gaze to Nurse Devlin. 'What do you mean?'

'Well,' sniffed Rose, 'I don't want Violet to leave. I've been trying to help her deal with something bad, but she's feeling threatened again. And it isn't safe for her to be living anywhere else.'

Nurse Latimer was trembling now and she had started crying, too.

'I think we'd all better go to the Nurses' Home,' said Maud, 'and try to sort this out.'

'What's up?' called Eddy, marching in their direction with her district nurse's bag in her hand.

'An issue with these two probationers,' explained Maud, still reeling from Rose's revelation, as she walked briskly, with them behind her and Alice bringing up the rear. Eddy watched the women as they walked by, and then she stepped into line and linked arms with Alice.

Once the whole party were up the steps and in through the entrance of the Nurses' Home, Violet Latimer started to sob even louder and Rose put an arm around her shoulders. Immediately, the door to Miss Merryweather's room clicked open and the superintendent emerged, closely followed by her sister, Elizabeth.

'Whatever is going on?' demanded Miss Merryweather, her sharp tone mitigated by the concern in her eyes and the way she went immediately to the sobbing probationer and put a hand on her arm.

'Come on, all of you,' she said, looking around the group, 'into the visitors' room.'

The whole party, including Eddy, trooped in and sat in a circle on the straight-backed chairs that lined the room. Maud had never been in there before; it still smelt and looked brand new, and the seats were stiff and uncomfortable.

Miss Merryweather adjusted her bonnet and motioned

for her sister to be seated whilst she continued to stand in the centre of the room, moving her steely gaze around to take in all of the assembled nurses. Violet was still sobbing and Eddy, sitting next to her, had passed her a large handkerchief.

'Now can someone tell me exactly what is going on here?' asked Miss Merryweather, firmly.

Neither of the probationers said a word. Therefore, Maud, sitting straight-backed in her chair, with her hands folded on her lap, spoke first and gave the details of what she had witnessed on the path.

'I see,' said Miss Merryweather, looking in the direction of Nurse Devlin, who repeated the explanation that she'd offered to Maud. She then added that she knew what Nurse Latimer's issue was, but it wasn't hers to tell.

'I see,' said Miss Merryweather again, gazing across to where Violet sat, with her head bowed. 'Nurse Latimer,' she said, her voice gentler now, 'are you able to tell us what your issue is? I can guarantee that anything you tell us now, in this room, will go no further. Are we agreed, Nurses?'

'Agreed,' murmured all of the voices in the room.

Eddy put an arm around Violet's shoulders. 'Come on, then,' she urged, 'don't keep it all to yourself. We might be able to help. All of us need help at some time in our lives, and I think you'll find that women help other women, and nurses help other nurses.'

Violet wiped her nose with Eddy's handkerchief and then she looked up, her red-rimmed eyes flitting around the room. She tried to speak but the words wouldn't come out, even when Eddy gave her shoulders a gentle squeeze.

Then Eddy murmured a few words in Violet's ear. She seemed to think about it for a few moments and then straightened up in her chair and started to speak shakily, her voice ragged from crying. 'I need to leave the hospital because someone knows where I am. I've seen this person outside the Nurses' Home and I daren't stay here any longer. All the weeks since I started my training, I've been worried that this would happen. And now it has. So I have to go.'

'Who is this person?' asked Miss Merryweather gently, her eyes full of concern.

Violet tried to speak once more but the words seemed strangled back in her throat. She went red in the face and then she was sobbing again.

Rose, who was sitting next to her, took her hand. 'Shall I tell them who it is and what he's done?' she whispered.

Violet glanced at her and then nodded, wiping her eyes again with Eddy's hankie.

Rose cleared her throat. 'It's her stepfather, and he has threatened to kill her so that she won't tell the police what he's done.' Rose cleared her throat again. 'Ever since her mother died when she was sixteen . . . he has been coming into her bed.'

A collective murmur of outrage and sympathy moved through the room.

Violet started to cry again and Rose squeezed her hand. 'And that's why, as soon as she was old enough, she took the money that her mother had left her and ran away to Liverpool. She came here to the Nurses' Home because she'd heard that it was a safe place and kept strictly for women.'

Violet was crying even harder now and Eddy was hugging her and saying, 'There, there, don't you worry, none of this is your fault.'

'And you came to the right place,' said Miss Merryweather, her voice clear and determined. 'You are safe here. I will deal with your stepfather, the next time he shows up, and I will tell him that if I so much as catch a glimpse of him again outside our Nurses' Home, I will go straight to the police myself. *None* of the women under my care will be threatened by *any* man.'

Miss Merryweather pressed her lips together and her eyes burned as she glanced around the room. There was a murmur of approval from all the nurses and Miss Elizabeth adjusted the leather gloves that she always wore, got up from her seat and walked straight over to Violet. 'Come on, come with me,' she said gently, taking her hand, and gesturing for Rose to follow. She quietly left the room, with both girls in tow.

'Thank you, Nurses,' nodded Miss Merryweather, to those left in the room. 'My heart is full of pride for all that you are and all that you do.'

Maud and Eddy and Alice were in tears themselves now and they got up and clustered around the superintendent as she patted each of them on the arm, dabbing at her eyes with her other hand. 'And I was on the point of dismissing the girl for lack of engagement and lack of interest in her nursing,' she murmured. 'We never know what's going on beneath the surface, do we? We should be more aware.'

'I felt the same after working with her on the ward,' confessed Maud.

'And me,' said Alice. 'It would have been terrible if we had dismissed her, though. I can't even think about what might have happened at the hands of that man.'

'I think her friend, Nurse Devlin, would have spoken up,' said Miss Merryweather, quietly. 'We shouldn't perhaps be too hard on ourselves, after all. Sometimes we can only judge on what we see.'

Maud, Alice and Eddy were all murmuring a response when they heard the front door slam open and a man's voice screaming, 'Help, help!'

'What the—?' shouted Eddy.

Maud led the way, running at full pelt into the entrance hall. She knew that voice. 'Harry?' she shouted, seeing him there, his eyes wide, gasping for breath, with a tiny baby in his arms.

'It's Flora! She's not breathing!' he screamed, clinging on to the baby, desperately scanning her tiny face.

Maud's heart was thudding in her chest, she never thought she'd have to see this child up close again. But she saw right away that the baby was pale, and her lips had a tinge of blue. Maud was ready to help in any way that she could. 'Give her to me,' she said, firmly. 'We need to examine her.'

Harry handed her over and then gave a huge sob and fell to his knees on the coloured tiles of the entrance, clinging to his dog. Eddy moved to his side and put a hand on his shoulder.

Maud tipped her head towards the baby's face. She could feel gentle breath that seemed not much more than the beating of a butterfly wing. 'She's definitely breathing!' she called. 'But only just, and she's very poorly.'

Harry glanced up and then he broke into another sob.

Miss Merryweather was already giving directions. 'Nurse Sampson, I need you to go back to the hospital. Run! Find Dr McKendrick and bring him straight here. If he isn't on the wards, he'll be up in Miss Houston's office.'

Alice nodded and neatly sidestepped Harry, before running out of the door.

'Bring the baby into my office, Nurse Linklater,' the superintendent said, marching towards the door, with Maud and Eddy following. 'Place her down there, on the chaise longue,' she ordered. 'Remove that shawl and her clothes, down to the napkin. It's warm enough in here with the fire. I'll turn up this lamp and bring it over so we can have the best light.'

Maud felt the heat of the baby's body as she removed her miniature nightie and then the tiny woollen vest that lay against her skin. The napkin was damp, but not saturated, so she left it in place, as instructed.

Flora's body was limp, her breathing rapid and shallow, and although her eyes were closed she didn't look like a sleeping baby. Apart from the steady rasp of her breath, she was completely quiet.

Maud heard the low whine of Harry's dog and she

could hear him still weeping outside the door. She felt a stab of pity but it was completely lost amidst her anxiety for the baby.

'Her fontanelle feels slightly sunken,' murmured Miss Merryweather, running a gentle hand over the small black head of hair as she leant over the baby.

'What does that mean?' whispered Maud, tears stinging her eyes now that she could see how very poorly the little scrap of life that was Harry's daughter actually looked.

'It means that she might be dehydrated, that she might not have been taking her feeds.'

Maud could hear her own heartbeat as she knelt beside the baby.

'We need to wait for Dr McKendrick's assessment,' continued Miss Merryweather. 'But by the way she is breathing, I think the baby may well have pneumonia. One of you go out there to the father. I'm assuming he is the father, this friend of yours, Nurse Linklater? Go and ask him exactly what has happened. And tell him he needs to put that dog outside.'

'I'll go,' volunteered Eddy, placing a hand on Maud's shoulder.

Maud watched Flora like a hawk, willing her to keep breathing. Seeing her tiny hand, with the fingers splayed, she stroked the back of it with her forefinger and then she grasped it between her finger and thumb. With her other hand she gently stroked the baby's cheek, desperately whispering words of comfort.

Eddy was back in through the door. 'Harry, the

father, says she was crying and unsettled all day yesterday. And she didn't take her feeds that well this morning. She vomited this afternoon but he managed to get some spoonfuls of sugar water inside her. And then her breathing seemed to change, and about half an hour ago he thought that she'd stopped breathing. So he picked her up and ran here.'

'But what about the mother?' frowned Miss Merryweather. 'This baby is only weeks old, where is the mother?'

'Apparently, she left last night. Packed a bag, walked out of the door and didn't come back.'

Maud twisted round to glance at Eddy, then she swallowed hard as the painful lump that she'd been trying to subdue fought its way back into her throat.

'Highly irregular,' tutted Miss Merryweather. 'But this man must be a good father – doing what he's done and bringing her here. What's the baby's name?'

'Flora, she's called Flora,' said Maud.

'Beautiful name for a beautiful girl,' murmured Miss Merryweather, leaning over Maud's shoulder again to have a closer look.

Maud blinked back her tears. She didn't want to see Harry, she truly believed that she felt nothing for him now. But she knew already, especially since she'd learnt that Nancy had walked out, that this tiny baby, clinging to life, was a very special little girl indeed.

17

'It is as easy to put out a sick baby's life as it is to
put out the flame of a candle.'

Florence Nightingale

Dr McKendrick slipped quietly into the room, closely followed by Ada Houston and then Alice. He came straight to the baby and knelt down beside Maud. She made a move to get up but he motioned for her to stay put.

Maud heard Miss Merryweather behind her, murmuring, 'Come on, Nurse Pacey, Nurse Sampson, let's go over to the visitors' room, give the baby some air and the doctor some space. See what we can do for the father, he must be beside himself with worry.'

Eddy rested a hand on Maud's shoulder before she made her way out. 'I'm going to go to the lying-in ward,' she said. 'See if I can find a mother who'll express some milk for the baby.'

Maud nodded and mouthed, 'Thank you.'

'She is definitely feverish,' reported Dr McKendrick as he gently passed a hand over her body. 'Her colour isn't good, and her fontanelle is slightly sunken. And her mouth,' he said, inserting a finger and peering into it, 'I can't really see in this light, but she has some white furring of the tongue, I think . . . Now I'll just listen to her chest.'

Maud and Ada waited in the silence of the room as McKendrick used his stethoscope on the impossibly small chest. He moved it gently over the baby's ribs, from one side to the other, his eyes focused on nothing. Just listening.

'Can you turn her on to her side, please, Nurse Linklater?' he asked gently. 'So that I can listen at the back.'

Maud placed one hand on the baby's delicate shoulder and another on her hip and rolled her, ever so carefully, on to her side, keeping the tiny body in the correct position for Dr McKendrick.

It seemed to take for ever before he removed the stethoscope from his ears and sat back on his heels. 'There is definitely some congestion of the chest,' he said quietly, looking directly at Maud. 'And I think there is every possibility that she could have pneumonia . . . and in that case, the outcome will almost certainly be the worst.'

Maud pressed a hand to her heart. 'Is there nothing that we can do?'

'There might be something to be said for treating her with steam overnight, to try to loosen the chest, and sponging her to keep her cool. And we need to get some fluid into her – from a dropper at first, every ten minutes or so. She'll need constant attention overnight, but it's definitely worth fighting for her recovery.'

Maud was nodding now, feeling the beating of her heart, as she gazed down at the baby on the chaise longue. 'My friend has gone to the lying-in ward to see if she can get some expressed milk,' she said at last, forcing herself to think of practicalities.

'Excellent idea,' said Dr McKendrick, getting up from his knees. 'Try her with boiled, cooled water first. But she will have to take the milk as well if she is to survive. And I tell you what, Maud, being here with you nurses will give this little girl the best possible chance of survival. There is nothing more that could be done for her.' He glanced back down at the body of the baby, lying pale in the lamplight. 'What is her name?'

'Flora,' murmured Maud, reaching out to take the baby's tiny hand again.

'And the father, I believe he's waiting . . .'

'Yes, he's Harry Donahue,' said Maud, feeling a knot in her chest when she uttered his name. 'He's in the visitors' room, opposite.'

Dr McKendrick nodded. 'I'll go and have a word with him.' Then he murmured a few words to Ada before he left the room.

Maud took a deep breath and stood up. 'We need to get organized,' she said.

'Yes, we do,' said Ada, placing a hand on Maud's arm. 'I don't know for sure, but I'm thinking that this friend of yours, Harry, the father of the baby, is your husband?'

Maud's heart skipped a beat.

'Yes, he is,' nodded Maud, miserably, feeling the knot in her chest tighten a little further. 'It seems the baby's been abandoned by her mother.'

'Right, I see. Well, we have work to do here, so there's no time to go into the matter right now, but all of this must be very painful for you, Maud. Do you want me to take over the baby's care?'

'No,' said Maud, very sure of herself. 'I want to do this.'

'That's all I need to know,' said Ada. 'Now, I'll liaise with Miss Merryweather and give her all the information. I think the best thing would be to put the baby into the empty nurses' sick bay overnight. I'll find a steam kettle and all that you need, and I'll ask Dolly to light the fire in there. You stay in here with her until we're ready.'

'Righto,' said Maud, stooping over to wrap Flora loosely in the shawl. And then she scooped her up and carried her over to the straight-backed chair beside Miss Merryweather's desk.

She was gazing at Flora's face, and monitoring every single breath that she took, when Harry came through the door.

'The doctor told me everything,' he said, his voice broken. 'Oh, Maud. Is she going to be all right?' he gasped, sinking to his knees.

'We don't know yet,' she said gently, moved to tears, despite everything that he had done, because of the love that he showed so openly for his daughter.

Maud could only watch as Harry ran his roughened

finger gently down the pale skin of the baby's cheek. That one simple gesture made her heart clench with pain. She knew that there was every chance that it might be the last time he saw his daughter. He looked up at her then and his eyes filled with tears.

'I'm sorry about this, Maud. So sorry.'

'There's no need to talk about that,' she murmured. 'Right now, what we need to consider is the life of this child. I need you to stay strong for her, Harry, do you understand?'

He nodded and then stroked the back of Flora's hand.

As Maud sat, she could hear the delicate rasp of Flora's fragile breath and the heaving sobs that moved in and out of Harry's chest as he tried to calm himself. Time seemed to go on for ever as the silence of the room unspooled around them.

Maud couldn't bear it any longer. 'Has she been baptized?' she asked, to break the spell.

'Yes, I got a priest that I know to do it. He didn't ask any questions.'

'That's good. And do you know where Nancy's gone?'

'I have no idea.'

'Whatever happened for her to walk out on her child?' She glared at him now, unable to control the outrage in her voice.

She heard Harry take a ragged breath, and then he looked her in the eye.

'Flora was unsettled all day, crying and crying, and

not wanting her bottle. And then when I got back from seeing you here, at the hospital, as soon as I was in through the door, she thrust the baby at me. Flora was screaming by then. Screaming. And I could feel how hot her body was. "You take her," she yelled, and then she picked up her bag and walked out. She wouldn't even tell me where she was going. I thought that she'd maybe calm down and come back, but she hasn't. I did get Flora to settle, though. I rocked her and rocked her on my knee, and I slept right by her so I could get up each time she whimpered. But all day today, things have got worse and then she seemed to just stop breathing. And now she won't wake up . . .' He was crying now, tears streaming down his face.

Maud couldn't stay angry with a man who was so wretched and heartbroken. 'We'll do everything we can for her, Harry,' she promised.

'I know that,' he sniffed, wiping his face on the sleeve of his jacket.

'Harry, you need to go now, and you have to promise me that you'll be all right. No going to the pub to drown your sorrows. This baby girl needs you. And I want you to come back here first thing in the morning. Do you understand?'

Harry nodded. He made a move to touch Maud's arm but she drew away and switched all of her attention back to the baby.

'Just go,' she said firmly.

'Goodbye, my precious baby girl,' he murmured.

Maud felt him leave the room.

'Come on, we're all set,' called Eddy, popping her head through the door. 'And we've even got a crib and some napkins from the lying-in ward.'

Maud pulled the shawl straight and folded it expertly around the baby.

'Can you manage her?' asked Eddy.

'Oh, yes,' replied Maud.

The nurses' sick room looked like a baby's nursery when she walked in, and Maud was heartened to see the fire lit in the grate and the first gusts of steam emerging from the kettle.

'This will do nicely,' she said, laying Flora down in the crib. 'I just need to change her napkin.'

'I'll do that,' offered Eddy, already rolling up her sleeves. 'We've worked out a rota . . . and you need to agree to this, Maud, there is no choice. I'll take the first two-hour shift and then I'll go back and get some sleep so that I'll be fit for work tomorrow. You can do the second stint, and then Miss Houston will come in to take over until the early hours – she said she enjoys night shifts – and then you can come back first thing, hopefully having had some sleep. And when you need to go to work, Miss Merryweather will take over.'

'Maybe, I should just stay with her, Eddy. I'll be all right.'

Eddy was smiling and shaking her head. 'You'll be worn out by tomorrow, and you'll be no good to anybody. We're all nurses here, aren't we? Let's share it, so we can all keep fulfilling our duties as well as looking after Flora. It makes sense.'

Maud knew it made sense, but she couldn't quite believe how bonded she felt to the baby already.

'You are the special one for her, though, Maud. We can all see that. And if there's any change overnight, or at any time of day, then we'll come to get you straight away.'

Maud was nodding now, and then she leant over the crib and stroked the baby's cheek. 'I'll see you in two hours,' she murmured.

When Maud returned, after forcing herself to eat a bit of food and treadling the sewing machine to produce a stack of bandages and compresses, she found Eddy in a room full of steam.

'How is she?'

'Just the same,' murmured Eddy, cradling Flora as she tried to give her some water, one drop at a time.

'She does seem to be swallowing some of it.'

'Did you manage to get some mother's milk from the lying-in ward?'

'They'll bring it in the morning, so it's fresh. I knew there'd not be much change overnight, so I thought that was best. We need to start her with clear fluids.'

'Thanks for doing this, Eddy,' said Maud, seeing the concentration on her friend's face as she sat in the chair giving Flora water, her hair now a mass of curls due to the humidity in the room.

'No trouble at all.' Eddy smiled, looking up for a moment. 'I'd do this for any sick child, but this little scrap just happens to be the bonniest baby girl I've ever seen in my life.'

'She is beautiful, isn't she, Eddy?'

'She is indeed,' replied Eddy, standing up to pass Flora over. 'And she has taken some water, but it's not enough, so keep trying her every ten minutes. I'll put some more coal on and fill the steam kettle before I go, and you'll need to keep sponging her with cool water – she's still running a fever.'

'Righto,' said Maud, placing the baby gently back in her crib. 'Leave that to me,' she said, taking the coal tongs out of Eddy's hand. 'And I can fill the steam kettle. You look tired, get yourself home to bed.'

Eddy yawned and then gave Maud a hug before pulling on her nurse's cape. 'Miss Houston will be in for the night shift. And then you come back in the morning, if you have time, before you go to work.'

'I'm always up early, I'll have time.'

'Oh and Miss Merryweather's arranged for you to have a half day tomorrow, so that you can do the afternoon shift. Is that all right?'

'Yes, of course,' said Maud, knowing as Eddy gave her a kiss on the cheek and clicked the door to behind her that, given the choice, she would have sat with the baby through all the watches of the day and the night.

Once Maud was alone, with only the lamplight and the flickering of the fire to keep her company, she rested back in the chair beside the baby's crib. She couldn't take her eyes off the baby girl as her tiny chest rose and fell and her body lay completely still. She leant forward to gently place the back of her hand against her body. She would sponge her with some cool water before the next round of drops – they had to try and keep the fever at bay.

Gusts of fresh steam were starting to emerge from the newly filled steam kettle as Maud took Flora in her arms to administer the drops of water. She swallowed the first, but the second dribbled out of her mouth. Maud stood up with her and rocked her from side to side, starting to quietly sing the words of a lullaby that she must have remembered from her mother – certainly her grandmother had never sung songs to her.

The words came out naturally, as if from nowhere.

As she sang, she gazed at Flora's dark hair, the perfect lines of her face, and the pattern of tiny blue veins on her closed eyelids. She felt that knot in her chest again and she sang a little louder to quell it, all the time gazing at the baby's face and trying to hold back the voice in her head, telling her repeatedly, 'This could have been your baby, your daughter.'

Maud sat back down again and tried one or two more drops of water and, to her relief, Flora took them. It still wasn't enough; the clean napkin that Eddy had put on was still bone dry. Maud wanted to sigh and grind her teeth with anxiety, but she held it back. Instead, she made herself smile and she spoke to the baby soothingly, telling her made-up stories and singing all the songs that she could remember.

Then it was time to put her back in the crib and busy herself with preparations, before sitting in the chair by the fire for another ten minutes. The routine went on until there was a light tap on the door and Ada came in.

'How's she doing?'

Maud gave all the details, as Ada stood taking in every word.

'Mmmm, so no real change as yet, but let's just keep going,' she said. 'Now you go and get some rest.'

Maud nodded obediently.

'And don't forget, Maud, I'm here any time if you want to talk. I can't even imagine what you've been going through in the last few days.'

'Thank you,' murmured Maud, 'but all I seem to care about right now is Flora. I'll be in to see her as soon as I wake up. And please let me know if there is any change either way overnight, I'm just down the corridor.'

'I know which room,' said Ada, 'and I will. Have they told you about the arrangements for tomorrow?'

'Yes, I'll take over from Miss Merryweather when I leave the ward for my half day.'

Ada nodded. 'Good night, then, Maud. Try to get as much sleep as you can. None of us can function properly if we don't take our own rest.'

Maud still felt wide awake as she closed the door of her room behind her. She would have loved to have gone back to the sewing machine but the noise of the treadle would have had the whole building awake. Instead, she turned up the lamp to the full and took up her needle to sew in the loose threads on the bandages she'd made. She felt the strain on her eyes in the dim light but it was the only way she could stop herself from listening out for the cry of a baby.

In the end, she must have fallen asleep in the chair.

She woke, fully dressed, with a crick in her neck and the needle still in her hand. She pushed it through the fabric then and went to lie on her bed, knowing that she should have followed Ada's advice and gone to bed properly, but now it was too late.

Waking again, at her usual early time, she felt groggy. She undressed then and washed herself with the cold water in her bowl before dressing again and fixing her hair, pinning it back extra tight before placing her nurse's cap square on her head. Taking the clean white apron that was neatly folded on her chest of drawers, she fastened it tightly around her waist and then clicked open her door to make her way along to the sick bay.

She listened outside the door but there was no sound, so she knocked gently and went in.

'Good morning,' smiled Miss Houston, extremely bright-eyed for someone who'd sat up all night. 'I hope you managed to get some sleep.'

'How is she?' asked Maud, going straight to the side of the crib.

'No real change, but she has been taking a little more water, and I think her fever's come down slightly. It's a shame we can't use the thermometers on babies, they're just too big, so we need to rely on the old methods.'

Maud placed the back of her hand against Flora's body. She nodded, 'Yes, I agree . . . maybe slightly.'

'But there's still not enough movement, and no loosening of her chest. The longer this goes on, I'm afraid, the less likely it is that she will recover.'

Maud nodded grimly. 'I'll take over now, until Miss Merryweather comes,' she offered.

'All right then,' said Ada, 'I won't argue. I need to catch up with some paperwork before I collapse into bed for a few hours.'

Maud nodded. She wanted to be left on her own with Flora. It seemed to be exactly what she needed.

'What else can I do, beautiful girl?' she murmured, as she stood by the crib after Ada had gone, gently stroking the dark hair that was so like Harry's.

18

'A few hours will do for baby, both in killing
and curing it, what days will not do for a
grown person.'

Florence Nightingale

Maud's body felt heavy and she placed a cushion in the
small of her back as she sat on the chair next to the crib.
The fire was stoked, the steam kettle full, and she had
just administered the drops of water, so there was nothing more to do just then.

She sorely wished now that she'd taken more care to
have some proper sleep; her eyes were heavy and it was
all that she could do to keep them open. Maybe she
needed to close them, just for a few moments . . . and
before she knew it, Maud was having a dream that a baby
was crying, a weak sound, just on the edges of her mind.

She tried to rouse herself but her body felt trapped.
She couldn't move, and still the baby cried. She had to
make a huge effort, she had to get out, she had to help
the baby.

Maud's eyes snapped open.

She wasn't dreaming. There was a sound coming from
the crib.

She leapt up and the chair screeched back on the wooden floor. She was wide awake now and her body was tingling, as she leant over to look into Flora's dark eyes. The baby was blinking in the light and moving her arms, as if trying them out for the first time.

'Hello,' she whispered, picking her up. Holding her close, feeling the warmth and the murmur of the tiny body against her shoulder, she rested her cheek against the baby's soft hair and breathed in the scent of her as tears started to well in her eyes.

Flora cried once more; the sound was weak, but it was still a very good sign. But then she started to cough, and for one agonizing moment she sounded like she was choking. Maud felt her heart thud, her eyes scanning the room for some clue as to what to do. She had never really nursed a baby before and that realization fell heavily on her shoulders. She followed her instincts, sitting down on the chair, holding the baby upright on her knee, rubbing her back, willing her to breathe.

Beneath her hand Maud could feel some looseness in the baby's chest. This had to be a good sign. Flora gave another cough, but she was struggling now, as if her air passage was blocked. Maud's mouth was dry and her heart was pounding. She lay the baby down on her tummy, across her knee, but that seemed to make things worse. She sat her back up again. She was making a high-pitched wheezing sound now.

'Oh my God,' cried Maud, 'somebody help me.'

Then she remembered the steam kettle behind her,

and she twisted round in her chair to get the full benefit of it.

Still Flora wheezed, her whole body wracked with
the effort of trying to clear her chest.

'Come on, come on,' murmured Maud, still rubbing
her back.

And then Flora gave another cough and something
seemed to shift and she swallowed. She was breathing easier now, and Maud almost cried with relief. But
then, almost immediately, she was wheezing again, the
high-pitched sound going right through Maud's body.

Right, Maud, you need to stay calm, she told herself.
Just repeat the process, keep her in the steam and pray
that it clears.

As Maud rubbed Flora's back and held on to her for
dear life, the door to the room clicked open and she heard
someone coming in. She glanced over her shoulder,
almost crying with relief when she saw Miss Merryweather removing her bonnet and walking straight over.

'The little one is awake, I see,' she said, her eyes
gleaming. 'It looks like her fever has broken, but this is
a crucial stage. We need to keep the steam flowing to
loosen the secretions in the chest. Now you hand the
little beauty to me, please, Nurse Linklater. I've sat
through many a vigil such as this. Before I came here, I
worked with women and their families at a silk mill in
Essex. There were many sick children and babies. Now,
all I need you to do before you go to the ward is to
stoke the fire and fill the kettle. My sister, Elizabeth,
will be along shortly and she has worked alongside me

with these cases, so this baby will be in very capable hands. I do need to warn you, however, that the little one could still sink – only if she has enough energy to clear her chest will she stand a chance.'

Maud nodded solemnly. Then she got up from the chair, with the baby in her arms, and held her close for a moment before handing her over to Miss Merryweather.

'And Nurse Linklater,' called the superintendent, as Maud was about to leave the room, 'these vigils are hard work. You need to go now, straight to the dining room, and get yourself some breakfast. I'll see you back here this afternoon.'

'Yes, Miss Merryweather,' said Maud quietly, glancing at Flora once more, before slipping out through the door.

Once in the corridor, she leant against the closed door for a moment before taking a deep breath and making her way to her own room to refresh herself. A nurse walking swiftly, with a glass jar in both hands, almost collided head on with her before she could reach her door.

'Where's the sick baby?' asked the nurse. 'I've got the expressed milk here that Nurse Pacey ordered.'

'That door there,' pointed Maud, smiling to herself. It felt like the whole hospital was rallying round to help one tiny baby.

Maud was first there in the dining room and the place was deserted. She was relieved; she knew that she couldn't have coped with any questions from Millicent Langtry, not this morning. She felt sick to her stomach but forced herself to eat a bowl of thin porridge. She couldn't manage any of the beer that was served at every meal, but she did have half a cup of tea. As soon as she was finished, she was straight up from the table.

She met Alice in the entrance hall.

'I've just been up to the sick bay to see Flora,' Alice said. 'I can't believe that she's awake. I was sure last night that . . . that . . .'

'Yes, I thought so, too,' murmured Maud.

'She must be strong, Maud. She's a little fighter. But all of this is so strange, isn't it? I've just seen Harry waiting outside, with the dog. He looks awful, like he's aged a hundred years. I told him that I'd come straight back out and tell him how she is.'

'Oh no,' gasped Maud, 'I forgot about that. I told him to come back this morning. I'll go and see him, I've got my uniform on, you need to go and get changed.'

Harry looked up as soon as Maud opened the door.

'She's awake and she's holding her own,' she called from the top step, seeing his body crumple instantly with relief.

'I never slept a wink,' he croaked. 'I didn't know what to do with meself.'

The dog was whining softly as Maud walked down the steps. She reached out automatically to give her a stroke as she continued with her report. 'Flora is fighting very hard and her chest is loosening. But she isn't out of danger yet, Harry.'

He wiped a hand over his face.

Maud reached out to steady him as he looked at her with swollen, bloodshot eyes. Beneath his pain there was a glimmer of something that Maud read as hope for Flora — but not just that, maybe. She saw something that resembled a look he'd given her when they were together, and she could still feel—

Instantly, Maud closed up. She couldn't allow any of that now. She'd reached out to him like she would to any relative of a very sick patient. That was all it was, she told herself, as she took a step back. She cleared her throat. 'Have you heard anything from Nancy?'

He shook his head slowly. 'No, and I don't care if I never hear from her again,' he replied, his voice husky.

Maud almost suggested that they try to find her, let her know that Flora was sick, but the words wouldn't form in her mouth. No, if she wanted to know about her daughter she would come looking. The mere thought of handing the baby back over to Nancy made Maud feel sick to her stomach.

'Is there any way that I could see Flora, Maud?'

'I'll see what I can do,' Maud replied, businesslike now, using the voice she used on the ward. 'I'll be going back up there this afternoon, and the Nurses' Home is more or less empty at that time. I'll have to get permission from Miss Merryweather, but I'll see what we can do.'

Harry nodded and gave her the ghost of a smile.

'You need to go and get yourself a cup of tea and something to eat, Harry. You have to look after yourself. Flora needs you.'

'Yes, Sister,' murmured Harry, a gesture towards the banter they used to share when she was a probationer.

Maud felt the intention but didn't respond. Instead, she set her mouth in a firm line. 'I'll see you here later, Harry,' she said, trying to ignore Rita who'd pricked up her ears and had started slowly wagging her tail.

As Harry walked away, Alice was coming down the steps.

'He's taken it very hard, hasn't he? How is he doing?' she asked, turning to join Maud, as they watched him walking slowly away, with his shoulders slumped.

'He's just about managing,' said Maud, linking Alice's arm.

'And what about Nancy? Is he trying to find her?'

'I don't think so.'

'Well, she walked out, didn't she? If it was any other woman, even though Harry is your husband, I would say that she had every right to come back to her child. But this is Nancy Sellers. We know her, don't we? She's never shown any sign of doing anything for anybody other than herself. And she's a bully – and I think, Maud, that she is pure evil, that woman, pure evil.'

Normally, Maud would have tilted her head to one side, thought for a moment and then tried her best to present a more balanced view. But on this occasion she said nothing.

With everything that had happened since the end of her last shift, Maud wasn't even sure which ward she was supposed to be working on, and she was glad of Alice's direction.

'You're on Female Surgical with me, and I want you to take it slowly this morning, Linklater. Do you hear?'

Hmph, thought Maud, we'll see about that. The more worry I have, the more I need to push myself. But she smiled at Alice and told her that she would try.

Thankfully, there were no admissions, or theatre cases, and the morning went by in an organized fashion. And, with great relief, Maud found herself actually enjoying working with Nurse Latimer. After all that had emerged last evening, she almost seemed like a brand-new person. Even though she looked tired, and she had the slightly swollen eyes of a woman who'd cried a great deal, Nurse Latimer was keen to help today and was actually engaging properly with the patients. The difference in her was remarkable.

Maud was pleased to find Mrs Martin propped up in bed, with her hair neatly fastened in a loose knot on top of her head. Night sister had reported that she'd come round nicely from the chloroform and had been taking fluids. They'd washed her and changed her and sat her up in bed.

'Good morning,' said Maud. 'You probably don't remember me, but I was the nurse who went into theatre with you yesterday.'

'Of course I remember you, my dear. How could I forget those big dark eyes and your beautiful voice? You really helped me when they were giving me the chloroform.'

Maud smiled. 'Can I just check your dressing? I need to make sure that it's clean and dry.'

Mrs Martin lifted the corner of the sheet.

'All fine,' smiled Maud, once she'd had a good look. 'Now you need to drink as much fluid as you can – water, tea, beer or wine, whichever you prefer. And we'll start you on a soft diet today.'

Mrs Martin nodded, then winced as she tried to sit herself up in bed.

'Do you need anything for the pain?'

'No, just a twinge. Night sister gave me some drops before she sponged me down and dolled me up in a new nightie,' smiled Mrs Martin, her pale blue eyes shining with good humour.

Maud returned the smile. 'I met your friend Mrs McCluskey at visiting yesterday. She seems to be a very caring person.'

'Oh, me and Cynthia, we go back a long way. We've lived next door to each other since we were first married. I know all of her children and treat them like my own. Every mother with a large family needs as much help as she can get, and Cynthia was always happy to let me look after hers. I couldn't have any of my own, you see. So . . .'

'That can't have been easy, Mrs Martin, but it sounds like you've given a great deal to others because of that.'

'Oh, no more than most,' she smiled. 'Do you have any children, Nurse?'

'Oh, no!' gasped Maud. 'Not as such. Nurses like me aren't allowed to be married or have children.'

'Really?' frowned Mrs Martin. 'But I suppose, with the long hours and all that, it would be difficult. You'd need somebody like me to look after them.'

'That is very true,' smiled Maud, starting to feel a little hot around the collar, thinking about Alfred and now Flora.

Maud began to feel more anxious about Flora during the final hour of her shift and she needed to keep busy. With the ward completely straight, she'd asked Nurse Latimer to go to every bed and check that the temperature charts were up to date. And she'd launched into a full clean and tidy of the sluice. Alice smiled when she came in through the door to find Maud with her sleeves rolled up, vigorously scouring the sink.

'Maud, what did I tell you about going slowly?' she laughed. 'You've just about taken the glaze off that sink. Now give that cloth to me, Sister Pritchard has said you can go.'

'What? Does she know about Flora?' said Maud, turning from the sink, with the cloth still in her hand.

'Of course she does. She had to agree to you taking the afternoon off, didn't she? But you know what this place is like, the whole hospital knows about the sick baby in the Nurses' Home. Michael Delaney gave me these this morning,' she said, pulling out a minute pair of knitted bootees. 'His wife made them. And there's a wooden rattle from Sister Law, a blanket from Stephen Walker, and a toy dog from Dr McKendrick, all waiting in the Nurses' Home. And apparently, Sister Tweedy was saying special prayers for Flora all through her shift last night.'

Maud smiled and shook her head, before placing a damp hand on Alice's sleeve. 'We are so lucky, aren't we, to be a part of the life of this hospital?'

'We are, indeed,' agreed Alice, pushing the knitted bootees into Maud's pocket, before reaching to take the wet cloth from her hand. 'Now, go on, off you go.'

It was pouring with rain, and Maud had no umbrella, so she picked up her skirt and ran the distance to the Nurses' Home. She arrived, breathless, in the entrance hall, dripping wet over the Minton tiles and leaving a trail up both sets of steps to the second floor, where she nipped into her own room to get dry, remove her sodden cap and change out of her damp uniform. Feeling the pressure of time due to her urgent need to see Flora, she didn't even bother to check her hair in the mirror. It had come untethered from the clip as she removed her cap, and stray wisps were now falling on to her collar and on each side of her face. She did notice one strand and gamely tucked it behind her ear.

As soon as she slipped in through the door of the sick bay, Maud could hear the bubbling of Flora's chest. She glanced anxiously, first to where the baby lay in the crib, and then to Miss Merryweather.

'Try not to be too alarmed, Nurse Linklater,' she said carefully. 'Her chest needs to loosen so that the secretions can come up. And that is exactly what is happening. The good news is that she's started to take the expressed milk, and I've been giving it on a teaspoon – as much as she can take, whenever she's awake.'

'That's good,' sighed Maud, rolling up her sleeves and going straight to the bowl of water to wash her hands with carbolic soap. Then she was straight to the crib, scanning Flora's face. She was sleeping, but she started to cough and then the crying came.

'Pick her up, that's it,' soothed Miss Merryweather. 'I know she's very small, but don't be afraid. The child is showing her resilience, and every time she coughs she is striving to get better. She is very strong. I don't think I've ever seen one so small with such a tenacious grasp on life.'

Maud nodded and smiled, hastily tucking another strand of hair behind her ear, before picking up her charge.

'Keep the steam going,' ordered Miss Merryweather, as she started to make her way out of the room. 'And I've placed a large bell, there, next to the fire. Ring it hard if you need anything. I'll be in my office and I'll come running.'

'Oh, Miss Merryweather, just one more thing,' said Maud, rocking from side to side with the baby in her arms. 'I spoke to Flora's father this morning, he was waiting outside. He asked if there was any chance he could come in to see her. I was wondering if, now, during the afternoon, he would be able to come up just for a short time?'

'Yes, I think we can do that. Anything that might help the baby recover. I'll keep an eye out for him. Harry, isn't it? I'll bring him up. He will have to leave his dog outside, however. As much as I like animals, I do not think that the nurses' residence is an appropriate place for them.'

'Thank you, Miss Merryweather,' said Maud, turning

her attention instantly back to Flora when she started to rattle with a cough. As Maud sat with her by the steam kettle, she could hear heavy rain on the window and big spits of it came down the chimney and hissed on the hot coals. 'It's raining, it's pouring,' she sang to Flora, as her small body began to convulse with another fit of wheezing and coughing.

It seemed like only minutes before Miss Merryweather reappeared, with a bedraggled Harry in tow. He walked sheepishly into the room, his dark green jacket almost black with rainwater and his hair plastered to his head. He seemed to have no awareness of just how saturated he was as he walked across the room, with his eyes fixed entirely on Flora.

'Take your jacket off, Harry,' said Maud gently. 'Get a towel from over there and give yourself a rub dry. And then you can hold her.'

'She's rattling, isn't she . . . how do you think she is?' He frowned as he removed his jacket, to reveal a clean white shirt clinging to his broad shoulders and flat belly.

Maud recognized the shirt, it was her favourite. She cleared her throat. 'Flora's improving. She's waking more now, her fever's broken and her chest is loosening. There's still a way to go, but she is a real fighter, Harry. She's strong.'

He broke into a smile then, and it almost brought tears to Maud's eyes.

Flora started to cough and she made that high-pitched noise as she breathed in again.

Maud saw the panic on Harry's face, and she reached

out a hand to him. 'It's all right,' she said, 'this is all part of the process. The steam is helping to loosen the secretions enough for her to cough them up.'

He nodded, but he still looked stricken.

Maud rocked Flora from side to side until the coughing fit had subsided, and then she passed her over to him. It made her heart ache when she saw him settle the baby against his broad chest. Flora looked minute, with his muscular arm encircling her, but he held her with such delicacy, as if it was the most natural thing in the world for a man who'd once earned his living as a bare-knuckle fighter to be nursing a baby.

He was talking to his daughter now, the lilt of his voice sending shivers down Maud's spine. She turned away and made herself busy, stripping the sheet from the crib, tidying up the pile of napkins and checking the expressed milk that stood ready on the side.

When she turned back, Harry had eased himself into the chair by the fire and he was rocking Flora gently from side to side. Maud didn't know if she was imagining it or not, and it seemed almost miraculous, but since she'd handed her over, Flora's breathing seemed to have calmed – and the rattle in her chest seemed to have improved, too. She'd even started to make little snuffly baby noises. Was it possible that simple contact with her own flesh and blood had instantly helped balance out what was going on in her tiny body?

Maud had no answers, and she didn't really care. As long as Flora was improving, that was all that mattered.

'You're sounding better already, sweetness,' murmured Harry.

And Maud could see that Flora was looking up at him, properly taking notice. And then he looked up at Maud with a broad smile and her heart jumped.

She looked away, she couldn't let this happen. Not again, not after Nancy. The fire didn't really need another lump of coal but she took up the tongs and placed one on there anyway. She checked the water in the steam kettle. She could feel him watching her.

Then Flora was coughing again, choking a little, and he stood up with her, rocking from side to side, whispering words of comfort. Maud knew that she couldn't weaken; it was probably only a matter of time before Nancy showed up and he went trotting back to her. How could she ever trust him again after what had happened?

In due course, Miss Merryweather was at the door to tell Harry that his time was up. There was only so long that the presence of a man could be tolerated within the hallowed walls of the Nurses' Home. In fact, apart from Dr McKendrick, Harry was probably the first man ever to set foot in the building since Dolly, the laundress, had taken over the repair and maintenance of the building from the hospital handyman.

Harry nodded and handed Flora back to Maud, so that she could feed her some of the milk from a spoon.

'Thank you for letting me visit,' he said, retrieving his sodden jacket from the back of the chair.

Miss Merryweather smiled.

He has a way with him, he has for sure, thought Maud, he can even charm the superintendent.

'Come again, at the same time, tomorrow afternoon,' offered Miss Merryweather, with another smile. 'I think it's very important that the baby spends some time with her father.'

Maud breathed a sigh when he'd gone. She didn't even know if it was of relief, or the reawakening of some other feelings that she was desperately trying to keep at bay.

'As long as you are getting better.' She smiled at Flora, as she took yet another teaspoon of milk. 'That's all that matters for now.'

19

'. . . I do so believe that every tear one sheds
waters some good thing into life . . .'

Florence Nightingale

There was further improvement in Flora's condition as
the afternoon wore on. The bouts of coughing became
less frequent and her chest was certainly sounding
clearer. Maud even sent for more milk from the lying-
in ward. Miss Merryweather had mentioned that she'd
asked Dr McKendrick to visit when he had a chance, so
that he could check Flora and listen again with his
stethoscope. As Maud sat on the chair by the fire, with
the baby sleeping quietly in the crib, she was expecting
him at any moment.

The door clicked open and Maud stood up. She
opened her mouth to welcome her colleague but then
gave a small, startled cry. There stood Nancy Sellers,
with a glint in her eyes and a nasty twist to her mouth.

Maud moved instinctively towards the crib. But
Nancy was there before her, grabbing the baby, waking
her up.

'Put her back down,' ordered Maud, both her hands
balled into fists.

'I think you'll find that she is my property,' sneered Nancy. 'It's a good job that I still have friends here at the hospital who keep me informed of what's going on.'

Flora was crying now and starting to cough.

'You walked out on her,' spat Maud.

'I told Harry where I was going. My father has been sick, I was going to look after him,' snarled Nancy, tightening her grasp on the baby, almost squashing her against the stiff blue gown that she wore.

'You did no such thing,' shouted Maud. 'Now put Flora back down.'

'Who do you think you are? Just because you've adopted some ragtag boy from the workhouse, you think you have some right to other people's children. You've always been above yourself, Maud, and now that you've come back from New York, you're even more pathetic. Harry always wanted me, he only made do with you. It was me he wanted to come back for, you know it was.'

'Nothing of the sort,' retorted Maud, confident at least in the knowledge that Harry loved New York and he had only come back to Liverpool because they had received news of Miss Fairchild's ill health.

She'd moved to stand with her back to the door, blocking Nancy's way out of the room. If she wanted to take the baby she would have to fight her way past.

'Stand aside,' ordered Nancy, the baby whimpering now as she held her clumsily against the smooth fabric of her gown.

'No,' said Maud with force.

Nancy grabbed Maud's arm and dug in her nails as she tried to pull her out of the way. The baby was screaming now. Maud stood firm, keeping her at bay.

Nancy let go of Maud momentarily and then swiped back with force, scraping a stinging line of scratches down the soft flesh on the inside of her forearm. Maud yelped with pain and grabbed her arm, off balance long enough for Nancy to push with her shoulder and almost get past her, with the baby dangling in one arm. Maud growled with rage and threw herself back in front of the door, setting her feet wide apart so she wouldn't be thrown off balance again. She heard Flora start to cough, and then the baby slipped down through Nancy's arm and almost fell to the floor. Nancy hauled her back up, holding her tightly against her blue gown, and then she leant right in, face to face. Maud could smell her cheap scent and see the smeared paint on her lips.

Maud stood firm, her breath coming in quick pants. She was acutely aware that Flora had gone quiet.

'Let me by,' hissed Nancy.

'Over my dead body,' said Maud, without flinching, as the blood from the wound on her arm trickled down and dripped from her fingers.

Nancy's face contorted and she tried to pull Maud out of the way once more, her fingers digging into her upper arm. Maud didn't know what Nancy would do next. Most of all she feared for the safety of the baby, who had now stopped struggling in her mother's arms.

As Maud braced herself for a further assault, she heard a voice at the other side of the door, crying out, 'Nurse Linklater? Are you all right?' and she felt someone trying to open the door behind her. She took a step forward, pushing up against Nancy so that she had to step back also, and Miss Merryweather emerged into the room, closely followed by her sister, Elizabeth.

'Nurse Sellers!' spat Miss Merryweather, narrowing her eyes. 'What is the meaning of this?'

Nancy adjusted the weight of the baby in her arms and tried to smile. 'Oh, Miss Merryweather,' she said, 'Nurse Linklater has been looking after Flora for me.'

'Nonsense!' said Miss Merryweather, straight out. 'You walked out on your child.'

The switch in Nancy's demeanour was terrifying to witness. Instantly, she was glaring with contempt. 'This is my baby! And Nurse Linklater has stolen her!'

Flora started to wail, a thin noise, with little energy. Maud kept her eyes on the baby. All she wanted to do was to take her back, check her over and make sure that she was safe.

Miss Merryweather drew herself up and puffed out her chest, raising her voice so that she could be heard above the wailing baby. 'I think you will find, Miss Sellers, that this baby is, according to the laws of the land, the property of her father, Harry. So unless you want me to call the police, I suggest that you put Flora back in the crib where her father has deemed that she be cared for until she recovers.'

Nancy's mouth turned down in an ugly grimace.

'Well, Superintendent,' she sneered, 'I bet you don't know that our Miss prim and proper Nurse Linklater here is a married woman. She is, in fact, married to Harry.'

Maud gasped.

Miss Merryweather didn't miss a beat, however. She looked Nancy in the eye and leant in to speak to her directly. 'Of course I know that. But, as you are completely aware, Nurse Linklater is now separated from her husband. Therefore, she is once again a single woman. And she is, once more, living in the Nurses' Home under *my* jurisdiction.'

Nancy reeled back, grinding her teeth with rage. 'This is not the end, Linklater, I will see Harry, and he will tell you to hand *my* baby over,' she hissed, thrusting Flora in Maud's direction, before pushing her way past Miss Elizabeth who stood, wide-eyed and defenceless, in the doorway.

'Is the baby all right, Nurse Linklater?' asked Miss Merryweather, moving on effortlessly, as if the incident with Nancy Sellers had never even happened.

Maud nodded, tears stinging her eyes, as she rocked Flora from side to side, desperately trying to settle her.

'And look at your arm, Nurse Linklater, you are bleeding. Did she do that?'

Maud nodded, reaching with her other hand to wipe the blood away. She didn't care about the scratches, they didn't matter. But Miss Elizabeth was already soaking the end of a towel in some cold water and Miss Merryweather was insisting that she hand over the baby.

'Sit down,' soothed Miss Elizabeth, pressing the cold compress to Maud's arm. 'The scratches are deep, they will need to be cleaned with iodine and dressed.'

Maud's head was still spinning but she sat, as instructed, and held out her arm. The scratches stung when they were treated and as she gritted her teeth, Maud felt a fresh surge of anger strike through her body. She couldn't deny that Nancy was Flora's mother, and some might argue that she had every right to come and reclaim her child. But she had shown no regard for the safety or care of her daughter, so intent had she been on wresting back something that she saw as a possession. Maud thought it through, seeing again the vicious look on Nancy's face and the moment when Flora nearly fell from her grasp. She was sure that she'd been right to fight for the child.

Once the bandage was applied, Maud was back on her feet, checking Flora. She looked over every inch of her and then stood gazing down at her as she lay in the crib. Where is this going to lead? she thought. Whatever will become of these feelings I have for a child that isn't even mine?

'I'm here for the evening shift!' called Eddy from the door of the sick room, later that day. Then, as soon as she saw the bandage on Maud's arm, 'What the heck happened to you?'

Maud pressed her finger to her lips. She'd only just got Flora settled after a prolonged bout of coughing, and she wanted her to sleep. Seeing the concern on her friend's face, Maud felt tears springing to her eyes and tried to smile. 'I had a visit from Nancy.'

'What?' shouted Eddy. 'And she did that?'

Maud motioned for Eddy to sit down on the chair by the fire. After she'd helped her out of her district nurse's cape and hat, and found a safe place for her medical bag, she perched on a footstool next to her and started to tell her all that had happened.

'I know you've ended up with war wounds, Maud,' smiled Eddy, reaching out an arm to put around Maud's shoulders, after she'd finished telling the story. 'But you're a hell of a fighter. And I would have loved to have seen Nancy's face when Miss Merryweather told her about Harry having the legal rights. I mean, it certainly isn't a fair rule, like all of the other laws that prejudice women. But in this case it really works in our favour, doesn't it?'

'It does,' smiled Maud, but then a fleeting look crossed her face.

'What?' murmured Eddy.

'Well, it's just that . . . Harry has assured me that he has no feelings for Nancy and that he only moved in to live with her because he feared for Flora's safety. But what if he does decide to take Flora and go back to live with her? What then?'

'He won't,' said Eddy firmly. 'I've seen the way he looks at you, Maud. How could he go back to her? She's nothing.'

'Yes, but have you seen the way he looks at Flora?'

murmured Maud. 'He might do it for the baby, if he wants to try and make a proper family.'

'Mmm, I see what you mean,' said Eddy, continuing to ponder as she ran both hands through her hair till it stuck out at all angles.

But she didn't seem to have an answer. And then Flora was coughing again, and Maud moved to settle her, whilst Eddy stoked the fire and filled the steam kettle, and no more was said.

By the time Alice called in on her way home, Flora was sleeping peacefully in her crib, and Maud and Eddy were back in front of the fire. Alice took a pillow and sat on the floor at the other side of Eddy. Once she had found a comfortable position, Maud and Eddy told the story of what had happened that afternoon.

'He won't go back to her, Maud. You've no need to worry on that score,' said Alice. 'But my concern is, now that Flora seems to be definitely on the mend, is he going to be able to look after her by himself?'

'Yes,' said Maud confidently. 'I think he'll take good care of her, he seems to love her with all his heart.'

'I wasn't really thinking along those lines, Maud. I've never seen a man who can do the basic care for a baby like he can. It's just that, he will need to earn a living as well, and he won't be able to take Flora with him when he goes about his business on the docks or, God forbid, takes to bare-knuckle fighting again.'

'Ah, I see what you mean,' said Maud. 'I've been so busy, I hadn't put much thought into any of that.'

'Ha,' blurted Eddy, 'he's a man. He might be thinking that you'll go straight back to him, and you'll look after the baby.'

Maud glanced from Eddy to Alice. 'I hadn't thought about that either. And I've been very careful not to give him any sign that I still . . .'

'You still love him, though, don't you?' said Alice, quietly.

Maud blinked. 'I don't know. Only days ago, I could have strangled him with my bare hands, I hated him so much. Now there are moments when, I just don't know. I'm still in shock, I think.'

'Well, no wonder,' added Alice. 'After what he did. And with . . . *her* . . . as well.'

'And that's it, isn't it? Could I ever trust him again?'

They were all silent for a few moments as Maud stared into the fire. Then she raised her head. 'I don't know what I think about anything any more. But one thing I do know is that I can't give up my nursing. I have to work.'

They all sat for a while in easy companionship, a little sleepy in front of the fire, and then Alice stood up from the floor and stretched. 'I need to get going,' she said. 'I don't like walking through the city too late on my own, even in the district nurse's uniform.'

'You go as well, Maud,' said Eddy, getting up to check the steam kettle. 'I'm on shift now for two hours, so you go and have a break.'

'If you're sure?' said Maud, glancing towards the crib to check Flora.

'Go on, off you pop,' said Eddy. 'She'll be as right as rain with Aunty Edwina.'

Maud linked Alice's arm as they walked down the stone stairs to the ground floor.

As they passed their old rooms, Alice smiled. 'A lot's happened, since we had our rooms there, hey, Maud? A lot in a very short time, when you think about it.'

'I hope there aren't going to be any more nasty surprises in store,' murmured Maud, as they reached the ground floor and started to walk across the coloured tiles. Maud began to open the front door. 'I've had quite enough for the time—'

'What?' said Alice, seeing Maud freeze.

'Uh oh,' murmured Alice, peering around Maud to find Harry waiting right at the bottom of the steps, with the dog next to him, both of them looking up expectantly.

'I'll leave you to it,' Alice whispered, stepping by her. 'Good luck.'

Maud stared down at Harry from her elevated position on the top step, with the warmth of her lamplit sanctuary behind her. He looked awful, she thought – unshaven, dishevelled, with lines of exhaustion on his face. It felt very different, being face to face with him out here in the open. The softening that she'd felt towards him when she'd seen him holding Flora was gone now. All she could feel was that hard lump deep inside her that had started to grow the moment she had seen him walk towards Nancy.

'What do you want, Harry?' she called down to him, her voice coming out unexpectedly strong.

The dog whined.

She saw the surprise in his eyes. He seemed to have been expecting the gentle version of Maud that he'd seen nursing his daughter.

'How is Flora?' he asked, shifting around from one foot to the other.

'She is fine. And given that Nancy turned up this afternoon to try and force me to hand her over, that in itself is some kind of miracle.'

Maud saw no surprise on his face, and she knew instantly that Nancy must have been back to see him. She decided to keep quiet for the time being and see what his reaction would be.

He straightened up. 'That's what I wanted to see you about.'

'Could it not have waited till tomorrow? I need to go back in to Flora soon, and there are any number of things that I need to catch up on.'

'No, Maud, I need to see you now.'

'Well, I'm here,' said Maud, allowing the door to close behind her but not showing any sign of coming down the steps.

Harry was looking at the ground and shaking his head. 'You are quite something, that's for sure,' he murmured, with a glimmer of his old self as he looked back up at her. 'My wife, Maud Linklater.'

'I am no longer your wife!'

'Well, there's a man of the cloth just down the road there, at that church, who might argue with you over that, Maud. But right now I need to talk to you about something else,' he said, trying to make his voice light and gesturing for her to come down the steps.

'I'm not moving from this step,' she called.

He made a move to come up towards her.

Maud held up a hand. 'Stay where you are, Harry,' she warned.

'All right then, Maud.' There was more amusement in his eyes now. 'Nancy came to see me after she'd been here,' he said. 'She seemed very shaken up, and she was crying.'

Something snapped inside Maud then. She marched straight down the steps to stand face to face with him, her breath ragged. 'Very shaken up!' she shouted. 'Have you any idea what that woman said and how she behaved when she came to Flora's room this afternoon? Have you?'

The dog yelped.

Harry took a step back. 'Steady on there, Maud,' he was saying, 'I'm only trying to say—'

'*What* exactly are you trying to say, Harry?' she said, pushing him back with her hand. 'Hey, *what?* Go on, spit it out!' She pushed him again, and he took another step back.

'Well, she was crying when she came to me and she said she was sorry and that all she wanted was to look after Flora. She wanted me to ask you if you would let her have the baby, now that's she's not as poorly.'

'Oh, she did, did she?' said Maud, her voice icy cold. 'Nancy asked you that?'

'Yes, and I'm not saying that I want her anywhere near Flora, I'm not saying that, Maud. But I was worried about Nancy, she's been having a very difficult time.'

Maud could only cry out in frustration, she couldn't form a response in words. She screamed and then she marched away down the footpath, not even knowing where she was going. She just needed to get away from him.

20

'I don't agree . . . that a woman has no
reason . . . for not marrying a good man . . . I
think some have every reason for not marrying,
and that for these it is much better to educate
the children who are already in the world . . .'

Florence Nightingale

'Maud!' called Harry, trotting after her. 'Maud?'

'Leave me alone, Harry,' she spat over her shoulder.
'Go back to her, go on!'

'I don't want her, I never did!'

'Well, that's strange, isn't it? Given that you ended
up having a baby with her!' called Maud over her shoulder, as she picked up her pace, desperate to leave him
behind.

'Stop, Maud. Please,' he called, his voice breaking.

But Maud could not stop, all she could do was walk.
And now it was spitting big drops of cold rain. She
turned her face up to the sky so she could feel it more,
wanting it to rain even harder and wash away all her
pain.

Harry was still calling out behind her, but she had a
buzzing noise in her head and it was starting to pour

now. She walked on through the driving rain, heedless of the water stinging her eyes and dripping from her nose. She walked on, even as the water from puddles seeped inches up her skirt, dragging the heavy material against her legs.

Still he was behind, calling her name.

Only when he went quiet, and she felt that he was no longer following her, did she seek shelter in the doorway of an empty building. She leant back against the reassuringly solid stone as the rain began to fall in a curtain outside the doorway. She was sopping wet, saturated, her hair plastered to her head and water running off her skin. She rooted for a handkerchief in her pocket but when she pulled it out, it too was wet through, and she had to wring it out.

Wearily, she wiped a hand around her face and then leant back against the stone again and started to cry, her tears mixing with the rain. She cried with her whole body, like a child, like the orphaned girl she'd once been. The sorrow erupted from her and she couldn't stop it.

Only when the rain eased, and her body began to shiver, did she start to take back some control. There were one or two pedestrians creeping back on to the street now, and a child was splashing through a puddle. It felt like the world was starting to resume. She needed to get back to the hospital, it would be almost time for Eddy to leave.

She glanced out of the doorway, hugging herself, trying to keep warm. She needed to move.

As soon as she stepped out and started to walk in the direction of the hospital, even with her sodden skirt dragging around her legs and her hair plastered to her head, she felt some life coming back into her. And then she saw him, standing, facing her, in the middle of the path ahead. He must have taken shelter before she did; his hair was wet but he wasn't soaked through to the bone. She decided to keep walking straight towards him. Why should he make her cross the road?

As she got closer she saw his face, pleading. Her heart tightened and, almost involuntarily, she started to slow her pace and then she was standing still, shivering violently. He was striding towards her now. She could hear his breath coming faster. He didn't say a word, but as he took his final stride he opened up his jacket and pulled it around her, enveloping her against his warm body.

It was warm and dry inside the jacket, and she could feel his heart thumping in his chest as she rested her head against him, breathing in the musky smell of his body. It was the only thing she felt capable of doing in that moment.

'Oh, Harry,' she sighed at last. 'Whatever are we going to do about all of this?'

'I want to be with you, Maud. There's no one else for me,' he murmured, his voice husky. 'Nancy never meant anything. And I was so drunk that night, I don't even remember anything about it. She never told me a thing about the baby, not till I got back. And Maud, I'm just not right without you. If it hadn't been for the baby, I might have taken meself down to the docks and . . .'

Maud could feel the heaving of his chest now. He was sobbing.

She reached up a hand to stroke his face, and he leant in to try and kiss her. But she turned her face, his cheek brushing hers for an instant. She pulled back from him, she could still feel the tingle on her skin where his rough cheek had scratched her, it sent a ripple through her body.

'I don't know what to say to you, Harry. I can't forget all that you've done, and I don't feel able to forgive you . . . but I think we can at least be friends. And you need to listen to me when I tell you that Nancy should not be allowed near her daughter. She is a bad person. A manipulative person. And I think the only reason she came to try and take Flora today was that she'd heard that she was with me. She's always borne a grudge against me, and she bullied Alice terribly when we were probationers. Don't believe her, Harry. Don't believe a word that she says.'

Harry was nodding now. 'I'll take your word for it, Maud,' he said. 'I know you always tell the truth.'

Maud was stepping away from him now and keeping a decent distance between them as they started to walk back towards the hospital, holding up her sodden skirt with both hands to stop it sticking to her legs.

'Have you any ideas about how you will be able to care for Flora when she comes home?' she asked as she walked.

'Well, I know any number of women who have their own children and would be willing to mind her for a bit of extra money. I was wondering if I should rent somewhere nearer to the hospital, so it's easy for you to visit? And then, when Alfred has time away from school, he can come there as well. And my work is what you might call flexible – I've got some good business contacts now in New York and they're going to ship goods over, that kind of thing. I can look after her for part of the day.'

'Sounds like a plan,' said Maud, matter-of-factly. 'There is one thing, though. Like I've told you before, I won't tolerate any drunkenness around Flora or Alfred. So you can't be spending much time in the pub.'

Harry nodded. 'I'll do my best. Oh, and I went up to see Alfred today, after I left you in the Nurses' Home. I told him everything.'

Maud stopped in her tracks.

'No, don't worry, he was fine. He just sat there and listened, and I didn't really know what he was thinking, but in the end he just wanted me to promise that everything would be all right between me and you. I mean, I didn't really know if it would be or not, but I had enough trust in you to know that we can probably find some way of . . .'

Maud was frowning now, as she started to walk away from him.

He jogged a couple of paces to catch her up. 'So, I said that we would. And then he said something like, "Well, that's all right, then," and he pulled a hard, dried-up piece of ham out of his pocket and fed it to Rita.'

He saved it, all that time, thought Maud, all the time . . . waiting for Harry to visit.

'I'll leave you here,' she said, stopping abruptly just before they reached the Nurses' Home. 'I look enough of a fright, soaking wet through, without being seen by the night superintendent with some man. I won't see you when you visit. But the way things are going for Flora, she might even be ready for you to take her home tomorrow, so you need to get on and make your arrangements.'

'I will,' he said, reaching out a hand and almost brushing her sleeve as she began to back away from him. Then he started speaking rapidly, clearly playing for time as he desperately tried to keep her attention. 'And like I was saying earlier, about the women who might look after Flora, one of them is the wife of the big fella, the man who I used to fight, you know, the fella who ended up in the hospital bed next to me. Well, his wife, Daphne, she's just had another baby and she's one of them that's been saying that she'd take little Flora as well. And she thinks she'd be able to wet-nurse her. She's done it before, for any number of babies. I think they need the money, that's seven children they've got now.'

Maud was nodding and had stopped backing away from him. 'Good idea. And when you start to look for another room, find somewhere clean and dry – with good ventilation. Oh, and it must have a good fire, not some smoky old dust machine. You need one that will give a good blaze and take a steam kettle, in case Flora starts again with a bad chest. And you won't be able to smoke in the room when she's there, she'll need pure air. That child is the most important business of your life. So you need to take this seriously, make a profession of it.'

'Yes, Sister,' smiled Harry, taking a step in her direction.

'I need to go now. I need to get back to Flora,' she said, holding up a hand to stop him moving any closer. Then she turned on her heel, picking up the sodden, dusty remains of her skirt and walking towards the Nurses' Home as elegantly as she could, with her hair plastered to her head and her feet squelching with rainwater.

Maud woke early, as usual, the next morning, but she was so exhausted that she couldn't get up out of bed. She rolled on to her side so that she could see her uniform. Thank goodness she'd changed out of it yesterday. It was fully dry now, unlike the gown she'd worn to walk out into the city – that still hung, black and heavy, sodden with rainwater.

She smiled to herself, thinking of how she'd struggled to get out of the wet clothing and change into her nightdress and shawl to go back and relieve Eddy. She'd felt so light, and almost giddy, as she'd tripped along the corridor in her 'next to nothings'. And Eddy had laughed her head off, seeing her in her nightie, listening open-mouthed as Maud told her about the walk through the city, pursued by Harry.

'I told you, Maud, I've seen the way he looks at you. He's overflowing with feelings. A woman could wait her whole life for something like that to come her way.'

Maud had dismissed Eddy's comment on the spot and found all kinds of reasons why Harry wasn't the right man for her: she could never trust him; he could be unreliable . . . But she'd known then, even as she recited her list, that there was something about her bond with him that couldn't be explained in words. It was a feeling so strong that, at times, it felt like a real thing sitting under her ribs. It made her heart beat faster and her breath come quickly.

She gave a small groan and rolled on to her back. She didn't want this now, not again – at least the anger that she'd felt after he'd walked away with Nancy had been clean and uncomplicated.

'Come on, Maud,' she muttered to herself. 'Get up, get dressed, you need to get moving.'

As soon as she was ready – apart from her starched cap, which she'd have to replace – she went along to Flora's room, as she now thought of it. Ada Houston was sitting by the fire, resting back in the chair. As Maud came through the door, she sat up and smiled, her whole face lighting up with it.

'Good morning, Maud,' she said, brushing back some stray curls of dark hair that had loosened overnight. 'You will be pleased to know that our charge is much improved. She's still coughing but not choking with it now, and I've even been using a feeding bottle to give the milk.'

Maud went straight to the crib, her eyes perusing every inch of Flora's sleeping face. She looked so much better, and it was very satisfying to stand and listen to the now quiet breath moving in and out of her tiny body.

Ada came to join her. 'She's a real beauty, isn't she? She's the spit of her father . . . and I suppose that makes it easier and harder for you, all at the same time.'

Maud nodded, still gazing at the baby.

Ada linked Maud's arm. 'Life can be hard for us women, can't it? Inevitably, there are difficult decisions to be made, and we are never really sure if we've chosen the right path or not. But in the end, we have to make a choice and stand by it.'

When Maud looked at Ada, she could see tears shining in her eyes. She held her breath, not wanting to disturb the moment, knowing instinctively that whatever was coming was personal and important.

When Ada spoke, her voice was hesitant at first. 'I told Alice about my situation when she was going through her own troubles with Victoria's father, and I have to ask you not to repeat what I'm about to tell you. But I had a baby once and she looked so much like Flora when she was just weeks old that sitting here, night after night, has been a very strange experience for me . . .'

'Oh, Ada,' cried Maud, her breath catching on a sob.

Ada gave Maud's arm a squeeze with her own, before continuing. 'I chose to give Leah up. Not completely, I see a great deal of her, and she is well cared for by a friend of mine who she thinks of as her mother. She is almost four years old now and we are very close. Aunty Ada, she calls me, and as soon as I come through the door she runs to me with something to show me, or wanting to play . . . and I adore her. But that means I have to bear the pain of missing her as well. I'm not there at night when she wakes and calls out. I'm not there to pick her up when she falls. I willingly gave her to my best friend – who is, without doubt, a better mother than I could ever be – and Leah is the happiest little girl in the world. But sometimes, I struggle with the sorrow of it all.'

Maud squeezed Ada's arm with her own. 'Thank you for telling me,' she said quietly. 'It helps to know that other people have had to make difficult choices. And don't worry, I won't mention this to a soul – except Alice, of course. There is one thing, though, and I know this might sound strange, but somehow I feel I can say it to you. The thing is, even though I didn't give birth to Flora, I somehow feel like she's mine.'

What had been said hung between the two women for a moment. And then Ada spoke, her voice gentle.

'There are much stranger things. And, knowing what I now know about Nurse Sellers, it seems that this little one is going to have the best possible start *without* her birth mother.'

'It does worry me, though. I mean, despite everything, Flora is still Nancy's child.'

'Mmmm, you're right,' said Ada. 'And if she comes back in a reasonable way and puts her case then it is only fair to give her some consideration. But somehow, Maud, I don't think that Nancy is going to do that.'

'You're probably right,' murmured Maud.

'And in Flora's case,' Ada continued, 'perversely, we have to be grateful to laws made by men for men, which deem a baby to be the property of the father!'

'Strange, isn't it?' mused Maud, quietly stroking the back of Flora's hand. 'It's a terrible law and affects women so badly. Yet I'm delighted that, in our case, we're on the right side of it.'

'Well, that's only because your Harry has turned out to be a good man.'

'I suppose,' murmured Maud. 'But I'm not sure that he's good all of the time, if you know what I mean.'

'Oh, I do,' smiled Ada. 'I know exactly what you mean.'

'What about Leah's father?'

'We exchange letters very regularly and he visits every few years. He's a doctor, always very busy with his work, and he travels widely . . . but he knows nothing about his daughter and, rightly or wrongly, I want it to stay that way. I don't want Leah's happy little life unsettling.'

Maud tried to probe further, but the moment of intimacy had clearly passed.

Ada was already moving away. 'I need to get going, go down to the wards and then hand over to Miss Merryweather, before she comes up here to relieve you.'

'Yes, all right,' mumbled Maud, still feeling a little thrown by Ada's revelation.

'Thank you, Maud,' called Ada from the door. 'I'll ask Dr McKendrick to come and check Flora over, but from what I can see she should be ready to go back to her father. It might be best if you accompany Harry, though, and help make sure that our little patient is properly settled.'

'Yes, of course,' offered Maud, as the door clicked to.

Female Surgical was busy, and it took Maud a while to get to Mrs Martin's bed.

'Hello there, Nurse Linklater.' She smiled, warmly. 'You look a bit tired today, I hope you've not been over-doing it.'

'Oh no,' lied Maud. 'And how are you today?'

'I'm very well. In fact, now that the soreness is starting to go, I'm realizing that I feel much better than I've done for some time. That cyst, or whatever it was, it must have been really weighing me down. And Sister Pritchard's thinking ahead – she's telling me that once the stitches are out, then I'll be able to go home. My neighbour, Mrs McCluskey, she's itching to have me back. She's got a copy of Miss Nightingale's *Notes on Nursing* and she's raring to go. I think she always wanted to be a nurse herself, but then she married and had all those children.'

Maud smiled, she could easily see Mrs McCluskey as a very sharp ward sister.

'Anyway, Nurse Linklater, I just wanted to ask you something – I've been hearing rumours that there is a very tiny baby being looked after in the Nurses' Home.

Mrs Horrocks in the next bed, she overheard one of the orderlies talking about it. I believe that she's only weeks old and a real bonny little thing. Do you know anything about her?'

Maud was incredulous. For a second she couldn't speak. 'Yes, I've heard that, too,' she said, in the end.

'Well, it's just that, I like to give something to all babies in trouble, or those without family. And I don't know the wee one's situation, but I want you to take these few shillings.'

'No, I couldn't, Mrs Martin, honestly.'

'Nonsense,' she said, pressing the coins into Maud's hand. 'They are for the baby. I've never had any of my own, and my husband was a shopkeeper, he left me well provided for. Please, take this and make sure she gets it. I've been thinking about that little girl ever since Mrs Horrocks told me the story.'

All Maud could do was smile and say thank you.

'Look what Mrs Martin gave me for Flora,' she said to Alice, pulling the coins out of her pocket when she caught up with her in the sluice, later on.

'But how did she——?'

'Like you said, everybody knows everything in this place. And there was no chance that she was going to let me refuse. She doesn't appear to know anything about the link between Flora and me, so it's strange that she chose to give the money to me, isn't it?'

'Things sometimes happen for a reason. It's like there are unseen bonds that connect us,' said Alice, her eyes wide. 'Maybe Mrs Martin is one who can read them?'

'Not long ago, Alice, I would have dismissed what you've just said as balderdash. But do you know what? These days, I'm prepared to believe anything.'

'That's the spirit, Maud,' laughed Alice. 'Now can you believe me when I tell you that I need you to look at Mrs Horrocks's wound? And can you believe me when I tell you that you are probably the finest surgical nurse in the whole hospital?'

'Oh, stop it,' blushed Maud.

Word came through in the afternoon that Flora was to be discharged that evening. Maud found Harry waiting for her to come off duty, in just the same place where he used to stand before they were married. Seeing him there made her heart beat a little faster, but she tried not to smile.

'Have you got the fire lit at home?' asked Maud.

'Yes, Sister,' he grinned.

She tried to frown, but she couldn't. She had to settle for ignoring him instead.

Once they were all packed up and walking down the stone stairs – Harry in front, carrying a large bag packed with extra napkins, nighties, the toys that had been given, a feeding bottle, two jars of expressed milk and a steam kettle, and Maud following behind with Flora in many layers of shawl – Maud began to feel a bit sad. She would miss knowing that the baby was just along the corridor and she could pop in and see her whenever she wanted. She hadn't even asked Harry where his rented room was; it might be right over the other side of the city, for all she knew.

Rita was waiting obediently outside and she trotted along behind them as they made their way through the city. It turned out that they were following the same route that Maud had walked every time she'd set out for Stella's place near Lime Street. In fact, they turned down a street not all that far from the railway station. I've been passing the end of this street on a daily basis, she thought, with no clue that Nancy was there all the time.

At the end of the street she waited outside the property, with the dog sitting politely beside her, as Harry put down the large bag and fiddled with the keys. She was at the point of taking over when he finally got the door open and, with a glance behind that revealed the shadow of guilt on his face, he led the way up the creaky wooden stairs to a room on the first floor.

After another clumsy fiddle with the keys, the door swung open. Maud took a deep breath and entered the room, with Rita trotting in behind her. There was a good fire, it was nice and warm, and the flickering light from it showed her the crib that stood ready, as Harry moved across to place his bag on the bed and light the lamp.

Maud saw the bed and her stomach tightened – this was the room where he had stayed with Nancy in those days after he came back from New York. The bed was unmade, as if they'd only just got out of it. Maud fancied that if she walked across the room and laid a hand on the sheets, they would still be warm. She felt a small shudder go through her body and then Flora began to whimper in her arms.

'What's the matter, my sweet?' she murmured, unwrapping her from the shawl, seeing the baby's eyes blinking in the light.

She sat on a chair by the fire, with the baby in her arms, and tried not to look at the bed. Harry was busily unpacking the stuff from the bag, his head down. She could see a flush of red at the back of his neck.

'I'll find another room as soon as I can,' he said, glancing back over his shoulder. 'This one's within walking distance of the hospital but I think we need a fresh start, and I'd like to be even closer to you.'

Maud took a deep breath. She wasn't sure now that she wanted him all that close – if only she could see the baby without seeing him.

'Yes, you do need to be somewhere else . . .' she faltered, 'and, well, I don't . . . I won't feel all that comfortable coming to this place to see Flora. And I will want to see her regularly, just to check . . .'

He glanced back over his shoulder again, with a glimmer of something in his eyes – hope, maybe?

'Right, Harry,' called Maud, as Flora started to squirm and thrust her arms out of the shawl, and then she was crying. 'That's a hungry cry. Can you prepare a bottle of milk?'

'On the double,' he called, jumping up, shrugging out of his jacket, throwing it on the bed and then straight away picking up the turtle-neck glass feeding bottle. 'Miss Merryweather showed me how,' he said by way of explanation.

Once he had the rubber teat secured on the neck of

the bottle, he was striding across the room and handing it to Maud. He watched carefully until the baby was suckling and then he crouched down in front of Maud, stretching one hand out to stroke Rita as she lay in front of the fire. 'And tomorrow Daphne's going to call by and meet Flora and try her with the wet nursing. And if that works, once she's strong enough, I'll take her to Daphne's every day.'

Maud twisted her mouth ever so slightly.

'I'll be with her every night, of course,' he added, hastily.

Maud glanced up, with her eyes narrowed.

'I will, I promise you, Maud,' he ventured, his eyes wide.

She had to believe that at least, in that moment, he was entirely sincere, so she nodded her approval as Flora continued to guzzle her milk and the dog gave a satisfied groan and stretched out even further in front of the fire.

Harry was back up on his feet now and over to the bag to finish unpacking. Maud didn't want to look at him, so when she wasn't gazing at Flora she fixed her eyes on Rita, stretched in front of the fire. She hadn't noticed until now but there were grey hairs on her muzzle and when she was lying down her ribs were clearly visible. Maud could see the slow beat of the dog's heart and for some reason it made her feel calmer.

Once Flora had finished the feed, Harry came over and held his arms out for her. He laid her against his shoulder and rubbed her back to get her wind up, and then he rocked her until she was sleeping. Maud held her breath as he tenderly laid the baby in her crib, leaning down, with his white shirt all untucked, to give her a gentle peck on the cheek. She had to clear her throat to stop tears springing to her eyes, and then she was up on her feet and checking the room, making sure that all was in place in case the baby had a coughing fit overnight.

'I need to get off,' she said to Harry, who was sitting on the bed, still gazing at his sleeping daughter.

He opened his mouth to reply but stopped short when the sound of two screaming voices reverberated up from the street – one shrill and male, and the other pleading. Maud walked to the window beside him and peered out on to the darkened scene. A woman stood with her head bowed as a man leant in towards her, his neck straining with the effort of shouting garbled words. The couple were beneath a street lamp, and it cast an eerie yellow light.

The woman was sobbing now and starting to shout back, and then the man grabbed her by the neck.

'No!' Maud cried, but Harry was already leaving the room and running down the stairs.

She watched him burst out of the door and go straight for the man, grabbing him and throwing him off balance as the woman lurched to the side. The man came back at Harry with his fist raised, spitting and full of rage. Harry ducked neatly out of the way and then threw a punch that sent the man up into the air before landing with a dull thud on the ground.

When Maud breathed again, she realized that her heart was pounding.

Then she watched as Harry went to the woman and put an arm gently around her shoulders, talking to her, nodding. And then she started to walk bravely away, without a backward glance. The man on the floor was starting to move, so Harry went and lifted him up on to his feet by the scruff of the neck. His nose was streaming with blood.

Harry had a few words with him and then pointed towards the end of the street, and the man staggered off. Maud saw Harry run a hand through his hair and then she could hear the sound of him running up the stairs.

His breath was laboured as he burst through the door. He was panting, his eyes were alive, and he had a streak of blood down the front of his shirt.

'Are you all right, Maud?' he gasped.

Yes, of course I am, she thought. You were the one out on the street.

'It didn't wake Flora, did it?' he murmured, going straight to the side of the crib.

'No, we are both fine,' offered Maud, moving to stand beside him at the crib. 'But you seem to have grazed your knuckles.'

'No, it's nothing,' he said, wiping his hand on his trousers. 'I'll give them a wash after.'

Maud didn't know what else to say. Her heart was still pounding and she was undeniably proud of what she'd just seen him do. She wanted to hug him, tell him that he'd done a good thing, but something was holding her back, she still couldn't let herself get that close to him. So instead, she pulled her nurse's cape more tightly around her, telling him that she'd have to be on her way, and giving him full instructions on how to use the steam kettle.

'I'll see you tomorrow,' she said, reaching down to stroke the baby's head.

He put his hand over hers and then held on to it.

'Harry, I . . .'

He started to pull her towards him. She could see his eyes shining in the glimmer from the lamp.

'No,' she cried, pulling away.

He let go of her hand instantly and stood with his head bowed.

'I can't do this,' she said, setting her mouth in a firm line. 'This place is where you were living with her, with Nancy, and whether you fully understand it or not, you need to give me much more time to think about everything. I can't just snap back into where I was with you, before I found out . . .'

'How long will you need?' he said quietly, raising his head to look her straight in the eye.

'I don't know,' she cried, exasperated by his seeming lack of understanding. 'How could I possibly know the answer to such a question?'

'But can you ever forgive me?'

'I really don't know,' she replied, unable to meet his direct gaze. 'And you need to give me as much time as I need to think about things,' she said, already making her way to the door.

He gestured towards following her.

'Stay exactly where you are,' she commanded. 'I'll call in to see Flora tomorrow but you have to promise me, no more of this. I will speak to you when I'm ready.'

Once she was out on the street, Maud glanced up at the first floor with her heart pounding. She could see the shape of him, standing in the window. He lifted a hand in farewell, as she turned to walk away. She'd promised to call by Stella's to see Alice, but all that she could think was that she needed to be near Alfred. It was far too late to go in and see him, but maybe if the gate was still unlocked, she would be able to stand in the courtyard at the front of the building and have some sense of him, and maybe it would help her somehow.

21

'A good nurse must be a good woman.'

Florence Nightingale

Maud found the gates to the Blue Coat standing open but the front door was firmly closed. Apart from the circles of yellow light cast by the gas lamps and the dim glow from some of the windows, all else was in shadow and to her frustration she could gain no sense whatsoever of Alfred or any of the other children who lived in the school. She stood in the courtyard at the front of the building with walls on three sides, turning to look at all of the windows but not even able to make out the detail of the stone cherubs. She sighed and started to walk back through the gate.

But just in that moment she heard an organ starting to play in St Peter's Church and she could see light cast out through each of the tall windows, and then she heard the sound of voices starting to sing. The music swelled and the voices grew stronger as she came closer to the black stone walls of the church, and her heart thudded when she recognized the words. The hymn was so familiar that she knew each and every word. It was just about the only thing that she'd ever been able to remember properly about her time with her mother: snuggling up on her knee, feeling the rough texture of her apron as she sang 'Amazing Grace'. Maud breathed in the words, as she stood looking up at the arched windows of St Peter's. 'I once was lost, but now am found . . .' flowed over her. She took a step closer, right up to the wall, and placed both hands against the soot-blackened stone. And this time she could feel the rhythm of the ancient church, almost like a heart beating beneath her hands. She rested there, listening to the choir, feeling each word, and not until the singing had stopped did she lean away from the church.

She felt breathless as she took a step back, continuing to gaze up at the light from the windows. Rousing herself, she walked around the building, aware that her heart was beating faster and her legs were stronger. She made her way along the church path, passing by the low wall where she'd sat, not so long ago, in complete despair. Once she was out on to Church Street, she easily stepped around other pedestrians, effortlessly making her way to Stella's place.

'How did you get on with Harry and Flora?' asked Alice, looking up from her chair by the fire where she sat with the black cat stretched out at her feet.

Before Maud could reply, they were interrupted by the sound of raucous laughter and a bumping sound as a visitor to the brothel lost his balance and fell against the kitchen door that she'd just closed behind her.

'Not like that, I hope,' laughed Alice, gesturing to the door.

'No, not like that,' said Maud, carefully removing her nurse's cape and hat and hanging them on the peg behind the door.

'You look different somehow,' said Alice, standing up from her chair. 'Are you sure you didn't—'

'No, Alice, definitely not!'

'Just wondering . . . you seem to have a glow about you somehow.'

'Well, that's nothing to do with Harry,' smiled Maud, not wanting to tell Alice about the church or the hymn, in case it somehow dispelled the magic.

'Well, let me get you a cup of tea,' offered Alice.

'No, thank you,' replied Maud, lifting her head and meeting Alice's gaze. 'I need a brandy.'

'Maud!' gasped Alice, as she moved towards the cupboard and started to remove two glasses and the bottle. 'Right, tell me all . . . immediately.'

Maud took a good swig of the brandy, coughed a bit, and then she started to recount exactly what had happened with Harry.

'It sounds like you've still got strong feelings for him, Maud,' offered Alice, as Maud slowly sipped at her brandy. 'And it might ease, in time . . . but you can't just switch off those feelings. I should know . . . I think about Roderick Morgan all the time, it drives me mad. And I don't have to see him on a daily basis – not like you will, if you want to visit Flora.'

'That's true,' murmured Maud. 'Unless I ask him to

leave the room and stand outside,' she added with a giggle.

'Ha,' laughed Alice, 'good luck with that. I've seen the way he looks at you. He's not going to be ready to ease away any time soon. And maybe that's not what you want, either?'

Maud sighed, and then she was holding her glass out for another shot of brandy. 'All I know for sure is that I need to keep working, I have to see Flora and Alfred, I want to live in the Nurses' Home, and I'm quite happy to use any spare time sewing bandages for the hospital.'

'You and that sewing machine – I could hear you treadling from the bottom of the stairs the other evening,' admonished Alice.

'Oh no,' cried Maud, 'I hope I'm not disturbing anyone.'

'Don't worry about that, Maud. It has a nice rhythm to it, and you're doing good work for the hospital – nobody can argue with that.'

'I suppose not,' smiled Maud, holding out her glass again.

'Steady on, Maud,' laughed Alice, topping up her own glass, 'or you won't be able to walk home tonight.'

'Oops,' said Maud, starting to giggle. 'Don't tell Harry, I've been on and on at him about staying off the drink. And now look at me.'

'Well, it's good for you, Maud. We all need to loosen up a bit, once in a while. And you've been through a lot since me and Eddy came to meet you off that ship—'

At that moment the kitchen door burst open, and both girls screamed in alarm as a figure hurtled in, only to fall flat on the floor. To their relief it was only Eddy.

'Sorry I'm late,' she grinned, propping herself up on one elbow from where she lay on the kitchen floor, still clutching her nurse's bag. 'All of my cases took a long time today, and then I had to help an old fella I found out on the street. His legs had gone and he couldn't get back to his lodgings. But he lived up three flights of stairs, and by the end I nearly had to carry him.'

'Are you drunk? Why are you on the floor?' asked Alice, grinning.

'No, I just tripped over a man's shoe or something, out in the hallway,' said Eddy, as she hauled herself up and clicked the door shut behind her. 'What?' she said, turning to grin at them. 'I was in need of a lie down, after the day I've had.' Then, seeing the brandy glasses, 'You two boozers!'

After Eddy had removed her hat and cape and settled herself at the table with a glass of brandy, Maud and Alice told her what they'd been discussing, and for once she sat quietly, without interrupting.

'Right,' she said eventually, putting down her glass and then running both her hands through her hair. 'Well, it seems to me to be a fairly simple decision.'

'Does it?' Alice frowned, as Maud looked hopefully across the table.

'Yes,' breathed Eddy. 'All of it hinges on whether or not you, Maud, can forgive Harry for his past misdemeanours. If you can, then there is a good chance that you can both make it work and you can build some kind of partnership with him that will allow you to share the rearing of Flora and, of course, Alfred.'

Maud was shaking her head. 'I just don't know, Eddy, I've been turning it over and over in my head. When I see him, I feel the connection between us, and it either makes me feel drawn to him or incredibly infuriated by him, there's no in-between.'

'That's understandable,' said Eddy, matter-of-factly. 'And it is possible that you'll never forgive him. And if that ends up being the case, then you will have to devise some way of having a businesslike arrangement with him, because anything closer will be destructive for you both – that lump of anger and resentment will grow and grow inside you, Maud, and eventually it will kill all that's good between you and Harry.'

Maud was looking down at the table now.

'None of this is your fault,' murmured Eddy. 'But you are the one who will have to forgive, and that is not easy.'

'But how can I do it?' asked Maud, looking from Eddy to Alice.

'Well, you could try thinking about it in a different way. Resentment is hard work, Maud, it's something that you need to work at every single day – it's exhausting. But you only need to forgive once. And then, if you stick with your decision and put the rest behind you, then you and Harry can make it work, I'm sure of it.'

Maud was shaking her head. 'I don't know,' she murmured. 'It doesn't feel like it would be as easy as that.'

'I didn't say it was easy,' said Eddy, 'but I can't think of anything else that would work. Forgiveness is all, Maud. And it is there for you to give.'

Maud tilted her head to one side, as if letting what Eddy had just said settle there. Then she looked up and reached out a hand to her, across the table, swaying a little as she finally got herself up and made her way to the door to retrieve her cape and hat.

'Maud?' said Alice, twisting in her chair.

'I know what I need to do,' she called. 'I'm going to go there now, on my way home. I'm going to tell him what I've decided.'

'No, Maud,' said Alice. 'You're not yourself, you've had too much brandy.'

'I'm not drunk,' said Maud, setting her hat slightly askew on her head. 'I just need to see him, get this sorted out, that's all.'

'What are you going to say to him, Maud? Which way will you go?' Alice asked anxiously.

But Maud just smiled and pressed a finger to her lips. She caught the concerned glance that passed between Alice and Eddy.

'I'll come with you, Maud,' offered Eddy, already grabbing her cape and hat.

As they walked, Maud was glad of being able to hold on to Eddy's arm. She knew that she wasn't properly drunk, but she'd had more brandy tonight than she'd ever had in one go, so she did feel a bit light-headed.

'This is it, this is the street,' Maud said, stopping in her tracks. 'Now will you wait here for me? It's just

369

that, whatever happens between me and Harry, I need it to be only the two of us. I don't want him to be wondering about what you might think.'

'I understand,' said Eddy, glancing down the street. 'I can see all the way to the last gas lamp, so I'll wait for you here.'

Maud nodded and then wove her way along the street.

She stood gazing for a few moments up at the window, where there was still the faint glow of a lamp. The door was locked and she didn't want to knock or shout up, so she searched the ground beneath the gas lamp for anything she could throw to get his attention. There were three seashells that a child must have been playing with, placed in a neat row. She grabbed them up off the ground and aimed at the window. The first one hit the right spot, but it wasn't really loud enough. The second she threw with more force, but there was still no sign of a figure at the window. The third she threw with all her might, and it fairly cracked against the window. She saw the glimmer of a lamp being lit in the room below and hoped she wouldn't have to wake up the whole house just to get his attention.

When she looked back up to Harry's room, she could see, at last, the shape of his broad shoulders and the shadow of his head peering close to the glass as he looked out. She held up her hand to him and he disappeared at once.

Seconds later, she could hear the key in the lock of the outside door, and he burst out on to the street in his stockinged feet.

There was a split second as they both held their breath, and then Maud looked him straight in the eye. For a moment, her head was spinning and she couldn't speak. He took a step towards her but she held up a hand to stop him. His eyes were round with expectation, and his breath was coming in quick gasps.

She couldn't say a word. All she could do was stare at him, with her heart thudding against her ribs. She took a deep breath and felt a tingle all through her body.

'Harry,' she said, her voice firm and clear in the night air, 'I forgive you.'

He took one huge stride and grabbed her. She could feel his heart hammering against hers as he lifted her up off the ground, crushing her body against his. Then he put her back down and she could see that he was crying. She reached up a hand to dry his tears and he leant down to kiss her full on the mouth.

Breathless, she broke away. 'But if you do anything like that ever again,' she panted, 'it's the end for us. Do you hear?'

Harry was grinning now. 'Yes, yes, I hear,' he stammered, and then he was lifting her up off her feet again and turning full circle with her in his arms.

And so it was that, on her next afternoon off, Maud found herself walking to the big house to see Miss Fair child, with Alfred and the dog at her side and her husband walking behind with the baby in his arms.

Harry stopped dead in the street when the baby whimpered. 'Oh, I'm thinking Flora's unsettled, Maud.

It might not be a good time for us to go and see Miss Fairchild, not if the baby's going to start crying.'

'You're coming,' Maud called over her shoulder, turning to face him. 'I've already written to tell her that I won't be alone and to expect a surprise, so we can't let her down.'

'Yes, but Maud, she won't be expecting this. What if she turns on me? She's a fearsome woman is Miss Fairchild.'

Maud was shaking her head. 'You'll just have to be brave,' she smiled. 'Because there is no choice, Harry. If you want to be with me then everything has to be out in the open. I don't want any secrets or whisperings. Not any more. Miss Fairchild has to know everything, and we will both have to accept the consequences.'

'Well, all right, then,' he murmured. 'But maybe you should go in with Flora and Alfred, and I'll just wait outside with the dog.'

'No,' said Maud, firmly. 'You are coming in with us. I'll take the baby and you can follow along behind, if that works better. Now come on, we need to get going.'

Cook nearly dropped her pan when she saw Maud coming through the back door with a baby in her arms. She couldn't speak for a moment but came straight over to have a look.

'Well I never,' she said at last. 'You kept this bonny little one quiet, Maud.'

Maud cleared her throat, a little daunted herself now that she was standing in the kitchen. 'This is the daughter that I'm planning to adopt,' she said. 'Harry's child.'

Cook narrowed her eyes and looked past Maud to Harry. He tilted his head to one side and raised his hands in mock surrender.

'That's a turn-up for the books,' she said, looking back to the baby. 'But what a beauty. So it's a girl?'

'Yes,' said Maud, unexpected tears springing to her eyes. 'Yes. She's called Flora.'

Moments later, Maud's heart was pounding so much, it made her feel breathless as she stood outside Miss Fairchild's door. She knocked lightly and waited, but there was no response. So she tapped again and then glanced down to Alfred who gave her a reassuring smile.

As Maud opened the door slowly, the baby was starting to make little noises and wriggle in her arms. Miss Fairchild looked up from her chair, Maud saw her frown, and then she smiled as Alfred skipped over to her.

'I've brought someone else to see you,' Maud said softly, as she walked across the room. 'This is Flora. I'm going to adopt her, just like I did with Alfred.'

Maud glanced behind to see Harry standing in the doorway, running his hands through his hair. She gestured for him to come through into the room, too.

Miss Fairchild tilted her head to one side. 'Well, Maud, I knew when you wrote to tell me that there had been a change of plan and I wouldn't be seeing Harry, that clearly there had been some kind of drastic happening. But I never expected you to turn up here with a baby. And it seems that you and Harry might even be reconciled.'

'Well, the thing is,' said Maud gently, 'this baby . . . she is Harry's.'

'What?' Miss Fairchild frowned, straightening up in her chair and glaring at Harry, before looking back to Maud. 'Well, I suppose there will be some explanation that I'll need to hear in due course,' she said, at last. 'But as long as you two are all right together.'

'Yes, we are,' Maud assured her, meeting Miss Fairchild's unflinching gaze.

'Mmm,' said Miss Fairchild, her face stern. 'In that case, all I can do is believe you,' she said quietly, beckoning for Maud to come closer. 'I would have known that she was Harry's, even if you hadn't told me,' she murmured, as she gazed at Flora. Then she held out her arms. 'Give her to me, let me have a hold. I've never been all that good with babies – I seem to scare them, for some reason. But somehow, I think that I'm going to be all right with this one. Oh, and look at her beautiful hair.'

Maud glanced back to Harry and smiled. He still looked nervous, but she could tell that he now saw that they'd done the right thing by coming here.

'She's called Flora,' said Alfred, stroking the baby's head. 'And she's going to be my sister.'

'Hello, Flora,' smiled Miss Fairchild. 'You are beautiful, aren't you?' Then, glancing up at Maud with a glint in her eye, she continued, 'Go and ask Cook to bring in a full bottle of sherry and some of her best cake. We need to celebrate our new arrival.'

*

As Maud walked back, with Alfred on one side and Harry carrying Flora on the other, she glanced over her shoulder to check that Rita was dutifully trotting behind. She smiled at Alfred as he too looked around and then stepped back to walk with his hand resting on the dog's back. Taking a deep satisfied breath, she linked Harry's arm. He was grinning now, and it wasn't just because of the few glasses of sherry that he'd shared with Miss Fairchild. Maud had seen him visibly relax once he knew that no grudges were borne by any of Maud's friends at the big house. What's more, he had felt ultimately accepted by Miss Fairchild when she had taken him aside to discuss the inheritance that she'd promised for Maud and her family. He'd already murmured to her that they'd be able to get their own little house for Flora to grow up in, and where Alfred could stay when he wasn't at school.

Maud had encouraged his thinking, and although she was still a little nervous at times about her future with Harry, she knew how he loved her and how he was absolutely sincere about his feelings for the children. As they walked back to the new rented room, close to the Infirmary, Maud started to look more closely at some of the houses they passed – solid brick terraces, with a bit of a garden. More substance in the world than she'd ever thought would be possible for an orphaned girl who'd started her working life as a house-maid. If all went well, she could see herself wanting to move into a place like that with Harry. And if it was far enough away from the hospital, no one need know that she wasn't living a single life out in the city, like some of the other trained nurses chose to do.

Mirroring her thoughts, Harry spoke up. 'That would be a nice house,' he said, nodding in the direction of one with a blue painted door and fresh curtains at the windows.

'Yes, it would,' she murmured, giving his arm a squeeze and then reaching across to adjust the shawl around Flora's sleeping face.

Alfred was skipping along behind them now, playing a game with the dog. He appeared at her side again, slightly out of breath, with his lovely smile and twinkling eyes. 'Please can I hold Flora when we get back home?' he said.

'Yes, of course you can,' smiled Maud, reaching out a hand to brush his hair from his face.

'Hurrah,' he called, falling back to keep pace with the dog. 'Rita, Rita! Maud says I can hold my new baby sister.'

22

'The good of an organisation depends on
every individual who is in it. School, hospital,
coffee-rooms, institutions, district nursing must
depend on the living life and love which are
put into them.'

Florence Nightingale

Some weeks later, as Liverpool withstood the grip of an icy wind from the north, a lone woman in mourning dress, complete with a fine black veil, made her way down a path away from a church. As she reached the lychgate where half an hour earlier the coffin of her father had rested, whilst she waited with the undertaker for the clergyman to arrive, the first snow began to fall. Individual flakes were sticking at random to the veil that she wore, making a delicate icy pattern that melted and re-formed as the woman walked purposefully away from the church where, bar the usual one or two church mourners, she had been the only attendee.

Behind the veil, Nancy Sellers was frowning and her mouth was drawn down at the sides. This was no pretence at mourning. She felt nothing for the man who she'd just seen lowered into that icy hole in the ground.

377

She hadn't been to visit him for years — not until she'd heard that he was dangerously ill in the Northern Hospital and she'd called by at visiting to take the key to his house from him. It had come in very handy indeed, all those weeks ago, when she could no longer bear to be in a house with a screaming baby. No, she felt no sorrow at the passing of Arnold Sellers.

With her mother long dead, Nancy had left home at sixteen after an incident with a middle-aged male customer in the shop that her father owned. She'd been working behind the counter and the customer had made regular unwelcome advances towards her, which her father had chosen to ignore because he didn't want to lose the man's trade. Although she was young, she wasn't naïve and she knew what the consequences would have been if the man had forced himself on her. So one night, she packed a bag, emptied the safe, and left without a backward glance. She'd easily found work in a milliner's shop and enjoyed helping the well-off lady customers choose their hats and think about colours. She'd worked there for a few years and become something of an expert, but in the end she wanted more. So she emptied that safe as well, one night, and didn't turn up for work the next day. She'd heard about the Nurses' Home and Training School from a customer who'd recently employed a private nurse who trained there. She'd been impressed by the promise of twelve pounds per year salary, and she knew that the best way to keep out of the way of any police enquiry was to have board and lodgings in a place that was completely closed to men. And, after all, who would question the moral fibre of a young woman who'd chosen such a noble calling?

The solicitor's office for the reading of the will was conveniently close.

'Please come in, Miss Sellers,' smiled a slim, well-dressed man, introducing himself as Mr Samuel Chambers and showing her to a chair at the opposite side of his shiny desk.

Nancy prepared a teary expression before slipping the veil back and presenting a brave face.

'Miss Sellers,' smiled the man as he fixed her with his bright gaze.

Nancy dabbed her eyes with a black-edged handker-chief, taking in the handsome specimen with dark hair, greying at the temples, who had just slipped into his chair opposite.

'I am so sorry for your loss. I didn't know your father, Arnold, very well but I do know that he tried his very best to keep the business going, even when his health began to fail.'

Nancy felt genuine concern behind her fake tears. What if her father had let things go too far and there wasn't any money, after all?

'He did, however, manage to ensure that, although there is no stock and only very little ready cash, he secured the property itself, so you will have a tidy inheritance, Miss Sellers. No vast fortune but a tidy inheritance.'

Nancy tried a sweet, brave smile and Mr Chambers reached across the desk to squeeze her gloved hand, just for a moment, before proceeding with the reading of the will.

As his well-spoken voice delivered the news, Nancy's mind clicked over the exact figures of her inheritance. That will do nicely, she thought, glad now that the sister who'd been born the year before her hadn't survived the bout of pneumonia that she'd caught at the age of seven. Given that she was the sole beneficiary, Nancy would have plenty of money. She wouldn't need to work for some time and, once the property was sold, she could set herself up in a house of her own or run some kind of business. She was done with nursing, at least for the time being, but she still kept up with Millicent Langtry and one or two others at the Infirmary so that she could stay informed about prim little Maud and her silly friend, Alice. She wouldn't ever let that go, not after they'd seemingly engineered a situation where Harry would have nothing to do with her.

Not that she wanted to see her daughter anyway. Babies were extremely annoying, and hard work. Even though she knew exactly where Harry was living, in that place he'd rented near the hospital, it was no trouble to stay away right now, no trouble at all. But give her a few years and that demanding baby would be a very cute little girl. Nancy smiled to herself as she pictured Flora at three years old – a head full of dark curls, big green eyes – and just ready for dressing up and taking out to show off to the friends that she would, no doubt, have in plenty, once she had some standing in the community.

*

Across the city, Maud was making her way along the corridor to Male Surgical for her daily review of Mr Langer and another surgical patient who needed specialized dressings. As she walked, her breath was clearly visible in the air. She shivered and pulled her nurse's cape more tightly around her body. 'It's snowing,' she murmured, as she saw the first flakes falling outside the window.

As Maud entered the ward, the fire at the top end puffed out a gust of smoke and those in the beds nearest started to cough. She could see Nurse Devlin there straight away, wafting away the smoke, reassuring one of the men who'd started to hack with a cough. Maud would have gone to help, but she could see Sister Law in full uniform plus a woollen shawl, gesturing for her to hurry up.

'Come on, Nurse Linklater, don't dawdle,' she huffed. 'It's far too cold to dawdle. Now, we have good news, Mr Jones and I checked Mr Langer's wound this morning and we were able to confirm your view that he is finally ready for discharge. His wife has been informed and he will go home with his family at visiting today.'

'That's such good news,' grinned Maud, and even Sister Law was smiling.

'Yes, it is, isn't it? I thought we were going to lose him. I've never seen a man make quite the recovery that he did. This new-fangled spraying and sloshing of carbolic acid at every given opportunity must be doing some good. But we're awash with the stuff, we'll be bathing in it next!'

Maud giggled, desperately trying to keep a straight

face; she knew how Sister Law was regularly exasperated, not by new ideas themselves, but by the often unfounded optimism they brought in their wake. But she could see Sister's shoulders moving up and down as she tried to suppress a laugh.

Maud cleared her throat. 'And is our other case, Mr Stein, progressing satisfactorily?'

Sister Law bit back her laughter. 'Yes, he's up to the eyes in carbolic acid solution, so all's well there.'

Maud giggled again, seeing the mischief in Sister Law's eyes. Then she spotted Mr Langer down the ward, sitting with a thick blanket around his shoulders in the middle of a group huddled around the fire. She called gently to him as she approached. He turned his head. 'Nurse Linklater. My saviour!'

'Well, it wasn't just me,' she murmured, feeling her cheeks flush pink, as she moved to stand beside him. 'I was working with Sister Law and Mr Jones, and our Nurse Devlin – she's the one who's been doing your daily dressings all these weeks.'

He was nodding, but wouldn't let it go. 'It was Nurse Devlin who told me about what happened that day I took a turn for the worse. She said it was your plan to use the antiseptic packs in the wound. And all these weeks when there've been murmurs about the wound never healing, you've been the one to keep saying give it time, we need more time.'

'Well, I suppose that is true,' said Maud, modestly. 'And there is still more time needed,' she reminded him. 'The very top layers aren't yet fully healed, and the district nurse will be coming to check your dressings.'

'I know that and I will be very careful. Keep everything clean, no cats or dogs in the house . . . but at least that means I can be at home with Clara and the children. Little Martha is so excited, she hardly slept at all last night.'

'Oh dear,' smiled Maud, 'poor Mrs Langer.'

'Poor everyone in the house,' laughed Wilhelm. 'We have two lodgers, and they are also at her beck and call, she is a little demon!'

Maud laughed. 'Anyway, Sister Law has checked your wound this morning and she is satisfied, so it seems you're all set to go home.'

'Yes, with the help of those,' he said, pointing to a new pair of crutches propped by the fireplace. 'Mr Jones has told me that the leg will always be twisted and shorter than the other, but I'm hoping to graduate to a stick in due course so that I can get back to work.'

Maud pressed her lips into a firm line.

'No, Nurse Linklater, don't worry, I work as a sugar boiler. It is skilled work and they want me, at first, to train up two bright young men who have come up through the ranks. So I would just be directing them.'

'All right,' nodded Maud. 'But make sure to support your lower leg with the splint and the bandage – you have to do that each and every day.'

'Yes, of course. Don't you worry, Clara has already been fully instructed by "she who must be obeyed".' He smiled, gesturing over his shoulder to Sister Law at the top of the ward.

'All right, then, it seems like everything is in order. I'm just going to see another patient, and then I'll be going back to Female Surgical. So I'll say my goodbyes.'

Mr Langer nodded, and when he looked up Maud could see that his eyes had filled with tears. She put a hand on his shoulder, tears welling in her own eyes.

'Thank you, Nurse Linklater,' he croaked at last, taking her hand and kissing it. 'I will never forget what you did for me, not till the end of my days.'

Maud took a deep breath. 'You take good care, Mr Langer, and come back to us if you ever have any concerns about the leg.' And then she patted him on the shoulder and willed herself to move away.

She noticed that the patient next to him put an arm around his shoulders and gave him a gentle shake. 'Well done, Wilhelm,' he was saying, 'Well done. You're ready to get out of this place.'

Maud left him sitting with his friends around the fire. And as she walked back up the ward, she slipped a hand in her pocket, quickly removing her handkerchief and dabbing at her eyes before anyone could see.

'Ah, Mr Stein,' she called, a little too loudly, as she reached the bed of her next patient. 'How are you today?'

Maud and Alice came out of the hospital at the end of their shift to find a good covering of snow over the footpath.

'Whoa,' said Maud, feeling her feet slide.

But Alice had already picked up her uniform skirt and was sliding along, cackling with laughter as Maud walked very carefully behind her.

'Whoa,' called Maud once more, almost slipping again when she was hit in the chest by a snowball. 'What?' she cried, as another hit her and knocked her cap askew. And then she could see Alice being pelted as well and she could hear outrageous laughter from the steps of the Nurses' Home.

It could only be Eddy. And sure enough, there she was, crouched down trying to hide herself.

'Right, let's get her,' called Alice over her shoulder, scooping up an armful of snow.

Maud did the same, slipping a number of times as she tried to run up the path after Alice. They both piled on top of Eddy and covered her with snow, rubbing it into her face and filling her hat with it. All three of them were sprawled on the steps, holding their ribs with laughter, barely able to breathe.

And then the door clicked open and who should appear on the top step but Miss Merryweather herself. She sniffed the air, 'Mmmm, it's been snowing, has it? I see.'

Maud held her breath as all three of them gazed up at the superintendent, all expecting a 'telling off'. But to their astonishment, Miss Merryweather giggled like a child, before stooping down, picking up a good handful of snow and throwing it at Eddy.

'You are no doubt the instigator of all this, Nurse Pacey,' she grinned, as she walked by them and then stepped spryly along the path towards the hospital, without a single slip, her shoulders heaving with laughter as she went.

Maud, Alice and Eddy fell back on the steps with a sigh, giggling again.

'Come on,' urged Maud, looking up at the sky. 'It's starting to snow again. We need to move, or they'll find us here later tonight like frozen blocks of ice.'

She managed to stand, but when she tried to help Alice up she nearly slipped again and Eddy had to grab them both. All three of them were laughing again now as Eddy dragged them inside, full of snow, and dripping wet over the pristine tiles of the entrance hall. As the heavy wooden door clicked shut behind them, any passer-by would have been able to hear the sound of raucous laughter from inside the building as the heart and soul of the Liverpool Royal Infirmary made itself heard.

Also by

Kate Eastham...

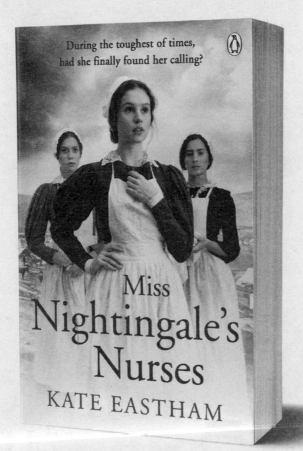

During the toughest of times,
had she finally found her calling?

Miss
**Nightingale's
Nurses**

KATE EASTHAM

Out Now

Also by

Kate Eastham....

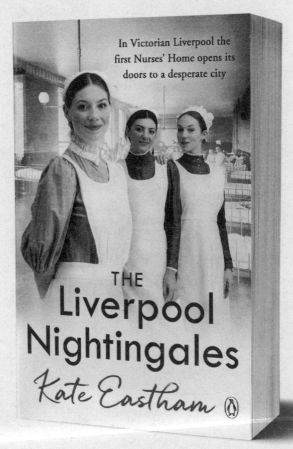

Out Now

Also by

Kate Eastham...

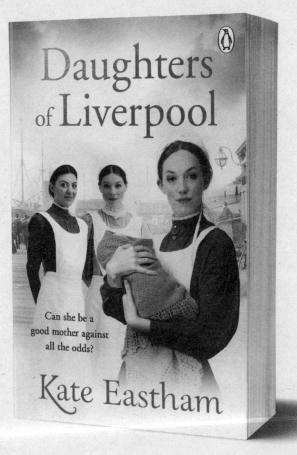

Out Now